The Slag of Creation

Richard Grossinger

NORTH ATLANTIC BOOKS

for Theodore Enslin

"A man may do that
once in his lifetime,
   and at its close.
There is something — a stone —
    inanimate
that mocks, or seems to,
   the living."

Theodore Enslin, THE TESSARACT

Late Spring – Early Summer

Wet wind in the maples. Touch of leaves on leaves in the static of the air. Light flesh body. Misty. Pouring from the calathus of elements half-lit. From a caldron into the calathus. And there is nothing at the end of the tunnel. For all these years calling it "the light". When I stop, that inside all is motion/is all in motion, flowing, living out, in swift separate times, the unfoldment of the whole.

The agon is frozen. The stone falls into the sobriety of the stone. That men quarry the granite for. The scene mimes existence as a simultaneous disclosure, a parallel procession of the difficulties of those who act. Within the light in the temple, thru the trees that overflow, the sky with light, the leaves sugary and topous, the life that has never fallen over the glacial precipice like water into the grotto, and to whose hollowness there is the echo of stones under metamorphic grinding in the throat of shape.

There is nothing beside this. The ceaseless dripping. The soundless scenery. Between dreams stands a statue, a proscenium of frozen rhythm. It is sheer time, in which shape and form merge into each other and the prospect of roads vanishes into the finished towns of men. Behind the elements, the elementals.

My numbness is a ceasing to feel, what continues against the dizziness into sunlight. The breathing is filled with the smell of wet leaves. The fish are churned to the surface, massive shapes of pre-history and enclosed waters. Dreams prove it beyond living. The resonance of living substance, growing as a fern, invisibly from the nebulous space of psychic potential into the littered sediment, the present soil, dull and granular, a tasteless fog, yet containing all the particulars, the matrix, ion by yron, of the sweet cabbages. Beneath the new grass and cotyledons, the old grass, dead and dry — is the ground itself, shell of a creamy beetle. Fibers of the unseen statue in the center of time.

At night the proximal mysteries vanish, and the arc is visible. Influences penetrate the stucco. We are alone in our house, in the light our house is, and ourselves, making dinner, being together, trying, behind the spawned images of a thousand such years, each second, to go there, to embrace alive who is there, pouring all that prickles from the spotted jug that holds it, the juices of suns that will never rise, the poisons they are, and must be, into tender fluvium, thru the warmth of joining. To make the numbness feel its hook. Who says we do not grow as a fern from a dream, the leafy garment flung in cells of more distant cells of, the lacustrine world trailing yarn like the unfinished blanket of the scientist who sits with needle at his seminar, tracing the surface by hand.

Even in this confusion, even north in the barren appletree grove, even dreaming of when there was nothing here, not even ourselves, as the wood around this house, once soil, once fire, once air, now fire again; the old railroad ties built into the slope as stairs, rotting, hollow, packed with fertile bugs. The memory alone is dim. There is the possibility of drinking its wine in mandibles, of lucid blossoming images, the old river running under the stone bridge in the city, (the golden dome of the capital an enigma of the all too clear minerals of the impoverished north). The water drops like industry into the machinery behind the village, in which it is thrashed, broken again into sheaths, as fire goes along these lines, down the barren back-roads, to shacks of the semi body of light.

Unquestionably there are times when we don't want to live it, when we don't see why we are living it. This alone attacks the slick optimism of the journeyman pleasure-seekers, of the farmers of the neo-Vermont revival. The soft presence of inert matter rims our investiture; our own animation, even as it attempts to examine and revive every figment, every dead ant, is no answer to the dead and raw material of a monstrous nature. The earth and stone and chaff is incredible; the space between campfires is immense and deadening. The loom has no angles from which to send bright threads into the flowering of its cloth. It is dust and crap, shit and planet-formation, even its sky is, though made of gentle light. We are no answer to the anima we cannot inhabit, throw it up squirrels in grey fur and clouds of nebulous proportion and the song of a single bird in repeated complication that wakes us from the sleep we fall into after making love, even when it doesn't. The force in the center of things is neither happy nor sad, as the chemical fires that issue from it in cosmic alarm and at crisis speed, even yet; it is no business with *our* feelings that *it* should have no feelings or whether the golden vehicle of the possibility of joy can be reinhabited in the beauty of twilight, whether I can smell the mosses and grass, or the dizziness of creation makes me less and less, even who pursues them desperately to be human. They demand simply that revelation go on, that the scarred matter, within that scar, whipped and broken, recoil, retwirl about the cavernous, swollen, seek out the spaces of its enclosure. And it is a continuous ache. No simple sorrow or ego-wail, but warm tears for all sentient things. It is a music that goes on. Even the master athlete and his cousin the zen must agree, as we all know, being the stream along which the manywaters flow, that it hurts all the time. It hurts all the time. Even if that water is a rainbow. And if it hurts all the time, it can't hurt, it can't be anything at all.

6

To this the elixir is mimetic, the lattice of nerves beneath each muscle, gnarl of roots into the tree, however far the leaves. There is no time for unrelenting perversity. We're not here forever. It is like drinking poison. The hole in the sky grows larger and larger. Our actions are recoded. The woods are not finite. The edge keeps alive the snake who, legless, winds his way thru the astral he is also in, twisting as the loop he makes himself go thru.

In the mirror our child, pulled as a thread from ourselves, the skein of living that makes us but a cell producing cells: yet in the holy chalice, the Malkhut of our life, we see him as if the young god, or godlike process, achieving full vision of a world we are in, hence enlarging it (not like a secret male or female lover we both have but, in the flesh, calypso provides the item: three).

II

Brief trip on a rainy day: we leave the lamplit, maple-enclosed wholeness of our house, the discouragements of inaction, drive 15 miles along Route 2, a side road across the mountains, the windshield wipers keeping our sleepy eyes clear, the other cars with lights on, and we do not transcend, either the storm or our state, but approach the larger world that hangs down thru us, like the vision we once had of being able to go infinitely far in any beautiful direction. Now the difficulty lies in the deep conservatism of the mind; however far the psychic explores, it is reduced to the space it inhabits. A visionary wind pours thru the static electricity of the medulla, awakening the passageways to light.

Mountains enclosed in clouds we climb upon. The fields littered with boulders as after a meteor shower, the sheep and cows grazing in the aftermath of a tragedy. The houses, temporary shelter, made of a forest that has since been plowed into the visibility of light. The grass and weeds grow up around the rocks. Long fences like glacial margin. In the center of the crops and in the yards, for children to climb on, the Immovables. And where they have left deep holes are small lakes, fenced by the antediluvians. No matter how much junk, tractors, cars, sheds, fallen barns and rusty troughs, they cast onto these fields, they will always be empty; an underlying sparseness precedes any amelioration.

Peacham Pond is the largest body of water we have visited since the ocean. The shore is still. There are no waves, and there is no salt. The creatures are born and die, frogs; they have long since been trapped genetically inland. The birds are quiet, more like minstrels than armies, though it is the same war, waged ever in camouflage. There is a barrier, the gums, which separates this puddle from the ocean: from the gulls and planetary tides. Thick to our perception, it is but a thin rocky interzone, outside of which the ocean still tears to get in and submerge the continents. The pond itself, glacial in origin, is geologically enclosed, grinding its pebbles in soft incisors, an innerplanetary mind fed by the alembic clouds, the cooler mountain run-off, no Greek or European history, no spicy driftwood, pure American in its reincarnation, Cooper's inland waters, with trails Indian not Byzantine. This pool Olson describes in our own center, beyond storms, beyond new-cosmology waves which burst upon us every instant.

An ancient voice is breaking the stone, is spreading its particles to a breathing god and goddess, on whose bodies, locked in an act of love, we walk, simultaneously their spasm. The cold wet forest. The leaves of autumn black but unburned. The first seeds have sprouted thru the turgid mat, now glow with the embryonic colors of the jewel. Long ago the glacier decayed into mountain lakes, leaving behind its teeth, large boulders covered with moss. In pockets of dirt on them small conifers grow, their roots not deep enough to know the size of the stone they enclose, nor yet whether they enclose it, or will be strong enough to crack it into mantle. The seed from the matrilineal has fallen here, and we are witness to the remarriage of a northern invader, barbarian as he is, his rough ice-eroded genes.
Clubmoss gathers deep and permanent light in the microcosm, and the world seeks intelligence in the movement of insects and their partisans, ally to the giants and cones of the upperworld. The cold lung spits in the branches; the rain has stopped, and the moisture is shaken loose in phases like music. Rhythm and tone are erosion; in nature alone are sounds connected, Schoenberg's harmony. It is a sentient and unintelligible world. We explore only the mural, a depth and field that vanishes beyond the vastness of original possibility — in ourselves the same hesitating enormity. These are shards of an existence before memory. Its touch is pale and cold, archaic and untranslated, incisions on pots of clay, left by hands, phalanges, footprints of beetles within the imago mundi glyph, frogs and salamanders nested like princesses in the rhizome systems of the literate biological world. Yes, genetic coda, forest scrolls.

Since we have known of them, we see that the world itself is an art. We wander in the distilled aromas of pine and rotting wood, a Bachelardian space, closed and open at the same time, in the limitless world of numbers and the finite geometry of our own perception. We can see the deep landscape in which we are aroused to life, and we can feel the drugged world that refuses to allow it, that drags it into the dull shiny present of a jive remote dialect we speak as if we could refuse the revelation the drops thru our hair onto our cheeks from the branches bring.

III

Not that optimism fails. But the line gets tougher. And we come to realize how much there is to this profane world, its nameless peoples, its mute materials, its despots and prisons and thieves. It's a density human consciousness must always be drowned in, as a butterfly beneath a boulder. Lemurian man, it is said, the occult records (whether of this world or another) claim, was able to change nature by his mind, increase the strength of his muscles, measure and enact the leverage necessary to move the boulder, however large. He imagined cities out of tons of psychic rock. Atlantean man had no need for cities; his centers were in jungles and caves, climax forests and mountain valleys, deserts and islands. An urban-size population sucked the clouds and flowers, and turned the sunlight into food. By the millions Atlanteans lived on lightning bolts and fields of goldenrod, literacy without technology. For them *The Slag* is a conquered text. So when the modern world age began, we find man struggling in those fields as a farmer, some rocks too big to move hence planted around, for millenia, until the powers that moved that stone destroyed also the web; then we knew the power to move mountains lay behind and not before us, and what was expected was the most difficult of all grails. Against such stone, and sheer grain size, to yield, to be human, to adapt, to be transformed. Or to prove consciousness by a geologic measure. If the line is tough, if civilization is granite, right into the glorious centers of secular power, if sun itself is nothing but a fiery stone, the Earth a melting bit of hail, this, ox on axle, is the human test.

No amount of will can submerge the trauma, good will or bad will; human action is retrogressive. Any conscious remedy hangs null in a suspended-lotus universe. The rest is dangerously final. It cannot be made conscious, be weakened by sheer content, and in its unconsciousness it cannot be renounced.

We are solid only to weak eyes; in living space we are balls of fire. We cannot keep order in our kingdom; we cannot prolong rule. Those billions of electrons and molecules and cells, arranged in synchronous orders, live their own lives, and tumble into a sensuous darkness we register only as the void. In those empty moments, when the path is flat and the resonance of being is a tinny clank.

The law is large and iron-clad. The leaders, in order to become leaders, have escaped into alien humanity. The whole sustaining mass, its unconscious balance greater than the national debt, might collapse and crush the world at any moment, the monetary system cracking like a feeble bell. This is not the dark moral purpose which lies behind social life, but the psychic purpose, whose poison *is* the heart.

Forget atomic stockpiles. There is a deterrent which grows exponentially larger everyday. We attack it with the alert flashes of our sense organs until they weary of novelty; the uninformed, unspiritual mass swells around us, to which ordinary consciousness is all too thin (expand though it does into the world of psyche, plangent with color and meaning); still there is the world of Wittgenstein, extracting its 90% due from what precious little remains, until in every parcel of water we deliver across the desert there remains but a drop: enough as long as we do not fail. For there are natural men and women on the other side planting vegetables, chipping bark, building their houses out of rawstuff, outlasting the winter by the sheer candle resonance ice transmits in them, these the neo-Lemurians.

There is no spatial mind; unconsciousness and consciousness are simultaneous oscillations, as when the rain starts suddenly in the humid air, or lightning strikes, a snake's fang. Our life, as a sun, is hung in eternity; its progress across linear time is purely semantic; what we seem to remember remains present in some other form; thus it cannot weaken us, as wasted recollection; it can only make us stronger, the oil and fragrance of the psychic flame.

Recent events are moons; we see them at all not because they are bright but because they are near; traumas, infantile desires, karmic messages, these are stars, and we know them not in their proximity but because their light crosses vast distances, because they *were* so bright, they will fill the darkness of our bodies with an intensity of remote design, like the zodiac on which their countermeanings hinge. We will never be done seeing them, no matter how far we go.

The condition is tenacity. What follows a storm. The way one board is hammered into another to make the back porch stand up, and is already beginning to collapse under gravity and the damp shifting ground, or the tin roof on the house, every corner of every room formed at right angles, the rust on that. It is very tight. What we do physically, however painstaking the execution, does change the world around us.

There is a place in myself I want to get to and it is as restricted as the plan for a house. The more I know the less likely I am to want to change things or get ahold of this planet fiery and hurtling in space; that was a childhood daydream; it took the energy right off the top like cream. Now there is no more cream, and even the sour milk must be swallowed, until the clear brook bubbles back up thru the medulla, like Thorne's crushed star. My dreams are no longer enough even to dream. If I were made king of the world, my brain would be blown to bits like an overloaded computer. If I started again on the planet of a Cygnet star, the problems of people and lovers and laws and shelter would be awesome. I am dizzied by the perspective up, and the flatness, that when you get there, even for the president of a nation, it's just a gameboard of seas and islands and icelands, strategic considerations; it's anybody's planet, a journeyman rock in space. When you get to the top of the ladder, there's no one to appeal to; even high spiritualists cannot make political contact with the sun. It's a beach-head in eternity, and a cosmic pebble could ruin it; its water is limited; it has yet to pass thru such badlands as once, in the veil of Lemurian protection, ramming the physical thru the astral not like a nail thru oak. The ceaseless, then ceasing crickets, likewise consigned, know no more than we do, and once *they* were king of the world. The limits, famous, of instinct.

In the local farm-country of anyworld, there is no brahman-warriors; any person could save us all, carries in him the holy power. The crisis is too extenuated to chronicle and all its swords too fast to see. How can we affect it when the charge of gold is as violent as an ant emerging from: which egg?, every egg! We watch under the microscope how viruses grow, our cell cumulus in paradigm. How absolutely after a rain the field is filled with mushrooms, and we cannot stop this, without starting something equally as big. Witness the platinum and concrete dams feeding the looms of Las Vegas. We *are* such a field, and in it, psyche and soma twine, like Spengler's spindles of history, mature into the kachinas for which they were seeded, each one of us. As we grow older our aberrancies become more firm, as the sun energy of childhood departs, revealing the actual magnesium flecking and marks of granitic scouring, reflecting unavoidable lesions in a dim and discerning light. Beyond which: our skeleton, and the limestone base of our life. This reduction is the only thing that gives us a chance, the only numerical hiatus in infinity we may yet know. We who once intended, by our inquiry, so much.

The world fills with leaves. The trees are conscious, and their consciousness is the same as their growth. They stand hierarchically above us: rich and sunlike. So how could any of us be king of the world? When these forests die a perfect martyr to their cause, without a peep, they leave behind the scar of their remuneration.

I return to feelings because they are what is left. The rest is heavy, uninhabited, and it is sheer exhaustion trying by desire to compel the world. The world falls back, like rain in a pool, or the continuous oscillation, dark and light, water into water, image, even in sunlight, suspended in the shadow that is suspended in the image that throws it back again and again into itself.

The literary relationships matter little, are a kind of pleasant dissembling history. The real germination of my vision lies deeper, gamma, in what I am. And that would have happened anyway, no matter who I was touched by, so that its perfection is its own evidence (it has no energy or romantic charm; it lacks even the brilliance which made it popular in those odd glistening moments of fact as it seductively undressed; so forget your enthusiasm for the meteoric display; it appears, finally, as any stripper, in the final condition of nakedness, without possibility or revision). The other world is subsumed in this one.

IV

That the time in Ann Arbor was blithe. Of course, it was not. But an active principle was everywhere; the blossoms on the quince pounded the window by their light, and the Huron was a sensuous mystery. The bees were hermetic carriers. Ther revels ended. Our friends became stiff china dancers. Our dance changed into trance-like realization, traced like the hands of many clocks.

The butterfly is about to be crushed by a boulder. The butterfly's consciousness is remote from this. Perhaps the image is from Nabokov, human life a caterpillar squirming between two eternities on either side. It comes cheap — pale fire.

12

The rock is more like one under which the centipede rests, his place delicately shielded from meteoric weight. The inert must be drunk, alkaline as it is, and we can't always count on the wind or the crickets. The soy is a kernel. Those who make text out of it are in a fragile position, for they draw the legions of false sympathy, a dread weight they must dance with, ever in the possibility of abandonment and betrayal. Thus, the perception of how the porch is held up, or the number of ceiling lights I have fixed, the several times moving, the infections on my fingers and ear last summer, all lie between now and the time under the quince, Frodo peaceful grey, Lindy with new baby. And these are more acute than anything in a rented apartment as a student in the early years of marriage, despite the softness and fragrance then. The ovary swells beneath the apple flower, and that fruit contains within it the chambers of the seeds which, if planted, duplicate the whole apple again: this is more than density of information; this is a gnostic vision of the depth to which we are into it, and the thickness of the roots we would cut if suicide were even a possibility, i.e., that they cannot be cut.

Some people try to weave the materials into lattices that stand against the darkness for them. They build houses; they cut in wood-lots; they breed cows they eat; they roto-till; they wire; they work out ratios of sunlight to heat and cut down on their fuel consumption. I don't mean farmers; I mean professionals, who come home from work and engage in this artistry. And though it be practical (ever more so with the dollar on the move and the pipeline in jeopardy), it is also their means of attack, the way they do not allow the vastness of the materials to stand against the animate tenderness of their lives and the acuity of their perception. It is measured out into boards and directed thru wires. So that when the plumbing delivers, when the wires carry light, they know exactly how the map was laid, where the differentials come into contact; it is not that they understand electricity or geometry, anymore than Newton understood color or gravity, except in an alchemical vision; it is that they have lined and insulated their minds with the actual connections that repeat mechanically in daily participation. They have reduced the anxiety of the inert world by rebuilding their psychic life of items of physical survival.

And because I don't, another messenger visits me beneath the apple, protector of the counterspace. When he goes away, it is like the fading of astral space. I am left in a field of glacial rocks, bearing the very electric lines over my shoulders. I can cast the vision only into other centuries of circuit-designers.

But the rest of what we inhabit is cambium and cortex. It is a beautiful cocoon, spindled by a technology whose occult origins we little appreciate, but for worms such as we it is a gritty inedible veil.

. And when we are invited to their houses, it is like being asked into their soul. The loom surrounds us.

And who would live there, would allow such a hibernation?

V

The creation was brilliant and from a center, but all this rest is suspended in time as we are. And the materials wither and fade of their own inner lack of strength. Proceeding from the nursery like an elephant-drawn carriage along that slick and globular dimension cast by time. They are the materials of a single beckoning, despite unending chemical resurgence, and they return to the heap, to be (recycled is not the word) back from the mysteries of their use.

Thunder breaks the hot sky; rain falls into the ground; the seeds are opened like maps, and unravel in the mystery of numbers. Pain is no issue. The weight is that of a clown, upon himself upon himself. The bright, almost-ritual colors of his mime. There is a spirit that moves things, and it is not the law by which things move. If we carry whatever exponential three billion years of traumatization within our apprehension of things, it *is* as a heap (the dream of the wart on the knee that keeps replacing its surgery until it crumbles leaving a black scar on the ankle). The argument that there is nothing to call pleasure but the absence of immediate pain, an only and incomplete solution to the riddle the first Freudians were initiated by, after salvaging, that for the whole of joy and partying in the previous century, nobody was happy, and were getting unhappier. Until Reich measured the skin by meter, and planted joy as any other seed in the garden; so it is no longer a question of the mythological origin of the image-fears of death, the desire not to go on. The energy present has a dark wing (copied again from the delicate scales of the Kirlian photograph in the years that followed): we are submerged in it beyond having drowned, and it is powerful enough to maintain a shape even after the physical basis of the shape is gone: life, breath, soul, call it what you will, is lattice enough to explain why the people at the party are unhappy, and cannot break the connection even by breaking it. Not the galaxies and

14

exploding stars in the space we know from ancient times but within that space must lie itself the wish and conduit, recording the changes of feeling along its twisted rhomboid plane. And thus laying, like a cloak for the lady to cross the mud-puddle over the century, a science of the inside of the inside. Working not at right angles, or not only at right angles, such that functional clarity is the best to be hoped for — but diamonded and flare-notched. The rest is a welter of false information, which is not like a lie but solely and efficiently the contingencies of one event to another, endlessly ramifying within the sequential structures, so that truth is not the test.

The death that awaits us all is different than the old age which also awaits us, its surety of death beyond. Death snaps the persistent cords of meaning and limits creation to itself; none of us will be a stone statue yet. The end of life is a road of concrete, year after year, the villas rise and fall around us, sun in their soft pores, the young get younger, the old get younger too, until we look back thru what is history and remember having been there. The world itself approaches that single intuition. Everyone is dressed in strange clothes.

The beauteous inner circuitry is alive, but the past miasma of possibilities, from the Maine islands and golden-wet seaweed on the beaches of the Moon to the wind-sculpted kivas and dry mesas of New Mexico, are one masonry, and that is neither possibility nor image. What is seen is swallowed deeply and penetrates where we do not see or feel it. We can travel and visit many things; we can delay the toxic passage, but the acids of change age too, like scraps of paper torn into unrecognizable debris or wood under the ocean's torso. They carry the images but they carry their own turgor, their own viscosity and salt of vita. We have the lives we have, and the time thru which they tremble, and where creation is hot and brilliant we are held to it, and seem to need nothing else, and go on living, loving, as if it would never end, and it never ends; the will is itself a dance. But there are the slags of creation, and day after day they haul lime from the pits, the dark counterbodies of the golden stone, and our philosophy is gone with the trash that text becomes. We are left with the replicas, the shells, the Nostalgia Stores; what we were given, almost by a holy grace that sought communion with us, we must carve again out of the toughest stone. And we are asked to make that the same.

There are cities, like Cleveland, Chicago, Detroit, which were once the cities of the New World, the New World cities; they now lapse into autonomic hulks; they lie, in their decay, upon the decoding; their complication is fleshy but inhuman, without the light thru the window priests guarded until light came thru, as even those Spanish counterparts, Rio de Janeiro, Montevideo, taking from the jungle they replaced the opiate of pure somatic growth, the woman who is not, despite her many names, psyche, or even Moon. She is one heap of rock, the slag whose soft light, whose menstrual tenderness, whose reflected porousness is only a distance, a reflection, as the rest of the parapsychic possibility the new science was to be. The atom itself a deep and inexhaustible coal-mine, but against the deadness of its hierarchical body and the unwillingness of that to be awakened, the debris of systems and the reduction of psychoanalysis to chiropractic in our time.

The world is distant, but it is also closest, and principle. In its presence our conduct, our very survival, is alien, yet brings back in confirming resonance the possible and flickering intimation of an eternal. We ride the myth as though it would bear us there, with its regal bloodlines and bridle of jewels; but where the myth ends we do not want to be, for the wasted suburbs that go on forever beyond the city, so people can keep on being born, the empty lots, the burned-out buildings of obscure violence never replaced (because the obscurity feigns to be explained), the children that are born and die there, the muffled lights even of the bioplasm, in the summer heat, so that they hammer open the hydrants and lower the pressure of the sacred fountain, a nectar which the scientists pray must fall from the sky so that we can drink it raw to get past this dilemma. The hope that our mind is also a star.

For the human is the only measure of it — not social realism, or the assumed need for revolutions in the Western Hemisphere, but to honor each event, each imposition singly as it arises. The numbers fail when they come to suggest classes of numbers, e.g., the thousands or statistical millions and billions; the powers are powerless, they diminish the single, they do not raise. Or it is in the heaps, where they raise the materials they no longer need, even the materials they need give off terrific wastes, and come to an end in their carnal form, yielding finally only shortages, while we still cannot measure the body and the shape of this thing. All on the illusion that plenty is literal. How are we now to shed the single golden apple tree our history has taken from us in all except the image anyway, which does have its branches and principle of fruit in the celestial, its roots in the alchemical dung du monde, and find in its stead the grove of actual bent trees, each with its principle, to be pruned, its locus of fruit. For it is to these that they seem to have fled the urban slag, to find that it is a rural heap also, and that the houses must be built of the standing materials, the heat and light must come from decay, leaving ash, even if it be the sun, the sun: core. The ash is their own burnt-out life, circuits, our own, even when we do healthy work, holy work, where the spark fails to register, where the gates lock for the old primeval law, in a closure we merely replicate, even literally that were we to attain every other costume we could no longer turn back into a fish or a frog, though the night is filled with them, and their voices reveal the bog where the horse tore up the ground when he was chained there. For the sun has roots also in an unstable source.

We cannot be everything. Where it closes, happiness is no longer possible, for them though they do not even know, or care to know, what happiness is; seems to close for some unjust and unrevealed reason, taking with it the lumina obscura, the angle to the cowfield, where those brazen creatures graze also upon some lighter principle. And yet this is clearly the shape for lack of which all else fails in time, all love dies, all happiness fades: our unwillingness to see that a door is also where there is no door and an object which is black can also be black by being explicitly white.

We are enclosed by the glacial hills, the stale water of minerealization, the gathering rust, plaque, disease, the dusty coating of the world and the genetic withering, the lack of an eternal flame, the geothermal spa sputtering as the elixir gives off a fatal immunity, nuclear plants located strategically on the landscape to save the vision of our yellowstone youth. The principle of life is endemic and pursuit can achieve naught, but dimmed perception and old age, and the wheel of the hag works, though we do not see it, lodged behind the single image-objects as creation in its vastness is lodged behind the single sprouts, making certain that the radius drains the circumference.

For thousands of years in the West they have ignored this, with almost shamanistic optimism at first, then the optimism of the philosophical enlightenment, believing in man's power to be conscious, and government to reflect that consciousness, the experiment of democracy in the young and primitive lands of the Atlantic. But consciousness does not last the night; there is another veil thru which leaps not only the nightmare but life's principle itself, the desire and willingness to be: not from the pursuit of happiness but from never-to-be-seen founts, piercing the sadistic shell, the feelingless impenetrable words that go on directing and fail even their language over time, as they harden, these words, the condition of their being become lax.

So the early Freudian belief was that pleasure brings pain always, for pleasure must end. The blissful states are sleep and dream, stone and uncreation, orgasm and unbirth. And this they offered not to rob us of the joy of living but to show how conservative our hopes of joy must be, so we could feel them instead of the great nostalgic leap for the impossible and the extinguished passions of memory. They said: *we are like broken sticks, and we have been broken.* Even if you should fight your way back to the first romance, then to the primal act, then to your birth — beyond that would lie the jagged act of your own creation in the womb. You could not pass thru this to the joy that precedes it; even if you did, there would be utter floodgates, beyond them only to leap at angles unknown into the astral body, and if there be none, into the void, or via that gilled and oceanic creature we were in the eternity, when we lived forever and the Earth was young by an equalization of size and time the fluttering of microcosm thru macrocosm and back is by light crystal faces hidden, into dark crystal, emerging not in womb but in egg, and beyond that the primeval ocean, outside the archaeological eras of the planet, unintelligent and unrestored, and if there were energy to sustain that leap, still the galaxies would pour from the broken jug, and that jug would ever be broken, and their fine fleece would spill, and would be stars and fires in the only theogony we would be given, would have the original heat, stored in the spas beneath creation, and would be farther than ever, for there would still be a veil.

*** *** ***

    The boards come out of the mill, shaved white by their creation, whether you cut the wood yourself on your land or buy it from the forests of New Brunswick, the man in carpenter's clothing, no houses built; it would all be possible then, he thinks, even as the pre-Socratics prophesized for all the complicated history that was to follow them, that wood is fire, that the fire is water, that the water is stone, and the principle of creation is none other than the creation, the galactic explosion suspended in the one time we see, as turbulent as the waterfall dashing the rocks we do not see, in stars, in rivers, rapidly strewing the minerals of the millstream, and if we got back to that, even in the psychic dream, even in the ultimate hypnosis of the grand magus, born on Alpha Centauri or in the Himalayas, he would still be one of us, and the twig would still be broken, and we would be here, either hammering the nail into the wood or paying someone to do it for us.

VI

Plainfield, Montpelier, then the highway toward Champlain (the lake he named, and these mountains covered with forests he called Ver Mont, in his exploration of the Western Wilderness, north to St. Lawrence, then inland, a vision different than Deserts Mons, where we lived in the early years of this book). For him as for us, the cities of the South lie in the future; we return today to the Seaway, the Atlantic opening. The imperfection of our eyes resolves against a brilliant pre-blue sky, the car vibrating, cutting thru the dross, using up America's oil reserves, to what obscure purpose of our own (racing drivers trying to burn the covers from that hot fatty sun). Indigestion follows waste, then digestion; sleep follows that, curled about dream, and the awakening comes as another day working in the garden, making a furrow for seeds, weeding, hoeing, playing roofball off the aluminum ripples for intermission, wasting the afternoon in the Grand Union air-conditioning of the modern consumerist fraud, of: we will go on as long as we can, until this cooling system becomes a crematorium, against which the blind and hapless skiers of winter twilight return to their glass lodges. Today, in the young summer: the haze of creation. The lakes and rivers across which speculators came (which the fact that they are still coming does not obscure).

Burlington, Winooski, St. Albans; vegetation is sparse and the land is flat, still the neat white houses of the American flag. In Quebec this same road opens a different landscape: scattered ir-regular lots and houses, mansions and shacks together, brick and wood, rounded spires and glass. Changing colors and textures, grease and machinery, stores and farms tangled in semi-circles. American products, French billboards, a curious slang upon the glacial field, false Holocene brightness, this semi-permanent bilingual era, that visits as a carnival, then packs it all in and moves on to the next eon, leaving this one as bare as the stones that ride out any temporary farm, any mirage of prosperity.

[And yet there remains a profound but empty sense of there having been more, something that cannot be recalled, proving how unobservant we are, filling our lives with moments we don't live, don't see, and if we do, don't remember. There is, in fact, along that road to St. Jean, a line of immense trees that go on as regularly as telephone poles, first on the left, then on the right. They are elegant and fertile beyond anything else the soil there produces.

The road is narrow and straight, three lanes, the center for either lane to pass in. The instructions are all drawings: what you can't do is a car with a line thru it. Everything habitable is right up on

19

the road, but there are also farms visible toward the horizon, beyond other farms. The machinery is elaborate and cluttered, with storage facilities and semi-exposed elevators. The crosses in the graveyards separate New France from Protestant Vermont. Small ornate objects are hung upon the houses and worked into their structure, without the fear that it will lower their value. Symmetry rises above function or standardization, and everyone has a different sentimental aesthetic. In the fields, long and flat like the U.S. Plains, are clumps of rock and dirt with vegetation growing out of them. No attempt has been made to dissolve them.

The color is incredible; surely if I forget it as image, it remains a subliminal gallery, mixed pop and impressionistic: a beer can, a sheep, a melted cheese dish, an automobile, eggs, all painted on wood in place of commercial realism. The doorways and windows of certain houses are colored differently than the house itself, as if a face, or separation were intended. Even the commercial billboards are not painted with the present American industrial dyes; they are the old colors we grew to love. A red coca-cola, too red. A creamy metallic yellow. Cobalt blue. The weather has softened the blaring indelibility, and we know that they won't live forever. The oranges have faded to tans and pinks; the purples are browns and magentas. In Montreal itself is a huge grainy foot with corn plasters that could hang in a New York City art gallery. The years have worked on it, screening and tarnishing; they don't even draw feet like that anymore, not so fleshy and massive and Donald Duck.]

We come to the highway, then swiftly over the St. Lawrence towards the city, the bridges visible in succession thru the haze, wound with islands, rotaries, in the distance Montreal, its single houses, the gatherings of large buildings. It isn't Champlain anymore, but it is the city he found in this place, having changed Indian hands in wars even since Cartier's passing.

From a car, the geography goes by too quickly to return to. The streets of suburban houses on the far side of the Seaway a blur as we pass the signs for Nun's Island (Isle Des Soeurs), then the warehouses and complicated intersections of feeder highways, small factories and industrial offices almost beyond human comprehension, if not collective human capacity. Suddenly to be in the center of the traffic, at the first stoplight, North America but no American city; North of Boston, North of the last communes and Vermont wilderness: Montreal is the center of another migration, the Orientals in business suits, the Africans, the European shops, reflecting not only the policy of the Canadian government but the planetary latitude and relation to Eurasia. Montreal is the great Northern city of of the world, wound around a central hill. A giant has fallen in the sub-Arctic, and is rescued by the complication and solidity of New World urban life, the people who keep such a being alive, though they know nothing of its real sentience, nor how to restore its dead and dying limbs (proud merely of their survival in its lair).

But Montreal is also the rich Renaissance city, adorned with speeding cars, Expo banners, colored flags, outdoor bars and restaurants. The neo-American avant garde is not here, nor any of our friends or fellow artists (not immediately anyway). We have been to downtown cities and uptown cities, and we have been to aboriginal cities and Indian cities, revival and Baptist cities. We have never been to Montreal. Because there is no preferable or familiar direction, we cannot be lost; we are not lost because we will be displaced no matter what direction we choose. So we drive up and down streets looking at the clutter, the people, the flashes of parks and institutional buildings, the big department stores and corner newsstands. We know no one who lives here; yet we have chosen this for our trip. And the question can't help but come back: who the hell are our friends? So we should so flee their irresolution in our life.

The city is noisy and full of traffic, steam, ash. This jives with our own sense of interference and disorder — the whole thing: marital patterns, cosmic patterns, psyche and language. Our rural landscape is unconfirming: everyone is holed up, either waiting for the millenium or, like the old people, convinced that they live in its aftermath. Here the Canadian stock market flows thru the life-blood, bulb by bulb in the storefront, and the optimism, the false optimism, that has kept us alive in the Twentieth Century, is evident everywhere, is not really so much false as stronger than we are, as we break at every conduit and altitude. The city keeps it alive, keeps the energy flowing thru the data, processing civilization with an equipment McLuhan and others have noticed joins the planet in a single t.v. show (though, sadly, the materials themselves cannot be teleported yet). Despite, elsewhere, population and starvation, rats and jaundice, Montreal lies on the wealthy cosmopolitan axis. The universal city has not been realized. The noosphere is not a practical alternative to the cash that, as lit numbers, flows thru the ticker tape, dancing above the local exchanges, from the Canadian prairies and the Maritime East, Bank of Nova Scotia, et. al., oyster farmers and cattlemen, oil and gold in the Yukon, the MacKenzie, eggs and cheese in Quebec.

There is no sidewalk parking, so we pull into a lot on Avenue du John Kennedy and rush across the street to a glass of beer painted on the outside of a restaurant. The captain speaks to us in French, then English. "Tavern. No Children." He points to us, then points around, and I see hundreds of people at tables over mugs, gesturing, arguing, laughing. We go back on the street and walk a few blocks to a small downstairs restaurant, its menu pasted on the outside. It's a brief retreat from our lack of decision; we have chicken and lamb; Robin eats nothing.

Once outside we try to think of where to go: a hotel, the aquarium, the park? We are watching ourselves watching ourselves, where we don't want to be, wishing perhaps that we were still young enough to bluff a gaiety. There are artists on the street painting people's portraits, creating a crowd just below McGill University — guitar players too. It can't be real; it's just a memory of some imaginary place Montreal itself might be. A big black man in a convertible, the radio blaring in French, stops at a red light, screeches off at the green, the little white baby shoes dangling from the rear view mirror. Quebec license. All Cocteau.

We approach the maps of the streets as the physiology of a thistle. I buy the NEW YORK POST and read the sports pages about the Mets, sitting in a NO PARKING spot while Lindy checks out a hotel. Too expensive, she reports. So we edge down Peel Street, past the business district, into an older city, the warehouses separated, by a complexity of roads, from the main drag. There we find the Queen's Hotel, a once-ornate establishment with an awning, giant sad lobbies, and restless waiting people. We check in. The clerks and bellhops are disinterested. A teenage girl reading a dime novel puts it down to drive the elevator to the top floor. It is gloomy and nostalgic, compelling the way memory is, or the shoddiest of desires we have failed either for desiring them too much at the wrong time or being unable to know what they themselves desired. The long dark halls lead past rooms weary of occupation, threadbare of history. We sit in our tiny room, the sheets all that is clean. The rug is clinging to scraps; the bathroom is rotting; the bureaus are splattered with some white substance which sadly wipes off with touch. The windows, of heavy metal, and without protecting screens, look out into a dark courtyard, better seen than left in darkness, for its hollow sounds. The day is hot and we fall onto the bed, weary of ourselves; it is without resilience and deposits us in the center. Robin wants to look out the window, but we fear the worst, so he plays on the floor with his cars. I retreat into the newspaper and its torpor.

In our own house in Plainfield we have rooms and rooms to ourselves, windows and passages thru maple trees and angles of sun and green reflected light. We have our work. Here, our spatial possibilities are reduced to a binary set, and we are imposed, in retrogression, on each other. This building might crumble and bury our lives here. Yet, without such an exercise, the condition of our home would approach it imaginarily, the static itself would lead us from feeling the sun, from doing our work. We would be forced to lie here anyway, without any of the benefits of knowing that the discomfort is physical. At least we can go home the next day and leave the numbness we brought here in this space that all too willingly receives it.

We return to the car and drive from Peel onto Rue de Notre Dame, aiming for the Jacques Cartier Bridge and the aquarium on an island in the St. Lawrence. Instead we drive the length of Rue de Notre Dame without satisfaction, thru one of the first cities built here: rows of markets, apartments, neighborhoods, full worlds with obscure names, belying the actuality of a single Montreal. The events are tight and contained, and one is thrown thru them, swift and uninitiated, memories of something in Kerouac, and the unknown poets of Brooklyn.

We come to the foundations of a giant network of bridges and rotaries way above us, the sound of heavy traffic upon them. There is no way to enter from here. Instructions at a gas station, followed by a tunnel, intimations of Flatbush during Dodger years; we emerge in the suburbs, the children passing between school and home. There are ballfields, small parks, supermarkets. We come to a dead stop on a street called Eglise, the church bells ringing. Just when the maze seems ready to swallow us, we find a bridge and turn onto it. We are re-entering the city; this time we take the turnoff for the islands and seek La Ronde. But we are out of season. It sits there in the distance, an unfinished stageset, the workmen fastening down objects of brilliant color, the painted buggies. The roads continue to circle the island, and we find the aquarium, and enter carrying hot dogs and lemonade.

They are enormous fish. One flick of the tail covers not only the whole distance but the weight they feel against their own. He comes at you, his total directed force, and then ceases at the glass. The giants repeat that single motion as if it were the only solution their shape suggested, their shape the only stimulus, or, like alpha waves, to balance the pulleys of their life, until eternity ends.

The small fish pass in complex Mercurial motions. The penguins, enclosed in penguins, swim just underwater thru the flushed power of the circle, their cousins sitting on the mural of the polar regions that has been built for them, taking it all seriously. Whether they remember the original and whether they think this is a good likeness has long ceased to be relevant. They bring up their babies in the plaster caves. This is as much the world as city the gods have built for us by our hands.

In another room, one semi-luminescent fish, transparent, is pressed against the glass, rising and falling in shimmies. The skeleton, visible thru the flesh, changes color. Glowing, it seems a man, a homunculus, something trapped. It is trying to reach out thru sinusoidal fins, thru flesh all too soft to penetrate, too hard to dissolve. Neither psyche nor eros. And because it cannot complete its shape or pass thru the glass like light, it throws off neural waves that are visible in stasis and frustration. The colors are bound to a primitive design, in their sequence, in their nearness to the intelligence they do not achieve. If Steiner is right — his human evolution descending — this is a man in chains.

The wind off the Seaway is heavy, everything blown in tatters. A foundation of stones is built up against the island, the fishermen standing above, casting. The boats lie in the middle distance, and beyond them, the Port of Montreal.

In the evening we sit at an outdoor restaurant in Dominion Square. The wind is still strong, and it lifts the menus across the plaza, smashes thin wine glasses. After a beer it is all very light and gay and summertime. The wind carries the water out of the fountain, and Robin stands at the edge of the spray, running thru it, bumping into the girls in short skirts hurrying by as they are soaked. We finish with strawberry tarts and carry him, sleepy, thru an underground shopping center filled with the dead merchandise of this present world. After the toystore wears him out, we carry him, asleep, thru the early evening streets, the sky barely blue, the lights going on. Beyond his weight and our own symptomatic exhaustion, beyond the hopeless possibility of a baby-sitter, the movies flash their scarred lightbulbs, porn kodachromes and slick black and white squares; stores, bars, racing automobiles. This is like a taste of poison to recall our vitamin, to drive the prior toxic away. It is too early to sleep, so after getting Robbie into pajamas, we haul him down to the empty snack bar at the Queen's where two boys, goofing off, fix us milkshakes, while in the back a policeman talks quietly to a nervous woman. Are they all tired of living? Do they all plan to live forever?

In the building next to the Queen's is a burlesque; on the outside are the pictures of three women who dance there, enormous breasts in skimpy flowery and metallic dresses. Recorded on film. Snap! Snap! Snap! There is a point in us where violence, masochism, and seduction overlap. They are like animals in a zoo, not sentient or conscious, almost not human — just the dance. And the prey. Staring down a dark alley. Thru their own (and our own) imperfectly-understood biology. But into what? Into what?

24

The Aquarian Family is unborn, and "anything goes" is still the motto of the Aquarian Age despite the Freudian conservatism that underlies it all. And the world pounds us, and the world yet contains within it a tragedy. There is a Kirlian torso of light, connected by intuition to a purpose that surrounds it. Surely the orgy will destroy us, the little we have saved from the last fire and the last flood, like the mantis devoured by the female in the act of fucking/ it so desperately seeks at the moment it seeks it (and we go on living, while the body rots away) — the famous darkness, the drunk flat on Peel Street, beyond his lover's recognition. The wick he burns, the oils that sustain the wick, lead in dizzying passage from house thru broken house. And he lies motionless. The material of the clothing and the size of the breasts indicate some missing context. The creatures of night, pretending to be women, pretending to allure, seek another victim to go with their own holy bodies, though they stand aloof. Why else would these places be here, street after street, unless it were a path?

Visible from our window, a girl undressing in some other wing of the hotel. We close the curtains. Sirens ring all night, and visions intrude upon dream, from old grainy newsreels, of Montreal hotel fires. To come to the Hall of Freaks and see one's self a freak also. The longer you look the more jagged your desires even to feel your desires become.

The morning throws deep humid robes on the city. We drive up the central hill to the park, and there we sit on the grass above the road, watching as the cars bend in and out of shape passing thru the frames of the glass buildings, the middle-aged men in their white shorts and tee shirts jog past us, each one twice on the loop. Robin and I roll down the hill together, but I am dizzy. The lack of focus seems a real thing, made conscious by a specific event. I can struggle to keep it in focus, rigidly, or I can fall back into the total dissolution of the edge.

At noon we drive down the hill to the Planetarium. The mystery there, since childhood, is that the lights go back that far, that the lights reach us at this distance. A hermetic reality is sustained though we call them stars and measure the tones of their incandescence. Science proper died in the Renaissance, natural and physical science; all the work since then has been neurophysics and psychology, exploring the possibility of ourselves as if it were total proxy, by writ of the senses, for all else in the universe, which remains changeless, while we pretend to change them, to alter their hierarchies.

In the middle of his show, the maestro plays a record of the pulsar received in Northern Canada. The dome above is dense with

projected stars. Uuurrruuurrruuurrruuurrr it goes. How steady, re-
surgent is the pulse, a precision beyond instruments or senses, de-
fining a random decaying universe we seem, on this plane, to be the
ghosts of. It is the sound coming thru the veil, though certainly not
the veil of light imposed by our recognition of its distance — coming
thru light it seems to, all the same.

Things do lie back in what are called x-ray or radio sources. Inside
the child is the skeleton of the angel. But it becomes harder to feel
that center as other centers awaken to us, as I fight it by trying to
know *what* it is before *it is*.

The Zeiss projector turns in the center of the room, an elaborate
astrolabe, precise as jade, thru which electrically-generated light passes.
It remains a human pi-disk universe, despite the zodiac of astrophysics
and the deep tunnels of starry space. We lie in a hollow cusp upon
the Aquarian sign.

That motion rocks me like a boat at sea. How yet I feel the mys-
tery and can give no name to it. It *was* the STARS, always. Even as
I approach knowledge of them, I remove myself from them, alpha
wave breaking as perception itself is withdrawn. For a moment I see
thru the window into infinity, but the window passes, carrying the
unnamed face down the other side of the track, and the fluids drain
into some other part of the nervous system, the price of being hu-
man. We could carry such displacement to the edge of the stars and
it would still be the Earth.

At an outdoor cafe on St. Catherine's we try having a good lunch,
but we argue about trivial things and feel dull and removed from
each other. The holy people gather for their trysts, two beautiful
lesbians at the next table. Or what is beautiful is what we feel in
ourselves, as ourselves, and can't get to. We are left as pale ghosts
with a sleepy child, having been abandoned by the inner romantic
principle we also wish to abandon. We have been changed, as by a
drug, by the time in this city, and are sleepy and dazed; the concrete
world wears; we wash it with beers, and then drive along the bumpy
access road into the terrific speed of the bridges and the exiting
traffic, old rock and roll on the radio, the windows open so that the
breeze from the water comes in, Robin's hair blowing; I contain so
much I don't know whether to be swallowed by it or to break free
of it into some higher state. I feel the streets, the people, my sense
of them, my memory of them, my imagination of their history and
geography, and the turn within that, the hermetic notions suggested
by that — the whole conflagration. We came here, in the bigness of
history, to be fucked by it; we charge back out like children from
the waves, changed not by what we saw but our engagement with the

deep and obscure centers. The flash of the girl in the dance hall (and that night in the middle of a dream something like a meeting with her, angelic and ephemeral). To equal in our consciousness of consciousness what seems to be invested in us, as well as the dark counterrhythms already there, the gaps in geometric objects. Ask of it nothing for it can give nothing. As the magus says: expect the worst, expect to be annihilated, obliterated, know that you cannot transcend, that you do not have the strength to go on, and from this fact alone, survive. We meet those two girls from the cafe (were they even beautiful?), where they are us, and enclose them.

Even in the cosmic moment the whirlwind passes thru. The numbness I feel, the fear that things won't work, are both the fuck-up and the tension that makes relief possible, where the music plays and the wind blows my hair. I see Rue de Notre Dame again, and thru it childhood New York, and thru it the steamy vision of an Atlantean city, origin of the human race, and thru it stars in the planetarium, city's sky, a relay, a pi-disk, see Lindy again, in the simple residual of having, finally, to live it out, for better or worse. That there is no answer to the question: at what level to feel, because it is possible to feel at all levels. But to feel too deeply IS NOT TO FEEL AT ALL. Down in the center of wanting and wishing, where nothing happens, the feeling like acid burns away layers and bubbles of itself, an eternal preoccupation from which there is no absolution.

***

We visit David in his shack on the edge of Geof Hewitt's farm in Enosburg; then the four of us eat dinner in town, followed by home-made raspberry pie at the restaurant, sit in the village square until sun sets, talking, while Robbie watches the teenagers speed by in their cars. Then we drive back thru the mountains along darkening roads; glens hang low over hairpins, waterfalls drop into pools beneath the road, our car glides thru, back to our own lit house, sit on the porch, a cool breeze in the evening leaves, the spaces blown out, out.

Goddamnit, we can be everything we want. But we can't be anything we want. Eternity strung out like stars. Hung in the turning Earth and its mountains: the turning of the sky.

VII

We throw ourselves against the boundaries of a world-age we will never know. It is not only the Poundians, in that immortal thrust to move the stone of language, but the anarchists in the street, destroying the institutional concrete around the lapis. The dadaists and science fiction script-writers, operating like surgeons, to deliver a world beyond which no ultras can attack or intervene.

As we gain context, we lose matter. We gain matter but yield context. We take on the dark and uninterpretable mass, to which life itself is a bare accident. Darwin, as Newton before him, warned, "It's nothing." The answer to the riddle, profaning the spirit in which the riddle was asked. What is life, against such a planetary vastness? Which cannot be mined like lead and must be moved, unhappily, each day, along with the sun, along with everything else, while its shadow crosses the sundial of continents with intrinsic ease. The Mediaeval priest emerges from the warm temple bearing a candleabra the non-winds of sheer inertia blow out. The butterfly delicacy is gone. Dainty as it was, it would neither tempt nor survive the onslaught of the cosmic thugs, who would have attacked anyway.

"Bury your science of rubies and jasmines; take off your Tyrian robes."

We have died many times, we answer, many times within life. And if your wonder drugs have cured us, the life they have given us is no longer real.

"Take it whichever way you want. The message is indelible. The Earth is anchored yet in ancient and traditional space, but you are blinded by the hoods upon your senses to a Sphynx you can neither solve nor overthrow."

Learning more and more about less and less, as they say down the street.

"But spheres arise transvestite and mutant out of this one; the drums will be playing, you will be landing on possible moons, travelling in bodies that today are mere esoteric figures connecting occult texts. We will impose *our* dada and space odyssey on your pastoral enclave, even as you have taken Blake's key and opened all his doors only to find less behind them than he found without opening them. And when you have all that, you can return to your farms and plant the forgotten corn. You can blind the wolves of conceptual space, unresisting upon the flesh-and-blood torsos of their masters. You can dismiss the Korean acrobats, the corrupt officials of state, and Mother Hubbard's rocket ship priests."

VIII

I feel the old pain down my back and stand in the center of my dream before the x-ray machine.

I don't want to know. Please. I don't want to know.

Feel this, it warns. Or feel nothing. A bottomless abyss beyond. From which, no doubt, I have risen. In that once-in-a-lifetime act of creation.

The old doctor of previous nightmares has died. There is a young doctor, more optimistic about my chances. He pulls out the pain by a thread; it tears loose of me, a skein of words and partial meanings, cells and incompleted acts. We go next door for a strawberry ice cream soda.

He is conducting a physiology class, and my body is the specimen. "Wait," I call out. "I thought I was healthy."

He answers that it is not so simple, and anyway, he wants them to see me.

(In a bright flash of daylight, naked swimmer in the pool, boys and girls sitting on logs talking, the sun high in the meridien).

The students are all female in medical robes, and I am prone on the table. They surround me, seduce me, and I begin to submit. Is this more wonderful, more horrible than the disease, or is this the disease? The fearful x-ray penetrates. "I am only flesh. Isn't that all I ever wanted to be, to be touched, and by so many, simple because I have, I have a body?"

The light passes darkly thru me. The girls are beautiful; they do not see me. I see them not seeing me, feeling me. This is what I wanted in the dream, isn't it? They see thru me. They are x-ray. They are more discerning than daylight.

I who will not submit to the doctor bow willingly to their treatment, just as fatal, just as arbitrary. That's the curse. I allow myself to be used, identifying with my body so that I am changed by what they are. Until recurrence touches the pain in the back, the fear of disease, and nightmare and sexual fantasy are bound, their unity of trembling overwhelming. My life is something else. Now that they have spent all this time rescuing me from the abyss, I want to live. I want to know what is happening, despite the consequences.

We are alone, together. Having made love. Having sent all those
signals from the brain into the body into each other. I cast around
in my mind, in my flushed nerves and empty scrotum. And it is
neither life nor death nor the wish for nor the fear of. It is full and
it is empty, and I see a lion running on a hilltop, down the other
side.

It's becoming more true each day, as if the sun were getting
brighter, our lives clearer, the memories less like memories and more
like a stand of pine trees in the present sustained and dimmed light,
the imperfect light of our imperfect existences. And the perfection
for which that is a laughing mime.

What holds one to the other is the conviction, that it can be ac-
curate (and is the only thing that can be joyous, that can make us
want to live, as the water is poured from the bottle into the glass;
why should you be thirsty?, why, being thirsty, should you even
want to drink?). Or the cat seen thru an opening in the curtains
running in the hot sun, panting, being a cat. I am laughing. It all goes
so far back it has no meaning, as I do, as I think I do, in the vibra-
tion of the moment.

Nor is it that man and woman fall away from their love surreal
and separate, symmetric; it is the love-making itself, the feeling, the
feeling that wants the feeling, no matter how passionately felt, that
comes to, now, in the dark closed-eye vision, what seems to be a
wave in darkness smashing against a foreign shore, and is not even
on this planet; is not even, in our sense of it, on this world.

In Parc Jarry I feel the yearning for something lost. Before base-
ball. Before even childhood. Because baseball, I have abandoned,
and reclaimed, abandoned and reclaimed so many times, it is both
the gaiety of the life I have not lived and the opiate, along with the
others, that keeps me from living it. But Jarry is the old forgotten
baseball innocence, Montreal itself the Norte Americano city that
never was, at least not in the U.S., where the game was invented and
the big leagues are now the whole global show. The President of
which is El Presidente of the world. Behind which Montreal lingers

in the northern sun-throw like an aging monk, lingers at a different archaeological stratum. Though it has its plazas and ceremonial architecture. We drive thru all afternoon. Squares with fountains and cubic institutional mass. And gardens. And narrow irregular streets. Vieux Montreal.

The arc lights are brilliant, gems of the modern century collection; they turn the field of late afternoon from a dwindling arena of shadows to a theatre stage. The grass and sod shine, and the players awake from their afternoon naps and loosen their reptilian limbs. The light is new each moment, as if the peeling of the gem reveals only a more precise and atomic gem within.

Only once, a flutter, does the power fail in the hot dormant evening. The stage is stricken like a ghost; the players begin to awake with a start; then the circuits revive and the tragedy is postponed.

The day begins in the early morning in Plainfield, awaking to our intention, the tickets in my desk drawer, July 5, Les Expos. I run Robbie up the hill to Center School, and we launch out in the station wagon to Montreal. The second journey demands a new confidence; we go right up St. Catherines, then on out in an unknown direction where a Chinese restaurant fulfills the strategy. After lunch, we come back into the Old City, park the car, and spend the next hour or so in the import houses, moving from France to Germany to Russia in rooms smelling of different incenses and with a fineness of craft and embroidery, metal-work and wood-work, that seems more the world of Marco Polo and the Venetian merchants than anything so uptown.

The Montreal airport is an insane international event. One woman is not sure if this is North or South America, but she's headed for Zurich. David arrives from the tailwind over the Atlantic as simply as from a teleportation tunnel. He is flying from "David Bowie's Last Concert," the teenboppers with sparkle and sequins on their faces, to the French-American baseball game in post-Northern Vermont. He brings us a picture of Bowie, one leg bare, the opposite arm bare, man and woman, in a spaceman suit, a Flash Gordon bolt of lightning across his chest.

We have beers and roast beef sandwiches around a table in Dominion Square by the fountain of the earlier trip. Heavy talk of America, England, Canada, Watergate, North Carolina farms we might buy, Vermont floods. Is it really outer space or just world culture? "This is as good as London," David smiles, leaving his fat shillings as a tip for the waitress he has charmed by his bad French of which I am jealous. The colored flags dance out an internationalism we find again on Laurentian as we head for Jarry thru the Hebrew neighborhood and kosher meat shops, Semitic alphabet, Greek letters, Italian names, until the city breaks down into parks and pasture. Most of the people are not there for the Expos but to play on their own amateur diamonds, tennis courts, or to walk with each other, children and baby carriages. The stadium sits in the center of this pastoral complex. No wonder they can still play the old game. After the sun sets and the sandlot fields pass into night (except for the one with the small light towers): the sense that the players and strollers of those fields will wander into the bleachers of the big game. Lindy asks why I switched from being a Yankee fan to a Met fan. "If this were Chicago," I yell back, "you'd have just gotten us all killed."

CBC is there with their long twisted pack of electric lines and plugs, but they seem a minor occasion, like assigning a single crew to a street riot. Perhaps the game is being sent back to the bars of up-town, downtown, midtown, and suburban New York, to Joel Op-penheimer and Fielding Dawson. But they know nothing of this gentle evening scene and the shouts of the kids in the fields beyond, how the blue-white strobes of Jarry light the whole scene, while the Mets, despite that losing streak, despite the 19 runs given up by the pitching staff two nights ago, despite the blowing of Seaver's 5 - 0 lead the night before, dance and jive about the field. Only poor Yogi is solemn, but he's getting paid for that.

Jim Fregosi plays first base with exaggerated dance-steps; then he pitches batting practice with elaborate arm motion and dramatic facial gestures, putting his hand on his hat, lifting one leg, and yelping every time a ball is hit out, kissing the baseball every now and then before he tosses it up, dancing to the organ music I have found so irritating on the radio, except that here the people are doing little jigs in the aisles.

The sense of cruciality is gone; the Mets are not going to win any-thing; they are out of the race. So it is just baseball, and they are the men playing it, despite and because of the intricate system of drafts, minor leagues, waivers, and trades that has gathered them here. They are men with a job, which, for their fans, may be everything. But *they* did not invent baseball. The Cooperstown-style history they make, sloppily called their "immortality" (which is true for each game and not just Henry Aaron's Ruth-passing home runs), is over-whelmed by a joy of living and playing. Teddy Martinez fields fifty balls at shortstop that will never be assists. Wayne Garrett smashes a few lightbulbs with a line drive against the scoreboard causing Jim Fregosi, who has lost two infield jobs to him, to prance wildly. This is Montreal, not Shea, and they are playing the game even as the kids are playing on Algonquian fields around them. The whole condition is early Norte Americano, the real Cooper's town: sandlot America, Frontenac's Kebec. Long before the coaches arrived with their stopwatches and pep pills and machine-drilled cadres and baseball academies.

The old city has not been lost, but the new city has not yet been found.

And the Mets are condemned to New York and the bigtime and those fucking intense sports writers who follow them like the summit conference. Who hooked me on it. Buzz Capra, who has lost three games on home runs this week, is juggling baseballs with Harry Parker. Jim Gosger and Don Hahn are telling jokes. Jim McAndrew, last man on the staff, is doing even better juggling tricks while a cluster of fans cheers.

Any way you look at it, it's a matter of attention, cruciality or ease. The global problems are too many and too complex to have any bearing. The farmers will never get back the money from the floods; the government will go deeper into debt; the victims of violent crime will be paid only in precious karma. These events will fill the newspapers along with the line scores of the games. The trees and clouds stand in material proof of another energy, of a stasis that overrides this one. The farmers do not care; their tax relief is problematic; their lives are short, like baseball seasons. Our lives are just as short.

I remember earlier in the season, when the Mets were still in contention, a nineteen inning game against the Dodgers David and I suffered thru on the radio (each time L.A. loaded the bases with nobody out in the bottom half, it seemed as though that was it). And the relief in '69, clam-digging for dinner while the Mets won the pennant, those ocean waves and stars.

It is as though we are doomed to make the wrong things serious, for reasons even Galileo suspected as he weighed the motions of moons in times of political crisis. Psychology and physics are both physics, are both children of mind and eros. We experience a false cruciality, when there is nothing there, nothing we can need or use or change. As George McDougall said so many times: "I don't go to games to enjoy them. I go to see my team win. Then I enjoy it." And suddenly, for me, it's not true, and I feel cheated by the years I have put in on pennants and standings. Part of it is sour grapes, with the Mets in last and going nowhere (George's Cubs back in first, though George has moved to Puerto Rico, frustratingly out of listening range, in pursuit of his career). Part of it is the wish to be free at last, to know where and why the cruciality goes when it comes to this, when it leaves this. I reach into twilight and feel only a hollow behind the life, the silence of everything that rides on meaning. I wonder: "Will this stay, or will this move too?"

The music enters the sky, the air darkening and heavy clouds gathering beyond the bleachers as the stands fill with bilingual chatter, and the jets operate between Dorval and Europe, above this ceremony, in the driver's seat.

Canada has its own preoccupations, like the number of French players you can have on a hockey team and still win, the French pronunciation of American and Latin ballplayers (and John Bocabella), and the spoof on the whole thing (i.e., Gene Mauch's sense of incredible self-importance, American ministerial, as he manages Les Expos, the fans seem almost to mock by joining in his cause with a fierce rooting both sincere and ironical). When the North American corporations take over, a lot of this will be blown on out. Already the p.r. men have dressed the usherettes in bright colors and short skirts and planned a domed stadium; already this has been touched by the banality of Mr. Curt Gowdy and others who sell baseball and the American way of life to us on every pitch. (And I recall the more perfect voice of Mel Allen, who loved and understood this game, and was fired after the Yankees' glory years, for mediocre salesmen, who pushed it without dignity or history).

The sky darkens and grows ominous; dark purples and violets are thrown out of the twilight, long streaks of brown. The sun sets in brilliant orange over third base, right in our eyes, while the Expos take batting and fielding practice and the kids in the bleachers scream. George Theodore, the Stork, looking like a classic hippie with his big glasses, signs autographs behind the Mets dugout. A father with his young son sitting in front of us is screaming at the players already; he probably can be heard on the other side of the ballpark.

Now is gametime, but the game does not begin right away. The Montreal Commission of Public Transportation, represented by its officials in a green bus, drives down the rightfield line and arrives at home plate to present an award to its favorite Expo, who turns out to be Bob Bailey. He comes out of the dugout and receives a statue by a well-known local sculptor entitled "Human Activity." It is presented to him by the leading official in both French and English; then he poses for the photographers with the statue, the bus, and the lot of them. It's like a New Wave movie on the American superstar in French Canada.

The American National Anthem is played, and an American couple on vacation in Province Quebec sitting a row behind us sings it very loud. I'm mum. I want to pass for pure Norte Americano. The Canadian Anthem follows, a more haunting and ancient tune, reminiscent of beaver and kangaroo totems, England in Canada, India, Australia, Hong Kong, E. M. Forester in India looking for Stonehenge; the sub-Arctic caribou-hunters are in my head, the Abenaki, and Champlain himself, hero of this riff, joined, in harlequin costume to David Bowie and Wayne Garrett, here in the forgotten republic of the North Atlantic, of the cod and seal, the quahog and the larch — the fans singing, some in French, some in Anglais, sun halfway down, its colors rubedo, tribal, sub-incisionary, hello Emile Durkheim.

Do not let the Anglo-U.N. Summit Conference culture wash out the mystery of the provinces. Do not let the removal of '50's atom bomb paranoia lighten our sense of Nixon, Brezhnev, and Chou, for in their world government we will always be the disloyals, the radicals of psychic liaison and intuitive anarchy. Better to worship the atom as the power that divides us now that the multilingual fire of planetary migrations is soaked in trade English and devalued pesos.

A cloudburst in the bottom of the first gives the Expos three runs when Wayne Garrett puts a wet ball in the Met dugout, and, after the fifteen minute delay and the tarpulin, the rain still mixed with moths in the lights, the clouds invisible beyond, Jon Matlack grooves one to Bob Bailey.

The game is one-sided; the Expos have base runners in every inning; the Mets go out quickly. One a running catch by Willie Mays in deep centerfield keeps the score close. After a couple of innings the Mets begin getting base-runners. Millan pokes a single every time he's up. No runs score until Rusty Staub, playing before the fans that named him Le Grand Orange, first baseball hero of this city, poles one out in right for a run.

All thru the early innings the huge planes leave Montreal for Europe, Asia, and Africa: Irish and Italian airlines, BOAC, Air Canada, 747's low over this game in the wilderness of the body of light. It's not Nebraska or Atlanta. It's Dublin, Antwerp, Rome, New Sydney, Zaire, the Indo-European natal culture, baseball cast against it as a single linguistic riddle in the global village, the voodoo church, the international city Montreal is, New York still is not. The exact and detailed baseball statistics sheathe, in the general numerical seriousness, the import-export diaries of the world, the continuous migrations. The jets are the outer determinants of the game, their wings lit, their position fixed as they approach and leave the earth beneath the clouds.

In the seventh inning the Mets load the bases on a pinch single and a couple of walks; Staub dumps a single into short center, and against the great relief pitcher, Mike Marshall, pinch-hitter Theodore hits the first pitch softly thru the left side; a wild pitch; then Garrett singles in two more. The Mets add a run in the eighth: 7 - 3. These are real hits, solid strokes with physical properties, even as Mays' catch was made in the traction of flying dirt; they are not Mr. Gowdy's relics or Mr. Kubek's archetypal replay; in fact, the ten runs are the first clean runs I have seen in five years, absolute and tingling in the rain-cleared Quebec air.

Beating the crowd by half an inning, rushing thru the night, down the dark avenues counter Laurentian, back into the city, over the bridges, sleepily across rural Quebec, checked out by a senile customs official, onto Vermont 89, Route 2, and home — in the silence of the cosmic broadcast.

Mid Summer – Early Autumn

I

The wind blows away the clouds, and blows away the hot air;
blows away the TOTAL INTERFERENCE, and lo, the Moon,
bright and full and as always; the night hollow and clear.

And I can *see* the Moon. And I can feel: my self. And there is
light shining from the edge of darkness to where I am. The Moon in
the center. Or the vessel for which the Moon is object. In my human,
emotional form. In my sympathetic form. On this plane. It has al-
ways seemed the Moon could be that thing.

Little matter that it is not the Moon.

Where the Moon is shining it *is* the Moon.

And until we have other object for it, the Moon will remain.

The lightning has struck in electrical mimesis; the river has flooded
and torn down the highway; the days have been long and hot. Now
the cold July winds blow the summer air clear. The feeling of chill
IS the clarity IS the brightness, the sense of a passageway I cannot
see; space is filled again with those familiar dimensions I have in-
tuited and that have intuited me all my life.

The air awakens my nerves, and I breathe the pungency of flowers
on whose surface the temperature has changed. Ancestry, trauma,
these obsessions, are sloughed. The croaking of the frogs is over;
their mating has ended; the pool formed by the horse's hooves and
filled by the river is now but a puddle. The toads, with dew glistening
on their vestigial backs, travel thru the high grass. I am alive and I
am larger than all the rest of them. My spontaneity is glee. And I
am. And I cannot fail; it cannot fail me. The sheer wonder of my
not being *there* when I am here.

The prior events I yield upon are nothing. Genes connect me to
my parents, and thru them their parents, the immigrations that
brought them to Europe and America. Someone left the water
running long before that. The granite-cutters, the fishermen, the
migrant farmworkers, the carpenters, the whole Asian continent of
agriculturalists and craftsmen: they speak an older tongue than es-
peranto, they prove the existence of a Moon. Their rhythm and
static blues fills the slums with simple music. Eric Clapton says,
"Play acoustic," and Howling Wolf answers, "Aw, c'mon, man. You
got to start at the top." A story Will Petersen tells me. "I was born
in the wrong race," he says to Muddy Waters. "Yeah," says Muddy,
"we all was."

However far I stretch beyond cultural and racial inheritance, there
are final boundaries, I bring with me into the world. Psyche's night

of Pluto's stars outlives me. The more transcendent forces stray only into the formlines of galactic centers; the stars in the center may shake the tables of Paris, the candles upon them, the flame in the wick, but the plumb goes to the bottom of creation, bearing, in its tattered arms, the child's hope of Justice. Even as I change the form, the form changes to receive me. Proof of the connection between two impossible lovers who twist to be together, who twist to become free.

In the oddest hours of the afternoon, and for no reason at all, I seem to want, I seem not to have. I pause in the torso and allow dream to precede me, breaking the world to mirror the dreamer. I feel the drop in the empty bucket; I hear the single echo at the center; I leave the banquet, granting a false smile to my friends.

II

In the moments upon sleep I feel it, this, this, my, the fragility of the brain. The arguments soften into reflex, which miraculously throughout the nervous system returns as thoughts. We have nothing, we know nothing, we stand on the brink of the eternal loss of intelligence; our bodies and minds are made of the same flesh; all we see, reflected in the sacred pool, is the bulk and immensity of where it lies, the mountains, the spires of stone. It crushes our senses, and we survive in the delicate dispersal we have come to know as Kant, Spinoza, Whitehead, Heidegger, Hegel. Rock quanta are translated into light, stars into thought. The material is strong enough, and we live our lives as giants in these hills. Which don't exist. That they threaten us to crumble, that they are figments. We emerge from brain as mind, unscathed by a chemistry either way.

The cosmos is strung desperately to the ends of it, which will return when the anchor is pulled back. There is no creation, and the anchor is but our link. The pulse plays as faint electricity upon the brain. The immensity is a fake. In these soft fingers which separate all meanings without even touching them I lie here knowing it is a dream. I sit behind and play it on some gossamer yet firm instrument, an electric, perhaps a harp. And the props move like shadows across the wings. As birds spring like sparks.

The liquid is a weak jelly containing small and powerful animals; it begins in the mountains where the snow melts (almost never), charged by the eel thru whose mask it passes, neural and resonant as the showers and storms that mix it from the navel's whirlpool. And when it comes down the other side, as the dancer within the dancer arches, silently disengaging her body, it will light eternity, retrieving that precious candle eros guards, even in romps of the sadist. The stone drops most deeply into the mercurial pool.

Why should it even conceive of vague faces, lips and eyes, should it associate features with the abstract friction it requires, as if personality itself were the edge? To pretend to desire all women, all beautiful women, meaning what, behind the curtain, behind the, behind, the human figure stands, either a man or a woman. The universe is filled with such paradoxes, the star-suns that in feeding themselves fuel civilizations, the cells in whose single hungers we maintain our grip on life, long past their dying. It is not the desire; it stands for the desire. The unfolding riddle of creation leaves everything serving its own ends, woven into the design by the quark of passion. It does not stop at anima or archetype. It couldn't. It is the source, tangled in the bolus beneath the tree. What we must see as contradiction is merely the plane torso bent away from us as sharply as it must bend to include all that it actually is.

III

The sun in the appletree pours light into the dark apple; the cats lie in the unmown margin of field. And down below, in the garden, the peas have grown too close together and without supports; they pull each other down, and the smell of yellowing leaves and pods fills the world with incense. Inside the blue cabbage furry worms are born, eating it out, their eggs not caviar, jellylike though in the acid slums of their gestation. No doubt they are a delicacy also, but one to which we are unable to respond. From under stones and dusts small toads appear, toads smaller than beetles, suggesting that whole possibility of spontaneous generation only hermetic sealing historically disproved. All about, nothing is sealed, and that is the proof of our world and the proof of proof, a posteriori, though everything is hermetic, entanglement of origins and properties leaving physics only, physical matter in its definitions. All other properties, as those of language, mingle, give rise to illusions, hide sources, nourish slight malapropisms we retain from the beginning of things.

I want to listen to the hollow sound behind life, the empty pool in which no women live, or in which woman itself has reached a form it is impossible to desire. Not only has she taken off the clothes in fantasy you would have her take off but she has taken off her body. And still she stands there fully dressed. The end of gender in pure incarnation, bearer of the lefthand staff. The rest is reality, or what, by being furthest from reality, suggests the same.

The sun, mingling its body with an arc of colors all of which we think of as blue, prescribes the day. At sunset it is difficult to pick blackberries. At night it is impossible, but sunset suggests what is happening, with the mosquitos, the armed shrubs, the cluttering shadows which blend into final blackness. The blackberries we do not pick will rot on the branches, the birds will eat what they can. So we fill small containers and put them in the new white freezer, wondering also if we should buy a whole or quarter of beef, how many peas we should boil and pack. Will the prices go up? What have we forgotten? This isn't the way, even for those who follow it.

The dim outlines of this are the edges of beyond the articulated, sounds that will never be heard but whose false, whose formed articulation allows more distant outlines to be intuited as the inarticulatible. Deeper and deeper into the wiring we go, a problem that is submitted to solution at the moment of waking even as it is submitted, less tacitly, to going to sleep. The unconscious grows wise only as consciousness, for it is a separate intelligence, as formal in its removal as a master or chief.

Where the river has washed out the road it is slowly repaved, though we rarely see the crews at work. By the time they get done, the snow will cover it. Now it is bumpy but rough. This is Northern New England, which most poets have abandoned for the other coast. "Certainly is a lovely place," Creeley says, of Bolinas, again and again, until I sense, as in woman, the form of wishing the beautiful place to be where the place itself is that is beautiful, object of desire at the spot where desire leads, until it too diminishes into ocean and stars, of which there are plenty, until all images are reduced to the blanched chemistry of eyes and nerves, and a more attentive chemistry is required. The aspirin, dissolved in the headache, simply gets you to the other, dull side of the foam.

Sitting in the wooden alcove with less than half a beer left, sensing perhaps the hollowness, perhaps the fullness that makes secret places hollow, sensing, in each gentle sip, the spacious outlay of the design.

IV

The growth of the world is hidden in the world, first as a sequence
of Platonic forms, again as the dirt and debris, fragments and signs
blown as pure chaff thru the habitable zones. From the seed-laden
earth, a jungle of weeds arises to the summer heat, the sun's densest
chords, as though the corona of, in its pulsing and waning were the
vines and shoots and flowers, the eggs in spots of moistness, the
stratum of fertile stone, equalling, in formation and decay, the debris
of the stars after the original explosion. Which, if not primary matter,
is the most basic posit and mulch we know. Yet this great Sympathy,
sprung from the Archer as his nerves, the sinew of his bow, has faded
into ionospheric disturbance and single meteors in the fountain of
air. A windblown dust, a fog, an erratic and oblique rain and rust:
this is the world we are in (not because it is any more the world than
the one for which the King received on his head the crown and its
touch, bringing lightness and light even to the husk of the villages of
the tundra). At this angle the image of reality is different than what
is seen on the visible surface the light strikes in the garden; the glow-
ing petals cup a withheld structure each animal suspects in his own
way. The Hindu philosopher sorts the strands of the Rope, at a point
where shape and fire converge, in an illusion of the Real, as, post-
Linnaean, artificial symmetry vanishes, and the seeds in the ovary,
the number and relation of the petals to the ovary, become strict
signs of real prehistoric events. The trumpet creeper winds around
the Jerusalem artichokes; the heads of aster and fleabane swell in
the shape of a flower with tiny flowers; the ground-cherry crawls
over the piles of old sticks. In the near distance, wild flowering
raspberry — beyond which, like a fire in the swamp, is a patch of
phlox. Queen Anne's Lace, the wild carrot with the soft white
umbels, and the young feathery domestic carrots, are divided from
each other by where the plow has made the garden and we have
weeded to keep the outer growth from impinging, indigenous versus
imported seeds, children of Nineteenth Century biology. An 1890
nickel found in furrowing out the pea-patch.

These images are nascent to my work and appear in blithe un-
guarded form in the early editions of the garden; "The Plant Book"
and *Solar Journal* are prototypical of a way of seeing, a simultaniety
of totem and animal, medicine and potion, fetish and taboo. Now
the vision, fresh with its source in those rivers, diverges, and in a
quiet field goes underground, into the darkness, before the next
great range of mountains.

What is hidden we do not know, but it is the same as the feelings, which almost seem to come from within. Where they cease is a space, like the room that was never filled with furniture, the monstrous mutant who cannot be born: outside the light, the knowing, yet attached to the building, no way to cut him off and no way to add him on. Thus a gesture, like a hunchback carrying himself and his bentness; with the twining of the vine, the causes accrue from within; it's not like signs or omens, we cannot tell from a man's appearance his fate and phrenology, nor from the flash of a zodiac at the instant of his birth, the condition of the instantaneity of his life; likewise he is not an arbitrary constitution of the forces combining to account for his existence. He is a strut in the flux of creation thru parallel and equivalent possibilities, bound as a handful of wheat, in this spot, where life is, where life is *not*/an abstraction, yet is *abstract* from the system which would seem to deny it its possibility of being anything more than the atomic process which *mimics* life, which is locked crystalline dance and passage of sediments, hushed fire that slides from ice age to ice age, from Pluto to Vulcan in the forge, and from cyclone to temperate sea, monsoon to thunderstorm, or what Charles Coulston Gillespie, in speaking of Lamarck, called "its lifeless residue spilling as chemical husks back down the other side," is but a giant, and we are the living units that crack on the whips of his exaggerated wight. This is why Lamarck, priestless and elemental, reached for the ingot Heraclitus struck so long ago, and why we have been unable to douse it in all the culture since.

The periods of growth are hidden within as numbers; they are pulses, cycles, ratios; they are the remains of a numerological manual for the excavation of a more ancient kingdom of matter, itself kept beneath the flow by a continuous repetition and interpolation of integers and matheses, reappearing, deceptively, as logarithms and progressive intervals, tensors and quarks. That in the garden the peas are the first plants to rule, with their lusty upfling after the spring rains, their bursts of flowers and pods while all the rest is small leaves and seedlings. Now they have withered, dried out, and fallen back, except for a few that grasp the fence and bamboo poles and continue to climb and give off a green shoot. The potatoes, quartered from kitchen stock, buried in the ground at odd moments, some even before the peas, presumed to be rotting or dormant, leap up between the rows of beans, and while the peas twist and curl downward, the potatoes develop secondary branches and stand over the entire garden, a small dark forest — as though their starchy slag will feed them forever. In another ten days the beans are so tall the potato tops are not even visible; their soft alternate leaves flap in the breeze and their curls blossom with butterfly flowers. The potatoes are invaded by hardshelled bugs who leave an orange secretion, as if that were their deep response to the green fluids they drank, who lay black eggs that yield softshelled young, so hungry and at such a rate the leaves literally disappear, until a powder made from the Asian derris root, a bug poison called rotenone, is applied, after which the potatoes abandon the chewed-up stems and meander along new lines. The cabbages, tomatoes, and lettuce begin to spread, and the kohlrabi sprouts hardy leaves. It is a combination of inner fire, soil, rain, sun, plus the no longer random times at which the seeds were laid in dirt; a shape is cast in the garden, which wanders as its coordinates take on visible values; joined by fatherland to the free growth around the garden, which has also been subject to wind, water, animal movement, perennial division, Indians foraging, early farms, etc., different only in that *we* are the ostensible source and interference causing domestic patterns to flare and wane, an overall disposition whose day has as little to do with our conscious mind as our dreams, happening under stars and Moon and in the twilight dew. Each full-born leaf opens, cools, and draws moisture from the thin fog.

Now the chard towers over the potatoes and beans, its unwrapping swallowing the tenderness and sparsity of the first leaves. The thick juicy branches part to allow smaller shoots to form in the center. And the lettuce, sown in the early hours of spring, piles leaves atop leaves, whorled and heaped as clouds in the hot day, become bitter as the rain is cold, unto a seething of black seed from which the first sweet leaves again emerge, the integers that fool us again and again, the genetics that damn us to (albeit the magic of) this world. The squash, planted late and in a mound, sprouts with a twinned cotyledon; in a few weeks these have vanished, and where they were are multiple trunk systems, thick and pulpy, bearing leaves bigger than burdock thistle; they cover the hills; in fact, like trees of heaven, they dissolve the mountain in which they were nourished, throwing massive replicas from the circuitry of the seed; the principle of vegetation defeats the aged Titan of stone. In fact, the section of the garden that was planted late, at the far end, has overshadowed the foreground, where the pea patch is in ruin and the lettuces tumble, the onions stalks point down (most of their action, as that of the carrots, is underground). The corn was planted on the last possible day; now the largest of them reach just over the squash, exploring from the kernel a size and vitality the delicate plants spurn. The transplanted ears are much smaller, needing, it seems, two weeks to regain their rootings before attending to the stalks. Perhaps I should have planted more seed and wasted less time transplanting, but the plot is small, and I seek changing rhythms and staggered growth rates, gardens within gardens. The brussel sprouts are as tiny and unbudding as a month ago, but the one tomato which survived the frost is full and flowering, with small green berries; the ones started from seed after the frost are still tiny cups of leaves and will perhaps only have begun to flower when the frost at the other end comes.

These rhythms and thrusts, as thick as squash, as tender as the peas' climb against the implantment from which they twist, as airy as tomato, as bolelike as kohlrabi, as taproot and underground as carrot, have the weights and senses of all the personal rhythms I intuit. And by noting this, instead of the herbal and the sympathy of macrocosm and microcosm, I have substituted a genetic psychology for a botanical astrology. I have allowed the reimplementation of the Earth by giants, who inhabit it also, and whether we shall survive by this means, by our houses and by the incredible structuring of the concrete cities, as from squash roots of civilization, blossoming before their time, decaying back into the rubble of half-manufactured, half-fused, disintegrating chemicals, before it becomes altogether archaeology, is dangerously unknown, as I am unknown, how I will grow, being a plant of variable and rhythmic emboîtement, with broken lines and sterile stems, flowers and branches so heavy with fruit they sag into the mud, spread seed, take root, and reflower. Now from this thin tendril on which I climb, almost gravity-defying, thru the hollow regions of my life, there seems to be nothing firm and macrophysical, poke as I may the small space in the log out of which I am suspended.

The city has lost its roots also, the possibility of its identification with the source, in Egypt, or Tyre. Once Platonic, the Merovingian, likewise Inca, it must also be real or the flared plaza of sympathies and streets would not have yielded dram, as it has thru the continuing ancient history of the planet. The connection is obscure, the infinitesimal and spidery chains which fill a prior world with precious and igniting spindles, in a mystery we have long forgotten (across whose subtle aura Kepler's vision of regaining the planetary cycles and equilibria of the tablets of Atlantis is but a faint shadow) of the Egyptian doctor guiding his patient thru dream to the source of the illness, to the origin of the disturbance, a moment so traumatically implanted and so weakly recalled, whether of the priest-physician or of the Egyptian locale, that in our hypermodern reading of it we seem to require an Esalen-like nakedness to reveal what lies within ourselves as people and inhabitants of the mystery. The body has become the social integument of the condition of being here, whose sympathetic and emotional origin is x-ray either of the immeasurable embryonic growth of the Janovian releasing wail (of the realization of the original moment: but of what?: ourselves?, the culture?, the creation?, the flow of what transiently-potent substance to these distant nervepoints?). The priest has become as false as he is akashic, withheld from us in another place, as thin as the selves we try to enter beyond the veil that the numbers and the plenty and the cornucopia of the world-game we are in, the technological-industrial orgy, has thrown over the coming Sun Age.

* * *

Small grasshopper on the rim of the garden jumps from one numeral to another, within a spiral mask, shaking the high stems in a ripple of its movement. Winged insect, legs hanging down, weaves in and out of the Jerusalem artichokes, following their margin on his sensorium, plus their own penetration of the world along hairy stems, gland knots, and large whorled leaves, the sunflowers yet to spring. A young fly, golden-linked in its center, lands on a flat leaf, a brief sparkle of sunlight from the segments, while the wind moves thru in a rustle. Ants crawl upon the lemmas of grass, dismantling the grain to build replicas of their eternal city. The bright blue bean flowers stand among the soft purple clover and the dry capsules of earlier years, whose juices have filled the herbals, their intoxication famous, leaving nothing behind in the mimosan leaves.

We have pushed this event into such visibility that we have lost the *Synopsis of the Quadrupeds and Serpents*, the *History of Insects*, the Great Chain of Being, and like quartos. The fins of the fish *are* the arms of the man, but only in the radial outburst of vita from the common center; life itself is the wonder, not man, who wanders into the garden a dwarf, seeking another resemblance, for this fire is surely not the Hand of God, Which lies, with the clover and its Hellenic qualities, in some other plane.

Realytie has come to mean to us: reality, and not the cosmic riddle or the so-called energy behind the veil. We think only of the sum constituent parts of the present system, dilated in time by the dimensional suspension; it is never something persistently invisible but a code which can be made visible, in taking apart the flower, counting the petals, establishing the embryonic origin of the structure, and uncovering, in the transition and survival of species, the nest. As by particle theory in physics, spectrographic analysis of the stars, we have gone deeper and deeper into a substance which may be totally foreign to Realytie, to the possibility by which we have been brought into Creation creatures of vision.

46

The trouble is that now the limits are the real limits, Marx not-withstanding (and glorious rectifying revolution after revolution); there is labor, there is capital, there is production; technological improvement of the means has no real effect on the human experience, this the Eighteenth Century discovered. As man increases, as any species, he goes into the sparsity of matter, the basic infertility of the Stone — beyond the fires that brought him into being — past which are the cold serpentine currents of the cosmic mines, where the alert Aristotelian animal dreads to dwell, or even to have originated. As man approaches the absolute limits of life, the only reason there seem to be no limits and the situation appears without danger is the imposition of an (albeit almost empty) space, like that of which between the Earth and the Moon is a present example, or thru which the oil drill goes after it has penetrated the glacial ice and the mantle. The bottom is reached only thru devastating exhaust and exhaustion, and then in mere vitated amounts, of fuels and energy and metabolism, to maintain the illusion of infinity and progress — more than Turner's sheer American frontier (overstepped in Southeast Asia anyway); the frontier of matter, beyond oil and beyond the rich supposed yield of atomic theory, from which to derive increased labor, security of the workers thru their unions, from which to build module houses and inhabit worse and worse badlands. This is the process to which we are consigned and committed, and if there is parallel or serial universe to our own, it is the last thing we will see, for we think we do not need it, we are set so as to be entirely dark to it, as it darkens to us. The limits we have set are the most unhappy of limits, for they are greedy and thoughtless of the greater wealth; they go in seasons and thru the false process of history, from year to year, naive of the Great Year, empty of meaning, except as we endow it with the progressive meanings of our civilization, as one war comes to an end in the beginning of another. And when we reach the end of that machinery, there is a hollow, that in psychoanalysis is called the unfelt reality, and whether unfelt or not psychologically, is certainly the psychic darkroom, the alcove and abyss behind life. This is the wonder of the bottom. We keep ourselves from exploring there in part because the energy is free, and the world has accumulated a giant debt we must pay off, as we will it to those within and beyond us, the myth behind the psychosomatic retreat from health. The light originates in the many veils thru which prakṛti are brought into being, in the Sanskrit identical to the Latin original of the later Neoplatonic design, thru shells of matter that endlessly pour forth and are filled with texture and sense, which leaves them even as we approach the boundary of what and where we are. Tangency in the system, as to land upon the craters of the Moon, just to get there, demands an outlandish squandering of energy, the kick into the rocket flask of the burning of the chaff, into men's minds the yawing computer mind. We seek the stirring of the true moving bodies, within the life, in the friction and flood, Lamarck's primacy of fire forcing a return to its own, its kindred instinctual diatom — to penetrate the dark unlivable space between here and there (to prevent systems each of which is holy from annihilating each other). Otherwise, man is a base intruder upon a world of cinders and stone, and the zooid itself, like the bug in whose armor it comes, is an accidental invader of a tomb.

* * *

I have stood on the shoulders, as they say, of the giants who have gone before me, but now they are forgotten, and their work is submerged in mine. History itself blurs: who Kant was as distinct from Hegel or Leibniz I cannot figure because, despite internal contradictions, they all do say the same thing. It is like being set down in the middle of a city on an unfamiliar block: how can you tell New York from Detroit? And now the weight on myself — that I have avoided history and have read only frenetically across its trade-route hierarchies for an occult object, Plotinus the unknown queen. I have climbed thru the intricacy of the caves, to get to the beginning, for which modern thought has substituted the end, a so much less frightening possibility, that nothing need be experienced in the inevitable because everything will disappear violently back into the fabric, in the same explosion that wipes out all our memory and all our pain, whatever we carry thru existence, whether it be this alone or the iota to which we attribute ourselves.

The beginning is terrifying and inalterable; at the end all is forgotten. At the beginning we reach the origin of what we are, despite Einsteinian simultaneity; for just because the Greeks and Phoenicians, the Romans and Hebrews and Atlanteans and Celts, the Polynesians and Africans, are brought back by the akashic force of omega and the resources of time, it is not the same as the moment they came into being, totally unapocalyptic, engaged in the habitat which demography assigned to them, the necessity that left them alone in the silence of their space, with an alphabet and ritual calendar, a plant-and-star science and a genealogy, from which no fugue was or is possible because history never lets go, and to which our vast unconscious push, our pure and vessel flesh is only the residual, likewise the weight that held the crane and supplied the rawstuff when Kant and Hegel built their cities, and why what they built are cities. We have the strange illusion that the contemporary is followed by the post-modern, and that the more radical the function we serve in the present order the more accurate it is to the basal energy of our condition.

The squash and cucumber twist and twine in the coefficients of genetic and chemical embodiment, a subtle fluid in their torsos, in the shimmering octave which winds around the world and holds it to itself, as erotically as numbers fit — because where there is an entrance in one, there is an entrance *from* the other; where three and four meet and breed, in four thirds or three fourths, is the binding together, the filling of the maples with wind and rain and light, the wild grass, the economic growth of nations, or the insect mincing along the thatched leaves of ground cover, is where we are within where we are. It is the explosion we feel, this pulling apart, the fabric moving outward at a speed and revelation that transcends the infinity of production or money necessary to live totally off the interest, to which modern America, in burgeoning inflation, similar to population explosion, similar to quasar discovery and Saturnian suck-off, to the richness of the microscopic vision, succumbs by denominations of itself.

* * *

It is beyond   feeling. The association has been lost.

It is humiliating to be this kind of a being, unable to translate literally the workings of an intelligence back into the gemmules of being. So the ultimate attack on meaning does not come via our philosophies; it comes thru our bodies, in the form of equally powerful arguments and transformations. The lethargies, the head-aches, the terrors, which punctuate this work at critical junctures, are not recorded in the text, except as captives; they must be discerned thru my evasion, as the part of meaning they form simply by chopping it — against the clarities, proving that the clarities themselves are not clear, sparkle as they do on the surface of this beautiful and recalled morning (entangled with the aura and resilience of the vegetable kingdom). There is a chemistry of doubt as well, and by evening it can literally crack the Moon apart in my head.

There are moments when, unexpectedly down a flat path that is more remote than I remember ever, sits the debris of a city. Everything is fallen. And as often as I thought in the interim: *I will clean that up; I will reconstruct it*, the actual circumstance is more sobering. The city is beyond repair. What is left seems less and less like a psychoanalytic exercise and more like the bird whose singing pierces sleep. Old smells of mown grass and the cold of spring water are returned in me, and without the pain of longing with which they were once associated, and which made them beautiful.

The physical envelope is no different than the philosophic envelope; they embody each other and coincide; hence the yoga, not to let thru so much imformation it must pry them apart. Even if this life is not sentient of other lives, this life unerringly leads us. There is no single casting of the die. The smell of the tomato plants is eternal, the vapors they give off. We act not to fill time but to postpone the anxiety of time, the devastating hole in creation time is. It is too late for me to reduce the text to a minimal system or to undo the complexities I have survived. The slags are calm, oceanic, almost eternal, and the small part of them on which I impinge, historically for reasons that I am made of matter lie in a single breath. The vessel will corrode, but I have roots as deep in the history of the world as any clover, which leaves me throwing up these nerves, like branches in the scarlet air.

V

Out on the rocks, the misty sweep of Champlain, a vision once as clear and young as North America, now the people like birds playing around the edge, the children diving off the cliffs.

The motorboats carrying cocktail lounges idle in the marina by the ferry dock.

I climb on the stones baked dry in the sun, slimy at waterline. It is so long since I have gone into the water that I become an animal, arms and legs struggling and paddling to keep afloat, beaver nose above the gentle waves. I kick my way thru the mud zone and swim out beyond the point of rocks and around to their other side. I sit on the rocks drying off under the total blue sky.

Then the oil spill washes in, dank aromatic prophecy, a mere 200 years either way. Why are we sitting in the back of Margaret's car going to the toystore? Why are we buying Robin blocks to make a city? Why are we driving to the lake? Why am I with these people?

We get dinner at the delicatessen and eat it at the Fresh Ground Coffee House. The chatter rises with the smoke and the smell of rich vegetable and root brews. The shadows fall thru the afternoon, the

50

buildings strung out on the street, and summer riding thru like a bicycler, until he tumbles off wearily into the woods, into a stream of aqua vitae bearing his sleeping form thru the land.

VI

I recall at this point a dream of embryos, tadpoles, sealed buds, and birds fused in their eggs, fish children locked in eternal radius; forms that will not be realized (and are not realized) are delivered at me in sequence, as a garden in which I wandered, and saw for flowers the expressionless faces of partial humans and fish. And the sense that they will be that way forever, that nothing can save them. In my own body, a curtailed nature, submerged forms of viruses, tiny skulls, wingless birds, rodents, and ancestral men. I perceive about me a second nature, a vast unfinished design.

Psyche lies dormant, without her lover, without her body, though her lover is whom we choose to be our lover. The mind is flooded with an underlying electricity, the form information takes when it must travel between systems, the darkness of time lit only in the clearing houses of the stars. There come, before and after, dreams of urban centers within somatic centers, going far beyond anything we can use or inhabit, even the madman or spinning dervish who, in their seizures of vast geometries, enter a mute countenance of partial wonder, partial unfelt pain.

I dream of a magnificent and dangerous bridge from peninsula to peninsula, constructed in the remote land where men have not yet been; the road map becomes a geological survey, and we plot our way sharply to the North. After a town called Figean, where the people celebrate in fire-heated bars and the winter comes with twenty years of darkness, there is another town, called Snowzone, or North-flake, which, because on the map the road is straight, we expect to reach by nightfall. We come hurtling off the superhighway at Figean onto a bumpy dirt road, barely sustained thru the closing tree cover, certainly no width in which to turn around, so we tumble on, in a laborious and inappropriate car, knowing now we will have to cross the bridge in total darkness and alone; then we will pass into the undeveloped lands, the regions whose roughness and coal-like deposits render them invisible, for they contain nothing of present value, by Earthly science; their ores have not been touched by life.

Who built these roads we do not know, which is why we dream them, and why we find them there, like the thin astral suspension we imagine between the subpeninsula of Michigan and the superpeninsula of Minnesota. "The embryo of the vertebrate animal is from the very first a vertebrate animal, and at no time agrees with an invertebrate," if set loose in the waters would prove not to be a fish, von Baer proclaimed a hundred and fifty years ago. We proceed thru strange and relict forms we contain within us, but they are of ourselves, not of the animal kingdom.

* * *

The night was warm, then hot, and at the graduation party bearded boys with broken red hearts on their shirts went around kissing bearded boys, as well as girl-boys with black masks; and girls sat in corners soul-kissing. There was no rain, but static on the radio, in bursts, and reports of drastic weather to the South, thunderstorm warnings moving along the dial, so that each station to the North forecast them half an hour later, that reached us in the middle of sleep, and awoke us partly, the sound of the neighbor's shovel building a channel to keep the water out of his house. Lightning was descending in every dimension, received into the ground like a crumbling meteorite; the water rang against glass and tin and thru the leaves.

We slide inertially between thresholds of dream, of noticing one another, of being transported thru the bells of the storm as if they were a progression, and awake in the morning with early plans to take the stray male cat with the swollen paw to the vet. On our way down the hall Lindy throws open the curtains, and our first sight is of our old white cat lying motionless by the back garden fence, far from her kittens, surely dead. Even as I hunt for the shovel to bury her, Lindy goes to check and finds her head moving, in visionless broken arcs, her pupils leaping in all directions, her eyes wild, as if all she sees is inside her, and inside that. She does not respond to water or touch, though perhaps a tiny part of her does, and is held in check by the harness within it. She moves her head in spooked repetition as if to unwind the fatal bonds, not that we shall ever know what did it, but from all the stories one unfolds: the storm moving over, close to the ground, armed with lightning and in all directions so that her nervous system is surrounded by enemies, as she tries to get out of it, as she tries to remember where she left her kittens, running insanely into the fence where she now lies, the record broken.

Perhaps it hasn't happened, it never happened, it is only in flesh, which fails to record it, even as the tablets of dream, confused in the sense of those who manipulate us, cannot be translated by the soldiers of language and light. And, damnit, if He was going to consign us to a world, why did He choose this one?; and why didn't He finish it?

* * *

At the same party was the sister of one of my students and the mother of both of them; the family stood there, ravaged by genetic design. The girl herself, having been rescued from lifelong commitment in a mental hospital by an act of violent perception, wrote, for her degree, a profound Laingian analysis of her condition, making it the creative schizophrenia. But what lies before and behind her in the seed?: a sister with a mute and frozen face, slouched and expressionless, the hulk, and a mother still shrilly arguing the condition from her doorstep, in pathological full humor — the pursuant oddity, that we call it mental, as our ancestors before the witch trials did, not just the Black Plague, but the omnipresence of an alien and hostile design.

Before falling asleep I lay in bed, on the surface of my tension, my blocked thought, my anxieties — all I don't let myself know because I think I could not survive the knowledge. They are there, just outside, the trusting ones, and conscious is the only, the perfect link. I tell them: I am here; I want you to know I am here, to understand where it is; I know more than I can ever say, about what I don't know. I will tell you, that it is possible, that it is okay, and in fact I will allow you, we will be electrical and perfect lovers, like the rough and unhewn phases of the Moon.

At the moment of greatest certainty the curtains close, and there is dream, and all that flies flies to separate levels; in the morning the debris of the storm is everywhere, the landscape altered in so many ways it is another landscape, as from an older dance; the witches have withdrawn, pleading that they are not witches, that they were not witches, even as they confess, even as they leave their handiwork in our midst.

VII

Grossinger, New York

The entrants weigh in on the scales, and we find out how much
they have lost or gained since the last incarnation, if they can even
remember whether it is loss or gain. Weight is health in some vague
and ominous way, so that inhabitants who cannot see each other see
only each other, how fat or how thin.

The construction crews work on giant new guest buildings, blowing
the urban dust into the air with the August seeds. When I was a child,
and came here from New York, this was the country. Now from Ver-
mont, it is the city; the individual cottages have become an apart-
ment complex; the streets are paved. No complaints. This is a business,
and they are building what the people want. Guests stand in the
lobby wearing turbans of towels from the health clubs, firing rifles
into the blue three-dimensional landscape, hitting World War I air-
planes, and jungle animals, and ancient warriors. Even on color t.v.
the German air force is blue-maxing a ground-army; click to another
channel and Arthur's knights have trapped the Goths with water on
three sides of them. "Now, let's put fire on the fourth," says Lance-
lot; so they cut down giant trees and set them on fire with their
arrows.

Yet even those few stars that are visible in the milky air control
this whole set, in my mind as well, and I look to them for history
and dynasty when Grossinger's itself seems only an architect's blue-
print of prosperity. The stars, not because they are visible, but be-
cause they outlast any individual meaning, because they are *not
visible* and all we see of them is a bent mirror of all we don't see of
everything else. What matters is the sparks. The rest is duration, and
ingredient, osmotic trickle, puts on beef and weight and plays golf
all day and gambles away its history, future, cared for like a babbling
baby by Nanny Artifice. Everyone thinks I look thin, and tells me,
with concern on their faces, or cannot remember how I looked, so
that the lightness I feel, the sense of being about to disappear, the
etiological disease, is my own inability to stand with them, vice-
presidents and lawyers and distinguished members of the board, like:
"Give me ten men . . . . .," and always at stake how much there is
of someone, physically, filling out, how vital the meat, how terminal
the interest, and how long the drive out of that dynamo to the
twelfth green.

The paper maché buildings go up like cities, and before the end
of the month the carpeting and queen-size beds will roll in. The multi-

million dollar bank loan is floated out on inflation like Noah, the golf course riding what was forest like a bronco buster, how it gleams beneath the daylamp, a green target; and how what is left of the forest, toads and rotting tree stumps, stands as a beggar, dark, scraggly, and proud. The fatal genes must out if life is lived long enough, must join the rest of the body. Either we develop the terrain or we go back into the young wild condition that gave us life, content that chaos is its own law. No Grossinger tombstone for me. Just the wind, which feeds sparks to unknown battlements. A windblown culture psyche will not forget, even when we are long buried in psyche's neap.

* * *

The music tinkles and the pool water trickles, blue, colored by sky and by paint on the inside. The bestiary is arranged in lounge chairs. And the left leg won't kick in swimming, so that I struggle against what is lodged in the muscles, to gain the freeline, ain't there, and swim against it back and forth across the pool, the smell of tar off the construction, the cold element on my skin, a high. There is so much food on silver platters I have become a camel and can no longer eat.

We flee the cornucopia along old Route 55, thru Neversink, toward Grahamsville, over the vast city reservoirs, past the revival meetings, the fields dense with corn — softly rising along the mountains into the light, coming down into Woodburne, its streets filled with Hassidim and late summer tourists waiting for buses. The bungalow colonies, just on the edge of the woods, no more than single shacks, with a pool in their center, are the entrance to something; it may be no more than an intense nostalgia, and it may be the uncertainty whether they are abandoned just this summer or have been abandoned for years. The crowds come now to Grossinger's and the other giants, to escape exactly that painful memory, the terror nothing will replace the love and joy they once felt, because it is somewhere else, in a bungalow in an old rusting shower in a shed the paint is peeling from, no luxury or immortality can restore.

VIII

It is more like music than anything else, botany as a living mathematics, the plants lured into meadows and barrens only by the varying moisture and warmth of the Earth, that old charmer, chimera, Schleiden and the German romantics found him to be. The numbers play, the song grows closer, and now in our century we pass from the polyp to the psychic, pursued by an image of an image of ourselves. The same law that has made us human insures that we are only human. The embryo breathes with gills and sucks its inherited tail. How young it was!

But the beautiful teenager has gone the way of the newt, whom we might once have seen in the mirror. There is only Socrates, and every line on his face, every wart, every ripple in his voice, goes back to a time before the Greek, inherited from what mind is, and with mind, even as the crocodile moves toward dark waters, to submerge his body in the delta. The questions to our answers incubate with scars that were birds and horsetails, that tattoo our flesh thru the coda of other lifetimes.

The seed matures while the scarab waits inside his golden egg, sniffing the soil and trace elements that border his kingdom — there on the edge of darkness where even the serfs are hooded, and the master weaves a winter blanket that can not be put on. The bonfire lit by the revolutionaries gives no light. The dadaists crowd the depot of the meiotic egg: the vestigial fantasy that all seeds are concealed in each other in Adam's loin played out in an age when our lives do seem the shadow of an eternal code.

IX

There are so many songs, so many singers, so much has been lost already, and these few records are what I hold onto, from all I once had, their grooves awakening to the needle always. Playing 45's into the late evening, real loud, I lie there defending a prickly calm, the distance of body and memory against which a self is measured. Gene McDaniels singing: *If I were a Tower of Strength!!!*, and Robbie, lying on the couch holding his blanket and sucking his thumb, suddenly perks up with: "He says, 'I don't like you. I don't need you. I don't want you,' and then he walks out the door. He's very mean."

And I realize that he can hear the words too, and they mean something different to him, as they will continue to, until the end. I'm not a teenager anymore. Lindy is sitting by him on the couch, blue jeans, no socks, tapping rhythm, pregnant. The songs are the same but we are different, deflected from them, so that their intensity is greater, like the sun behind the empire, behind the swollen boll, that is being human. It is how far from what I was I have come, and at what cost, for though I no longer suffer the indignities of then, and though for the first time something real in me can be fulfilled, there is also something lost and empty, for which I keep returning, as if it could be found and forged with the new being I am, as if it might be the writing itself.

Sam the Sham: *Hey there Little Red Riding Hood, you sure are looking good*; Al Wilson and *The Snake*; the Four Seasons, *Big Girls Don't Cry*; Jimmy Rodgers: *tell 'm what The Wizard said*; looking for story songs that make Robbie laugh, and: "You better put those ones with my records," as well as: *people talking with*out speak*ing; it's all so beautiful!; and I know I'm going to miss you/for a long long time.* The landscapes flicker and verge, a triple-exposure holograph film in purples and violets, responding like a sine wave and its alpha tailwind to a landscape that is only harmonic, as in an old comic book of Mars the orchestra has horns, woodwinds, and pianos, the crowd is dressed for the symphony, but instead of sound, colored musical notes come out of their instruments and blend in the air. All this begun by the *Monster Mash* from CHUM (Toronto) blending in with the final inning of the Mets' 1 - 0 win over San Francisco on WHN (New York), both 1050; *it's a graveyard smash* in the counter-rhythm, while gaining force on thru it: *Bond dives — and he can't catch up with it; Boswell rounds third and comes in to score the winning run . . . . it's the Monster Mash*, so that emotions and associations are literally juggled. It is not that these songs are any more precise than the thoughts and memories, but they are more human, more —pathetic, and oddly off-center the vision. They so little knew, in the studio, in the moment of heat when they sang, what time would do to all of us, so that now something like a generation has passed, and *Rolling Stone* and Watkins Glen, with the rock singer as culture hero, politician, and yes David Bowie, false prophet, have wasted for us that melancholy Martian landscape, albeit to make our vision muddy, bloody, and real, i.e., the drugs as immediate and direct vision, the music as twisted bio-energies, beyond which surge of youthful and Roman confidence an older race has faded into a sorry Druidlike cavalcade. The obliquity of their songs, as remote messages, as Wolfman static, left them broke and bankrupt, dishonored

57

among their followers, in jail or o.d.ed, or coming back to their people as castrated social workers.

The brilliant sunlight of today. How working outside with the black typewriter in the hot light I brought back some more pieces of the high school novel, reading, in my own words, that even then I listened to songs on Friday night, their irrevocable sorrow, their promise of a day of unimaginable brilliance, as eleven years later I sit here with the same text. The blue sky, against which the clouds visibly grow and break apart, and the cumulus hang in island-like clusters beneath the distant bands of cirrostratus, an older more fluid Earth.

Forget it, all those voices seem to say. It's only your life. You've remembered it too well. It's special only because it *seems* to have happened to you, and cannot be changed, for a whole lifetime, as you remember it.

Dead as the bird the cats have caught, killed, and laid before their kittens, which was alive and on a branch earlier in this day visualizing the same blue world I was in, or another one like it, the body now like stuffing on the ground, torn apart as filler for the kittens, to chew up, to play, the feathers, themselves shafts of a plummage nature bursts with in residual lacquers, stuck on their mouths and noses. And the fear: what if the devil created this whole thing, we delude ourselves in, if in the end we come face to face with his order, and he tells us: *you are my playthings; you are mere decoration; there is no hope for you*, his mask the anesthesia that deadens the plundering raping warriors to their victims, until they deal pain as pleasure; to face him, as one can *look away from* the damage the cats have done, brings our very existence to a crisis of meaning — for in the end we know that, by any law, the dimension itself shifts before the final recognition. No matter how strongly he says it: *I am the devil and it's all for me it is done*, he remains inside us, where he cannot be proved; we wouldn't know or respond to him other- wise, dead or alive though we be, or think we be. Terror and dis- tortion are limited by the scale of nature, the bird's body torn apart; process falls into the disguise of the enveloping levels within levels, so that that which perceives, in its sensorium, lies both with- in and without that which is perceived, and the seal is absolute at any crescendo of the scale. It is a fact that cannot be changed, no matter what the carnal scourge turns us into, no matter what chaff is left behind to fill a world with its materia. It's now, here, we better make sure it's not the devil inside us, because when that's turned in- side out, it's the blue water that's going to be the fire in our nerves.

Still, after dinner, the methodical labor of cutting the chard from

the bottom of the stalk, filling the white bag I drag behind me, think-
ing about how fertile these green leaves, how far they would go,
filling with sun in Vermont, standing on the street corner in the city
slum dispensing them for free until they run out, and then driving
back to Vermont for more, a mechanical song I develop in the sheer
leafage, as I cut the stems from the billowing geese and pile them
separately in a big carton, sheer form we cut and cook and preserve
on our own terms, spinachy sun-absorbing layer we rip up only to
turn into blood and shit, turn back into the ground via the mulch
heap, pure bran which floods and fuels the fire of life, only to be
eliminated as the darkness of life and the starless night that expands
to fill the wintry universe, only to contract to a nodule, to have life
spawn in it again, how hopeless, as I get more tired, as dishonest
people come back for more, and sell it to the grocery markets down-
town, and work into the night, boiling stems, with the ballgame on,
filling cellophane bags with them, and piling them in the freezer.
How essential the mass, in one form or another, to keep us going,
and how slim this mortality they have given us if they were to give
us anything, which god knows they didn't have to; how I must
cringe and hunch to protect it, and grow weak to be strong, lose
energy by capturing energy, the mass of the body responding with
such iodine sensitivity to the currents of brain and mind, the memories
of posture and stances of uneducated martial protection, still
grumbling like a sluggish giant thru a world it must be told to be in
even as it sees. And then it all softens, it all responds, as the family
sits in the living room listening to these old records, the high music,
the harmony of jive voices, remembering, so unconsciously, so simply,
it must be okay, and I will continue this text, the two of us, child,
child in embryo, even though our balance hangs in a deadly and un-
predictable lesion, whose momentum outweighs our lithe sensibility,
our life upon the heap: but what else is there?, who have always
trusted in transformation, layer by layer the onion peeled, more a
description of it than the rings of the oak or the fat of the whale.
That's where it comes from, as we seem to be doing it. They could
have given us nothing, instead of this room filled with junk. They
could have wasted us on jewels. And we have the key to it, the
melody, which alone gives it motion, which alone, in the mind,
is still the dream of the mind: transports it, battered and sonic, thru
a body lighter than air.

X

The warm air meets the coolness of night, the fog rising in an early morning enfoldment of vision. The world is unquestionably softened. The flowers glow with a richness so fragile they could only be alive, the mushrooms on the tree stump, shelved and violet, the toad's green. The day is hot, and the shadows are long; the first fallen leaves blow thru the field. There is the beginning of the pungence of decay, and a cycle that falls within our cycle, and so is revealed to our senses, the corn ripening thru the pneuma of wet fleece. There are cycles of stone also, sterile as monuments, that fall outside ours.

The beaches of the cities are crowded with those driven out of the apartments and streets by the intense chemical heat. They exist in a black and white newspaper photograph. Vermont is part of this hot spell also, but the vegetables can be picked, boiled, and frozen for winter. The beans, still flowering at the tips, tumble in the center with the weight of their pods; the ears of corn begin to twist away from the stalks. The cucumbers lie in the leaf-shaded herbal, swelling with pulp and seeds.

The white butterflies move over the garden in their scale, encircling in their circles the patterns of planting. The grasshoppers sing in multitudes, but their single song is inaudible as the sky is invisible, until the shrillness touches the breakwater of blue, and they run together in a horizon of visibility and sound, a landscape so precipitous it hangs over this one, as another hangs over *it*.

Our modern psychologism, with humanism at its breast, assumes that our dilemma lies in our inability to feel what we perceive. And yet the hermetic dream is to be able to see, the dispassionate vision of an intelligent outer order, whose existence frees us from the dark regressive nerves.

We hear the song of the crickets and see the blue of the sky in the depths of our being, without feeling, or we recall the tissues in ourselves, the cords that join them to the rhythms of our living. The issue is, of course, a false one. Cold dark streams feed streams which rush into sunlight. Vision embraces the dancer as the whiteheads crash against the gradient stone. The Jung-Pauli riddle is more simple than we might have thought: it is the whole of nature that is simultaneous with us and not just our being drawn as lots.

The late August days *are* hot, and by noon such philosophy is impossible. One may look behind to the spring winds or ahead to those of winter, but immediacy determines who we are, not those accidents and deliberations that brought us here. If put into play again, they could move us again, indignantly, to some other place.

Or, insofar as our condition is Plainfield, we could migrate, but only the book-maker would gain. Better not to fight it, the boredom of the long Labor Day Weekend notwithstanding: no movies, no restaurants, no ballparks, only the informing mood of this journeyman's paradise — the real issue, for all its vagueness, to absorb the tension, as I sit here in silence in lieu of being with friends, scanning the trees and grasses and clouds. It would be this way anyway, for behind our activity is an inertness deeper than death. We are altered directly, moment to moment, by karate chops so painless and deadly they could only be called subatomic, and yes, again, simultaneous.

The opening comes when we least expect it. When the work is done we begin the work. When the work is flowering, the possibility vanishes. Which is why I say: swallow the heat; soon enough the frost will come. And the other morning, after working in the garden, I had a sudden rush of Spanish mediaevalism and windmills. I picked up *Don Quixote*, a copy of the book I have owned unread since high school and, expecting maybe to do 10 pages, found myself 150 pages into it by sunset. The cars were gone, the heat was gone, the summer was gone; it was not just the Mediaeval knight consigned to a profane world, or even the tales of lovers wronged and wronged again, or the disappointment of dragons and crusading armies, the dangerous reverse of sign and object, but the sheer intensity of the narrative now that time has left it where it is and there is no possibility of its being continued, of its sequence being altered. The next morning I grab *The Tessaract* of Enslin, and read:

> *The work opens — infinite —*
> *draws, even as it seems to close.*

I take Robin for a long bike-ride (in the seat on the back of the bike); we go above village, into the hills, the house and farms visible across the valley in a subtle and radiant light. We ride the old railroad bed between Plainfield and Marshfield to the spot where it is totally washed out, the stream now a mere trickle over pebbles, chunks of granite and toppled trees dumped over to fill the divide.

> *It is a hard sojourn*
> *as if all the reading*
> *were done in a language*
> *unfamiliar and coming through*
> *less so — not across to where I sit*
> *or think or hear*
> >   *anything at all.*

We cannot force the Sign or hinder the Scales, whose balance lies against us. This ailment is the very cure health cannot permit. The zodiac twists and winds thru a tunnel of concealment, along its shape (not its distance, not its brightness), for it is darker than the sunless sky at the end of history. Bats replace butterflies above the garden, singing erratically thru the cornstalks, their evasion that is interception. And of this bestiary within the zodiac, Enslin writes:

> *The little horseman, Alcor,*
> *fiery to a steady eye*
> *looking there, aloft and north*
> *I may find him.*
> > *He will stay,*
> *a constant in variable winds,*
> *aloof — but faithful —*
> *Ah, seagoose and snowbird,*
> *why not you?*

Here in the village the men's groups and women's groups turn difficulties of vision into difficulties of feeling; there are no informal exchanges left (as for all the conscious dialogue and narrative I put down, I am drawing in hundreds of times that in final and formless texts beyond). To make a crossing of the river in naked daylight is not the same as to cross it in dream. It is like an elderly man who visits a prostitute at moments of uncontrollable nostalgia, the cure so much more secure and faddish than the ambiguous malaise, which could be a woman one day and a vast herd of impalpable horses the next. For pleasure? What pleasure? The design itself is only an indirect and artless diversion. Better to worship the tree, as the Martian astronomer must, in its changing color and thrusts of vegetation across the jungles of a planet. The direct resources of the enlightenment are like the accessible resources of the machine age; they lay a mournful blanket over a jagged and sepulchre landscape.

Earlier in the week, in the wasting heat of mid-day, we drove to the rumored site of Wilmer's Pond, led by Robbie, who had been there with the daycare group. He pointed off Route Two, and we turned, onto a rocky washed-out road, bouldery in fact; from it, a foot-beaten path up thru the glacial topography, pits and sheepstones, to a small fence, torn down in spots, around the pond itself. To whose actual level of the landscape one must ascend, so that it becomes visible, slightly out of breath, as a gained and not a sequential level. A small cowpond: there are hundreds of these in the hillsides. But the ascension is simultaneously modern and ancient, those photographs of Woodstock in *Life Magazine* more dated than the naked quabbalistic bodies of perfected natural history: bathers around the pond, men like satyrs and bears, young woman emerging from the water, smiling, her eyes meeting ours almost directly as we come over the edge of the hill, a lens thru which it does not fade but become more intense, an otter burrowing in the water, a human being, the blush in ourselves automatic, for something inside us is more bare than bodies can ever be. As clothing is literate and suggestive, body is animal. The nude photograph, despite its many devotees, is merely another literary genre, distracting and erroneous, misleading as to what nakedness is.

In the visibility and physicality there are animals, like the cows who once grazed around this pond and lived in the crumbling barn beyond. We are human only in the recognition of our desires, not just to touch what seems beautiful and be moved in being touched, which any animal can do within its own masquerade, but to feel that *we ourselves* are beautiful, abstractly, not only in the aura and the self, but naked; that we are enough.

Swimming on my back, I see myself thru the amber water, and feel the hot and cold springfed currents thru my loins, where there is a golden glowing body, the dark treelike and forested penis in the center, rippled thru the water, its immediate association with the wildness of the field as it climbs beyond the pond into the woods, which perspective throws against the clouds. Not as thru the chlorinated window the wriggling flag of bathing suit color – and one more totem – but fleshlight itself, refrangible but uninterrupted; the swimming, reconstitutive in a way it has never been for me, because I take those associations so damn seriously they are as catalytic as what I drink, and my response to them is as direct as potion. The image frightens me in its closeness, which has always been true (both the fear and the closeness), and which I have been able to flee as a creature of land and air, but the tabernacle now seems to glow without an external light, not the letters of the alphabet but the flesh of that alphabet's realization. I swim a frog's strokes and feel like a green frog, thru the sight of myself, sight and feeling together.

Skinny bathing is not a social issue and has no interest in and of itself; it is blatant and obvious. The painful degrees by which the veil is lifted are something else. The one social issue: that Vermont laws allow this freely – sitting up on the hillside among the bleached rocks, unseen by the traffic that pours thru on Route Two, from New York to New Hampshire and Maine, general American tourists scanning the continuity of scenery that is false reality's best trick, almost bumper to bumper, and the big VERMONT TRANSIT bus in their center. For as well as the film-clips and postcards circulating in the heads of the see-ers, filling a humdrum unacknowledged rhythm of thought, turning lye the desires which bubble up, distorted and as if disconnected, there is also our own synthetic landscape, beyond what we imagine or fool ourselves we desire (that at the Barre Fair a man loses his temper during the frog-jumping contest, with $50 at stake, and in trying to stampede his frog into a leap by stomping behind, squashes him, while the auto-racers warm up, and the various spectators trade in their metabolism for this dull spectacle). Instead we are becoming part of a community of unconscious beings, who unconsciously join our community, beyond the uninteresting embarrassment, beyond the boredom and wasted time, both of which engrave the hard capsules of plants in the late summer as they are blown and spread, as mites dash on the water surface. There is still the revelation, and it is historic for those who stand utterly on either side of it, unable to strip, or stripping all too readily. Post-Woodstock, and over the limb of Aquarius, we approach a public nakedness that will only destroy the vast romantic orgy to which we have been subjected. For the revelation any person undergoes is radical beyond content, beyond massagists searching for magic bones, and beyond biofeedback machinery and velvet orgy. Throwing off more than all clothing, throwing off the styles that hold motions to the body tighter than dress. Still, by degrees of hypothetical nakedness, we will not get there any faster. As thru the sun in multiple series of veils, removed one by one at sunset, aurora on the horizon of civilization, turns white again, beyond the three-dimensional perspectival planetary systems, the backbone of the unknown force that is *dearly known*, beyond all of which the goddess of light bathes on a beach that is also light.

Thru the words of the master we are aroused to sensations he did not feel, or even know of, when he wrote them, but meant us to feel by his writing of them, as we mean him to feel by recalling them, if we bear anything, together, beyond those various memories which clutter process, to give him for the eternities of labor he has poured into us.

Enslin, again:

> *Colors I had known as a child,*
> *on the little hill, one day, the stones*
> *picked up, bright blue,*
> > *but dull*
> *when I took them inside,*

the sky's blue out of them.
The black stone, dried out, to grey,
after I had fished it from the brook.
And now these autumn flowers —
phlox in the abandoned fields —
what color's blue in them?
or lilac?
      mauve?
            How much is in the eye
of the beholder?

XI

Cold winds evacuate the fire, summer heat vanishing thru the starry
sky. Each morning the thermostat registers a few degrees less, until
at 61°, the first flush of hot air fills the pipes, and the metals of the
furnace stir on signal from the diode, breathed thru our memory of
when the hulk was last filled, in June says the postmark in my winter
coat, as I reach into the pockets as though someone else's, or well
before the word about supplies of oil, so that our sensitivities to the
gauge are subtler, as all bodily things are, as season by season the
Earth is altered toward millenial things, happening in minute stages,
neither fires nor flood but the series of perceptions that seems to
make them known. The onions are all pulled up, dried, and stored by
the furnace, next to the old bottles. Now the green tomatoes, in
expectation of a frost, are set beside them. The corn continues to
grow, with a smell like honey, though hardly at all after the tem-
perature drops, we read in the pages on corn, so half a dozen ears
are boiled and frozen. The cucumbers are plentiful beyond need,
and one night, with the ballgame on, in the kitchen, and Lindy at a
poetry reading, I devote the evening to turning them into a vast soup
we can freeze; I bake them and grind them and reboil them, until
the bitter stench of the poisonous vine of which this is a domesticate
fills the room, crystals of sour cucumber on all the windows, against
the night, to which Lindy returns, giving me a flash of perspective
on my obsession, not just food, but money, house, books, building
fires. I throw it all out into the mulch heap: gruel and unmashed
cucumbers and cooled bags of soup; we'd never eat it, better to face
that now; the cucumbers flatten in the cold and then are covered in

the husking of the corn.

The lettuce sprouts yellow flowers, and the peas and beans are overrun by grasses and fall weeds, but it is not all over. The kale and broccoli and cabbage and brussel sprouts are in various stages of shape; in the mornings the cold rain they feed on looks silver, like frost, against their skin.

The temperature is reckoned against the sky, and the falling leaves. A body is flushed from the body, into the memory of summer which is now pungent as a flower. Lindy's pregnancy fills her, a gourd beyond the spring, when it happened. And families move into the village, closer and closer to the flame (Robin discovers child by child) — the single cameo of this house, its lights orange as blood thru flesh. Darkness falls swiftly with cold, enclosing us to what was left unfinished in the spring, and other springs (the Apache music and Gregorian chants on the record-player), visitors unexpectedly after dinner, for coffee, Peter with a bottle of wine, the fire burning, making heat visible as long as the image glows and crumbles and the furnace is quiet, as we talk of past and present, and make a shape, transient, of now, say goodbye, turning on the porchlight for him, opening half a path thru the maples, where the old driveway used to be, into earlier autumns more than a summer in which all these things that are now continuing began. THERE IS A PRINCIPLE OF GREATER DECLIVITY, despite our continuum.

In the early morning blue a gibbous Moon floats, not upon the sky but in the tension of the sky beyond. The cool winds blow down the hallway, exposing more and more of the housing, blasting out the nasal bone, clearing what blocked it without regard for eternal return. I am aware now of how feelings and images fold into each other all our life, covered in later images and selves, lost while they remain, in both their evasions and their proximities. A flash of a field from childhood, remembered with everything that was intended then, so different. Riding my bike along the road at college to a stand to buy pumpkins and grapes — even the grapeness of the memory, so that the fruit can never, as such, be bought again. The ocean that first winter in Maine, how it crashed against the rocks this time of year, the violent preciousness of life in such cold. Even then, remembering the grapes. The walk between grade school and the candy store. It must be, if it is the same body, the same tunes and strings. What was sought remains, incorporated beyond consciousness, changed into being. I have no choice, in the music of my life now, beyond the responsibilities maturity appears to have given me, but to pursue the remnants of these moments, not out of the romantic possibility still left in them, but in the exact

66

exercise they suggest, as part of the tangle that must be undone in approaching what I am. There is no form of banishment, which is not itself the explanation for how to return, and we are condemned not to where we are but to the circumstance that fails to read condemnation as the map of getting back. The very rule which makes it impossible for us to contact God directly makes it impossible for Him, as Memory, to contact us, without the intercession of visions, angels, and active imagination: intelligences with whom we could talk man-to-man if either of us were to transcend the hierarchy that divides us. But the galactic explosion has placed us in the hermetic flask.

As I teach in these pleasant buildings around the Northwood ponds, I sense the final disjuncture, as the divergence of two roads, which will rip apart any body that tries to go down both of them. All these other moments hang between, waiting not upon a revelation but a softening, within which vision is clear and unmistakable. There are some, like Mr. Mattuck and Mr. Sheedy, to whom the education of the youth, in the context of this college, is a holy mission, and one in terms of which they have achieved their maturity; in their teaching they are grown men; yet I sit here talking like a ghost, a strange repository for my own words. My articulateness belies the depth of my haunting. Would that it were always as easy as Allen Ginsberg in his twenties deciding not to be a marketing executive, and the spiritual-poetic mission that followed from there; not only would he have been miserable at it; he would have been the buffoon of his profession, and of himself. Yet there are millions of aborted marketing executives and professors wandering around as Allen Ginsbergs. The declaration comes only when the voice is already there. Such is the just decree. In between those dizzying mountain passes, thru the needle of psychosomatic tension, there falls an anchor, and will go on falling until rock, as clear as the Moon.

XII

A beautiful moment of vision. Nothing like it in eternity. Oh yes, that's what I've been doing, that's what it was all along. And I don't have to be any better. Just this. David Bowie: "Love will clear your mind and you'll be freeee."

Numbers and forms, shapes and rhythms, an energy which gives us life, gives images to our consciousness, though it cannot be conscious. Despite the dionysiac, the sadian, the tantric, we are on the brink of a terrible nightmare, shaped like an embryo in the hard flesh of unremitting transmission; no wonder the Freudian id wanders between a deep mirror of man's source of being and outer jungle beasts, who are all appetite. And what other identity have we, except as that too is shaped in a vessel? Life stands against monster and Inca and sun, which *are* life, holy books that are wordless, or stone the medusa throws back to the shape which petitions her for immortality she cannot give.

What lies at the beginning leaves an imprint obscure even to archaeology, the clay shifting upon the hidden wheel. To put a mask over the torso, to take the mask off: the same thing; to cut off the Count's sixth finger changes the gene not one iota. Bounty cannot prolong what is stasis already. Though there is nothing outside the mind, our existence depends on the tension and discomfort of a world which draws us from the oysterlike slumber of psyche-id, where we might live forever, into the golden clarities of a text — the sun behind, the sun not behind, the same mountains. The cold night wind turning the squash leaves purple, the birds feeding off the fallen corn. Rain trickles down chutes in the tin roof.

You wanted to be someone, you said you wanted to be me, you said I wanted to be me, I said you wanted..../even that stops.

Or as a mercurylike figure passes (sometimes a woman, sometimes in a dream, sometimes I forget, and sometimes I remember). It is music only after it has been written and played; it was once the wreck of an old apartment house, a childhood, a theatre backstage. Stop the physical system the way a film can be stopped and you see all the state variables hung in a space curiously diminished; the eye searches for the implicit quality that gave it motion. When the movement starts again the source is obvious: the swaying of the tops of jerusalem artichokes, their sunflowers beginning to form, is obvious yet unknown. And without us to disturb the silence of its riddle, the lotus in the wind, it would not be there, either to be stopped or to begin again.

XIII

It is much later in all our lives, but the dream pulls back the old apartment in the city, 96th and Park. It is as though I have come back from all these years since to find what they were doing then. My mother and stepfather have another child now, a tiny girl, in the bathtub, younger than my sister. I call her by my sister's name, but she giggles, knowing that is wrong. I realize I have never seen her before.

How can my mother have a child? My sister is in her twenties. She has been divorced. More than that: she has denied, thru psychoanalysis too indulgent and too late, the entire past, from which all her children came. She is the child now. Yet the baby girl seems as indelible and real as a newly discovered moon of Jupiter.

I am alerted in the dream to a very loud knocking on the front door. My stepfather is trying to get in by banging on it with a hammer. Before I can let him in, he has broken the hammer in half. The superintendent of the building is standing behind him, quite angry his hammer is ruined. The scene has changed from the city, and we are standing on the porch of the house in Maine. I know where lots of hammers are, and I go to the basement and bring up two whose heads are bent out of shape; the superintendent accepts them in exchange for his broken one. There is a coffee can filled with nails on the kitchen table; my stepfather very rudely grabs for some nails; I offer him a few and then take the can away from him. He walks outside and looks around. We are in the country; there are no buildings and streets; the sun is shining in the trees, the famous consolidated dream sun, of olden memory and present fact. It is more than that history has left him no retreat to the city; the city is gone; its buildings are not even represented by slums; there are just old wooden houses, blowing away, the forest reseeding and returning almost visibly before us. It is the end of his world. He is dead, as he is dead in my mind, a sham man our lives together, but his aura goes on feeding off the fact that it once lived. I was close to him in his prime, but now he must suffer the fact that I hold his world as big as a globe in my palms.

The dream shifts suddenly, and I am both older and younger in a more complex sense. We are going skating, high school friends and I. We come down from the mountains where the ice is hard as stone and end up in Burlington, Vermont; instead of Lake Champlain beside it there is Bernard, Maine, on the ocean. We are coming back to shore in a little rowboat, and though it is the ocean, the immediate waters around us are a gentle lake, filled with lily pads. There is much activity, with lobstermen pulling up exotic amulets and extinct fish, rushing into the wharf to sell them at auction prices. Wendell shows me an enormous eel, with meat enough on its coiled spine to feed his family for a year. The fish is an old Abenaki ancestor. The rowers are laughing and we are having a good time; the boat is hardly steered, the waves bringing it up on the shore sideways. We get out, and my friends board cars to go into the mountains (which I sense we have just come from but in another sense). I put on my skates, which is foolish because there are no cars left and I will have to walk. I put on the rubber skate-guards and try to follow them in this awkward manner. All the way up the mountain the water is soft and warm like the ocean; I approach ponds, hoping to skate across them, but there are animals in them, infusoria, ceaseless mitosis and creation. These are sacred pools I cannot step in, qabbalistic remnants; their mirror is fluid and inhabited. I remember now not only how this is like dreams I used to have (the repeating dream of the ice-skaters and the unfrozen pond), but how I have written about the ice-skaters and wondered what metaphysic they represented, what it would be like to be one of them. I find the place where the cars are parked, but the other skaters have gone off into the woods. I find myself with a car and driving and feel that I have cheated, not so much because I didn't have a car going up the mountain as because I am younger now and don't know how to drive. I am faking it to keep the dream going, to keep my pursuit.

I drive the car down a narrow forest road; as I go along, the weather is getting colder, and there is frost on the trees. I am hopeful I will not have to take off my ice-skates.

I see the others thru an opening in the trees, and I park the car a little bit in the woods and get out. The air has become warm again. Before me a puddle is melting, and has melted even as I test it with an ice-skate and get the tip of the blade wet. I am worried now that I won't be able to get the car out because of the long narrow trail behind me and the angle at which I am turned. The experience has many parallels; it is like roads I have been stuck on since coming to Vermont, or if not stuck, from which I have made a narrow escape. Living here has reduced me to a state of almost not being able to drive because regular vehicles, such as the ones we have, cannot make it across the roads to many houses. The real drivers have jeeps and pick-ups, and our lack of such makes us quasi-children.

Meanwhile, the people who started out as high school friend ice-skaters with cars have become barefooted volleyball players, the net extended between two pine-trees. I am quite late, perhaps ten years late, and it doesn't look as though they are going to let me into the game. This is a partial converse of a waking situation. About a month before the dream, we were invited to a local commune by an old college acquaintance who lives there during the summers. Lindy and I felt uncomfortable about going and had several arguments about it during the day. I felt we hadn't really been invited, but that she had encouraged them to ask us. She felt this was accurate in only the most limited ungracious sense. When we arrived at the commune, we found ourselves in the middle of their diurnal schedule. They were not really ready for dinner. The goat had to be milked and people were taking saunas. A few stood around watching an airplane pilot do stunts over the mountains. The plane kept circling back to almost directly overhead. And we weren't the only guests. The father of two of the boys in the commune was there from Minnesota. Someone suggested a spontaneous volleyball game, and everyone joined in enthusiastically, except me. Actually, the commune women didn't play either, but Lindy did, making a curious symmetry. My own stubbornness about not wanting to play was painfully reminiscent of a childhood stubbornness, when, for years, I refused to play any other sport but baseball and would sit out football and basketball games. It was as though the childhood means of fighting authority had been transferred to the commune, where such group spirit was probably benevolent. Something in me wouldn't believe it. But I also wasn't that child anymore. I joined in after the first game and found myself wildly in the center of the whole affair, diving to keep the ball afloat, not the impassive, but the gay manic child I once was too. The noble presence my stepfather was on the 97th Street ballfield, before the nails and the barn-shingling in Maine. In the dream, a poet named bp (like the Toronto poet of that name) invited me into their game, he himself not returning after chasing a ball out of bounds. Then I find that I am unable to serve. The ball is alive in my hand like a fish. It keeps flopping off. They grow impatient. I hit it badly and lose my serve, I stumble into water, but when the other team serves, I move into the game and play smoothly.

Vague lingering sense in waking life of not knowing where I am, and it seeming a problem of whether I am in the city (where I grew up) or the country (where I have come since and my child is growing up). If one is to be a man in the country, he should know about wood and pipes and sources of heat and water. He should have good hammers and plenty of nails. The commune at which the volleyball game occurred was a co-op of carpenters, and the volleyball was like an American Indian busk, in between laying the sewer pipes for an ideal village in the wilderness. Not only that, but Bob Barasch, whom I see as analyst once a week, in attempting to recover and interpret a text I was given on Central Park West in the New York City twilight, is a farmer and horse-breeder from Alabama. He breaks our sessions if the horses whinny unexpectedly or the baler arrives. I see him riding on his horse down Creamery Road thru the town. So Vermont or New York: stands for what other issue? As Bob says, maybe you have to forget that you were ever supposed to be crazy forever: maybe this is just to prove those years of psychiatry were all along something else. So it must be for the symbolic sparsity on which this northern sun sets.

The dream ends on another level. From high in the Vermont mountains I look down and can see the entire geography I have crossed, as a mythological migrant. The ocean, invisible at first, appears gradually, until I feel myself drifting just above it. *Book of the Cranberry Islands* is on the left side of my typewriter, as draft pages, and *The Windy Passage from Nostalgia* is on the right, so that I seem to be writing directly into it.

I awake from the dream feeling it is part of a trickster cycle, which itself is unravelling toward the creation myth which lies at both its beginning and end.

XIV

This is the time, as summer ends, of the quiet rundown of the baseball season. I sit in the living room with the ballgame, reading against the pleasant static, rooting gently for a few Met wins while attending more to the September rookies and their sound in the line-up — a sense of autumn as the world becomes cooler. And then it vanishes altogether, it is no longer on the radio.

Suddenly, beginning with the second game of a doubleheader in Montreal, everything changes, a three week wipeout high. The Mets are still in last place, but they have won the game on absurdly daring baserunning and a diving catch of a bunt by Tug McGraw, and if the momentum is right, they can make it, it can be '69 again. Part of me doesn't want to get into it; I am resigned to calm autumns, the rhythm of the game like the wind thru the trees, simply the sound of the world in which I come to the form of my mind. I don't want to betray that withdrawal, but I also don't want to betray the tension and heat that underlies the whole listening, that keeps the game alive during fallow years, all the way back to 1952, when it began.

I'm there, hovering in anticipation, hoping for an early lead, after which I settle back into a book, as long as they hold it, until the crush of the late innings. There are no other fans. People go about their lives in Vermont far from the crush and ceremoniality of the city. I listen thru the night air, the game half blotted out by that Toronto rock and roll station, warbling between a faint negative of the announcer's voice and a buoyant clarity that seems to be right in the room as though the broadcast tower were out on Route 2 by the Barre skating rink. In the day it's impossible; the car aerial must be touched to the garage roof; a New Hampshire station blots it out with banal jingles, and I worry about why what I want to hear isn't equally banal, its only grace that I can barely make it out, the score thus an obscure and significant message, bearing a momentary link between Plainfield, Vermont, and New York — absolute, speedy, and off-center. If I'm moved by something, it's not baseball. I am moved in myself, but the game brings me there without explanation. It's not that I miss being in New York; if I were in the city, the Mets would be part of a shared social space, the classic frolic of the rabid fans. Here, in this house, in my life, able to let it fall hundreds of miles away with the click of the dial, it is a specific channel, a tuning-in made cosmic by the tuning out that follows and the being tuned out that precedes. It *is* airwaves more than baseball. American children of the last war, if we were to learn any exercises of deliverance, any surrealistic radio connections, it would be by the most unlikely and profane devices. "It's like a gift," says Lindy, as the hectic vibes dance thru the house. "You have something none of the rest of us can." And I realize, as in Montreal, how it stands in the way of my arrival and yet how I associate the jig I do off it with a free and transforming space.

The game pours out of the radio each night, and I join in, yelling and clapping, commanding the whole downstairs like a revival meeting. Brief hiatus when the Pirates win a big Monday night game after knocking out Seaver. The next night maybe it's all over; the Pirates have a two run lead in the ninth. Then Beauchamp pinch-hits successfully, and Millan triples, tying run on third. Tense two-strike pitch to Hodges, his whole history, as a sub-.200 catcher in the Texas League brought up to fill in for injured players; he doesn't strike out; he singles. This is like nothing else. A few more base-runners, then Hahn is up, a three-two count, and I yell, "This may be the pitch of the season," Hahn himself a refugee from Tidewater when the Mets ran out of outfielders. Line drive over short for two runs. They barely hold it thru the bottom of the ninth; Apodaca makes his major league debut, called from his home in California after the minor league season; he's too wild; Capra replaces him; it's a one run lead, with the bases loaded, before Sanguillen pops up a three-one pitch. You can listen forever to ballgames, but this is what you wait for, and you can't be deaf when it's happening.

It's a month-long climb from last to first, exhausting. My dreams are filled with the halved and broken names of the Mets' pitching rotation, Sooman and Keaver, old high school friends wandering thru abandoned stadiums and subway stations, how George Stone, the fourth man in the starting rotation, is 12 and 3, reprocessed again and again thru the trade in which the Mets got him and Millan from the Braves.

The next night, in New York, the Pirate-Met battle continues. Cleon Jones settles it with his second home run of the game. A night later they find themselves a run down in the bottom of the ninth, two out and a man on base; Duffy Dyer, without a hit in a month, and without an RBI most of the season, lines the ball up against the wall, and the tying run scores. Later, in extra innings, with Sadecki mowing them down like clockwork, the Pirates suddenly get a two-out baserunner and follow it with a line drive by one of their own rookies, Dave Augustine. It looks like it's going to go over the fence for a home run, but the ball drops on the top of the railing, bounces back into the hands of Cleon Jones, and he throws out the runner at home plate. The next day thousands of New Yorkers claim it was *their* psi-waves that stopped it. And maybe it was. I see it on the news the next night at six-fifteen and realize that something must have been there. Bottom of that inning, two strikes on him again, Hodges out-battles Giusti and drives in the winning run. This is too good to be true; they're not only winning, but the rhythm is fantastic; they're doing it like a run of one-in-a-billion cards, which is the only way a statistical madhouse like baseball works. The next night Seaver and the Mets and a full house at Shea, and me in Vermont, blow them right out of the ballpark. The Mets are in first place. And they find themselves on national t.v. the following afternoon, the first time the whole thing comes as an image rather than a radio-message; in some ways it's not as good. Kubek and Gowdy try to own the phenomenon, but they're latecomers, as usual, to every scene, too phony dramatic, too unspecific to count. Still it's a joy to *see* them. Garrett homers and Matlack shuts out the Cardinals, and they hold first place (the old thing of: it's one thing to get there, another thing to stay there). And it must be a dance (though I can't hear the music playing), and since I can't dance slower it must be faster, faster, until it ends. Is this what it's like? Is this what I want it to be like?

On a sunny blue day in the mountains, we drive into Burlington to meet Stan Brakhage at the airport. While Lindy is shopping, Robin and I hang out in the town like brothers, the wish on both our parts, in different ways, to be equals in each others' worlds. We eat lunch together at a tavern on Church Street, then visit the toystore, and hook around the city to meet Lindy on the way to the airport.

Driving back to Plainfield with Stan thru the later afternoon. The light on the altered trees he notices like flashfires in the hills, and so begins to call attention to the visible visionary event. That evening he gives us a parable of the creation of creation by light: phos appears, followed by lumen. Pictures of older worlds are cast, beyond the focal plane, thru pictures of pictures and the light which makes up any image, the present blue and red spilling over the lens, absorbed into the inarticulate brain. A fable whose moral is *life*. There is no center to the screen or vacuum of vanishing lines to suck us into a Hollywood town. Creation passes in and out of dimensions, between the numbers one, two, three, and four, for which the integers stand, we never see because it is buried husk in husk giving only the illusion it can be taken apart in layers. The perception comes after boredom, after I feel I can't sit there any longer in the chaos and maelstrom, when I have exhausted the wish to be engaged, comes swift as the positrons cloud chambers catch only after the fact, our lives the impressions of. The residue is light, sparkling as the laws of physics will allow, right down to the pinnacle of wave and particle. These films are long signals from the cosmic thud.

A night later he dishes up "The Act of Seeing with One's Own Eyes," the film shot in the Pittsburgh morgue. The autopsists hollow out the bodies like canoes, until there is nothing but a bark vessel filled with blood. They remove the faces as masks, taking the persona from the sensorium, the tangle of nerves behind. The liver and intestines and kidney lie together, marshes in a storm, amidst muscles, veins, blood, white fat, no conceptual space between them — one lobe in electrostatic simultaneous profusion: the current of feeling and desire, the food-digesting sacs, the muscles twined with the arteries. How could I have thought the functions of the body were separate organs and chambers? Did I imagine the physician could ever be master of this, which exists only violently and alive in the time of its happening, leaving not a moment or spark in between? Surely in a dream of robots I must have been.

Inside the glitter of the social world, just beneath the decorative surface, is a gnostic world. Or what for us will suggest ever the alchemist and priest more than the surgeon. The dead are made of the same flesh as the living, and the living are made of the same material, not only within each body, but body after body. How utterly the gene orders this world, whatever the origin of life and its codons, how terrifying and final the condition that makes and remakes Adam, without vitiation, without translation to another plane. "I stood among carnage," Brakhage says.

The riddle is unsolved, and we stand back out in the cold air of the mountain night, trying to breathe a thousand times, the wind having cleared things for the stars. We drag these bloody embryos home, and into them put ice cream sundaes. We carry death within us, as life. But for the evening I take Tug McGraw chanting, "You gotta believe!," and David Bowie's: "And I want to live!"

The next day after lunch David Wilk and I take the car up East Hill, to the top, hopefully to pick up the Mets from across the mountains, and from Chicago, where they are trying to hold on. There is nothing but static as we feed dirt road into dirt road. The leaves glow yellow and red from the landscape, an aura, partially transcendent and partially alive. It is not the Earth but, as Olson said, the brilliance of Earth, blue now the color of, as light pours from all the trees, the grass, the eroded colors of the hills, the mountains in faint clinging intelligence, against the hierarchy of creation itself, set in time. From here I can see that stone is alive too, at a different speed.

We come back down, strangely beyond the game, pensive and calm, in the magnificence of the interference and the staggered and tilted geography in which it happens, the oblivious farms adding to rather than detracting from the cruciality, the farm-wagons heaped high with hay.

I leave David at the house and hurry to Goddard for the Sufi class, meeting Stan and Lindy on the way, as they have come from a pouring of hot metal in the sculpture building. The day is mysteriously warm, and the class forms by the pond, sits in a circle on the grass, and we talk about Avicenna, Ibn Arabi, prophets and imams, the worlds angels flee from visibility into, and how yet they are seen, the timeless magus whose hieroglyphic transmission is a monument in hidden space. And we sit in hidden space. While one student reads a description of the many wings and eyes and rainbow colors of an angel, I lean back, and then fall back, and look up into the utter sky, blue blue over the world, without a single cloud, just eye interference and the erosion of having lived, in itself a flood of sensation and passage. I think: of course there is no history, it's all right now. Myself and the occultation of my being here, in a spackled bundle of nerves and minds.

There was no game anyway, rain in Chicago, where Brakhage is going, having come from Pittsburgh, weather which reaches us the next day, alternating wind and rain, clear sky, then billowing clouds, as the shape of the mountains guides the turbulence. On the car radio, barely audible, the Mets lose the first game of a doubleheader to the Cubs and lie on the precipice. I am sullen and belligerent, wondering why I am so hooked — which becomes a cluster of runs for the Mets early in the second game, postponing the issue. The game neither easy to hear nor moment-to-moment crucial, I begin playing a zany game with Robin in the driveway, rolling the old wheelbarrow tire full-speed on its wobbly edge, he chasing it, we chasing it, trying to knock over the blue cup, or to pick up the hook of the driveway so it keeps rolling, as he runs ahead to steer it off the path of the little brown caterpillar in its ball. While I listen to the end of the game, he tumbles in and out of the back of the station-wagon; we race for an alphabet block, throwing it thru the open tailgate. All this energy and bounding lies upon a sense of fragility, my whole life spent just one step ahead of the hounds, and why? — until I go to sleep, where my dreams are, in that big brown body where mind and matter heal each other. I want to make it with this family, here, here in the frame of daylight and the space of the maple trees and flowing aura, this wife and child and coming child, the eternal vigilance to end. For the world, in its geological outlay, its starry origins, has struggled, rocky and barren, sun-orphan, to be here today also, in post-glacial degradation, the Neolithic family born of the remains of the Palaeolithic tribe, surviving the madness of others, not only to show them I could, to show them it is possible, on the other end of consciousness, but because I want to. So, for a moment, the ballgame is a rich and heady drink, shared with Robin in another way, beyond the fantasy to be in many worlds, this drama hinges on, and can go under like any dark river sustaining life.

The Monday after the season should be over, the last rained-out game is played in Chicago. The stray tabby is sick, and we take it to the vet, no choice. In the center of Barre, daytime reception improves to unprecedented clarity, so Lindy and Robin take the chance to check out the thrift shop while I drive around town looking for the optimum position, settling finally on the Grand Union parking lot. The Mets struggle from a 5 - 0 lead to win 6 - 4, and, with the game, the Eastern Division of the National League. The season ends not in New York City, where the change in mood and energy would be visible; it ends, thru a mass of static, in a Vermont granite town, where a continuously-operating machine by the railroad tracks seems to boost reception. The town is old and white; the stores are still dressed in 1950's fronts; the customers, mostly elderly, from a granite renaissance long past, leave the Grand Union with their bags. The traffic pours down the street, past the construction, where a few people stand watching because a whole building is being levelled. The school children rush thru the streets like mercury, past the old folks sitting on the benches holding their canes. There is no response in Barre, and that's the way it has to be; like Cocteau's Orpheus, I sit in the car dialed into another world. We leave town with second-hand pregnancy clothes, two toy trucks, and three vanilla ice cream cones. We sit in the three-dimensional sun outside our house while a measureless calm rises thru the maples to the sky.

I go to bed with the beginnings of the flu, and in the midst of several dreams of childhood, there is something that is not a dream. I am under an enormous body of water. I think of it as the ocean, but something tells me it is the ocean at the beginning of time. A moment comes, and I know I must swim to the surface and breathe. At first it is simple and buoyant: a dream of being underwater and propelling myself upward; the images of life rush by me, other dream landscapes, some of them New York and Madison Avenue uptown, others Michigan and dark blue twilight on Packard, troll-like ferries to Maine islands I slip aboard, more like starships, like the ships on which the Irish migrated here, narrow strips of land along the coast on which we rent a beach house, long Vermont pastures filled with boulders. I have dreamed these sceneries before, it seems a thousand times, and recognized them each time as something I come back to. Now I realize they are also prehistoric landscapes, scenes from before my life. I am running out of breath. The water becomes exceptionally dense, as though it were another element; at first it is just heavy; then it develops knots. I find myself lodged backwards against a stone. I try to twist away, to throw myself free, free of it, but the stone is everywhere. I am trapped complexly beyond any space imaginable. Someone is whispering to me, but there are no words. Someone is leading me. I turn more than upsidedown; I tumble thru a lifelong dizziness, thru six-year-old car-sickness and deep viruses. I am not moving, but valley after valley of dream landscape brightness is imposed on me, until I see it, and then it passes, I am past them, I have turned completely, and am still being led. I think, "It's alright," knowing that it has never been so good before.

I have seen beyond my life. It is not a surface I can reach for by rising, but, in the spinning, an opening, split and underwater, containing all the dimensions that ever hindered me. It's my whole life the plummetting upwards at unknown speeds, straining to be there, to throw out the head and breathe. Without ambition, it is given to me. I am promised it will be there.

XV

The tabby is dying in the kitchen. Something is wrong with its
blood. It struggles to stand up and falls over. In the general failure
of the support systems, the cat and I face each other glumly; our
diseases face each other. I want to be soft and whole. I can't save all
the cats in the world or keep the rooms warm, though I understand
there are better ways to heat than this furnace sending air thru the
vents, the joints and woodwork filled with cracks and pores allowing
a general entropic draft. The gas tank on the red mustang is so rotted
the radiator shop called it a "pin cushion."
The rain falls, the leaves grow more brilliant before fading; the sky
dwindles and winter appears on the horizon. We are not ready. I
worry about how much a new gas tank will cost, how much to get
the cat well, plus the amount of fuel to make it thru the winter on
the new prices. The college may fold also, leaving us with no support
systems, simply in a sparse northern town in a big old house with a
dying cat and Jackson Oil at the door.
There is finally no other way. I can't just watch the cat die. My
work precedes me with a grace I am barely learning. I fight thru the
resistance, put him in a cage, and drive back thru Barre to the vet.
Thirty dollars for a complete blood transfusion, he says. Okay. The
situation isn't desperate yet, not for us, and if we don't respond to
the sympathies we have left, it's all over anyway. What's money
after all? Just another one of those American secrets. People with
twice our income complain seemingly everytime we see them about
being broke; people with less than us live with an upper class ease.
The fact is: we don't really know what goes on, and no one tells.
Like, off what do you live? In this country it doesn't matter; people
just live. Their cash-flow, like their terminal sexual honesty, not-
withstanding. All so problematic, hypothetical. One more excuse
why we can't or won't expand into the world. You're waiting for
better times, are you? The cat bounds, its shadows from the candle-
flame. As if there were a choice not to live.

XVI

The world an illusion: the treetops fill with light. The plan ful-
filled, planet by planet, note by note on the musical scale, in solar
silence. The maples with roots in the Egyptian stone, translating the
hieroglyphics, the light and the matter, into the burning literal mask.
Bird, having smashed into image of sky on the window, lies dazed on
the green planks. I look into the glass it flew into and see eternity,
more beautiful and spacious in its reflection. So that's where it was
going: the strange attraction of a lefthanded world. Lindy picks it
from the porch and sets it on the branch of a nearby tree; its tiny
feet cling but its eyes close, stay closed. It could be on the point of
death, then suddenly is gone into the wind.

Reports of war. Reports of God. The spiritual gradient rough and
bent. Light left in the universe from warmer days. Robin and friends
tumble down the hill in a big cardboard box, into the pile of leaves,
Lindy full with child and raking, hauling bundles in a sheet to the
mulch heap. Nervous energy. Crucial pennant game on the t.v. The
living room the control center: the information comes in and is in-
terpreted. No longer just me and the Mets. They've gone national.
And the clarity is even more devastating than that. The news is filled
with UFO's, and the vice-president resigns during a Met rally. If we
were on a starship, the stadium would be the single image, the flow of
leaves and debris and the ten thousand games brought down to a single
encounter. Intimations of a global something.

Greg visits for the first time in five years. He's in a different place
now, profoundly sad and romantic. The last time I saw him he was
on the crest of a big wave: mathematical insights and visions, a girl,
a less rigid more dancing shaggy self. It's all gone. No. It's never all
gone. It has passed into another next stage. The marriage is broken,
the numbers mock him; he has discovered, he thinks, that at heart
he is a sadist, because he has thought about it so little before. So he
becomes an underground press photographer and a humanist, trying
to talk to schizophrenics in the mental hospital, fighting the shock
wave doctors at every step. All this in England, under the aegis of a
young Marxism, the fervor of emerging from abstract topology to
radical economics and Laing at the age of twenty-six. His discomfort
is central and he doesn't know what he needs. "How can you sit
here?" he asks me. "The world is full of starving people." I stay up
half the night talking it thru, but he fights me every inch of the way,
as if I were pure topoi, for my seemingly dispassionate transforma-
tions. What are you so angry about, Greg? Why are you destroying
yourself because what can't be changed can't be changed? Why not,

instead, change it? In you. And, in the wee hours: Greg, do you know, I mean do you really know, what those people want? He shakes his head. We're those people, Greg. It's our responsibility to get out of this too. There's no back door.

It's because our psychology is so desperate anyway. We pretend we're responsible, making it that much easier to live on the go, and heroic, than trying to stay someplace. Where there are more people, the danger is greater, the future is exponential. Suggesting as well the depth of personal trauma, which cannot be solved, and thus must overcome any marriage, any human contact, except the revolution (he thinks), which burns off it as fuel, and delivers it beyond its own silence. Albeit the source of the city in the garden in the sun. The lettuce plant on which the condition of the streets depends.

He leaves on a night bus to Montreal, to meet a plane to an English city not London. And the next morning we take the hornet's nest off the tree and bring it into the house. The hornets are dead; they fall out of the hole and blow across the porch. The nest is set on the bookcase, its branch is hammered into a shelf. It sits there, the whorled and maché mask of a face without eyes molded by creatures who have no such sense of a human being and are no bigger than one of its eyes. A flashlight shone into the hole shows a hollow sphere of complicated surface inside another hollow sphere, dead creatures lying along its hallways, as if a planet had been wiped out by an invader with death rays. The nest is unsafe not because the hornets might come back to life or their young arise from the obviously full nursery within. It is unsafe because it is a whole world; although it fits in our house, it is larger than our house. This distortion will engulf our dreams and put us inside its terrifying alien sense of interior space.

Playing the old songs at night brings the old feelings: *Some roads lead forward; some roads lead back; some roads are bathed in light, some wrapped in fearful black.* It's a long smooth high, as though the spiritual is upon us. Other times I lie awake the first hour in paranoid vision, scheming, planning, shooting machine guns, taking on and abandoning projects until sleep clears the brain. What is there to wait for if it's happening right now? Having to do it over and over because it's done to me over and over. It seems so long ago, the closed loops billions of years of evolution have trapped us in — that must be broken, right?

I realize idly: most poetry is terrible. I've indulged it for the wit and spunk of its creators. All that counts now is the dictation, transmission of the unknown weakness in eternity, we can penetrate only by dropping our strong right hand, the flare and hipness

that go with its use. After all these years of trying to woo her, of try-
ing to be her lover, we're the only ones she loves. And that's what
holds creation together, experientially, beyond the Mediaeval argu-
ments of necessity or will.

XVII

The water pours across the present, a source in the mountains we
do not see, rocks and slabs, having tumbled from that same terra
alta, overlying each other to form small pools that catch and churn,
that redirect it like radiation over the edge. Some large enough only
for bugs and fish; others in which the people bath, their sensoria
awaking in the streams of temperature, bled from ice into transient
heat. Our life is. Made alive by the ripples against us, we dance to
them, seek not to be constained. We believe they are real, are really
what we feel. Splashing its way down.

Peter's sculpture, made up of three white pieces, blown
glass in the shape of musical notes or frozen force-fields, each
piece somewhat round and somewhat lineated, covered partly by
leaves and knocked out of shape by the children playing on it, his
life is, so best leave it, to leave it change as it will. And so define, in
what it is, what it has always been. A modular unit. Or at junctures
(like now) to drag them back into exactly their original positions.
Shapes harden despite our best attempts, memory likewise, so what
is left is always *both*, whether we see them or not, from autumn to
autumn, and in the changing conditions of a post-genetic world in
which they each must survive.

A worn hose, across a rock, diverts the stream water into a pool
in which a child's wooden boats are anchored. Leaves have been
pushed against the opening, allowing a bare trickle until my fingers
clear it, dislodging the leaves; the water crashes on down gradient.
And all littered with broken planks from a bridge higher up, across
which wood was sledged historically, split by the rising river this
summer.

Hopping from rock to rock and crossing back and forth across
the water, we come to the deepest pool, a delta of falling rocks,
which larger geologies will surely crush in their time; the water stays
here longer and circulates, continually fed. The path leads thru the
ragged secondgrowth, white stones with skimmings of life, along

heaped boundaries of older farms, and the litter of sugaring, logging, sledding, and less explicable human presence, down into the sunny field where milkweed is everywhere; as I loose it, is blown high into the light, across the stonewalls, obliterated in brightness and micro-scopy, exploding past the faces of those behind me, in my fingers wound around the bent wings, the cone shape familiar to all the plantworld of this post-Mesozoic Earth, unravelled from the pod where the deepest numbers store it, against the sparsity, equally certain in the darkness the light of day hides.

We drive back into Plainfield, into the center of town. It is like an old warehouse, the cold October sun silent in the almost bare trees. The big kids sit on the stonewall by the church, their legs kicking, their hotrods revved, talking, and silent, before the absolute winter. This image sits there too, a boulder, inert and frozen as society be-comes, against, in my head, the fire of the last World Series game, about to begin on t.v., from childhood October glory, flames illu-sorily blown into being in the city I imagine now was the scene of my youth, this last game a memory before the winter of the outer-most declivity of my life. A false excitement time will vitiate, if not my body, my bones, and bring me back a frog, in the brutal calm condition, set, in a single pale sun, kin to ice age darkness, against the stonewall, numb to the senses, that brought them into being, that they will bring themselves into being, again and again, an omen of what my heart is made of and how empty this if I pur-sue it, a cold and profound pregame warning, the graveyard on the hill above, where the wind blows.

XVIII

The road from the town leads into the mountains; there, in the omniscient sky, the ranges that parallel and encircle this one are becoming visible on the rim. A rising from the market zone into light, a psychic correspondence, people seek in building their homes at 1500 feet. The rubber cable is laid in the furrow, and Chris and Ellen are pouring on fine sand before the plow covers the rest. Months before he was thinking about a windmill, a complete emergence in earth, air, fire from an ondol, water from a spring. Now he is satisfied to keep the cord beneath.

In the garden below, hundreds of frozen tomatoes litter the

ground, having become red after the frost. The cabbages are fat, and their hearts are frozen, the days of sun not long enough to thaw them. No matter. Ice is the condition. The house is on a knoll above, a spot Chris chose in the wisdom of severe intestinal illnesses, when he was able to feel, further out on the ledge in the superficially more attractive spot, how hard the wind blew, and how one position alone lay in the eye of the disturbance, protected in some karmic pact the visible landscape had all but done away with. Still, there is air where it is, sky where it is, mist where it is, stone where it is — a fat pegmatite quartz in the center of the house, rising from the projected basement into the living room, part of the Cambrian beach, jewel of the mountains' upheaval, the comets of prehistory, bared by the glaciers of the onset of our own temporary time. And this cannot be changed. The unseen rider draws the reins, and the reins cross, and we draw in the reins, and so draw ourselves, because we breathe the air and walk on the earth, and because the snow falls against our even finer flesh, and is recorded there by the fossil of thought; what is left where we are is nothing but to make those processes conscious, and then the processes suggested by them, until the sun does seem to touch us thru mens, seraphin, cherubin, potestates, archangeli, angeli, caelum stellatum, saturnus, iupiter, mars, sol, venus, mercuri, luna, ignis, aera, aqua, terra. Terra Earth. Touch us as fully as its heat reaches us, and at the same time. Without which we are surely damned to death in windy caves. As a friend says: *we are dead*. With which also. in our time.

The day is cold now, but the last bits of summer remain on the Earth's axis, seeds that will be blown away. The furthest mountains are hidden in haze, but the suggestion in the broken torso and its rocks is migration: whiteman, palaeo-Indian, liquid stone. Pebbles and sand into the cement mixer with the Portland powder, mixed and poured into the plywood mold (Chris is a potter also, and knows, between the sun's furnace and the icicles that fall a hundred feet to their liberation, the point of slump, having but a single failure, one whole wall littering the dirt, poured when the potter was in sunlight and all the hills around were in storm; then the clouds blew in and smashed his pot with fresh stones). He says, at 1500 feet, the man who sat in my *Moby Dick* class and wrestled with Ahab as lightning-struck, as trauma-scarred, whose own trauma puts him in these hills like a bear with his harmonica, hooting to keep away the small game hunters, "I want to be rooted in the Earth," clenching his fists, his house a twenty-two sided polygon, again and again losing the number four which comes, twice, in the removal of zero from the real numbers, not from the fourth dimension; "but I want to be in the sky." And god knows what will come out of such a northern sky in his lifetime.

It is not just Chris. These shapes fill the Vermont hills, half in apocalypse, yet more in the invention of number. And the antipodal hills too, for an Australian named Ron Smith, mistaking the title of my *Solar Journal* for a source on solar energy (which it yet may be), writes of a subcontinent sparkling with private generators, solar, pneuma, and the famous but lost hermetic city of the sun.

Chris' madness will still carry him thru this journey of materials, as Ahab's could not for his break with the domestic. Chris will patiently make his peace with the demons. From that initial circle of stone it is hard to visualize enclosure or warmth, and the winter will fill it as a bird lays its egg, in the straw to keep the heat at the joints. Ellen calls it Stonehenge, not inappropriately, the tools of its makers scattered around, and Michel's vision of a yet purer power conducted by shape alone, in monument, of which Reich's orgone must be a later siren.

When the wind blows, it is very cold, and the trees beginning a stand of forest that runs for fifteen miles into Groton sing harmonia mundi, and it is a sound so high and harsh, voiced as it is with bark and needles, that its spirituality, to use that dangerous and possible word, all but eludes us. The suggestion of what a climax Earth would look like, its ground fertile with pine needles, named by the Indians within it the Cathedral, and the small medicinal spring from which the water comes thru a black hose, decorated with sacred ferns and called Bloomingdale's, for the city that is no more, and the memory of the city which our body has changed into some other thing, Chris' father himself a contractor in suburbia, a training he is playing out once and for all, building the house freeform, a spun pot, form rising organic and utensil from the human shape which makes its circumstance necessary, because if we do not build our cities, we must inherit them, from the aliens who came before us, and pay their enormous debt.

Chris speaks of how far a single log, decomposing at the speed of rust, can go in life and light, here in the forest, in potentially, the darkest and most alone of all worlds, though it has been settled before, logged and potatoed, merely adding to its remoteness of soul, from which three deer in the spruce and red pine only seem to flee, now inhabit the sacred prefiguring of the space, so that it's not the edge of darkness, but in our own hands — from light, into which cement is poured, and family, not for eternal duration, but making it possible to live inside, while we have yet years, to observe the time of our life, and in which to grow from seed into what we

85

are, thirty and forty years along the prototype. And so I will honor
the occasion of their house with a benediction from Robinet, the
French natural philosopher who was thought a fool for having be-
lieved in mermaids, by those who do not know either, even now:

"All the modifications which our senses observe in Nature consist
simply in the variation of the limits of extension; as soon as we are
compelled to give up this extension we seem to be confronted with
mere nothingness; we come to a stop as if there is naught beyond.
We do not give heed to the fact that the material or visible world is
an assemblage of phenomena and nothing more — that there must
necessarily be an invisible world, which is the foundation, the sub-
ject, of the visible world..... There may be forms more subtle, po-
tencies more active, than those which compose man..... The invisible
world is the collection of all the forces which tend to ameliorate
themselves, and which do so in fact, by incessantly extending and
perfecting their activity, in the proportion suitable to each of them.
There is a gradation of forces in the invisible world as there is a pro-
gression of forms in the extended or visible world."

Passing Beneath the Scorpion – The Winter of the Comet

I

The images flash and disappear, reappear. Nothing else. All we are given almost more complicated than we are. And what history has done with it. To bring us into it. Patching pure Mediaeval holes.

Small Vermont town carried thru the axis of winter, receiving less and less of the sun's heat though a Whole Sun is still visible. One day, the faraway light in the appletree, a warm breeze, and David and I throw the ball back and forth across the frontyard, recalling mid-summer motions whose frolic nothing will allow us to repeat. The next day a gray sky, cold wind, people shivering, no one dressed warmly enough. And we are upon this winter, which is called, by some, a test of our civilization, strangely prophetic in other senses too. The fuel which fills our house is a remarkable transfusion, its Arabian origins hidden in Boston harbor — the sense that insulation is the real issue, for if the house were tight enough, our body's heat which keeps us alive (and alone which) plus the heat of the light bulbs, would be enough. Yet we are not even close. Suggesting that civilization itself is a condition like winter, coming from far in the past, at too great a speed for us to know or control or soften in our time, made of the same shorn imperatives ice is, and those lost in a wind that sweeps our oblique plain beyond any choice we have left. Living or dying. And if living, be damn sure you know by what implicit grace.

The food itself now dependent on dangerous monocrop, the prairie better left to the buffalo and the orgone-tip agriculture of the pyramid, which calls the water from the air as life calls life (and not the dead harvester machine), which has been forgotten in a slumber we do not even know we are in. Is it that the resources are scarce, or only that psychologically we are scarce, and have come to the end of what such a material civilization could mean to us anyway?, and thus would seem to use up the rest as our spiritual debt, the fire of Nine-teenth Century vitalism unable to be relit. The four hundred years of coal, the natural gas in the American intestines, the tropical oil beneath Alaska, the oceans, years before their time, the whole pulp material Moon, pulverized into energy, to sustain this winter sorrow, this lack of meaning. It is the least highly regarded events of the former world-age which determine this one, whether they be the Alaska purchase, the funding of national science, or the dispossessing of the last Indians.

And there is still a path bare and barren, not unknown to us but unknown to us: how cold it really is, a mystery, along with what our lives heat. I renounce a culture I have never been part of, but whose lease and allotment on me has been a tangible security and warmth. Wilson Clark brings with him, from D.C. to Vermont, the image of hordes of urbanites pouring out of the ghettoes and high-rises, long in breeding behind Lysenko's veil, to the North or South we do not know. Alan Van Newkirk, the Nova Scotian, fears a far-reaching American invasion, along the bright windy turbine, hungry, future-freaked ad-men and state workers. David, headed to North Carolina and some sort of farming imperative, thinks they will inevitably follow the warm winds. The psychic again, that cutting North Atlantic breeze which is not the South Atlantic breeze that warms Gerrit's passage back thru cocksure Maryland lovers and Ricky Nelson, down, lightless yacht, to Fort Lauderdale itself, and New River Lane; it blows out, over the glaciers, the Detroit LSD flashbacks of murder on the Lodge Freeway, a woman incinerated in a car while the artists, in the dryness of their French metaphysical madness, watch from their coffins, on the verge of revolution. But there are only *people* in the Northland, and the slum madness will sustain us no longer; the wind alone blows the wheel and fills the mind with images. Barry McDonald proves to me that Nebraska schoolboys raised on Willa Cather, who reject her for Mallermé, in some ironical but Aquarian sense return. With all the poisons in our land, LSD flashback is becoming greater and greater, and even in the pale bars of Barre, it sputters and sparkles, and then scorches, with electrodes, the depth of trauma in the Holocene. Jumping from crisis to crisis without a plan. If there's lightning in that to sustain a farm in the North Atlantic, all the more power to the systems, but this we don't know, and on a Buddhist hunch, better to let the systems cool out before demanding them to turn on again and light the lonely universe.

It is not only famine and cold, or the deadly plutoniums of the breeders, which hang against our time; there is also the deadliness of our lives and the masks, the cocaine Halloween party, each distortion submerged in a more complicated one. Harvey is processing his moods and feelings out of a black bag. My brother writes of sorrows that have gone on almost a year now in their present unaltered form, dreamless thorazine nights, a letter received on my birthday, November 3rd, wishing he could see again my films of 1967 Michigan autumn, the cold blue skies, the wind blowing the leaves off, shaking the twisted beans, the blue getting darker and darker until almost no images are visible, until the snow falls in the car headlights, wet black shadows, because he wants to feel something in Maryland, even cold.

The party goes on past midnight, and Wilson says that we will not make it thru this winter, that civilization will collapse, 'the coming dark age,' the *Burlington Free Press* calls it, as if to apply it to someone other than us. People with broken marriages and uncertain psyches sitting around the fire, an emotional plague, waiting for what is inside them, outside them, to come to its conclusion. It is a good party, cohering with a melancholy we cannot combat, laughing in the wine, the walls and furniture spinning, Lindy and David reading their poetry, and John Todd, the new alchemist, flooding the room with warm oceans, till five in the morning when Alan freaks and sees Detroit again, when John goes, brrr!, back out into the stars, and we go on crisis mentality, the hours switching time zones in our body, Atlantic; it is the old mysteries in ourselves with which we fear the end, and what our lives have been until then. What, after all, is it we are defending and protecting from such a night? Why survive it? Why survive it too?

The land outside, called Vermont, is not ours, alters thru occult degrees into a slab that passes thru the sun. The only perception we can have of the resources now must begin with how they were never real, thru the additional nihilisms of inexplicable war, the luxuries that give the illusion of longevity and pleasure, while the crack in the sunlight breaks down into man looking at man. God we have tried so hard and claimed so much, why can't it be the way we want it, and if it's not that way, why don't we want it?

It flows together: the draftiness of the house, Lindy's sixth month of pregnancy (and headed for a new red baby in mid-winter), the faraway sources of oil psyche has ignored in her plans, and dreams in which John Todd of the New Alchemists, as farmer/torch-bearer, is confused with Rusty Staub of the Mets, their blondeness, the fact that they both have origins in Montreal, and Wayne Garrett, figure of an earlier dream, is found far from baseball, on a commune tilling hay, fighting monocrop, bringing back weeds and wildmen and diversity, for our memory is not as good as we thought it was; when the habitat is destroyed, there is nothing for the chromosomes to return to, no matter how hermetic the seal. And the problems I cannot solve or even absorb any other way, past five a.m., past birthday, get blended together in dream, and dream eases them into a meaning they can have only for me, while all around are drinking wine and laughing too.

The images John brings from his Sun City are deep figures. Tilapia, the Egyptian fish, the lost cabbages of the 1920's returned seed by seed, the flowing fertile fish piss, the pigshit heating indoors, the windmills with Enyalion on their tails, the watermills and solar houses, flashes of Pico and a hermetic landscape; their name: the New

Alchemists, but where: in Cape Breton from the wind? , on Bartlett's Island, which I once saw across the miles of powerful tide? , in Wood's Hole, where the Sea Museum is another unintiated Hermes? , or on Martha's Vineyard, a mutual help community? Is it only an image? Wayne Garrett borrowed from the Met scenario to be the farm-boy magus, to be John Todd, Mirandola, myself in the center of my dream, the railroad tracks out of Harlem and Manhattan leading no-where, and in all those brick buildings the same feelings, the same flu, and how can you say this dark vision isn't real?, as the patients are wheeled from hospital to hospital dying, and Wilson says: "When it begins to wobble, and it's wobbling now, the whole thing falls." In the November fireglow of our living room on a world we possess so little as to have been born into only, no more intimate link, as across the snow the fox charges and sinks his teeth in the deer: who starves?

This proposition begins in my work with the lobsterfishermen, creative materialists and source figures, whose actions I followed, and in whose life motions I rediscovered the depth and darkness of my own geographical world. I carried the text into the telepathic, the psychic, the Mesolithic, into the reincarnate and traumatic, the memory and the joy. And here I am, back again, at the origins of raw technology, oars and rotors. No longer the extraterrestrial scribe. I am back to the slag, the clear domes over fishponds, heating with the sun's wafer, diaphonous, but still material; the wind machines that pull from the astral the power of our homes, still wheels and circuits, currents; the mulch of a physical order, used properly, filtered back into our life as health-giving substance, is almost not a slag anymore, is almost a psychic quantity. If the massive wastes of our civilization crumble, as the city has crumbled, a hermetic landscape arises, a ghost technology Aldous Huxley and Gary Snyder spoke of in the interim, from Northern Vermont across the Arch-Atlantic — in the interim, geometric houses, self-cooking chambers, Ashley stoves running on each single log tree by tree till eternity, windmills wireless in the mountain-stirred drafts, food co-ops as di-verse as Edgar Anderson's garbage heaps of Mesoamerica. What is despised shall return, the crone as magus, the pest as grain, the de-centralized market as the new cultureplace of Pythagorean man. This is the beautiful princess whose hidden form in the gestalt is an ugly hag. Which do you see?

I think of all the mishammered shingles of Maine, and the weari-ness I've had with an axe or hoe, and John says it isn't that way: you work with things and find you're able; it's not lost back in a childhood we never had, either the love or the capacity to build. We are still free.

And Harvey brings with him word of a different order: Chögyam
Trungpa, speaking about our physical envelope, no thought that we
can leave it lightly, in suicide, and feel any better; the pain's still
there, only worse, because it's not located in any resonant place;
it doesn't even have *that* distraction, our whole world is. Gurdjieff:
man is very sad, nothing we can do about it, has no soul, must get
it in this lifetime, otherwise must come back — and of Katherine
Mansfield, who died with *images* of revelation and transcendance:
she died like the rest of them, a dog, without a soul. Taking from
her even that last hope, in his brutal honesty. And who can doubt
it, news films of people moaning and shaking at a mass funeral in
Israel. It can't be changed; it can't be made better. They're not
wrong to want to destroy the enemy, though, of course, they *are*
wrong, in the end, exactly and precisely wrong. But who can doubt
the realness of their sorrow and that it goes to the emotional depths
of which they are capable?; who can doubt that they are really sad?

So the Halloween-Scorpio weekend becomes the famous meeting
of the poets and the biologists in this lingering century, with a joint
declaration that word and world, gene and djin reseed each other,
that the pure sources of information are specific worms on specific
cabbages, removed by hand. Which flushes back into the confused
and amalgamated present, everyone gone, and the Sunday air cold
and blue.

On Thursday morning Chris and I work together in the wind,
loading his jeep with four foot logs from the fallen tree of a decade
ago that lie on the hill behind our house. By the back porch, we set
up a sawhorse and cut them with a heavy antique chain saw,
taking turns holding and working the blade. I am exhausted; I reach
back thru all last winter's flus, imaginary and real, for some prior
strength, thru the psychosomatic at the end of which is exhaustion,
is a new being I want now to be me. There is no time for debate. The
air is cold; the saw is dead metal; my arms are tired; and my fingers
shake and are numb in the vibration. Yet the world is clear, and as
Wendell prophesied once of seasickness and hauling traps from the
ocean floor, it is possible to get beyond this, to not have every
task *be* the traumatic one. Though Harvey points his finger at me
in Scorpio, I have none of the capacities as they are in him, the coke
or promiscuous sex, but am working in the same body at getting my
head clear, thru the brown and entangled mass. That Chris cries while
listening to David Bowie, from the inside, as cold winter approaches
from the outside, is perhaps all we have, in this book, the slag, out of
Nineteenth Century biology and Greek alchemy, that in their vision a
home of concrete and wood, in my writing about their construction

a vision and fire passes thru the cord, thru the inertia and resistance, to the pool in the center where it arises again in purple sensuous robes, Virgil's nymphs of pre-eminent beauty. As we build what we are made of, and though the whole point of the slag is that there is so much of it (natural resources, they call it), and so little of everything else, it is also alive in our using it, our need for it, our care for its needs, so that we don't waste it, even in its carnal galactic sleep. All this creation until remade beyond. Van Newkirk seeking the old farmlands of Nova Scotia restored by city spiritual breakdown, as the archaeology covers and is covered in successive tides, an experience the spiritualists, the Witnesses, in their greed to own the slag, or to dump the slag, are without. The world predicted by Reich, his hands and brain teeming with bions of a New Atlantis, is, in memento, the world of Stonehenge and Palaeolithic man.

The comet enters our skies, its tail blown and brilliant, from the sun, the inescapability of that, as Nixon's strong Uranus, albeit it an image, is the real thing that will go thru the heart this winter, this many years past the cracking of Hamlet's mill and the building of a new one, the deterioration of profane shells from the astrum of stars, as the eagles swoop down on Venezuela and Laos, in our name, and the government learns that that Uranus terror has no name, but is an aspect and changes, changes even while it is still, which are the numbers that lie within as if the brain lay without, setting down in darkness what thru the darkness of psyche and city we will see, perhaps in our lives, perhaps in the golden eyes of our children, that the dead material, like interstellar space, is radiant, and we are born again in it, as the shining candle, in love, before our ultimate chemical breakdown, the Osiran druggie trance, loading the old barge for the Sun. It is a wonder that we feel at all, after all this deprivation, after the solving of trauma *by* trauma and impossible acts of fucking, the sexual desire still fresh and unexplored each time.

II

I dream of us finding ourselves back in Ann Arbor looking for a house in which to live. Time is flowing in two directions at once, for going from Vermont to Ann Arbor is retrograde the sequence of our life; at the same time, we are in Ann Arbor originally again, in some sense that includes Maine and Vermont.

Someone who wants to live in Vermont has traded us their house in Ann Arbor for our house in Plainfield. I'm not sure if this is how it happened, or if I remember it that way to fill in the gap. Perhaps we have sold our house in Vermont and now have money to buy a house in Ann Arbor. Lindy and Robin and I seem very young.

The fear is that houses in Ann Arbor will cost so much more than houses in Plainfield that we won't be able to buy anything. This is a ripple in the dream, an anxiety whose roots beneath the lotic flow can be transformed by moving to a different stream; the waves want to go on. We have already bought a house, miraculously before the current real estate boom. It costs only $10,000, and it is right on the University of Michigan campus, beneath one of those big green trees on the mall. There is another possibility: the dream is a contracting force, a deflationary environment, and money kept in dream banks becomes thicker rather than thinner, more rather than less valuable, even without interest.

From the outside the house looks small and unspectacular, but I remember from earlier dreams that this is no testimony to what the insides are. Once we pass thru the door we are in a cavernous building. The settled part of it, the wood-finished part, is only a small corner of space, rough and unpainted, with many openings in the bare planks where walls and ceiling were supposed to go. Above us, as we move our things in, are giant rooms and galleries stacked around an open core, one above another on rough stone and dirt walkways as in a round museum. The house *is* a museum, one that was closed years before, and not because its relics were unimportant; it closed around its collection like a magician guarding amulets in a robe, an eagle on bald mountain with jewels and nuggets in its nest. Everything is intact.

At first I think it is like any old house, a few curios lying around, the bulk of the valuable stuff gone with the auctioneer, but the auctioneer was never here, and as night settles and the Moon shines in, I see that it goes much higher than I had thought, and all of it full. Our electric lights are no more effective than a candle would be in an auditorium; and they are just as effective, for we see what we are supposed to. The rest is stone, massive hollow stone without any visible source of lighting. I cannot even see the ceiling, and at times I have the sense that there is none and I can see the stars. They are schematized as chalices and emblems, Pawnee buffalo robes, in the upper exhibit halls.

There are rare books, coins from Asia, stuffed animals, vases, tapestries, raw gems, cut gems, triple gems; it is a combination of the

Museum of Natural History and the Cleveland Art Museum. It is Nebraskan and Mandarin, Alaskan and Yangshao. We go to sleep in our corner of it where the kitchen and bedroom are crammed together like a two room apartment.

Morning awakes the museum like the forest. Not only does the sun reveal all its treasures and the complication of its exhibit halls, how they twist beyond present possibility, it lets in thousands of people, or finds thousands of people already there. The museum has come back to life. I wander among the visitors, feeling vaguely responsible, hoping nothing is stolen. I also have the sense that *nothing can be* stolen, for the museum and people exist in two different time zones and are not aware of each other. In fact, the people may be no more than the crowds on the street hurrying to work. I decide to explore underneath. There is a brief corner staircase to the basement. The basement itself continues to lead down, past exhibits of butterflies, past Egyptian tombs, past volcanic geography and halls of dinosaurs, until it breaks off sharply and seems to enter the Earth. A guard stands by the opening, menacing but un-alert. It is like a coal mine or Howe Caverns, but exponentially more dire. There is a sense that the guard is a cosmological sentry and stands there not to prevent us from entering but to remind us, significatorily, that this is a dangerous hole. Because it's our house, I have a certain confidence; I walk to the edge and stare in and see people lost in a bleak desert landscape, crawling across lunar pumice and grey sand. Other dreams have taken me there, and I don't want to go back.

I have a sense also that this incredible wealth must be left in place, must not be tapped; it is the relic Earth, but it is also the other Earth. The Australian native may touch it on his cave walls, but we have departed from that interface forever, and wisely so, for any return brings us back again to where we are: before the ogre of dimensional space. We put a sign on the outside: SOLD TO NEW OWNERS. We try to get the people to leave. We find that guards have been posted by the door, but people continue to pour on thru. I walk up to individuals and explain the situation to them; everyone I speak to is gracious and gladly leaves, but the inflow far outweighs the single departers. As twilight comes, a Moon appears, and once again the halls are silent, and their treasures appear in the faint silver light, suspended beyond us, while we cook beans for dinner, and clean up, before making ready a place to sleep. Where could we put anything without losing it? The answer would seem to be: EVERYWHERE.

The following morning I go out to explore the old or future city. Ann Arbor is changed; I find a book of mine, yellowed with age and crumbling, available at the antiquarian bookseller for $700. I cannot afford to buy it, and it is so fragile I cannot even look in it to see what I have said. It is a book I have not yet written, or perhaps it is this book. We are in the far future, but the scenery is Nineteenth Century, with carriages instead of cars and very few houses or stores, even in the busiest section of town. As I return to the house, I realize that trees and dense second-growth forest have so overrun the campus that our house is hidden in shrubbery in what used to be an area of open traffic, especially between classes. It reminds me of the Phi Psi house I lived in at Amherst, which was right across the street from the school dining room, yet rural, with a glen. There are flash additions from fraternity houses at West Virginia University and The University of Vermont. It is also very like our own house in Plainfield; in fact, as I return to it, I have the distinct sense that I would be back in Plainfield if it were not Ann Arbor. With the forest overgrowing the campus and a small town emerging where there was once (or will yet be) an urban and geometric college, The University of Michigan has become Goddard, or Goddard has become The University of Michigan, as it was for those few days of the Ecology Conference when dozens of scientists and anarchists poured over to our house in the evenings and used our living room as a coffee house. If Goddard were as big as The University of Michigan, our house would be on the campus; or there would be something on the campus, with the proximity of our house, where people could gather for tea or wine or food. It is one of the depressing oddities of Goddard that it has no such space; after dark the school disappears for those not in the dorms, a condition that amazed our visitors from civilization. Of course, our house was seen as part of the grounds; as hermeticism and causal myth embraced biology and community planning, the spiritual-prophetic space of Goddard was at least the size of The University of Michigan for a weekend. And Vermont, in its underdeveloped snow and wind fields, its aesthetic removal, is, like an Africa-Kuwait alliance, the blueprint of another world age, in which Michigan, with its Wolverine football players and bureaucratic research buildings, is doomed to the spiritual famine issuing from Detroit and the general Midwest. Which is why the museum was so wealthy, so full of things that are not in our house or any house. It contained the unwritten and never-to-be-written texts of the entire race and planet. In my own life, it contained the matter uncontacted, the possibilities of a work, plus the fat unpublished binders, as big a weight on the lived-in and domestic portion of our house as the whole museum, up to and in-

96

cluding the stars, would be. Coins and owls and galaxies, as I have
used them, as I have been proprietor and clerk. The museum suggests
that I can issue the actual written work in a series of folios under
the logo of North Atlantic Books — lying as it does on the inter-
zone between the public and the private, the emergence and the
forever-buried.

This museum was not only closed years ago; it was closed before
the Cambrian; it is a museum of the last world-age, and the items in
it are so rare because they *did not* survive into this present time;
they exist only in our intuition of them. I can't hold it; I can't keep
it; the words flow back thru me, beyond the uttering of them, the
superficial record. I don't want to sell them; they are neutron star
wealth; they are centripetal beyond any matter or mohur, any alter-
ation of specie or change in the currency and accessibility of land.
They *are* the beautiful islands Cabot had full passage of, and the
Indians before him found unoccupied — that most of the world,
the world we are born to, is unknown, undiscovered, and beyond
ecology, beyond conservation and resource, as an endless psychic
energy and flow of forms. We seek to give matter life and image
meaning, to preserve from dream the vastness of transformation
and possibility, and the ceaseless duplicating and converging lands,
sometimes Vermont, that go on forever in our heads.

III

In the dream Lindy and I are supposed to be on separate planes,
flying to give readings at different places. It seems that because we
don't want it that way, we are both on the same plane, heading
West with a pilot who resembles John Todd, the New Alchemist
farmer. It is a small plane, but he flies it well and we drift along, al-
most effortlessly, above the clouds. The landscape below is choppy
and brilliant, and everything gives the sense of incredible distances
and vast connections. At this point I recall earlier dreams in which
I am in a plane that is flying below the tops of the buildings and losing
altitude. This dream moves in another direction, and a land totally
aboriginal and green, floats below us, the suggestion of Indian
tribes within, and Viking ships, if we could fly high enough to see
the sunrise, curvature-thrown, upon the world. Just as the flight
reaches its most euphoric Vinland high, we hit an air pocket and

are pulled down, so fast, that as we regain vision on the gradient, we see the heavy cities of the Midwest: Cleveland, Detroit, Chicago, all deserted and bunched together. We are flying so low we whistle right thru the holes in their buildings, thru caverns made of crumbling avenues. This is confusing, because it is in these cities that the readings are supposed to be. I am thinking about the transition to becoming a car; if we were any lower we would be going too fast, but in order to get higher, we must speed up; the conflicting directives break our motion. I tell the pilot about previous dreams in which this occurs, but he is unworried. "We have time to get out of this one," he says. So I sit back. And then I realize we have crashed and it is over with.

The dream continues as though we have all parachuted and are safe. We run into each other separately on 57th street and Sixth Avenue, by a Horn and Hardart Restaurant; there is a crowd viewing the wreck of a small plane that has crashed into the building above the restaurant. I am surprised at how tiny it is, given how big it seemed when we were in it. It is as though a raging river in Vermont has become a rush of sanitation water down the city avenue, and I am stuck with this dream diminution for having grown up in such a city and having it so deeply inside me. It seems bigger than the whole planet, with little chance that we will get back to where we were, or where we were going, in our lifetimes.

I have left my car up at high school, and I am wondering how to get to it. The difficulty is not only the distance and the rush hour. It is, as in the earlier dream, that I didn't know how to drive when I was in high school, and I am coming to realize, as the dream continues, that the lack of mobility stands for all sorts of other lacks. This is superficially confused with the fuel crisis, causing too many people to be on the subway. The crowds are chaotic and push and shift in waves thru the station. The trains are going too fast and are disordered on their tracks. I worry that the electricity might go off after we get into the tunnel, so I leave, conceding my fare, and come back onto the street.

I am in the old apartment where I grew up, and the loss of mobility is terrifying. I am almost lame. My child is born; it is unclear who is who: who is the father and who I am in the scrambled scenario. I am driving in the old family car with my sister and brother, and I realize that he must have come out of the mental hospital in order to be here. I see that he's been reduced to an idiotic condition and is making no sense. I wonder whose child this other one is. It must be mine, but it is born precocious, upright and speaking, and not only speaking but using words like "anyhow." There are, clearly, threads from previous dreams flowing into this dream, as the one in which the child walks out of Lindy like a big humanoid bug and takes its place among us. We are driving thru Connecticut, and I am aware that back then it seemed like the real country, sunny and green and far-away. Vermont is hierchically beyond, and that's why we can't get back.

I am walking uptown, but I am totally uncertain about where I am. It is a far northern city, perhaps Ottawa or Fredericton. I am es-caping from summer camp by going further North, and no one has discovered me yet, or realizes that I, the grown man, am the child that is missing. *Io* is in many bookstores, but only as a rare book. Some of the issues have been reprinted by those who came after me, and their names have been changed to suit the times. The dreaming cuts through webs and lesions of space and time. This is a city I have never been in; it's Twenty-First Century Halifax and Eighteenth Century Akron at the same time. Either undeveloped or advanced.

I am walking in a slum. I remember that I have been on an air-plane that has crashed. The street is filled with awnings, and I find that I have emerged from the northern city on Park Avenue in the high Eighties. There are doormen standing by their buildings at twilight. I look at the sky thru the city. I am coming to my childhood home from the wrong side of the street. A man who seems to be blind, carrying a tin of pencils, reaches out to me, then puts his arm on me. I think: he must not be blind. Then he tries to wrestle me to the ground. The doorman closest is not even aware of us. I sense that there is no way out of it now, so I wake up.

IV

New light from old bottles. Seas of fire at the threshold, memory trapped within thought, thought giving memory a name. Old bot-tles.

This is consensual reality. And still the waves elude the wild alligators, the giants who watch us thru their dreams, that our dreams can seem so hard and real to us, inside the sleeping. The higher system is indelible; we are initiated without confession. What is spilled van-ishes quickly, without name, into the heavy sands.

Firstness and Secondness, the philosophers called it, to distinguish, on an artificial scale, the relation of space and concurrence, suspended in an eternity of blinding sense. The Firstness is the pitcher, or is it the shape of the pitcher? If the stars reach us by light that both is and is not their bodies, are the stars First or Second, is the light Third, is there a star to which fire itself is the pitcher?

As dreams lie far from their masters, so objects which appear to be enormous are small brown nuts, when their cloaks and comas are stripped, and they rest before us, freed of the Second and Third bodies imagination has given them.

The background noise, which we do not hear in our lifetime, changes everything. I make no attempt to sustain critical arguments because there isn't time, and whatever safety I might gain is circumstantial, as long as I am what is acted upon, ephemeral in the same way it is. The knowledge is cheap; the hands that cup the knowledge are dear.

Our lives may take on the innocence of a sampler, but the wolves wait at the door, the same wolves whose bodies are sold as steak at the market. Since the merchandising does not fool him, we should not let it fool us. The blue jay who comes with morning to feed on the bird seed comes from a place as dark as Pluto, as cold as where the Sun is but a morning star, and yet he survives while he does, a bitter reckoning. This is the connection tyrants cannot break, for it is the birthright of the created. This is why, in their cosmic paranoia, they are tyrants, why they try to break it.

The music that plays in our homes, holy music, comes from a nuclear reactor miles away, right thru the lines. You can't renounce a system when it survives in you and around you, even in decay and negation. We suffer from our failure to know where former technological civilizations are buried under the oceans or ice fields of this planet, or on other planets of this system, or planes and planets of other systems — an oblique clue, by which to test our own power. How tricky and deadly the real riddle of the sphynx who, composed of matter, stands grey and neutral against us in our moral and sensual plight, inside us like a collapsing house of cards set in motion by a series of Chinese puzzles, in simultaneity, at different times, from the phased zodiacs of different centers, composed by the attractions that tie all objects together.

The inner universe of Hinduism and the outer universe of astronomy are equally perfect crystal, tied together in crossover Secondness, Thirdness, meeting to form a complete paradoxical system. Ocean, dream, star, agriculture, mythology, Greek etymology, expanding universe are one sense, with the first snows skimpy on the ground, the cats moving thru the sun, stalking the jays, because it's they, there, in their bodies. The whole toughness and raggedness

of it is defiant and subtle, because we want so much, under the real
crisis of wanting nothing at all.

V

It is not perfect, nor will it ever be perfect again. Awaking from a
dream of Florida, or some sunny beach we walked on, I see beside
me a cone with hieroglyphics in it. And although they are thin,
although they only scratch the surface, I know how long it will be —
until I remember, until I forget. Each of these marks is needed.
All life happens around a crack in vision, the sun streaming in.

Even technology has no origin artificiel. The solar accumulators
and solar houses arise in a blueprint of the sun, the wheels turning
by themselves in the metaphor of the solar wind. Photo-utopia. The
color yellow, its intensity a hint of the colorless white, and the
silence with which the wind fills the storage batteries.

The city people who have left jobs and bought land hold their
communal suppers, meet in the Grange, now the Food Co-op, to
divide the grains and beans. Where the answer to the question is: to
survive somehow without killing each other. At the equinox of a
world of plenty, the t.v. filled with sacriligious costumes, false gran-
deur, bloated confidence. The first European visitors to North
America sought inland channels thru Asia, where the Vikings saw
only woody islands. We still live, so few generations later, with the
Indian threat of fire and snow on our doorstep. The world market
is no longer a way out.

The circles turn in the wind, taking and giving power, and with-
out distraction; the love-hate relationship grows into a way of life.
Because there is only a stone. And if not that stone, were you
planning to spend all your time counting it anyway, as if it were
partible?

The river is frozen, but water comes from under the ice and flows
along the ice, in a dark channel ice makes. As cold as it could be.
The spiritual power of sanity, our fingers in these waters, the frosted
leaves on stone. Both verities, both laws the same. If you want the
madness to end, cold water. Frost in crystal scrolls on the window,
a language that precedes sanity, but also precedes thought: is one of
the forerunners of thought, subject to an archaic version.

The photo-satellite is swept into the size of Jupiter, and while still far enough away for there to be one image, makes a picture of the planet. Vastness covers vastness, and yet it is held in a single atmosphere, the materials drawn into bands of strong and weak interaction, always-shifting bands, each of them many times the size of the Earth — a planetary volume into which 1318 Earths would fit.

Our experience cannot be multiplied that many times. Between the singleness and the diversity, where the tunnel ends, where the tunnel goes on forever, is a wave of indistinct formations we have come to see as space. Our conception of it is misleadingly resourceful: the oil that runs factories *is* oil. The resources are limitless, the photo tells us (not where does it stop, but where does it go on?), and then falls into the darkness behind it, and proceeds beyond intelligence, figure for the dreamer who leaves his body to find the fabulous jungles on the threshold of all such dreaming.

The children, seed of the bloody husk, moving, hugging, crying in the dark rooms behind afternoon. Starlight accumulates on the snow, and every bright beacon seems, if not the comet itself, a planet of critical information, equally immersed in the unbroken chronology, the music we can neither stop nor decipher, in its own stops and divulgences. Against the tautness of the lyre and the obliquity of the extended field. A bright object like the sun in our midst at night, and in us the knowing, the lens of pond algae become the tissues of the brain. We feast on cannibals. We use the trick by which the sound is silence to make silence a wellspring of sound.

Latitude by latitude, going North from the Equator, from the single rings of remade Spanish gold the natives wore. Cabot on the St. Lawrence pushing toward the copper industries of the Great Lakes, always the fires of some later unknown peoples on the horizon, the secret-bearers, the true lost tribes. The world is least understood by those who know it best, as governments fall, and the disease mocks its many cures. We use the sun as source of oil and history and mo-tion, wheat and beef, but its largest body is ignored, its greatest mass undigested, our sense of moving into space linear and unabated, to Jupiter's magnetic field. In the South, inside the Earth, another omen, the same vastness, unknown. And though it will not swallow us — as we approach it on tether with the false majesty of our cul-ture — we will cease to be.

VI

If I stop writing, surely the images will come anyway. The water rolling over the giant rock. For I am excavating a dark tunnel, and need to bring all this into daylight, to see what it is and to join it to the rest. Those creatures who leave the tunnel and then return, while daylight is elsewhere, must be caught again. A calendar and memory system is the only justification for this being text. And yet: will the images come anyway and always? The answer: is yes.

The energy that is in me roars to the surface and twinkles in my eyes. I feel it around me, heightening the definition of sky and stars so that we buoy against each other and the creation actually floats.

The alternative is superstition, biblical prophecy, or the illusion that we can survive alone, in bomb shelters and rebuilt civilizations, with only our cosmic warnings. The figure of the comet and flood is older than Nostrademus; even the strongest of us, the most self-sufficient, is light as a feather before the lines of the belt. And this is the reckoning in which we must sit forever, the emperor cordoned off from the court astrologers, in a space in which the comet is no more than modern astronomy makes of it.

I bring back to you only that you seem to dictate to me, from where you are, and certainly not with the blatancy of a spirit thru a medium. In the complication that is everything we have, myths are always and never realized, archetypes bind and vanish, alone or in choir. For me there is no answer, Seth, only the broken geography of a world, all of which must be accounted for. You say it too when you say that the dream goes on dreaming even after we awake from it. I defy you as I receive you with open arms; you are warm and friendly, and the gaunt figures in sackcloth await the downfall of our civilization in an intuition that is frozen, an expectation that has nothing in it for us either way. Though I wonder why *you* wait, here at the margins, if you are able to go on. And if it's not that you wait, how in the great smashing and reconstitution of the same glass, the voice comes thru you from where you are, and I hear your name not in me, but from where the ocean ends and the stars, all billion upon billion of them, begin. Are you the son born to Adam in his two hundred and thirtieth year, discoverer of the Hebrew alphabet and the celestial signs, inventor of the holy calendar, namer of the stars and the five planets? And if you are, why have you come back to us now?

VII

I have a flash of an old daydream. Flying saucers, friendly aliens, dimensional travel. I stand over a wild native planet, about to begin again, from the beginning, with everyone I love. And the sense, now, that the dream is a distraction. I see myself at a distance as only a poor actor in a science fiction set.

It has become empty and tawdry, dissolving thru neurotic longings, into a pattern symptomatic of the inflexibility of growth. This alone roots them; otherwise they are rootless in desire. A desire I can now discard, from the middle of a life I am turning out to live.

Though it's filled with happy people, the daydream is lonely. We could not gain such means of transport or survive the passage without complications, deadly complications. Better to be as it is, without such possibility. Or we'd never understand. We'd throw this type of romanticism into the workings at every opportunity, and we try to anyway.

There is nothing static and assured, and the dream to be so, though narcissistic, to bring everything together in a happiness, is less a source of pleasure than of pain. And even as we know this, we keep the dream as a record of something else. It cannot be altogether discarded, for it dimly outlines the shape of my life.

VIII

A strange December heat. The fields a somber green. The trees bare. The sky a bowl of steam. Rain and mist pouring thru the lower world. The softness of what passes for creation, when it is intermediate. The sense of wondrous things yet to come.

Who knows/surely we do not know — who fall from background to background, from warp to woof, in the intimation of sticks in a watery loom. The core Royce called the self found only by contrast with the environment, the will a piece of coal, which burns, which burns out, a nameless child floated upon the billion stars, the graves of the most ancient philosophies littering the Earth like leaves. Which Egypt? Which Atlantis? A stone beneath the Atlantic Ocean? Or the whole immaterial world?, thru which the surge of consciousness came even as it is now red with blood, the brain nomen for the thoughts, which pass over the brain itself in waves, ground fog sustaining the living, that what we create is as rough as what we see, and as it chafes us, it roughens its own landscape, and we grasp at our presence in its disclosure.

Whose comet is it? Nostradamus, who lived four centuries ago?, or us, the present selves of past incarnations?, concerned about the weather, and, more than prophecy — how much rain today; how wet the fields, how muddy the roads. A veil uninterpretable for its intimacy with ESP and astral metaphor (for there is no way out), and yet, because it cannot be read literally, because its impressions go so much deeper, because they use our voice to speak, it dogs us all the time we live, with its unfilfilled proposal, history denies and buries, as events unfold, only to receive us again as the late guest at the masquerade. A depth and ingenuity to which we cannot plunge, not in our present shape. A raw simulacrum of the angel of design.

Thousands of passing, connecting worlds, and we sit in a pew in a hollow church. Patterns, as we are patterns, occupying our space, fooling us with walls, or going right thru walls. There is an absolute interlock of all times, systems, languages. At one minute blatancy, at the next moment a weird and inexplicable obstruction, perhaps in the brain, perhaps in the space itself. It cannot be shattered and it cannot be brought into being, and so it must be lived, in the deluge, no matter how deformed, until it returns us, like crystals on a beach, to what we were.

When the woman rises, her belly holds, dream within dream, the new form, allowing it to happen because it happens thru our agency, as the waves that do not let us sink and do not let us swim. A thousand creatures once, now a billion, all of whom have lived before, a destiny no puzzle can protect in the cradle of time. The comet and crossing of Sun and Moon put their finger on a spot from 800,000 years ago. When it becomes visible, you will recognize it, not until then, the men with yellow raincoats at the gas stations, the lines of a hundred cars. They labor to hoist a tower in the middle of the city, to bring an object into the center, without any reckoning of whether it be inside or outside, dealing their energy-scarcity cards between the depth psychologists and the oil diplomats, in a game they refuse to play. All the rest springs, ceaseless but uninterruptible into every chasm and along each arc, brilliant flowing into the waterfall crashing at the mount of the stars, into the rocks beneath, as the sky darkens and rich spume blows thru — the winding and unwinding of the tentacles, a windblown clock whose accuracy is such that it measures even its own lacks of timing, spilling as a single filament into a single pool, where the child hangs in Lindy, the rain collects in the furrow, hangs like a pear, attached by the tip, breathing before it breathes, eating before it is given food, sensitive to colors before it knows the feel of objects, in the state of eternity before time.

One tires of doom, and the parts of being that go to it for solace, so that none of this, in its infinite sorrow, will have to happen anymore. The world has a certain unexpected resilience, and at the moment we are willing to discard it, and the life it has given us, the specter begins to laugh, to find us enjoying ourselves on this dark Saturday night back street. The old chef who cooks dinner at the *Thrush* smiles while he cracks the eggs, putting them on the black greasy grill, whose counterparts in the big cities to the South are blacker and greasier, or so we falsely imagine. The stealth of the crab, the snake and the maggot: the world getting darker but not earlier, intensification but not condition. Because it's made of some flatness in self, some previous sorrow.

The electric plants sputter on a sparse diet, staggering the arteries thru snowy nights. The nuclear jewels, the queen's greatest disappointment, certainly of this radio century, continue their dance, down the decaying stairways of city tenements, where human beings mark each half-life, mark, like scientists, the actual crimes as they occur. The power goes off, taking away the foam crashing thru gateways to generators, not taking away an image that was never there. Only a socket in the wall, half magic, speaking Spanish, like speaking Cherokee when De Soto grilled them in Spanish. The golden cities. Cibola? Sevolla? Where? Where? Coronado dying with only a vague notion of where he came from and in search of what. The Atomic Energy Commission equally baffled. The sputter of coal and steam insoluble, the dark half of the pendulum tumbles into the vat of poisons without will. A wandering priest named Cayce calling "Egypt, Egypt!" thru an American vernacular as persistent as a prairie plague. Corn and soy, that's all there is on the Nile. The spark is extinguished on the loop of the body of the warrior, who trades impenetrability for feeling, in an eternal dream of a dream of going deeper, of living for it alone, recoiling in starlike accuracy from the pelvis along the spine, while arbitrary yet connected thunderstorms whip overhead thru muffled night.

Murray brings us to the tavern for this Saturday night dinner, aftermath of the Ecology Conference, lingering warmth of the people gathered there. The outer crisis is real and impinges on our meal as a constant debate of political philosophies, Murray coming down hard on Lévi-Strauss out of habit, substituting the critique of Stanley Diamond — which seems like the old game of destroying the totem by raising the Western political consciousness of the shaman. Does Murray really think *we* try to control nature, and that's the blunder in a nutshell? What about nature controlling us, even Murray, in his assertiveness over dinner, instead of easing down his meal? What about the difficulty that we *are* nature, in a doubling of circuits that lights the plan for the city long before the city? "All this," says a student coming off speed, "assumes that we want the human race to survive. It's just one more fucking achievement." So the Meeting to Save the Earth wears out when the participants decide to go home, abandoning their NASA ships in orbit, ignoring the hysterics of a roomful of technicians, computer freaks, and eco-prophets, telling them there's no other way.

An energy swamps the Earth, swamps me in feeling, in more than I know; it is processed thru full-blown ideologies into things that don't refine it, that don't even work. The sadness is old and the sadness is young. We cannot use history for our purposes; history uses us. God Who can no longer save us; Who, in an age of Information Theory, can only *be* us.

God Whom Murray would like to kill, in the name of the Revolution. As if this terrific tide of unconsciousness, light, creation, dusk, fire, violence of elements, stars and quasi-stars, jaguars and totem-jaguars, could be quelled, by the dialectician's bid. The inhabitants of Florida (Laudonnière) "painted with devises of strang and divers colours" do not shed their rainbows, their incisions, their robes, their subtle and intertwined clans, to enter the European school, to be liberated by the priests who seek them even yet, as the fodder of creation within creation, baptism in the name of a holier post-Judaeo-Christian world. It is as Ribault said, then and forever, forever opaque and disclosed by its own design, "made in the watter with great redes, so well and cunyngly sett together, after the fashion of a labirinthe or maze, with so manny tourns and crokes," unmistakeably in the warm waters beyond Canaveral. It is not a windmill; it will cycle neither people nor volts. It is a geometry with roots in the Code.

I sense an invisible ripple in the pattern, breaking into and breaking away from it, like the ocean except larger, from beyond its archetypal source. It gives off diamonds we recognize, storing diamonds we do not know. It sits, as no accident, in the Flemish painting of The Whole World, seen thru any clearing, the Windmill. The detail is Fifteenth Century, pre-Swedenborgian. A science of which Dante was a master, in his moral geography, at the origin of gravity, for this being an inhabitable planet, for there being an Earth inside the Earth, an inner consequence to the outer tapestry, for coming into being by light and mesmerism and sense, borne also in a robe of letters and numbers, numbers and letters. And this doesn't mean that the wind didn't blow. Those blades, yet in pigment, in Whole World iconography, spun in a turbulence long since eased.

The flatness is a cold that freezes and does not restore. The rhizome lives, but the stems and berries are dead. I run down the frost-covered grass behind our house, that stiffens beneath my feet, my head thrown back to see that powerful other. The Moon, its ring of cirrostratus on Earth, whose every ounce of rock, dense and hollow, is an inlet or outlet of water, of air. There is a confusion of paths within paths, all of them involuntary, all the time we thought we had felt when we were merely led to the feeling. Until we were here in the clearing, in supernatural light, fed by circles which were spheres in constellations which stood for time caged in space. It is a juxtaposition, always unravelling, always reimposed. Previous fears and obstacles lift. I am being loved, in the warm brook, in this wooden cave, in the afternoon, behind the frost forming on the glass, and the sense, the senses, that the whole world is just the world, form by form, vista after vista, no matter how wide or contained. In my head is a movielike image of Eskimos on the edge of their frozen shelf, hunting along leads, trying to tell the shifting ice from the stable ice, to distinguish the current from the wind and the movement of the ice they are standing on from the movement of the larger water around them — snow at their feet that condenses to stone, stone that darkens, turquoise and black, in the ocean around the breathing hole of a seal. All the time the wind may shift, the current dissemble, and we might find ourselves at sea, having to swim for it thru the almost-frozen waters, our teams barely afloat — the sky neither daylight nor darkness, the dogs groaning as the barometer. Because the landscape *is* artificial, made of crumbling paths and disappearing hills, trails that converge as the water pulls them into itself, smashes them against the shore. Their whole survival, to use that equally dangerous word, depends on each momentary reading of this bedlam: water locked in stone, displaced in currents and wind, snapped, melted, remade in pulses of sun and sunspot, on the distant shadowstage of which we remain a local manifestation. The patterns curl and wind on the glass we see thru, as we pull bodies together, the light that falls translucent, robbed of every drop of sun but one, we do not use and barely see, but read instead the texture and resistance, thru our resistance, that leaves it all an open system, within the rules. Coming to you opens those scrolls of ice in a moment of wordless resumé, makes them currents, in which my body trembles, its own currents, wrapped around your legs, the magnet in which they also are prefigured. Beneath which all creation, minute stones and stellar waste, reaches us — as walrus and water, language and crystal, our tongues on the cold surface, leaving an intricate trail thru the labirinthe: from the tip of the glans rushing and falling into living fibers, ripples under ripples, in whose full and bloody angularity we carry mere buckets, and they are the whole of creation as we spill them, as is our lot. Even if this is sloppy and inconvenient, even if this cohere to exile like the snail to his shell, I will come again, there is no other way. The bodies and veils are penetrable by our use of them, and we play across impinging worlds, atomically, autonomically, on lutes of attention and the very small, because there *is* no other and because it comes in the same way we do, though in our posits we may be 10 minutes or 10 billion years behind. We arise thru worlds seemingly as substantial as this one, which dissolve into cinema and phenomena at the gates.

There is a sound in the stars of a windmill; the blades thrash out light and life, the crosscurrents pile in quantum pools. However cold it gets or how the frost forms similar to and different from our skin continuing to form: we expect nothing and we want nothing, and can be nothing. There is growth and design, not conspiracy or will. The ice forms along the glass as we conceive its sheer plane, as our lips form words and wordless gestures, mutter their own puckered shapes. We spin out our verification, weight in the well, and find the means at hand, gene in bloody gene, because we couldn't be here otherwise, asleep on the wooden floor, still generated, in the proximity of the loom, by the mind in whose mind our love arises.

IX

The sky as blue as sun. Cirrus fibers stretched across it as far as anything will go, either to return or to transcend, the two dominant countering intentions. The winds that have done this are higher and rougher than the undisturbed air below; they are cosmic winds, groomers of mares' tails. The curvature in the Earth, reflected in the curvature of the sky, is real; an iceberg blocks the shore, just outside the horizon, and, in the perspective it has on us, there are no waves, only the waveless procession of air.

The words are barely visible, light eats away at them; the signpost to CALAIS and NORTH MONTPELIER. Stiff huts sitting in the holograph of fire, the curious, almost implicative three dimensions. Brought back again, as if this were at last the realization of their physical properties.

The astral body of Kohoutek, dragging a spiritual mass the size of our debt, appears first in the vicinity of Jupiter, a major portent. Is it a mute pebble, twenty-five miles across, or a vast four-dimensional source? Does it come to Africa and India also or only to the Western World, for its powerful observatories, that allow it to see the end before the end comes? Measured by war in the Holy Land, measured by conjunction of comet with Jupiter and Venus, measured by oil withdrawal and daily future-shock world yaw, marked by the day, the day Sun and Moon align and draw with the same arms, tides visit the Carolinas with the fury of the Spanish Adelanto, heir to the instability of the rock formations on which commercial centers now sit. Cracking the West Coast into a tank of hot white lethal history. Synchronous with the precise dilation of the lens that brings it into focus long after its seeds have been sown in the loom like scraps of red thread in the tapestry of an August sky.

The wine and roses of the Renaissance have been drunk, and a stern Buddha visits these shores under the banner of the immaterial universe we have not squandered. The proposition comes down to this: evade it though we will. We can escape hardships and terrors we fear and project. Forgetfulness absorbs the wounds (into unconsciousness where they are reinflicted painlessly). We escape nothing; whatever happens to us goes on happening, inside and outside, until its circumstance is resolved. There is only one protection, for the harshness of Buddhism is neither punitive nor tautological. *We must yield to them and give them everything*, because we do not know where we are, we do not know how to defend ourselves, we have no rights, and our bodies are carrion, even in the best of times. They can do anything with us, and they must, from necessity, from generosity, and we must allow them, however we pretend to resist.

And it does not end with death. (Why should it? How could it?) It continues until we renounce what we have no claim to, thanking them for their persistence and the justice of their sentence. Harsh? But how much more harsh the alternatives. Unresolved dreams may sustain a decade or a lifetime but could hardly be food for a god. Galaxies whose distances defy space and time do not defy us, and thus stretch our interests across an impossible chasm, where they crack, breaking our hearts.

No need to pretend they might go easy on us or that they might not see: we have given up that privilege long ago. And those that didn't, have even less than us (in the center where we nurse the brown nut that will not crack). Nor do they want to crack it. They want to give it to us. They want to pull away from our attention, all else.

We will be born again in a world of sunshine and warm waters, but between here and there is the assignation of the comet with the fields of Jovian ice. And if we could choose our omens, if energy (psychic, nuclear, or solar) from outside our birth could change things, back then, in the subtlety of our dreams, we would pass as ghosts between barrierless worlds. But we are not ghosts, which is why ghosts exist.

The South Pole is a desert without rainfall; the granules of sand travel restlessly and in swarms, seeking the sun. We visit each moment of our life, a bee sipping flowers. The nectars are transformed into giant combs that adorn the attics of our summer.

The self-annointed prophet hatches egg after egg visions of what morning will be like, what grade of sunlight, fuel after fuel, mass market after mass market, nations straying like mad dancers thru costumes and stages undreamed of in national policy. Though we babble, the secret will stay with us, not letting our tongues reveal what our songs and visions tell so lucently. Prophecy is a recurrent degenerate condition, that says things so right, that says things so wrong, as the whole arises, snakelike and hermetic, from the collective meaning of its past. Not only the meaning with which we have endowed it, but the meaning history found when it left the carefully-guarded campfires of the Gothic scribes and wandered thru night's woods and lunar hallucination in search of the planet it was losing, the meaning of the unrecorded semi-Mediaeval zones it inhabited and plundered all the same.

In the total North the Eskimos are still and landfall, studying the directions of winds and stars, in the endless succession of blizzards and sorcery. Their life is a dancer, the dance of on-ice, with walrus, skin boat, and seal. They do not communicate one piece of significant data to those who visit them, except the physical properties of eternity, though cosmic properties afflict them more direly than any Westward astrologer. Violent winds come from the South, to solve the North, in the middle of which the dogs begin howling, to mark transition. All day stars in the night, nights coned within nights, and single bears wandering on the outskirts of the zodiac.

The comet fulfills its own cycle, as any seed. What it sows will arise among us a millionfold, apart from the orbit in which it continues its journey, or why it chooses the name Kohoutek as we trace that riddle back into the dawn of etymological time. Why Seth dawdles here at the crossroads, to speak thru Jane Roberts, a question she cannot fully ask him, or herself, and a darkness from which he cannot answer, thru her particular brain (though the reasons he gives flatter her, telling of a significant unresolved connection in former lives). Is it the truth?, even if it is? When incarnations, troubled incarnations, lie both before and behind him? He projects a great and generous joy. He brings with him a certainty that it is all by choice, his most precious gift, making of violent wars and irresolvable famines a shadow play of causeless causes, a cinder landscape within which the real harmony, the inner creation rests, safe as the egg profane geometry cannot hatch. Just as we are willing to concede the world its leverage of billions, its dire momentum, its poisoned seas, it swings out light and reconstitutive as we are.

In a series of late movies, Ivanhoe, though victorious once, must return, broken of ancestry, to invent another way to do the same thing again. They bring up billions of gallons of oil from the Earth, I would ask them to leave there (but must use if they release) and another 30 or 60 or even 1000 years to this industrial renaissance, ultimately, ultimately beyond which is the comeuppance, for us here or for those who will be here, and surely for us where we are, in the frozen descent, just as we are responsible for the means when the sun explodes and then dries into a pip, and a corrupt technology palls before the challenge, while spiritual energy is asked to do feats previously demanded of a man on horseback with axe, against ball-and-chain, as a trial of God. It is our responsibility, for they are *our* blasphemous scientist-priests; it is our boastful victory cry. The life of the heroine is not specifically at stake, and even if it were, submarine warfare and mindblowing drugs would take Ivanhoe out of the picture. This will look like a science fiction story before it's over, words passed at a gas station; for the duration, Lewis MacAdams says when asked how long he will live there. If a transformation is at hand, the seeds must grow: again and again thru the zodiac as they were planted from the zodiac. Perhaps not as simple as the Friends of the Comet would drink directly from psychic Kohoutek, as if she were a prostitute, a beggar of immediate design, but deep within, before and beyond the neurosis that makes of women women and men men.

He goes by the name of Seth, which is not his name any more than hers is Kohoutek, but must enter history by that name, so that I find him in the Chronicles of Malalas, where he was a Phoenician king. Abdi, son of Adam, sends me, via the campus mail, a relevant quote of Guenon: "Seth obtained re-entry into the earthly paradise and was thus able to recover the precious vessel (the Graal) . . . It can therefore be understood that Seth and those who possessed the Graal after him were, by this very fact, able to establish a spiritual centre to replace the lost paradise, and to serve as an image of it."

And we ask again: what does he want of us that he gives us so much?

The Jovian image is neither how violent nor how methane, how far or how huge; its center holds beyond any diminution, in the center of this sun system. We stare on it, single mind by single mind, each one of us the whole thing. The energy, mass in the Jovian sense, comes in thimbles by aeons, to use, abuse, use up. "You are not the physical world anyway," Seth says. "Why weep for the dead? Why feed the hungry? Learn to control your minds and the shape will change." God knows, when consensual reality breaks down and we meet only occasionally (and unexpectedly) at the fountain in the center of town, it will be a new time. We had better skip the excuses and find ourselves out of the maze we wake in the morning projecting of dreams we have spun, like milkweed down, into eternal lines that take them.

X

On Receiving the Amherst College Biographical Record (Living Alumni, Class of 1966)

It is all put together: then, now, and back before it happened. Vital statistics. Desperate facts. Things that draw us, as though to ourselves, which we had better forget, in some blinding zen removal of character, if we are to survive even in the most minimal sense.

Those people who were at Amherst in the class of '66, their birth dates, their parents, their mothers' maiden names, their prep schools, their fraternities, their degrees, jobs, publications, memberships, marriages, wives' fathers, children, residences, business addresses. All these in a tiny paragraph, with sequence confused and genealogy mixed, the only women (mother and wife) listed by father's surname, plus obvious errors in attempts to fill missing information (my old Maine address is listed as my business address, my present Vermont address as my home address; in some cases, the home address is given as the one from which the person enrolled in Amherst). The particular collection is alarming, though it is not easy to say why. Perhaps it is because the time-then, at college, is the focal point, while all the information suggests the subordination of that time to the other events in peoples' lives, as though the school were only an initiation center in the mainline of American occupational success. Perhaps it is because it suggests that time which is no time and so calls into question a relation between our inner life as we discover it and the outer life which is available for institutional use.

So much time has passed since Amherst it is hard for me to remember why I acted then as I did, why I remember what I remember and how it relates to the rest of them, most of whom I never knew. Some seemed so little like people, in their inanity or unreasoned cruelty; now they are lawyers, astronomers, geologists, high school teachers, psychologists, people whose counterparts I meet and befriend in these places I have lived without any knowledge of their own excesses and perversities back then, having buried those, as I have, in a family and a private life, or having transformed them, thru confidence and sensibility, into the world's business. The time-then seems only to have made us more desperate and crazier. We acted out romantic fantasies, either of love or sadism or community, but there was nothing in them. Some essential closeness or honesty was both undiagnosed and missing. Even though we lived together, the space we shared was aborted; the downstairs living rooms of Phi Psi seem now as much a dream space as the attic in which we slept like passengers strapped into the space-ship for a migration between stars.

There can be no real aloofness toward Goddard from my Amherst experience; it was a rich and elite world, cut off from the human space we might have shared, leaving us uptight and with no place to go. People, of course, went places, many of them to other great academies on the mainline, their real inflexibility submerged. Perhaps it is symptomatic that the people who felt most optimistic and free at the end were also the ones who most fully understood and accepted how little was necessary to be a success in the exterior America, how little on top of the Amherst degree, and the ones who felt the curtains drawing on them were experiencing the deeper emptiness in that same society.

I can complain about Goddard, and its low energy, until the cows come home; but its continuity with the world beyond, in which people live, is beyond reproach. "Downwardly mobile" is the joke about Goddard students, but Goddard is a different sort of tunnel thru America, based on a heretical interpretation of the text. It is

114

as meaningful to turn kings into beggars as beggars into kings; in fact, if one is happening, the other must happen also. There can be no Goddard Biographical Record; the people come from no such places and go to no such designs. Their time here is not hidden from the rest of their lives, is not focal of data. For many of them, the community around Goddard became the real college, and they have stayed, as carpenters, farmers, glassblowers, bartenders, typesetters. Some have begun communes, like Sam Clarke, who would have been in my class if he hadn't transferred to the North — the amazement in finding out that he had learned at Goddard a trade not taught at Amherst. You couldn't stay at Amherst and become a carpenter; yet few of us even dimly realized then what that meant. Sam's not in the biographical record even as my dead friends are not: Pardee, Bloom, Jenkins. That's excluded too.

We fought each other on Freshman dorm floors. My own perversity attracted the countermadness of others, trapped as we were in the blinding collective forests we threw into the same limited L-shaped halls. I was locked in my room, the room set on fire with lighter fluid. I tried to get out, smashing windows and people with a hockey stick. So much violence, so far from a possible meeting-place, so unavoidable, so impossible it was to see what we were doing, even to admit that there was something to see. Too cool; everyone was too cool for that. And writing this piece, and not being able to remember exactly how it felt, brings me to *The Amherst Literary Magazine, Winter, 1963-64*, and my story "Elmer the Cow." The righteous indignation is excruciating, as excruciating as the hip boy-girl jive that surrounds it in the other stories of more polished less freaked-out writers. Could I have written it? Yes, something in me did, something that is still there. But someone else wrote it too, and he is gone forever, along with those who tormented him:

"The wind blew and a loud whistle came from it. The trees shuddered snow and the Amherst snow symphony swirled. Barrett was frozen and dark; the road was slush. My window shook."

The trouble then, to hit one obvious thing, is that I wanted to be a writer more than a person; I had some lingering hope I could evade life, heroically.

"I walked back to my dorm — feeling the frost break through in the drafty-warm halls, watching the girls and boys lie in the hall under special blue lights, hearing sighs and sobs and wondering who ever loved whom in this world."

What could I have been complaining about? It was between those who wanted to live and those who wanted to transcend. I had my half. If we were in each others' ways, it was instructive, not war.

Jeff Tripp taught me that a year later. "Enough of this fuck-
ing Elmer the Cow. You don't really want to be that. I wouldn't
have anything to do with you if you did." Jeff, who didn't
graduate, before any of us knew what else you did, who grew the
first beard, who left to live in the forest with Eric the Rat and play
guitar.

Other people tried to get high, to find each other, to be in touch
with the spirit or meaning of their all being there together.

"I left and went into the dark snowy night, and I tasted the snow
like frozen puffed rice and watched it stick to my boots like Elmer's
Glue, fluffy Elmer's Glue. Think of Elmer the cow. Oh yes, think of
him wandering in that cold snowy night. Think of the snow numbing
his warm cow's back; think of him mooing into the moaning wind, a
lost Elmer-the-cow.

And think of me beneath the lantern wondering if tasting snow
would help — just a little bit. Oh, how I was trapped by the dark
night, the mountains, the snow, and the beer bottles warm in the
drifts. No stars!

'Oh, Lord Jeffery Amherst was a soldier of the king, and he came
from across the sea . . .

A group of drinks singing, I thought. Let them sing. I will walk
the other way.

'Silent Night, Holy Night: All is still; All is bright . . .

That formed and rhymed in my mind as the chapel bells were
bonging twelve; that hummed as my own eeriness answered the
eeriness of bells in the night — chanting an undercurrent to the bel-
lowing laughter from the dorms where all were happy and warm to-
gether."

We knew nothing then, nothing as succinctly as the Biographical
Record was to pose it: our mother's father and wife's father in one
rush, our high school and graduate school, fraternity and job, birth-
date and child's birthdate. We knew nothing of what was before and
what was to come, though I remember long discussions about whether
suicide was noble and incest immoral with Sid Schwab (now, the
book tells me, University of California Surgery) and Al Powers
(teaching English at Berkshire Community College), room-mates
then.

They come from single houses on single streets in Rye and Coopers-
town and Attleboro Falls and Portland, Oregon, and go to single
houses in Washington, D.C., and Little Rock, and Houston. And it
is over, over long before and long after it began.

The Biographical Record continues the tradition of false intimacy
and false association. In some remote sense it addresses the question:

116

whence came we, who are we, whither do we go, and by giving the illusion of an answer, in the most profane sense, it shows again how poignant the circumstance and how we cover our loneliness with fake lists of friendship and fraternity. And how we omit the Bardo and the dead, even as Al Powers said back then, that he would take his own life someday, so that no one else would take it for him, and Sid only thinking about the corpse and whether to will it to some medical school, to get an extra $200 to make it thru winter weekends. Al knew somehow that if we didn't make the corpse ourselves, they'd send it to us, as they have truly sent it to me on this winter morning.

The college was not a big commune; we learned nothing intimate about each other, and we were trained in the hiding of real information. In that sense, the communal spirit in Vermont and New Mexico well justifies the burning of these records as dead accounts of what no longer can be resolved or made up or made close, any more than all the oil company executives and state lawyers and environmentalists and English teachers and class freaks can be brought back together because they were all in the same year at the same Ivy League college, to impose some moral and shared order on this country, or to renounce, collectively, the football weekend that is still draining the last years of our youth. If there were any closeness in the nation at large, it would show up here, but this isn't China Class of 1966, and there are only differences, as great as those between the living and the dead. Greater.

At Goddard the attempts of teachers and students to share lives, to do real things together, practical, emotional, and to admit the lack of substantial hierarchical distance between them, brings its own confusions and madnesses. But it is a clarity also, and saves some of what Jeff Tripp, after Dylan, called "our precious time." At Amherst you felt they moved in another century, and their solemnity and sadness, the melancholy of their lives, most of them, seemed not only beyond my capacity to feel, but beyond my whole lifetime. They were a different species. And they weren't. The masks and formal parties made only the play real, and when they fell, something uglier always occurred, because they were masks of some desperation. Who cares? I don't want to be the elfish critic I was then. Part of me will always feel, without acting out, that we should strip ourselves bare and go into those hills and learn to live with each other and the world of sentience that surrounds. The Biographical Record fosters a deadly illusion that something can be gotten from back there even yet, where there is nothing. Its lesson, in boastful certainty, is how little I know about anything, and how

much there is to know about the people who live here in the world
with me, and who will leave the world with me. Whose life is it?
Certainly not theirs either. And what shall become of us, as we move
from town to town, breaking the ties before any of them become
real? And those of the failed communes: what biographical text of
their comrades do they carry into the future, as their hopes dim?
Or the Chilean poor? Or African and Eskimo clans at the ends of
their long history, though their members be brought back to birth
again and again thru the centuries, as long as the totem holds?
Will we ever know who we are? Will we ever be able to burn these
lists so that they go back into the universe from which they came,
or will they be with us forever, like the memories? The mystery of
our survival, posed against all the rest.

XI

From all directions the blue jays come to the seed, their wings flap-
ping, their heads thrown back to swallow. The bowl rocks, an
unfinished cobble, abandoned in the log from which it was cut
because the concavity was dug off-center by the trembling carver —
stacked with his firewood. He spent too much time high on the
ouija board for wooden bowls to cool out. The air is warm and has
melted its ice, freeing the seeds that froze there during days of
rain and snow, so that as the birds peck away in the pool of mois-
ture on the waning stone, there is more and more for them to feed
on.
The trees stand like sticks, the blown thread of their sugars mea-
suring time and light, as the years pour down over me, warm water
on my back. The past is gone and must be forgotten, except what
is remembered, when the winds blow it bare.
New clouds settle in the near sky. The laws that bring them into
being continue to fill them; the essence is enriched, the seeming
substance of their bodies, that will tumble, dissolve, over this land
or some other, day after day descent of the actual, of the conse-
quential, until we are what we are. Beyond them the atmospheric
clouds are blown apart; their fabric breaks and they are scattered
as dust. A moral lesson. Enacted almost casually in the sky. To
show us how calm and casual must be our own response to the
knowledge. Clear, so clear. And why, it asks, is it clear?

118

The tire swings on the rope and the long sun throws its hole thru a series of phases on the snow, like the moon, as it turns, from full to gibbous to half to crescent, to shadow, and back again. A lesson in geometry concealed in selenomancy, a late Palaeolithic philosophy of the inner sky, demonstrated as lucidly on cave walls in Spain. The principles have been here as long as this world has, in this sector, and the errors, the ripples of cosmic bodies, become trivial when one stands at the centers of old cults, in their temples, and sees that nothing has changed by as much as a whole sun or a whole moon, even the nature of civilization.

Patterns both of survival and meaning, which are everywhere demonstrated again and again. If I see it as didactic, it *is* didactic. The ice dripping like milk into water. The brilliance of the snow reflected back on the bellies of the birds, onto the daytime moon. The clouds thrown into the mill. It is alive, what gravity and molecularity, chemical and electrical make-up sends to its completion in an unceasing continuity. Nature is set in motion by nature. There is no sense that the fire must be relit elsewhere, no sense that it has been burning any longer than a second.

In a dream of the hospital as hotel I have fallen down the elevator thirteen stories to the ground, the dishonest elevator man has been killed, and I have crawled up a tunnel, throwing chunks of ice away as I fight myself free, twisting and reaching upwards for the holds, until I come to the first step of the staircase, beginning in the mud, and climb back up to the maternity ward on the 16th floor, from whose window I see the sun and field of high school and the baseball game going on as it always was, menhirs casting shadows across the turf. My dreams are encased in one another like domes, and I awake from this one to find myself as Lindy, fucking childhood friends who, like myself, lived in a world without women, my deprivation from them solved by me being the woman. It is a mechanical dream, like a semi-esoteric, semi-pornographic exercise, and I awake from it swiftly to a dream in which a wise man, a psychologist with the cap of a wizard, is pointing out to me relationships in the dream from which I have just come, telling me that the confusions of people in my life are on an unconscious level, and that I don't fully appreciate them because I make their information esoteric, as if conscious. He cannot say too strongly that I *never* experience fully the degree to which my body is confused with Lindy's, Lindy's with my mother's, and the birth of my child with my own birth, *never*. He adds that the doom prophesied for the future is an unconscious memory of terrible things that have already happened: the miasma of childhood, the blind attempt of my mother to kill herself in me, these are diagnostic. They are the hollowness, the psychic indigestibility in my soma. They become the physical knots of my accumulating age. Accept them, he says, with a vast sweep of his arm to sun, trees, birds, in a tropical landscape; accept them, with all the rest. And then vanishes. And I wander thru the city of childhood until I awake to people in my house, voices downstairs; it is quite late in the morning, and I have overslept; Lindy has decided not to wake me up; she figures in due time I will come on down. I walk down the stairs and see Victor, having come all the way from Toronto, but as he moves forward to say hello, I cannot see him; I blink my eyes and wake again, and am sitting in my bed drenched with sun, having truly overslept.

There is a fixed point, from where I am, into the snow, the sky, the things that move with the wind, the flight of birds, beyond the kinetic depth effect, in the vault of creation, as one event conceals and animates another. There are no bubbles in creation. There is not a leak. Not even a cosmic geyser spurting between starry geometries.

I cannot predict what this world will become or is becoming. The fictions that *Plain Truth Magazine* spreads via the t.v. are sheer poison and spite; they call it prophecy, or they call it "plain truth," by that meaning to set the living against each other for the possession of life. God do they fear the darkness of India from the whiteness of L.A. But I don't want to live that life; I don't want to be at war. Here in Vermont the old metals really rattle, as people try to do well by each other, and not have so much that their guilt turns them into fortifications and bright red carpeting. The metals rattle as the houses heat, as the parts of structures not fully attached in autumn wait for spring. I have an incredible sense of peace, an almost frantic sense, from this disordered and dangerous landscape, that the motion arises from my motion, and for all the despair and disrepair there are remarkable powers of recuperation. The moon in the tire. The utter depth, volume by volume, in the sky in which the clouds move. The shadows, and that they are shadows. The light unimpeded, color impeded only, in its polarities of yellow and blue, by sinuosities of air. This is what it is, forever, and if we are going to get past this point, under rough legislation, it has to be translated from what we are.

Damn the histories of literature and philosophy, that seek to steal the continuity of our visions. They are too rigid to prove anything. They are forced, horribly forced, in the alien-ness of mankind. The Aramaic and Egyptian clutter an obvious modern diction and tempt us to spend lifetimes, like bluejays, sorting grain.

The light on the snow. The color white. The wind. My dreams. The domes. The clouds. The moon in the tire. The moon in the sky. The premonition of feeling. The clarity which the light suggests, moving in photons along the cracked-paint surface of our house, is the clearness I feel when I break the webs and set the fiery insects free. Talking with Lindy in the living room in the sun, where we build fictions and watch the wind take them out in the sky. Putting coffee in me until I shit. Sitting in the bathroom where the light from outside bends in pulses and shifting fibers of yellow, the swinging tire on the snow, the slight warping of the glass, making the shapes soft and internal, where I can move them, as I move my head and my insides, and pick up, along a parabola-like trajectory, the sparkles in the landscape, from corners of metal and moisture. Shadows of smoke and haze flow swiftly across the snow, the tangled branches cast crisscrossing sundials. The birds fluttering in the branches, the single leaves strewn like ashes, the house creaking in the changing heat and wind against its box. Yesterday's footprints frozen from the subzero night.

And how the clouds keep coming overhead and thru because that's the proposition, and how, where the light gets into the house, it shows deep hues in the prints of Will Petersen and Nick Dean, the oils of Thorpe Feidt, orange by purple across stray figures larger than the world; and the books on the wall, in their particular combinations and colors of jackets, a music. All the reliefs terrible and intricate and exhilirating, for having to be known. A total personality uses my lesser one, guiding me, though I peversely reject him. The light so strong over the tops of the clouds, suggesting, as I have always told you or he has always told me, *eternal light,* for which this sun shall stand, in this creation, do what we will with our shadows, misuse our bodies as we may. And that's our choice this winter, beautiful in the limb of despair, Lindy's breasts prenatally full, biological law sustaining karmic law, giving nothing to those who would ban the world and steer our children out of it.

The birds keep returning, in sequence, raw music. Black necklines, white patches on their wings. Exact and zigzag. A single leaf, blown, almost steered, thru the sky. The cards flow; brilliant and faint images are interposed, while reality embraces them, and us, and what it is: dashing false history into t.v. and newsprint. So what if it never becomes easier, it only becomes harder, all our lives. Because if not here, then somewhere else, we would have to drink the brown water of the river when the master offered it to us, disgusted though we were, with our bile. We know this between moments, where, in the roughness of our torsos, the gears of the watch are so worn that there is time which is not timed, or is timed in such a way it is out of mesh with the rest. Still no fear can replace the joy that softens, the light which must reveal it because it is here, as we are, at the same moment in the same system, and brings us to itself until we see.

XII

The Earth lies between itself and unimpeded fire, the atmosphere passing by degrees into the next appearance. There is no real night and day, no calendar except the elaborate one Egyptians and Mayans give us. These large orbs are ground in orbits about each other, held to seasons by a mystery Newton called gravity, a mystery with no physical property except itself.

Part of the Moon's geography is sunny; the rest is night. As the triad of motions is recorded in the local atmosphere, Vermont passes thru stages of blue into darkness, and the Moon becomes brighter and sharper until the daylight in its airless valleys and down its mountain slopes is the only daylight we see, except for the planets that appear in the empyrean sky (as Vermont is taken away), and they are indistinguishable from stars: the sun on their deserts, clouds, snowfields, and oceans a single clear beam. We cannot make out a grain of matter where earlier every imperfection on the side of the barn was clear. Little consequence now that Jupiter lies out beyond us and Venus moves between us and the sun. The night sky belongs to ancient history and its observatories. 5 x 584 = 8 x 365 was the key to a chart which was not the sky, in which Venus entered the history of men as a figure who could articulate the riddle of their existence as well as herself be a star.

The Moon sparkles, and the warm day in its hills preens, where no one has climbed with knapsack and picnic lunch and no one sits — history and prehistory suspended in each other forever.

We pull the sled once more up the hill and go flying down on the ice, between the trees, bumping over the frozen footprints. One last look at it before we draw the curtains, the spindles of protoplasm continuing choppily to wind the thread that no longer connects planets and suns. We pour this unknown liquid from goblet to goblet, and the essence seethes thru the markings on their sides, hieroglyphs that form as if the silver were alive with birthmark and tattoo. So one series determines another: where wetness ends, colors begin;

where color ends, sound begins; where sound ends, light begins, ending behind the relativistic sky in which are distributed the objects of our cosmology. From there we pick up a sound, like that of a turtle shuffling across the sand, both alien and familiar in the sheer multiplicity, the whiteness of its noise. It evades our attention, but it is the material of which attention is made.

XIII

The green new world of Virginia, the Carolina Outer Banks, onto which those first ships fell like butterflies among clover. Campfire lights mingled with stars at the Atlantic horizon. Coves and inlets in sun and shadow. San Gabriel, Saint Augustine. Florida, realm of forests and barbarian kings. Chestnuts dense as blueberries, walnuts big as stones, trout visible between the rocks, vines drunk on grapes. The deer walk up to John the Baptist, who slaughters them, who initiates them into the order of Europe (June 24, 1588, Vincente Gonzales, Portuguese in the service of Spain).

And then the English:

"The second of July, we found shole water, which smelt so sweetly, and was so strong a smell, as if we had been in the midst of some delicate garden, abounding with all kinds of odoriferous flowers, by which we were assured, that the land could not be farre distant: and keeping good watch, and bearing but slacke saile, the fourth of the same moneth, we arrived upon the coast, which we supposed to be a continent, and firme lande, and wee sailed along the same, a hundred and twentie English miles, before we could finde any entrance, or river, issuing into the Sea" (from a document circulated by Walter Raleigh).

What was lost is lost now again, sulphurous decay, in spa and spawn of bubbling highlands, turgid lowlands. Abulafia, in Italy via Spain, bearing the throne of God, smuggled from Galilee by an Indo-European riddle, wed to Queen Alchemy, to raise a finer nondual gold the East had already envisioned and spun. The West continues, its vehicles trapped in snow and ice, spinning wheels, rearing horses, ships colliding with ice, to carry the thread beyond the "other" into the foundation, the source atoms of itself. And in South America, while Christ is born in the Crescent, they are moving stony debris, to leave images of spiders and lizards, microscopic details

123

transferred to figures so large their outlines are misread until aerial photography, the desert undisturbed for millenia; even the Pan American Highway merely slices in half.

Pastoral and sedentary. Explorer and fisherman. Gatherer and migrator. Priest and Powhatan. The raffle continues, item by item, but the prize is unclaimed.

Roanoke, Choanoke, Ooanoke, and King Menatoan of the New World. Trails the Europeans reported but did not see, they who risked so much and travelled so far and were treated with such beautiful visions. Iceberg separating from iceberg as section of sun separates from section of sun in the tabernacle of light. The optimism not just agricultural but stubbornly ontological, in the full Mediaeval promise of plenty ("......*but shall constantly remember to give the rows of Indian corn their education by pairs: so long shall Christians be born there, and being first made meet, shall from thence be translated, to be made partakers of the Inheritance of the saints in light")* — redone in Puritan metaphysical splendor by Edward Taylor and Samuel Sewall (above), finding themselves in Eden without the wise beaver or the changeling loon, treating Menatoan as the beggar instead of the host, pretending they could keep the temple even as they mocked its priest. An error corrected later and in almost-mural condition by Cooper, via the humanitarian museums of France.

"Hee sent us every daye a brase or two of fatte Buckes, Conies, Hares, Fishe, the best of the worlde. Hee sent us divers kindes of fruites, Melons, Walnuts, Cucumbers, Gourdes, Pease, and divers rootes, and fruites very excellent good, and of their Countrey corne, which is very white, faire, and well tasted, and groweth three times in five moneths: In Maye they sowe, in July they reape: in June they sowe, in August they reape: in July they sowe, in September they reape: onely they cast the corne into the ground, breaking a little of the soft turfe with a woodden mattocke, or pickeaxe: our selves prooved the soile, and put some of our Pease into the ground, and in tenne daies they were of fourteene inches high: they have also Beanes very faire, of divers colours, and wonderfull plentie: some growing naturally, and some in their gardens, and so have they both wheat and oates." Raleigh.

Break in the alchemical tradition. Texts of ice, copper, and pearls. Texts of maize and fruit trees. Texts of rivers, red timber, Indian chiefs lame but learned. Filtering into Europe from the East beyond the East, the West beyond the West, the expanding evasive geography itself.

"There is an herbe which is sowed apart by it selfe & is called by the inhabitants uppówoc. In the West Indies it hath divers names,

*according to the severall places & countreys where it groweth and
is used: The Spaniardes generally call it Tobacco. The leaves thereof
being dried and brought into pouder, they use to take the fume or
smoke thereof by sucking it thorough pipes made of claie, into
their stomacks and heade; from whence it purgeth superfluous
fleame & other grosse humors, openeth all the pores and passages
of the body: by which means the use thereof, not only pre-
serveth the body from obstruction; but also if any be, so that they
have not been of too long continuance, in short time breaketh them:
whereby their bodies are notable preserved in health, & know not many
greevous diseases where withall wee in England are oftentimes af-
flicted"* (Ralph Lane in his report to Raleigh on the Roanoke
colony).

Who would think of Marlboros, Raleighs, and Lucky Strikes, gold
mines and cowboys? Yet here we are, and we are not at the end.
The medicine is as fine as spruce needles, as white as birch, as potent
as the foot of the blind spider. The resiliency is the American
resiliency, the "drifting clouds of krill," billions upon billions of
them invisible, feeding fish so plentiful that buckets and baskets
thrown overboard come up full and explorers stranded on cakes of
ice find the tidal cracks, that threaten to separate them from the
spinning mass, filled with delicate red shrimp, food of royal whales,
so that they sip a broth of the icy sea. Living dreamless and filled
with stars that generate themselves directly, against a low northern
sun that circles the world in a year. Not snow for water, but pressed
against the body's heat, like the grape in the lower latitudes, near
30 degrees, the brandy melting it, the vines wild with seed on the
edge of the Arctic, ethnobotanies of pine and lichen, of the tribes
following the caribou, in whose bellies they find sacks to keep them
warm and, filled with water, from which to drink, killing yes, taking
apart the body as if it were an object, yes, hunters, but with a
haunting charnel remembrance of some palaeo-Siberian Buddhism,
a sparsity and attention to detail, taking things as they are and living
from them flat, as the whiteman could not in his honey and paradise.
Because the plenty is purely hypothetical, purely mental, and purely
creative. To drink from the brooks and blocks of atomic space. The
thirsty Uranus of De Soto, De Leon, that never understood this,
and whose children wander thru the cities still twisted by a painful,
alcoholic, romantic sun.

The mysterious Croatoan, signifying to John White so much
and so little. The colony he had not intended to abandon, as a man
goes out for a walk after dark and never returns (Hawthorne's
fantasy already old in America). Detained by the Armada, pirates,

the Embargo, angry shipmen, mutiny, forced to return to England twice, and then, in Virginia at last, finding nothing where he had left everything, and his promises. 1590. Or the thing that the whiteman must always find, be he Pizarro, James Dorsey, Castaneda, Columbus, or Charles Olson, and make of that what he will:

"Presently Captaine Cooke and I went to the place, which was in the ende of an olde trench, made two yeeres past by Captaine Amadas: wheere wee found five Chests, that had been carefully hidden of the Planters, and of the same chests, three were my owne, and about the place many of my things spoyled and broken, and my bookes torne from the covers, the frames of some of my pictures and Mappes rotten and spoyled with rayne, and my armour almost eaten through with rust" John White on his return to Roanoake Island.

But this far back there is no answer, and even the Gold Bug of Edgar Allen Poe will not bite. Lost persons and lost continents, and the baby Virginia Dare.

XIV

Sunlight rampant. In this the most present of worlds. Snow drifting off the branches, blown to the ground. Children in dark jackets dragging sleds thru the streets. Smoke rising from the chimneys, going straight up thru the cold crystal into the sky.

In her eighth month of carrying it, Lindy finds her baby coming closer and closer to this world. As in its salty birth-waters it rotates, forms itself, subtly within the senses, so gradually, from our standpoint, it seems a stillness, a pure accumulation, happening to itself as rapidly as clouds form in the sky, passing points with a terrifying speed which cannot be gone back over; that is, which will serve it forever. Though blood-ties bind us, and there is a science of the ovum and its spawn, the cross in this cannot be solved. The stages of pregnancy and birth, in their simplicity, and seeming to follow, disguise an unfolding of a different order. The body of Adam is there, God's own body — and whether it is the God of Aristotle or the God of Israel, our data will not deliver us of this riddle. Adam's fall is a metaphor, because we no longer perceive how it occurred upon an actual body to an actual being we are joined to as descent. This will not excuse us from the responsibility; the exile is real, beautiful though its stages and children be. We are so close to our own closeness to it, happiness and sorrow now flow together, and our not being part of the Body of God comes to resemble our being part of It. So the holy books vary from aeon to aeon, in their design of salvation, and not so much in the actions required as how we shall understand those actions, what we shall feel when something that must happen happens anyway.

The world of pregnancy is biological, and its demise comes for the best of all internal reasons. The embryo is hermetic; it hears the voices and communications of those who knew it in other worlds; it is guided. It touches spheres we cannot see as spherical, harmonies of pure circles, continually inscribed; it reads the utterly lucid light of psychic fields. The end of this gnosis must be terrible, for it would seem as though it could be that way forever, the yoga balancing all tremors of possible incarnation. But as spheres are joined to higher spheres, so are they based in a zone of dumb breathing creatures. The embryo makes its peace too soon; its meditation is fed only by the intercession of a rich and unknown world it cannot avoid if the embodiment is complete. Like any chrysalis, it will grow too big for this exercise, from whence it will spring, on its eternal passage.

There is always the slightest cosmic disruption, perhaps a movement of the mother not absorbed in the watery interzone, perhaps the unpleasant bloodiness of the food it receives from the slaughter of other beings, whose faintest echoes, of leaving life, ring out all around it in a field it can hardly, or barely, attend. The slightest disruption, and perhaps no more than the imbalance of an unfulfilled karma, whose feathers sift from layer to layer on a scale whose vastness measures stars and atoms without ever losing touch or count, that knows it cannot rest, yet; for in one sense or another, and they converge, it has chosen here and now for its manifestation, and when it grows too large for the delicate ontogeny that bears it, it begins the descent thru the organs, with little sense where this journey will end or that this new motion is linear and has no saving transformation, it will seek all its born days, the shock that there is another world outside that one, and inside this one, a world so large and bright, so small and flat, so abundant and crude, so perfect and lacking, so chafing and soft, a vast and repeating replica of the kingdom itself, which it has never seen, and thus could almost believe. It doesn't feel right, the stiffness of its construction, the phlegmatic disposition of its giants. In its first moment it would do away with all of it like a small bubble in its lungs, an alteration of breathing perhaps, to restore a more perfect lotus within. But the world stays, painted and sparkling gibberish in all directions, the spinning sword that keeps light in and out, like the obelisk we stand before the rest of the time, undecipherable, and yet so obvious we lose sight of it and forget that for all the letters incised in its surface we can read none of them. And it is not even there.

The baby is smothered in colors and lights, beautiful sounds and intimations of eternity; these do not fade easily. The sudden light is too bright to mean anything and the sounds too loud to be any but the rawest attempts at alphabet. It is confronted by a crisis of survival, and its most implicit wisdom tells it to forget, that it will do it no good not to survive now, even if it should crack the wall of pain and bone and get back to before where it came from. No remission until the form that has its seed now cast in this infant reaches its proportion, is realized as a flower is, and then softened and allowed to die. It must forget everything, for its wisdom is nothing in this creation, unless relearned as the distance at which it now lies, which is true of all wisdom, even should the dead send memory maps back to the living. The knowledge cracks at every seeming threshold and is left behind in shatters, while the new sun comes up over the world and lights the day, even in the minimum of a light bulb in the delivery room. Wait till it sees how far the stars are, and how the obelisk is hidden in them.

Unreal, it thinks, in the Atlantean language no longer and never spoken on the Earth, of which it is the only extant speaker, while all the rest utter and chirp. It will forget that too; it will forget that it laughed when the sun thought it could fool it, that it mocked such remote intensity, when its body was already *of* the sun, and that was commitment and ransom enough. Far, far apart, at the breaking of the waters, at the holy juncture, the aged priest in his cleansed robes sits but does not know he sits, having forgotten beyond forgetting, in the bloodstream the chant of Amon-Ra, and is not the sun, though the sun carries it with its rays of light to the outermost. A blinding obelisk without relief.

*The doors of the underworld are open, O Sokaris, sun in the sky.
O reborn one, you are seen brilliant on the horizon and you give back
Egypt her beauty each time the sky is pierced with rays, each time
you are born as a disk in the sky.*

XV

We pass thru sparse mountain towns, their streets dug and redug
out of the snow so that banks line them. Drifts in the air, thin as
sand blown off the rooftops. Because there is less here, they will know
more, they will come to the condition sooner. They are worn not
as decay is but because extreme conditions prevent their restoration.
In the used furniture store in Morrisville are medallions of crescent
and star, polished gold, 1899 Mardi Gras; in the window a small
mountain cat stuffed and frozen in threat position, with dishes
and plates, a roulette wheel, and old carriage wheels. The yellow
bulbs in the bank at 0°.

The sun moves on a remote limb thru the edge of the sky, over
the Wolcott railroad station, where there is no longer a railroad,
where the boxcars sit on a section of track. The pond reeds are stiff
in the ice. The lungs dance. In thru the nose and out thru the mouth;
in thru the mouth and out thru the nose. Making me a fast-moving
white fox. The sense of body to which we have been wed, no quest-
ion of ceremony long past or sexual connections. Despite the
misshapen people moving slowly along the sides of the roads. The
animal is aroused by such dangerous and absolute sensations.

Bright Venus and more distant Jupiter appear in the evening
sky, accompanying each other from opposite sides of a sun which
is now a silhouette of trees on the mountains. The comet is invisible,
though on television we see its soft coma, from a jet telescope,
thin etched disturbance accompanying Venus in a different plane.
The moon is brighter than it will ever be again, the sun in conjunc-
tion. This day stands alone in our lifetime. And the world is large
and eternal, the theatre of terrestrial astronomy open, we walk right
in, hooded like birds of prey, are marched down an aisle marked
now only by conjunctions and oppositions, are given in that sense of
wedlock to another physical mass, imagined as a woman or a man —
though no longer hooded, a ceremony we are too cold and too
close to see.

XVI

The air settles, like night in day, the river steaming as it burns thru icecakes. The world sticks to the nostrils like a mask, each breath stunned, then awakening to itself. As we go deeper and deeper into the landscape.

What we see is unconfirmed; what we don't see, likewise. As the mask changes, the composition changes, and we know how, in a very short and sudden span, it could be something entirely different.

On the hill above town, seen from a lesser rise thru the old railroad bed, the children are sledding, leaving trails in the snow like jets in the sky, until they are on the bottom and there is, behind them, a series of crisscrossing lines. We can see them as clearly as if we were there, and even more clearly, for we can see everything, where the hill begins and where it ends, and each of them as they move along it, beyond earshot and beyond the sense of speed.

The snow grinds under the boots, and there is so much light, reflecting, running from its initial source, that most of it cannot get in, and rebounds, and rebounds, thru the cemetery, scorching the photographic plate. It is not warm for a sun; it is as cold and brittle as it could be and still be this.

Night comes with certainty and sparkle. The Pleiades in the core, the stars return because they are there, in the absolute zeroes of the interstellar, a sense of dilution and even microdilution, how pinpoint and intense the condition. The smoke pours from the chimneys and goes straight up. Long plumes, iridescent and dissolving, gentle warmth at their base. The scroll of history, figured from our point in motion-time, is read against the vastness of suns and worlds; harshness is merely the condition of our going against it.

Certain old desires and longings have vanished into the wonder that I ever had them, as winter deepens, as Lindy has grown more pregnant with bright cold moons. The unresolved has seemed always pending, despite its obvious resolution in things like stars and snow. The possible trip to Florida flashes overhead, a comet filled with images of oceans, coconuts, Everglades, vast palatial interiors, a warmth and closeness to my father that is not possible because it does not jive with the beginning. Nor do the wishes to be anywhere else but here, despite the cold, and despite the distance from movies, restaurants, ocean, friends. We make new friends; we walk in the snow. The rest is distracting and remote, as houses also last only two or three hundred years. The design of gravity drives their stones apart; the winds gnaw at the molecular wood. The image is just that, a fantasy trip thru the air, landing in the tropics, visiting childhood temples kept by the servants, despite the change in every-thing else. Other friends go and return changed/unchanged. The brown fingers of the sun on their seeming skin. Nick calling from his porch in North Carolina where he sits in his shirtsleeves, observing the same changeable moon.

That it is 40 below here seems a mere flick of the horse's tail, and not very interesting or significant, no more so than the money it costs to keep the rooms warm, which is burned off anyway, no mat-ter what the oil-producing nations charge or how overweighted the zodiac with comet. I have the same feelings; I get the same warmth from inside my body; we twine and come together under the covers.

Outside the cold barn of the people we are visiting for dinner, I have a jolt of sudden alley depression, penetrating in the bitter wind, joined to the darkness beyond, as far as it goes; I move to it and with it, and for once, in my gentleness, it dissolves, until I see the barn again, the lights where they are, in the background noise of forest, snow, and winter. And I realize I have a choice: the world is beautiful by the same guise that it is melancholy. The feelings of being away from home when I am home happen for just a moment, and happen forever. They are buoys in a larger sea, beyond my immediate warmth and family. Things I think I have wanted turn out to be things I have not wanted, and have been placed there, in that differential state, to keep an image alive, a way out. As if I were Flash Gordon. With none of the personal intimacy that would seem to be their whole usefulness. Better to sled and tumble with Robin and chop wood in the afternoon if such sadness, if such intense re-call is just on the other side.

The dispossessed, either in us or outside us, might not exist, but then we would continue on this warm craft down the smooth lake across the imaginary summer skies. The stones would remain in the field; it would not be done, and it would continue not to be done, given the weight of granite and the counterweight of galaxy and star. The wild vines would go unplanted in the garden; there would be no one to restore and open the scaffolding, the masonry; there would not have to. There would be no warning. The roughness of wood and the deadweight of a handful of seed is only an invitation. The light is inside, no matter how many the suns. The loneliness is made of this; so is starvation when there is no food.

XVII

To put outwards an obscure and intelligent design, Rob moves from
the Norse and Finnish originals to a house he now builds in the for-
est, from the limits of etymology to the equally etymological limits
of wood. He cuts and hews the logs, and then sets a frame, with each
piece bevelled and dovetailed in another, so that the structure stands
on gravity and right angles, without a nail. He will not accept the
drawing of Jungian mandalas as an end; it must be something larger
and inhabitable. Dumézil's mythology of the Aryan is not sufficient
without the resin, the experience of carving and placing it, so that
Vermont encloses a forest of Lithuanian origins. He is making a large
piece of furniture; he is building a map, nails would violate the
topological qualities of; for it is the discovery of previous and struct-
ural limits, like the translation from Norse, which makes his text,
line for line, correspond to something real, what a house is in North-
ern climes, that can then be a life.

It would seem at first that he is abandoning a text of great inner
beauty, along with the Vikings he tracked in his own domestic mi-
gration, but his passion is to project psychic quantities into forests,
fields, and wind, a skill the local landscape demands. One day the
Vermont farmer finds he has gone over the edge, his heavy labor comes
to an end at a moment of exquisite exhaustion: the cows, the wood,
the axe, the sledge, the barbed wire, and, boom, just like that, it's
alpha rhythm the rest of his life. He hears a hum. The day passes in
a moment; the days pass. Something happens, if not to the weary
mind then to the cells of the mind, and the bony skull. In a time of
limited masters and dwindling gems, to come upon the place he did,
with stone, with wood, the logos he made, to build a house, to keep
warm, to feed the animals, eat, live a life of that. Without troubling
questions of etymology or Norse origins. And still come to a complete
construct within the whole. But a construct similar to what? To the
Norse scholar? The Poundian poet? The Icelandic farmer? Who has at
best Normandy in his genes?

And how much of the space we are to occupy is human, how much
of what is not human we are to make human, not by synthesizing
or recreating it, conversions we hardly understand, but in *their own*
limits and the abiding fact that they arise prior and simpler to us
in the same system, reaching beyond us both ways to what else
we are. They are cellulose and sugar; they will never come alive as
we do, never again; but without them *we* are not alive. What would
seem otherwise, in the cold, and the snow that accumulates on it, its
distance from the glyph, and the ownness of the deer that run on by,

thru their forest, in our forest, becomes the needed property be-
cause there is too much of what we need, too much for us to need
it anymore. And we must sustain those we sustained automatically
once, by our very living. We must sustain not only their minds and
bodies, but their skeletons, and the systems of suspension that give
those skeletons credence in the face of mighty and disparate winds.
The basis of material is still natural, and the natural materials are mon-
uments, sources in our moments of sorrow, as the stars at sea, the
outlaw finding his way to Iceland, Newfoundland, Vinland, the New
World itself a deluding repository of everything that was needed,
when the truth was, and is, that we don't know what is needed, and
whether it is lacking, and how much of it there is in Alaska, if that
is the end we seek, or merely that which seeks our end, in a mirage.
Even in the face of uncertainty, the hum remains, and can become
a house, if necessary, en route to the physiological basis of mind.

We can be sure that what we keep almost painfully conscious,
for its value in weaponry and strategy, is sustained by the billions and
billions of unconscious atoms — facts, like wood, like marble, like
yarn, which have become conscious another way, so conscious, in
fact, that they have passed into a hammer-and-saw trance guiding the
architect, the dollhouse-maker, thru a high the Vermont farmers know
but do not describe as such, for the dumbness of their ecstacy, but
which the dropout urban professionals suspect on their folklore
excursions and interviews with craftsmen and laborers, a farm
appearing with the morning sun, as gracefully as the miller's daugh-
ter would have spun gold had she been able. The bottle of rum is
broken over the center of the frame, and they are spaced beyond
Valhalla, the wind thru the trees, the snow on the cells, the cellu-
lose in the blood and nose.

"Aren't you ever bored?" he asks the old neighbor.

He doesn't know what the word means. "It means 'lonesome',"
the man's sister tells him.

"Yeah, I've been lonesome at times."

And with all the stone and all the wood before him, and Pound's
ABC OF READING, the SAGAS, and Piggot's PREHISTORIC
EUROPE behind him, the option is there, to go on for 25,000 years,
baking bread and not even feeling it. The first time, with stone-axe
and cave-paintings of the phases of the moon, it was derived directly,
and in concordance with hidden voices, perhaps inner voices, owls or
owl-like in their stealth and staggered appearance. Now he can go back
thru the materials and choose from among original Germanic languages,
the precise etymology, Shaker and Mediaeval, he will try to project
into the darkness of matter. It is like seeing it all over again,

as it was never seen, and choosing it anyway, under the darkness and the brightness of the stars.

So we walk out of the woods, the sky hazy, the temperature up to zero, and the snow still ankle-deep, across the deer's footprints, and it is not only by chance, and it is not only fortuitous, earlier in the evening around the woodstove they were singing, or recalling and singing:

Last night I had the strangest dream
I never had before...

Guitar, harmonica, voice, and jagged ancient harmony, like wood feeding off air in flame.

Or is that only how I remember it.

Dark and open, as the frame, and covered with snow, unfinished, against the stars.

XVIII

from Wendell Seavey in Bernard, Maine

Merton Rich an I went after shrimp but didn't do much at it along with many others. For about a week and a half we done good but it didn't last very long. If it hadn't been for one spot we found we wouldn't have done much at all. Many did not even find that one spot. That was my first try at dragging. Although we were dragging for shrimp I know that fish dragging is done basicly the same way. I can tell you I don't like it. As far as I am concerned it destroys to many other forms of life for what you catch. And I don't like that one little bit. I like fishing that doesn't hurt other forms of life or if it dose it is as little as posiable. There is something about dragging that to me seems very crude. I dought if I ever go again. I think it is high time we begain to start taking care of this old earth. We are going to have to reconsider our ways of doing things and our outlook of it. I think man's selfish outlook and ways of doing things are now starting to back him into a connor.

I no longer think it is man and God on sides against the devel and nature. I am beginning to think man is too selfish to give a damn what eather nature or God thinks about his actions as long as he can git what he

134

thinks he wants.

It is funny how a man can get an idear in his head an go along with it so long an be blind to any other thought. Well I guess you have lissened to me bitch and rave long enough in one letter so I'll go on to something else.

XIX

The January thaw is sweeter than spring itself. We awake to the sounds of water on the roof, in the driveway, falling from the branches.

After breakfast Robin and I climb the hill across the street, the unknown hill from behind which the sun appears, making this the last village street in Plainfield, on one side the old railroad bed and the parking lot of the feedstore-apartment, the other side dropping sharply into the campgrounds of a revival church that functions for only a few days each summer.

Water trickles down the slope, and our feet slip back in the mud; we pull our way up by loose branches, skidding over patches of remaining ice. The scenery changes rapidly as we ascend. The thaw flows sparkling thru the town, a map of the drainage from the hills. A mist from the snow, unnoticed when we were in it, places the village in a fog, the houses resting on seeming hot ponds. The pine needles break from the ice and are crushed beneath our feet, their hibernation essence richer than a California forest. White Kitty, running ahead of us, sniffs the ground and dances, bounding on and then looking back, using our protection from dogs to explore this strategic ground.

We sit at the top looking at our house from an angle we could not have imagined. We don't mind our seats becoming cold and wet; we are exhausted from the climb. It was always this way, even when a child myself, the possibility of having a child and climbing his first hill with him, the incompleteness of that hung in the incompleteness of this, so that one discloses and explains the other, pulling together the synchronous pieces of a life.

Looking into the church grounds, we see that they open on the hill not the road. The heart of the operation, the church itself, faces us as squarely as a billboard, on the front of it a large orange JESUS SAVES. What a fucking lovely trick!

135

Half-falling, half-running, into the wet field below.

* * *

The next day the cold returns bitterly; the thaw is taken into the
ground. The road is a mass of ruts, and crystals of mixed dust and
snow fly up behind the noisy cars. Below zero all day, and the chim-
neys smoking. We walk on the crust, from behind our house in the
other direction along the river, across the town fields, to a branch
where the water meanders below houses on crumbling bluffs. The
slope is littered with uprooted trees, fences, tires, cans, apparent in
the texture of the snow, the summer's floods having carried away
the bank, leaving the houses on a precipice. The aluminum saucer
roars along the new ice, spinning as it picks up speed. We bear with
us a wooden boat made at Clockhouse, a number of blocks of
different sizes and shapes hammered together on a long flat piece,
with flags and sails, and crayon coloring on the wood. The nails are
bent, and the wood is irregular and cracked, but the basic figure
emerges. Robin brings these home at the rate of three a week, but
this is the best and biggest. Our length of string is attached at the
highest nail, itself made of all the strings from the Christmas pre-
sents tied together.

We stand on the cutting edge of ice, inches above the water, and
throw the boat out. It rests for a second and then is picked up by the
speed and surface of the water until it is way below us and bound-
ing in white gushers. The critical moment comes sooner than we had
expected, but the string holds, and at the point of tension the boat
goes underwater and resurfaces upstream with a sharp pull. We
guide it back thru the turbulence like a piece of wood thru a saw,
knots where there is foam, indicating roughness over stone, breaks
in the current and force. The string picks up a thin coating of ice
which cracks in the tugging as I pull it into my hands. The ice is
brittle, but not the line, for the boat returns, and we welcome it hap-
pily, with mixed feelings about sending it out again, but cannot re-
sist. There are times when it stalls against the shore above the rapids,
times when the string gets tangled on sharp rocks and we almost
lose it. Robin pulls mightily, and I stand behind him with the end,
just in case. After twenty minutes of sitting on ice and handling ice
we are frozen creatures, having to run home before it is too cold to
stand, our hero safe in our arms. We pick up the path in the village
and come across the back of our acre, over the frozen orange
and grapefruit rinds in the mulch heap, coffee grounds on our boots,
the air delicate and aroused. Tiny stonelike crystals everywhere on

the hard Earth, the edge of the Moon silver, hammered in the sky.

XX

Sudden waking up. The sky in violet interchange. The famous
dawn hour between lives, between precious stones. You say, "It's
time," and I awake again, not from sleep, but from waking, my
body shuddering not from cold, but it is cold, and a world not of
our choosing, neither the wind, nor the feeling the wind brings with
it, nor the loneliness the feeling brings with it even though I am with
you.

It's close to one of the gates — and there are only two. Most of
our life awash between them: stars that suck us violently up, as
glorious and transcendent as the aura, as degrading and painful as
to be washed with sewage over the edge of world, the edge of the
dimensional principle we know as world.

Half asleep, broken record of a dream, can't haul stone out of
the quarry. Blue light in the tree, reminiscent of the insoluble eter-
nal.

Now dragged out of bed: not awake but in one of the many states
body is in, unconscious, mechanical. Robin waking to a day in his
life that begins a ceremony younger than he is, *less initiated*. He has
been the neophyte in this temple; now a chela appears from the deep
innerwound dialogue, pushing against the envelopes of Lindy in
which it has spawned, languageless, formal unto a design older than
cities or farms, the tattered windblown rags our lives leave us barely
clinging to, as the priests wander down the hallways of the empty
house crying for their masters lost, their lost masters.

Robin heads straight downstairs, dragging his blanket behind him,
his thumb still in his mouth, turns Captain K. on the t.v.

The raw closeness we have lost these last weeks is restored, sug-
gesting where it has been, suggesting how late we are, now that the
time is here, and we touch, and

in the road, the car warming gradually, the steam of the river
rising thru the trees, freezing on the branches, the water a dull metal
churning gas, clear blue sky, an open sign, and this follows us all the
way, with a tail of the ominous ten miles long. What do you think
at a time like this, when you refuse for once to do their thinking for
them?

The brilliance and certainty of the Earth, the tightness of the fit, the spruces white with snow and mist; I have carefully and gradually avoided these images, and yet they are right, all right — the declination of sky that fills it with color, the molecular quality of water that causes it to rise and condense, guiding, guided by it all the way in to the Barre turn-off. And I know now that the issue is whether to take them (as they are given), and what to use them for in a world where they are the only message, and thus subject to repetition, unconscious reuse. Once they were everything, in the novelty of awakening; now the world is hollow, and the gas stations and restaurants stand in an emptiness no economic turmoil could produce as thoroughly as our disillusion. There is an autonomic thief, we train to fine craft, who turns on us, not ungrateful, but to exchange for the lesson the lesson. Still I have gone sledding with Robin this winter, and we have tumbled down the hill on ice, and rolled as one laughing hulk. And there will be world enough for this child, I won't make the mistake of guessing boy or girl, those things don't begin at the beginning, but long before and long after, leaving the roulette emotionless, and suspenseless too.

In the hospital hallway an old wrinkled woman on a stretcher being wheeled like so much mass, the bottles connected: a condition equally proper to this port. It is the same simultaneity that brings these events together. There are thoughts in Lindy's womb, not of being born but of rhythm, and there are thoughts in that body on the other end, arising as effortlessly as the mist from the water.

Sitting in the downstairs, waiting to be called back up, half-remembered dreams lost on freeways in Philadelphia, of Michael McClure, and a crash, and a scene after the crash, as though birth is an accident, from which the living are carried like victims on the road. Reminding me too that this is a mammal hospital, and we are mammals, despite all the accoutrements which seem determined to relieve us of that burden: the gift shop, the financial records, the speaker with the doctors' names. Because they are all running scared. It is not death they flee, but waves of feeling, mammalian longing for the forest and the ocean, to die free and blown, to be born whole and naked. They do not want to get wet. Better to be an idea.

"It's handmade," someone says, and in my sleepiness I find that the words stretch apart: HAND MADE — HAND MAIDEN

Lindy, yes, I will take those images from the river, the white laden branches, the steam all the way in. I have nothing else, and even if I did, nothing is as beautiful, is as much like me, in seeing it, as it follows its own diurnal inevitable course.

It is no bravery to abandon the elation, to force the terror to sus-

138

tain it all, because it is there behind things always, to which I will remain susceptible, like the memory of the old nurse who took care of me in childhood. Things are terribly wrong, and the things that are right will never make them better. Yet we must let them. Otherwise we spend our lives in preparation, and find that it makes no difference. Not in a universe where everything has already happened, and we merely wait in the margins of the explosion, to be blown on thru.

"Feeling better?" a woman to a man, youngish, business-suit, corpulent.

"Still hanging in there," smile, grunt, mammal talk.

The cold steel of the gas pump in my hand, filling the car on the way, disguising moods and heartbeats: this could be a happy day; the joy could literally stream.

The anxiety moves across me like a little motorboat running out of fuel — chut, chut, chut — but never empty, and if I could hear the motorboat it would be like the plane seen from the airport beyond, in the hospital parking lot, rising in chops thru the cavern of blue, the optimism of its present power, carrying it, despite the fact that it is everything else, into the air.

In the brightness of the room where there is no soft angle, Lindy becomes the shell thru which the shell passes. The head rising, as from behind the mountains. Pulled out of hiding: like a bug in a cocoon the wind drives into daylight. Wearing the blue light of creation, the red of Lindy's blood dripping from it, the wound that ties it fatally to our line: so Miranda appears, naming herself. She is not a land animal at all, or even a mammal, folded newtlike, having dwelt in a mineral equatorial sea, buoyed in the eternity of life, of memorylessness. She has not only never experienced air; she has never experienced gravity. We have given birth to a wild thing, and the nursery, and the hospital, are but pretences for the pagan ceremony we enact there.

This moment is the first moment, but it is unrecognizable as such. We cling to meaning by a thread, everything so much more impacted in it than we are. We do not know what happens. And in place of that, the shock rings out, before and after, all our lives. Somehow we will try to remember it: the participation of the doctor, Lindy so high on gas she is on the ceiling, the masked faces of the nurses, my tears running into the gauze, the turning of the animal so it can leave the animal, the scarred and sloppy emergence, swept up into the procedure of the room. Because we struggle just to get beyond exhaustion, because we are mentally tied to the fulfillment of forms, it is not appreciated, its directness is blurred. We sit in the recovery room smiling at each other, nothing left to do or say.

Lindy comes home on a snowy day, relatively mild for Vermont February. The large fluffy crystals are crushed in the windshield wipers, and the road is wet and musical. Picking up Robin at Clockhouse. His new sister. And what should he do about it? The difficulty of that, and having Lindy back at the same time.

It is like taking a hammer head and smashing the glass between worlds: she sits there full as a flower in the covers of her basinette. Not only do we domesticate her, but she turns our triangle, unmercifully, into a rectangle, setting us all on diagonals, before we are even aware.

* * *

We fall together in a passion recalled of everything, and of missing each other, and become ourselves in the fire in which it began, not just with her conception, but at the real beginning, when we let ourselves see, and so made the rest of this unavoidable.

Lindy is the river, comes thru me, surrounds me as her, in senses that are my own, and so much her, her mouth on me, I wait for, heave to, her altered body alert to mine: a ginger moment, sore and open, but the only moment that makes this have to be.

Thaw

I

The air is filled with rivers passing thru town. Their friction. In muddy channels. Sounds from the whole spectrum of the radio universe. Faraway the breaking ice howls; larger rivulets reap the music and coins of the mountains, as gravity brings all things into the valley. Thru the disappearing snow appear dog shit and tin cans, scraps of aluminum, and sawdust where we cut the wood. The layers fall away, their detritus converging, to reveal exactly what they bore, nothing more beautiful, nothing more foul. Small pools surround the trunks of trees, overflow, trickle across the ice into the road, from road to road, the tireprints so exact, crisscrossing thru the mud in myriad interlocking patterns, yielding softly to each new imprint.

Once again I hear Holst's progression of the planets, pounding the archetypal if not the real boundaries of creation, bringing the magician's work thru the zodiac into the seasons. The blue sky distills into the pool of water, becoming white by correspondence, and I reach not for the colors, which too often are colorless, but gold itself, suspended in a neutral medium, become purple.

Clouds form and dissolve and re-form, of rain and ponds and mists, now whipped thru the celesta over the mountains. Ranges that were once shoreline, to which mussels and jellyfish clung, leaving a stranded sealike archaeology, snowpeaks which were islands in the Atlantic, bearing forests which douse their fire in leaves, now the sap beginning to run. Frogs found asleep at the bottom of hundred-foot wells awake convulsively to sunlight; a family of toads, brought from nine feet down, trying still to huddle together as the unborn principle; the wand of the elemental smith prods them into life.

We live at the doorway of a famous and old villa, kept by the wise descendants of a once-wealthy family: the heretical hermetical chemistry everyone denies, but which speaks for itself, even as the iron in our blood rushing to thoughts, as it burns in oxygen, as the coal to crumble carbon into dead ash, which is never dead molecularly, nor is anything. The keeper is gentle, though his line is cruel. We lie upon the tesserae, the single stars of frost and lime which form at angles to the rills, break apart in wet currents. Where else could they form so completely? What other system would allow full manifestation of their starlikeness, with consistency the only clue?

The Planets move from Mars to Jupiter, the rhythms themselves, heavy-handedly aware of nature's philosophy, gathering and dispersing like birds. There is another set of memories and another nostalgia which has nothing to do with the childhood one. It has nothing to do with this life either, though the living of it is everything: the face of the Roman emperor who appears at the beginning of world history, indivisible, reduced from the Pharoahs even as Mars, Deimos, and Phobos fall back from the sunlikeness of Jupiter. In place of memory is an intuition of occult figures, the herd of buffalo tramping thunder thru the zodiac, the stars distributing themselves thru threads that play in the billionmost division of the sky upon the roof of this world. Yellow and blue, which twain the creation between them, lie now at the edges of what alone is visible.

II

Robin plays with his cars in the mud, driving them along roads he shapes with his hands, forcing them over ridges with loud engine noises. The driveway is filled with snowmelt and puddles, the ground shrinking and expanding, popping with holes, as the stone is removed from its blood, a surface so attractive he stays with it for hours, his tiny cars scaling out a landscape of highway systems, roads, hills, elevated thruways, parking expanses. There is no blueprint for this event; he works within, his attention never leaving the paths the cars follow, the lines and clumps suggesting natural passages and obstacles. If he were to look up in the middle of his play, he would be disoriented, his own size not the least of it. His perspective is eye to the ground, connecting as he moves from region to region, sending different cars out into the unexplored quadrants of the map. His imagination *is* his physical participation, and he does not notice his boots filling with water as he stands in pools too deep, his gloves dripping with mud. He has made a perfect delicate image of the Earth as it is today, its wetness and malleability, its glacial lakes and sierras, the distances between its monadnocks and the heavily-travelled connections of civilization.

The rivers flow past, carrying the waters of the hills. It is not just the Winooski anymore, or the Great Brook. Most of them would show on no map, including the stream along the side of the driveway and the glistening animal beside the garden. There is an overwhelming complexity of particulars no imagination could duplicate, no life other than this could be, and the sparkling clearness of death, that is not a mask, that is not a memory or an image, that it comes with the sun, white, and prances along the girth of design. Law rules. Freedom from law rules. The water follows a path. The water slops all over. My mind is logical. My mind wanders. Discursively. Non-discursively. The uncoiling seed holds a deep golden rectangle, a series of parabolas that bend against each other in quadratic clasps. This evades the law. This returns to the law. In the zone of their wildest departure, madness and chaos are prodded by seriality, are driven back into the rills along the road, and the billion average haystacks of atoms crumble to sustain the fact of creation.

He takes the larger trucks and washes them in the water, observing how the ripples carry reflections of clouds and his own face, which they shatter and restore. The water is dirty, but the water, on the metal, makes it clean; the richness gives a strong mirror for the world to pass in, the Earth borne closer to its Sun, making a zodiac a necessary proposition, as we move thru it, scattering foci and images. Without such seasons, such erraticism, there would be nothing. All the hoops on the barrel, seen thru the cosmic window, are the single surface of a single sphere.

The roads of Plainfield must be graded and regraded, as thaw and freeze alternate, until thaw wins. Today the equation rules, and the heavy equipment is kept in its barns; it could not deal with such thorough dissociation. Everything pours into everything else. Paint peels from under the eaves, is carried with water down onto the tin roof where it picks up glazing compound from the window replaced in winter, now lies on the slabs of granite before the front door. The dripping off the upper roof pounds away the snow to reveal the dumpings of cat litter from the early winter before we decided to leave them out; Robin finds a penny, wet on top, still stuck to the ice beneath, he pries loose.

The torn-ness, the splatteredness, sloppy as the musicless whistle, is tight as a lyre, a melody recovered by archaeologists and linguists working together from Hurrian tablets, played today in California, as once in the Mediterranean, on a duplicate instrument, so that the Earth does not lose implicit motion and distribution, given energy at some remote juncture, displayed in variants too complex to reference the source, yet all continuous, back into the mind in which Druid and Mayan roads were planned, in which the possibility of the music precedes the writing of the song. Lindy leans over me from the upper step and kisses me, what I feel of it, while I lie there watching Robin, almost warm enough, and we continue kissing, the sun in our eyes.

He kneels by his highways, his shirt coming out, his cuffs dragging mud, plus the grains that will show up only after he dries. He has a turtle's deposit, for which we will use the porcelain tub, to wash the sediment away to some other meadow. The trees bare, the grass pale, the kiss lingering, not in memory but on the surface, where light is pretending to be an external object, the phenomenal world at war with the noumenal world, the noetic bearing its birds into the higher Eastern sky. Fat birds, black birds, who grow of some other food.

Everything flows with a spiritual intimacy, like antimony or arsenic in their original forms, from the inside of the Earth, when this was a pot on the wheel, from which the fires depart leaving two counter and opposite images in a single paradox. We will not wait like Coleridges for that secondary principle to find us, to want to contact us; we will develop a primary intelligence, thru which the secondary images can be reached, however ancient, however kin to geohistory alone. The Hurrian song. (And in the dream I am visited by the Nova Scotian whose body splits in two, one on either side of me, to show his power, just at the moment I *question* his power: now I *assume* Crowley's astral connection along the English-Mongolian railway).

A spider, born somewhere, rushes thru the pale grass, to my seeing of it, onto the rotting wooden steps, is stopped by Robin's shadow across it as he come to visit me. Now it moves again, both of us watching. It rests, very accurately, on a small crack in the wood: six legs, three pointing forward, three pointing back, and in the middle: a body. It begins to move, swift silent paces that cease, begin again.

It is not a question of how little there is, or how bereft, but how much, cut off from each other, by cobalt towers and moats of nickel, currents whose electric glue also shoots an adhering object halfway across creation, until the whole engulfing figure looks like the galaxy, fires passing between dissipating sources, drawing single yarns into formations, from the central deepmost stars to the centrum of spider, either a quiver or a nerve, while we sit on a planet of the edge, on the stone shelf, counting the pieces which, as single minds, inhabit the *Wind in the Willows* forest. Man might disappear entirely, his industrial towns burned out above a bin of Jules Verne coal. Like a game of checkers with burnt coins instead of characters, annihilating protons on the bare edge of modern linguistic theory.

Spider, having crossed the entire staircase, now rests on a bleached pole, its shadow cast on the sundial thru shadows of sticks and grass. Within charred wood lies charring oxygen, colored rust and broken bricks. Vanadium is a corpse for billions of centuries, but ultimately its escort arrives and it is led down Creamery Street into the world. The evening breezes begin to blow, and there is a touch of warm summer Mars in them. Scootchy sits outside the grey feedstore building a dam to hold the water in a reservoir in which to sail his boat. When Robin and I arrive he is frantically piling up mud, but the water is carrying most of it away. Robin brings small stones and I wedge them into the earthwork; Chris comes with a shovel and begins slapping down patties of hard ground, diverting the current around the side, joking about what Freddie Fowler is going to say when his apartment building is floated away, then running a pipe thru the center of the dam as a causeway to relieve more pressure (though Scootchy does not understand that he doesn't want *all* the water). Finally the boat is lifted and floats to the center, the secondary rivulets crawl off with the bias and continue sparkling down the street, golden evening mud carrying its microscopic coins, all of them alive, our hands in dusky molecular substance, rich as the unplanted garden, packing it into mud walls as Mesozoic forests were crushed into oil fields.

Memories of *The African Queen*, seen again on Friday at the co-op, the river so large, so warm with life, bringing the man and woman into the vast open sea, stormy with electricity and winds, almost darker and deeper than their psyche can bear. Just as surely as the sluggish backwater breeds myriad flies and leeches and crocodiles, the oft-cited Egyptian ooze, so does the lotus sea of New Africa receive its water in the evening; a flash rain lifts their dreaming barge from the dried muck and carries it in a chorus of angels into the unconscious reservoir, that restores their life, that almost drowns them (from the twisted jungle, they have come into an expanse of water without horizons, hot and bottomless, drawing fierce elements thru its center). They are rescued from the broken sticks of the *Queen* and taken aboard the German ship they will yet destroy, if not by their bodies then by the body they brought into this tumult, married on the gallows, then saved before the rope is cut, a latent and millenial event repeated in the *2001* trip to Jupiter, where the hero also casts his ship into a body too large for him as soma to survive, hence his mind to survive as seed.

Driving along Route Two with Robin to the wholesale meat farm. The sun near the horizon hits the land at an archaic angle, so that the fields below us appear as the whole Earth, seas glistening and lands rippled, and we are a space capsule. The puddles are as large as ponds now, surrounding trees and telephone poles, the ice beneath them yielding fluid, coursing across the highway in thin lenses. It is swampy and sedimented; it is sparkling and palpable, the farm implements and wagons sinking, abandoned sheds covered up to the windows; *The Terran Chronicles* are scattered now forever in creation.

Above the big turn on the road, the retaining wall trickles with water, thru which the color of the rock appears in the filtered sun, all its silica and granite variation, the melt squeezed down between the bricks. It is placer, granular, vital: carrying in its worn and textured coat the last vestiges of a material mechanical universe in which we suffer all that we suffer only in our surety that the materials are dead and no longer have characteristics.

Watching the trickle in the wall, I feel something floating inside me, something that has always been loose, the ale I drank settling on top of it, softening it. There is a fountain in the city park, and there are streets I grew up on; now I am with Robin in his different childhood, the car with a nimbus of spray. It is a feeling without an object, but it is almost now comfortable in the grand covalence, that the runoff does correspond and answer, the flat notes as well as the sharp ones. There is another feeling rushing in my cells, unreceived till now, made of the wind blowing sheets of water across water and ice, made of a radiance my attention has brought me to, very late. but still with time to see. The water runs out of the wall, and the vast planet lies beneath, with herbs and ground nuts, sweet needles of pine and grain, and the sky darkens, throwing the vision into an eternity of seeds and motionless winds.

III

Out of the rotten log as it splits under the axe/falls a cluster of dark purple ants, their curled bodies blown away in the wind. No resistance in them. As the cork opens like butter, their stain left in the pulp.

They are not alive. They were not alive. Their bodies can be burned with the log, but they will not be burned. They are not ants; they remain to show that ants have been there. The similarity of the one to the other is misleading. A whole winter has passed since their death. They were frozen. Now they are blown away like straw.

A waterfall drops from worlds beyond to worlds beneath us. Silver at the top, crashing wine red into the rocks, dispersing water and gravity, delivering visible matter. The yellow warblers rise in a single motion to the branches of the trees.

A science of facts, but: a non-science of forms. The clouds are blown apart in the wind. *By* the wind? Heidegger: moving-into-nearness. In gloss upon Heraclitus. The intimation of form is eternal.

The maples are alive and dead in sections like temples. Some of them are bright with sugar; others are almost hollow. The rainwater cracks the bark leaving a black gum at the joining of trunks, bright moss feeds off them. When they are dead, these sections will fall away, but the tree continues to impose maple-like forms upon a largeness that opens to receive them. From water droplet to galaxy the lens is smashed, is broken, crushed, and reconstructed, but it is, curiously, the same lens, and these distances lie in the same direction along different planes; there are no dimensions.

The billion leaves of the forest are tangled with the stars. The branches are senders, receivers. There is no electrical interference because the connection is not electrical. No radio noise except the excess static of creation. Dense biological interference. All nature, which cannot wait for light to heal its aberrations of mass and time, scatters and returns to its parts, all at once, the semblance if not the reality of a message. A code, bar source. The singing of suns is the wind thru the trees. The newborn milkweeds tremble again and again at an inexplicable twelve. The medusas quiver and invert, soft bags of symmetrical nerve patterns that never complete the shape they never cease completing. A babble dominates. The prelinguistic understanding, which language comes to be, does not need a nervous system. Its connection is enough. Trees on planets that circle other suns, and *these* trees, restless in the same turbulence, keeping silent rhythm of the sap.

Elementary particles are not reductions but *ideas* of matter.

IV

The village sits in the world. The light is sharp, reflected from the April snow. Robbie, awaking, says: there must be more than just water in snow.

Sentience, slower than mind, is a mineral intelligence. The body is uncertain, connected to the mind as a house, or as another mind. The culture is inflicted directly on the body, by which it becomes the mind. The poison, subjected to linguistic analysis, vanishes into the system; the shadow of the war approaches long before the war.

Number will always be a mystery.

The fertility of North America was a coin too rich for the European treasury. The islands of the North Atlantic were shrouded more in myth than fog, more in their non-complementarity than in a difficulty of locating them by map. We are born on the other side of that Mediaeval sea.

It was not so long ago Cabot visited the North, and before him single Irish priests explored an object too large for sanctification, thus were absorbed into the Algonquian. Which has remained, even for us, a definition of paganism. Not religious, but monetary. The relicless Norse-Skraeling wars. Single unconscious Indians stranded in the European blood. Feudal Greenland swallowed by a vast Eskimo text, whose daily survival survived the Viking quest for an escape from history and Europe. Because the Norse could become Eskimos: the Eskimos could not become Norse. Their farms are testament, are testimony, in the patchwork of moraine and driftwood hearths, before the glaciers, of the Palaeolithic substantiality, from which primordial Man came.

It didn't work as the North Atlantic, for the ocean was still Mediterranean, and the Mediterranean was the center of European consciousness, the Romans coming very late in that affair, to lay their roads and issue their pax; the Holy Roman Empire was later yet. In the obscure pre-Greek unfolding of a topological grid, Atlantis is merely the tip of the pyramid. Whether it be within the *Odyssey* or beyond Hercules, and whether Brandan's voyages take him to the Carib Indies. Charlemagne, who casts the distant figure of Barbarosa-Napoleon, is himself the shadow of Caesar Augustus. Only the Basque and Biscayan edge of the continent held the arts of Mesolithic fishing, held them thru wars and changes of kingdom and lineage, and it is their pure inheritance which makes possible an Atlantic. The Norse were absorbed into Normany and Britain, evading the Neolithic only to blunder and return. In sagas of remarkable likeness to the large stones the ground is also littered with.

It was finally the South Atlantic of Spain and Genoa, the invention of Inca gold from feudal silver, counter-stroke to Islamic minting and Mohammed's control of the Eurasian seas. Brasil is a figure for that conversion — how many times it was lost as an island or port to the east and the west, until it was lost forever in the country of that name. It was the Azores; then the Azores were Labrador;

then Labrador was everything.

The record does not show that North American Polar Bears performed at the court of Mediaeval Egypt, white creatures from beyond the Viking-Sufi link. The cod of Breton was different than the grapes of Vinland; it was preserved and mulched in peasant Europe. The Irish hermit alone knew the pagan escape thru uncharted stars. From the early days of Christian scientism, the mysteries of Empedocles endured, the legend of a wandering dervish-scholar, fragmented in Proclus and Plotinus, retained as the indelible heresy even in the holiest.

But by the Nineteenth Century the theosophists had wings that were too heavy. Their occultism was gluttonous. To fly out of here into a maximum angelology like an eagle. Forgetting those bare worlds the Norse rightly called Helluland forever, never to be found again, though Baffin Island lie upon a thousand global maps. Flat Stone Land. The needle swiftness of the Tibetan. Non-mentation. Beyond memory. Submitting to a broken thread. Until even memorylessness is filled again with the recurrent visions of this world. Because the split itself lies behind the split. So many western islands disclosed by that same sun, in a misty sea, worlds in a magic show. Endlessly headlands. Endlessly inversions of air and light, suggesting forms, leading to landfalls. Columbus altering the log.

The condition of life, the violent fact of the crossing, is bent under the weight of the living, electronlike, like the dreams of sailors of lands beyond consciousness, which those who trust their migrations to sailors must also dream, even in the best of times and even in Irish potato famine. The sailors cannot bring us back into day without the guiding suns of night. And those suns cannot return day to the same map from which it took them.

There is a mask in Magdalenian bone, needing a Moon, or the numbers deriving from successions of moons, to escape time, to come into time as a hunter. To survive as a creature in mind-body. To escape the werewolf and the changeling spook. The broken nerve falling to the East: Sahara, India, Nepal, Gobi. The psychic warrior emerging beyond the fisherman-explorer. A timeless Buddha across whose chest Marco Polo passed like a tin bug.

There is a lost root we have plied for all its robes, all its waters, all its illusion that light is light and we are they. Numbers lie only between worlds of form. Gemstones. Hoofprints. It is a new Sun each day, the fires dismantled and re-roped. The stars are chipped again from inertial stone. All thru our history we have returned this confusion to quantity, pretending to find, in the order and triangularity of a pre-activated system, the castles of which our world is the ruin. As the waves carrying the partial bodies of great ships break each day upon the shell.

* * *

Aquinas: not that we know what God is, but we know *that* he is. The intuition more powerful than the superstition. Behind the quandary of occult numbers and astrological signs is a landscape raw and unfinished, a connection of forms, like lagoons, in the rising sun, so beautiful, so unattainable, it reminds us of everything. In its perfection we are consoled as imperfect beings. Our certainty the same as our molecularity.

* * *

Awaking from a long nap in the car, Robin sees the city of Hartford around him: the golden dome, the Lovecraft towers, the graded tempos of cars and spaces thru spaces. *"That's* not a dream," he says.

* * *

Behind the construction of the endlessly new is the old decaying face of the hotel. The junk is stripped from the sides of buildings, and a new front is put on, connecting three separate lodges. It would take many millions of dollars, and the interest upon them, to sustain this illusion, to plant Parisian gardens, to build the fountain, and hang many-mirrored chandeliers. Thank god they don't have it. So the weeds return with the late but dwindling frosts of spring. And violets fill the golf course.

In their own blue and refracted galaxies, in rooms with magnificent carpeting, the pinball machines register the movements of a planetary high.

It is a very real complication: sending a man into space and bring-
ing him back, a riddle which faces us all our life. Astrology is our en-
tanglement, and as its involvement with us increases, our problems
become finer, axial. Saturn returns after twenty-eight years. We be-
gin again. Childhood bravado will no longer carry us, only those
things we can do with patience, we can do as our molecular energies
dwindle. Saturn returns, the chef, the hangman, the warrior-priest.

The binding is rough; it is not just a passing of cosmic mischief.
It comes upon us determinatively as birth.

If there was a way out, all hints of it are gone. If there was no
way out, suddenly we are given quasi-rocket ships and open quarters.
Our old vehicles are taken away.

The planets continue to draw the bodies of men and women in
the heavens, long bodies, opening so slowly we do not see them.

* * *

There are skies of sea where Eleatic clouds transform watery clouds.
The Moon is a semi-stable fog, the comets poxes in a sublunary mael-
strom. Even if it is a gas, we are gaseous beings, and submerged in it
we do not know the difference. If it is an interference, we are inter-
ference also. We go on building as if it were hard and resistant. We
count as our achievements, our no-need-to-worry-about-anymore,
that which has been constructed: the pyramids, the buildings of
Manhattan, the sculptures of horses in city parks. We attribute the
decay likewise to the hardness of abrasion, not the underlying
ephemerality of the mode of composition.

It does not matter. If we have to use something, better to use *it*
than wishful spiritualism, better to have it seem real and be our con-
federate. It will not go away. Its actual property is nil, but its ap-
parent quality is all-embracing. If we collect amulets of air, it is our
desire that air be the gem. Clouds on a warm and windy day. Let us
cast them back when their worthless jewelry is shredded before us.
But not until.

* * *

Geneva — late April

The field lies between our rooms and Lake Seneca. Once the
grounds of this estate, it is now a thicket of planks, brambles, cans,

parts of old plumbing, paper. How fast and suddenly the chief has fallen. The land slopes in stages of hills, railroad thru them. The frozen body of winter's snake lies half in the hole, half stretched across the unopened dandelion; it has thawed and is limp. Robin stares long at it. The forsythia flare up like sunspots, and blue escaped flowers commemorate the garden that has been lost, the people who tended it, who have died and whose time has died. The lake sits, beyond linearity, a fossil, blue and horizonless, blue in every manner blue time will allow. Our seeming slice of history is a cultivation returned to wilderness, by a dark route.

* * *

The apple stands are boarded up, their paint peeling. A few golfers play on the sopped ground, their course passing thru the edges of commercial orchards, land purchased no doubt from the mestizo. The trees are bare with the hints of buds, their traceries visible, the network that dries always behind the fruit, sensory fibers flying out of rugged arms. Each tree is a lineage map of the whole creation. Although these orchards were not here aboriginally, the dwarfness and entirety of the field, the glacial stones and human abandonment, are reminiscent of Vinland and harbors that seemed so much like home, and seem so yet. Beyond the present of vacation homes, one senses the passage of Cooper's Indians. A conflict of landscapes, resolving in a semi-habitation.

* * *

Lying in the backyard on the cold spring ground, trying to get my head together. The sun. The peeling blue paint on the houses. Beyond the fence, in the next yard, the kids at basketball with a red, white, and blue ABA ball. Telling each other: "Fuck off." and "Quarter for a blow job." The sheer embattled energy, of teenagers, of America, of teenagers in America. The little ones on their trikes. An angry red-headed kid is firing softballs at everyone. Infinite distraction.

The decision hangs, like church bells, then fire sirens. The wood and paper and corrugated metal that centuries in mud will decay like a Viking boat.

Hymn to heroism.

* * *

153

Robin to the lady next door picking flowers: "You shouldn't pick flowers. They do much better in the ground."

"But they're so pretty."

"I know it. But do you know that when you pick them they cry?"

"Cry?"

"Yes. And you know why you can't hear them?"

"Why?"

"Because they cry so loud."

Robin to the child on the other side: "Do you know Jason Wincuinas?"

Matthew: "I know him."

Robin: "*The* Jason Wincuinas?"

Matthew: "Yep."

Robin: "The Jason Wincuinas of Plainfield?"

Matthew: "I do."

To me: "Does he?"

I shake my head.

To Matthew: "You don't know him."

Matthew: "Okay."

* * *

Grossinger's — early May

Spice and seed North America. The trees in bloom are golden. The plowed fields are beginning to blossom, not with crops but wild spring flowers that have sown themselves. Everything is as delicate as magnolia and ginkgo. The burnt-out house and collapsed barn on the roadside feed the blue and yellow endosperm which bursts up around them as the psychic life of plants. The bogs of dead trees awaken with skunk cabbage, thistle, and marigold. For all the tons of fertilizer poured on it, the herbal Earth yet recovers. For all the metallic medicines with which they have been deadened, the medicinal streams flow again, by microdilution, from the source. And so do we, victims of the same planetary physician.

For the herbal Earth is invested with billions of years of sun, nocturnal-diurnal sowings of moons and planets, stars and comets, correspondences that go beyond all of modern life. It is so much more fertile, its fertility is so much more sympathetic, not only to our dreams of the golden city but to our nourishment today in the darkened glen.

Matthew and I climb the hill across the street from his house and

154

look down on the countryside. Even the hidden motions of spring are becoming visible. The discordance of signs moves in an approximate harmony. We sit and talk, reviewing, as if they were rivers leading innocently to the present, our lives, which rivers are not, for all the scoured stone and rust and drain-off from these fields. Mica into calcium. Corn into egg yolk. It is reminiscent for me of college friendships, but the problems we discuss are new, and about which we have learned to be secretive; life has made us superstitious. The valley itself is open, even clear.

We drive from Glen Aubrey to Binghamton, to Liberty on Route 17, tired, numb, the Met-Giant game on, Lindy, Robin, and Miranda asleep, toward sunset. The browns and greys on the hills are emergent reds and blues. Color the cosmic mystery. The lithium cadmium stand-in. It is clear the soil is more dirt, is tasty and edible, though our tongues are not delicate enough, as spirit precedes matter thru a wet, pocked hulk. The tons of worms per acre swallow and excrete sunlight and sugar, apple and leaf. Vitamin is original also, ballast to the dregs, the dissociation, our psychological processes bring to it equally, healed in the vegetable-sunflower soup. The decay of the cities, breeding viral oceans, is simply the time we have already lived, the collective corpse of that life. It could be spread on these fields and in the forests, in our imaginations, and give rise to the continuity of those friendships for which we yearn.

* * *

The wind blows dead shells, and the mass piles up. But nothing is dead. Everything was once alive. Everything, tossed without will into the heap, will be alive again.

* * *

No more *Mysterium Cosmographicum*, no docile geometry or series of perfect solids to which a bogus wildman submits. We have reached the specific, the ceaseless, the variable: the mind of matter confronts us in the mind. And the lesson is everything: every nail, every molecule, every electron; spread as thickly and individually as the blanket of wet moss, as thru the rainforest are a billion trees, seen by a billion different animals, from the angles of their long repose.

The gem which was astrology, set in an Ionian dome, gold and mysterious, over the baser metals of astronomy, has been cracked and tempered by the unforeseen fires of its lesser stones, now is born anew and set in a dome the stars will never reach. For all things happen in point-less time. The reality we see is a bright spot on which the sun shines, dust drifting thru the frozen eye. We have come from the encircled orbits of Ptolemy thru the imaginary off-sun foci of Copernicus; we have come to Kepler's *harmonice*, and the grand inertial music the volumes disguised in masses contain. A spirit cast out from the substantial Sun, though insubstantial, holds trees and mountains in place, holds the Moon to the Earth. The Martian orbit in the Egyptian-scroll sky is a pagan Yahweh, a silent God who speaks thru Hermes, who never ceases, by numbers and words, to draw us to the pyramid behind them.

* * *

Robin and me whirling our shadows in partial moonlight on the stone side of the house. Moon blown thru clouds, dense and knotted, luminous and unapproachable, "Where is the Moon?" he asks in hundreds of ways.

* * *

We sit among impeded artifacts of a withheld creation. The cirrus clouds are blown out across the sky, are the work of 24 hours of wind, since past. The sun disperses heat and light, the trees arisen of it jagged and timed, shaped by the hard master. The birds' voices are in the present, the sound the sound gives rise to. Three white doves spur thru the newly-flowering stems. The houses stand in time, their material ripped from molecular imagination and set in the mind. They will not last because memory will not hold them.

My father notices that the odd cones Lindy has set on the dinner table look like shelled insects. "Nature repeats herself," he insists. Yet the search for a design is interrupted; the jaggedness, which is the harmony also, keeps us from gentler merging: music of the spheres played so bravely by Kepler at the onset of a Thirty Years' War.

The symmetry refines the brutality of the whirlwind's path, but there are events which cannot be restrained, flowers, branches, clouds, orbits, geometry forever clasping the secant to the ellipse though neither are needed for this Palaeolithic procession.

* * *

Galileo was a Viking without a ship, but his new worlds in the sky made possible the Americas. Tracing the red spot across the face of a mathematical Jupiter. He established linearity, quantity; he invented the apocryphal universe.

* * *

The things I write are the same. Only my vision of them changes as I return, at different points of my own unwinding, to their hiatus with me. I once described these landscapes as histories and settlement patterns; then as angels and chemical designs: I come now to their essences, the memories and fragments of oblong systems. It is the return which touches me, the ephemeral quality of my own connection — not that I value myself above all, but I am the only link between the sheer expansion and the turning in. On the hinge lie the trees and cottages, the fantasies and clumps of spring violets. And while this goes on, this seeming coherence, my life flows away from the pieces of its broken egg, is restored in my resistance to that fact. I dream of integrity and entity, but most of what I love I sacrifice to what I am, ruthlessly.

The sensible properties are evasions. People open like flowers and are blown away like ashes. Better to be the ashes, to seek the emptiness over which the harp bends. For it will abandon us. It already has.

Denver — mid-May

Air New England

If composure goes when the plane rocks, this itself is a case of: inner state dependent on outer confirmation. I listen to the pilots' voices for a clue. They are, at best, bored, overconfident. The mountains between Vermont and Massachusetts lie before us, and the plane ascends gently thru currents of driven air. I allow myself to think about crashing, in all the detail I would have the luxury of on the ground, and I realize even that will not disturb the flight. Nor will the mad woman raving about death behind me.

You have to want nothing, not even the plane to get there, not even one's seeming self to be happy. You have to move beyond this whoring submission to the plane's safety. And when you do, the sky is beautiful, the sound of the engines elating and horn-like, the speed itself a gift. But who would give us such a gift, and why?

Having come to the site of my nightmare only to realize that my nightmare is true. But, for all my dreams of plane crashes, the dream is not the plane. And I see at last the reason I don't want to be here is I don't want to know my nightmare isn't a plane. Already I see the complicated space I am getting into; as the fear of crashing is resolved, an almost physical weight slides into the clearing, a gap of false shape. As hard as I try to penetrate it by my mind it throws me out. That's the trouble right there. The plane is just another American machine. The figure the plane suggests, the archetypal energies contacted by the possibility of broken flight, are dangerous beings, who pass just enough into consciousness to waste our relief and prayer on trivial episodes settled long before our birth.

Such stern justice. Such kind justice.

Why should its nature be to evade me as I seek it, and so seek me, by leading me over the rough country of its deceit?

* * *

We are hooked on this heroin material world; the dealers are everyone: the butchers, the gas station attendants, the police, the children on bikes. They lead us to believe. They sell us the big boy. And we know in our hearts he must be dismantled, he *will be* dismantled. Water comes from the faucet. We fail as revolutionaries, and a Red Guard a year will not get it back for us. Maybe some other better species. But not us. In any of our Lysenko or Mendelian varieties. In any of our transcendent spiritual guises. Plotinus' angels, too ashamed for their bodies, obsessed with sex.

* * *

Famously, when they know the place they lose the motion; when they know the motion they lose the place. And the absurdity of an economics based only on demand, as if that ox were going to pull that cart forever.

The mind of man is like a star, but you can't just pour in gold and expect it to come out golden.

* * *

Denver

The sad cows, and the long brown squares. The brown men, their cars and planes, transporting beef between Colorado, Texas, and Kentucky. Two years of moisture for one crop of wheat. Desert beyond Dorothy's Kansas I showed Robbie from the plane with the beginning of the mountains, the waterless marks of dead rivers.

Beyond the Parker feedlot sits the lit water-well, working below the sand while the Moon rises. A multi-thousand dollar investment, at prime interest rates, in hope of condominiums, as Denver heads South along Cherry Creek, the East plateau dry. Below this desert is neither an ocean nor a lake, but the fast-running arteries of the Earth, which, if tapped at the pressure point, will gush enough to sustain a city for centuries.

We are taken for a tour of the feedlot at dusk, Lindy's rancher cousin driving, drink in hand, the car weaving, as he boasts acres, heads, fucking EPA politics. The man who was her father is dead. His sister's son is pleased with the ranch *that* part of the family got together. His brother from Tampa is flushed from drinking away the memories. He's the last one. Uncle and nephew discuss investments, development, interest rates. Uncle damn well admires his nephew's spread is, in fact, envious.

Red Lodge. Bridger. Bozeman. The Hough land stretches South to Wyoming and Colorado, East to Florida. Population Density: 1.7. Population Density: 4.6. Setting down his drink as he steers: "The truth is: *no*body wants people anymore."

Journalist, oilman, drylands cynic, uranium false prophet, sentimental poet: betraying them all, and even again now, with his funeral. Betraying their success with his brazen and proud failure, his refusal to have been the same as them, so that the nephew from Parker and the uncle from Tampa must compare fortunes and mortgages, to keep on top of their own sense of: what's it all for.

The brown cows bolt from the oncoming car, bump into each other in retreat, in the sadness, a mirror of ourselves, in which Mipam of the story broken down and wept, spending his coins to free beast by beast from the slaughter. Until his money failed, the animals seeming to awaken as he led them, in recall of another, another life. But in Parker their abrasiveness as men is their defense against this cosmic lesson.

In the background of my head someone is singing from Finian's Rainbow: "... *follow it over the hill and stream.*" An Irish voice, a brogue the Plains absorb. Or is it just the bent-over way in which things reach one another, imposing themselves clumsily, yet gracefully, with an exactness that defies precision.

* * *

While Vermont struggles on the verge of spring, a lynx testing the water, in Denver the summer is already effortless. It is a flowering city.

The deepening evades me: the edge of the garden, the fenced separated houses along the streets, an order false and true to different things. The Moon faintly beyond. The Sun in the sky's center, always a sense of behind-the-Sun, which is not infinity, not space either.

There are circumstances I postpone to remain here. The birds on Earth. The domesticated, the tame, the numerical. It is where each thing rests, and calm finds me, only thru the anxiety. Confronts me by not confronting me.

An initiation withdraws from the cheap scenery. And I am aware, the more I look and listen, of what artifice has gone into the necklace of flowers the conqueror wears.

* * *

As the body ages, the soul merges with the body. The hollow lines fall into place, and the golden boy is sacrificed to the reincarnated master.

The body is not the ashes.

The remnants of a life scatter quickly without the person to hold

160

them together. The suitcase he took to the hospital — clothes, watch, wallet, glasses — leaves as a tagged collection of objects. His soft hat remains on the back seat of the car, parked on a suburban street, the newspapers yellow from the sun thru the window.

This is what it comes to and this is what it always was. We wrestle with metaphysical problems all our lives, but the death neither solves nor even identifies them.

The ashes are not him.

The apartment, now that he is gone, is filled with the shapes his mind, his soul thru his mind, could reach only by relics, material things. African and Australian figures brought back from the notorious trip around the world (when he served as guru-guide and clown for oil and uranium investors seeking global resource perspective). Masks and statues, including his own wood-carvings of a dodo and purple cow. Gadgets. Old transportation tokens, mills, foreign coins, stamps, polished quartz, souvenir tubes of sand and water. Labels from his many businesses and hobbies — Green Mountain Books, Bighorn Books, *American Indian Resources, Euthenasia News, The Oil Reporter, Rocky Mountain Arts, Denver Post Poetry Forum* rejection slips (he was the editor). The collection of books and journals by his bed mark an intelligence interrupted: occult, Western Americana, *Penthouse*, physical exercise manuals, Southwest geology, collections of favorite poems with markers and checks, tapes of his poetry groups.

The high school yearbook entitled *The Kyote* (1925), of which he was business manager: so quickly the time from then to now seems to have passed because there was nothing in the way to stop it. His words then read like his final words in the journal he kept in the hospital:

"This trusty Tomahawk has carries us on toward this great day when we may look back upon our completed work, feeling well satisfied. In passing from our hands to yours, it carries the hopes and best wishes of the departing braves and maidens of the tribe of '25."

Departing for where? Those lives already over. And a letter from the superintendent of schools thanking him for his work, dated October 5, 1925, sent to Mr. Henry Hough, Missoula Mercantile Co., Missoula, Montana. The surprise that the high school was in Billings not Red Lodge, a minor point Lindy had taken differently, a point basic to his life. And now stands disclosed to her without his saying. With all the rest.

Down to the secret romances and the love poems of Jamie Sexton Holme: *"He lived to see one evening star/Swim in the pale green*

161

twilight skies;/He lived to see one crescent moon,/To watch one drowsy morning rise./See now how cold and pale he lies,/How amorous of death."

Whether the mystery was this, or something else this suggested, has fallen beyond us. And between then and now are the notes and diaries kept in the Thirties and Forties, right up to the last minute before the last sleep, trying to describe a persistent fantasy, trying to buy off a romanticism that never relented, so that his death can be laid to the finality of its cumulative depression. The women at the end he wanted to caress him, his intentions unclear — whether he would not identify with his body because it was mis-shapen from childhood polio, or whether his absolute identification with it led to the masochistic fantasies, the delicately ephemeral poetry — either way, an eccentric and lethally naive path to resolve what the bent-ness became within him.

The reason these do not age, and the reason the ashes are not him, is that a person, like time, like the receding galaxies and images of light that are somehow carnally bound to it from our vantage, is everywhere. The brilliant asymmetrical images of the infant and the snuffed imagery of the elder join and determine each other. The deeds of youth are carried out with foreknowledge of maturity, even as the last events in a life recall the first. It is not that Henry Hough has come to this point and vanished, and that his ashes are left; the *Kyote* proves that much. It is that the thin line of light and pungency we follow like a hypnotized audience under the spell of the stage magician has fallen upon this moment, in his life and ours. All the rest exists, but in a darkness he will not let us see; all the rest is as real now as it was then; the days beyond a death confirm the haunting substance of the life that cast them, perhaps only more sharply than we saw them then.

He was reborn all his life, as inner knowledge, to see beyond, into lives he touched, as they are now knotted around him. In this week given to honoring of him, all gestures are flawed as he is flawed. The battles in which he was engaged continue on their own, mesmeric, for beyond a certain point he is no longer needed to activate them. His greatest virtue stands out now with excruciating lucidity, to challenge the living more acerbically than his presence ever could: that *he failed*, he failed at being a success, as an artist and a businessman, as a member of the family and community, he failed willingly and perversely, and made of it his prophecy. The images of male dominance and power, wealth and stature in the society plagued him, for he never gave them up entirely. His life drove the failure of American materialism into its equally evident success, never consumating a merger that would free both. The investors from Tampa and Parker are melancholy; this is a funeral they feared from the beginning. The minister, though a gentle man, does not know what to say; he makes Henry Hough sound like Thomas Edison. And everyone knows that's not true, no one more clearly than Lindy's mother, who refused to indulge him in that error and so lost the marriage.

"I guess I was married to a genius all along and never knew it," she remarks acerbically after the service.

Despite her present triumph she is doomed likewise, because she evades those indulgent romantic schemes without admitting her secret complicity in them. For not remembering her part, she turns it, as fate, from conscious acceptance into unconscious inevitability. As he turned depression into desperate withdrawal and planned death, she is left with only the vague memories of clinical depression, in her apartment with artifacts that are too lovely, the ransom of gold and silver that she now must be guardian of, beyond grace, beyond, as well, his own purposely tarnished and funky trinkets.

He accepted and even idolized Lindy (and his mother) as none of the rest. Only they did not seek his rehabilitation (despite their chiding words). They confirmed his eccentricity. He could allow Lindy, despite her ongoing critique not so much of his poetry as his qualifications for being an expert on all poetry, including hers, because she did it in a way that made him the father of an equally eccentric daughter. Although she could never have the father she wanted, she was the ideal daughter, and so could never lose track of him quite as accidentally as the other daughters, who were closer geographically, just where he could not use proximity. He tricked and misused them all their lives. But Lindy was his unacknowledged confederate in the cause, and god knows, in his blessed obscurity, despite the mediocrity in which he graced and hid it, he has passed that cause on to her. She alone can absolve those pained and obscure lines of Jamie Sexton Holme, and make them into something real and livable. She can restore the Red Lodge-Billings ancestry. She can reclaim a heritage he most clearly gave her by never taking it himself.

There is no inner world in sentimentality now, any more than in precious ornaments, even those shaped like hearts. The emotions are not the inner world. The inner world is not a list of events. Yet Henry Hough listed his actions, day after day, for years — people seen, things bought, places visited, ladies courted. No imagination. No landscape or spirit.

It is as though he had a sense of himself as incredibly important — the one accurate and moving sentiment in the entire work — but

163

instead of using it and seeking the origin of the indulgence, he took it on its word and listed the mechanical events of his days in the unquestioned belief that the diaries of such a man would assume their own depth and grandeur; instead of accepting his humanity, he tried to make it into his witness before the world. He might have known better, from writing vanity biographies of uranium queens, et al. And, as Lindy's sister Polly points out, he made the entries almost as though he expected the people to read them after his death, concealing everything in the niceties of the original time, making his private thoughts seem identical to the politeness of his public gestures, as though to confirm the original superficialities by the pretence, later, that nothing else was going on in his head, even then.

The ashes are a chemical reduction of what his body was, the last sick body even he did not know. On which he reported too, like a journalist describing foreign wars. Or shale oil locations in the Southwest. He kept even those secrets at the end.

In the last seven days he tried to write his big autobiography called *One Whole Life*, a lesson for mankind he called it, with intimations of a Shakesperian profundity. Like all the rest, it failed the impulse and became another maddening collection of facts, beginning with the oldest facts he could remember, set in Montana, told in a conventional genre, marred by his dwindling faculties, with total disregard for the space he was in and the knowledge of death he now had access to — but wasn't it always so, with New Mexico, and uranium, and the Arapaho; wasn't this simply the last stride of the programmed dominance of the ego, in its weakest shell, to assure no last minute breakdown? Even as his mother, in her nineties, sits in her room in the rest home, making minor changes in her four unpublished novels, hoping no one has stolen her title *The Wheel of Fate*.

[The inner life must be free to range among time and vision, to shake itself of reason and conventional beauty. It must be informed directly by the world as well as our use of the world, otherwise the dark obsession with our own existence.]

The body is not the ashes.

But down at the base of the stairs, by his apartment, where the newspapers have piled, ants eat a beetle. Up on the sidewalk the sprinkler is watering grass and stone. There is a smell of weeds, deep and engulfing, activity in the avenue beyond. A bird, a sparrow, sits in the water and washes itself. Time is clearly everywhere, and cannot be stopped or tamed. For lack of any other solution, we work all day packing up the paraphenalia of his life, watching the years spill, out of order, onto the floor, until something fine is blown away like dust. Then only the objects remain. The swifter we dispose of them, the better.

* * *

The zoo is a vision of the astral sphere. The flamingos running in flock. The vulture and his beautiful eyes. The lemurs with their babies. The gorilla dancing with a pail on its head. Elephant. Polar bears pacing in the heat. As the Renaissance zoologists saw so lucidly, the nature of any animal is also its spirit. The raw physical event is so complete it withstands any possible disincarnation.

The zoo is wild and disordered, and the zoo-keepers are tired uneducated men. The sense of it as a playground is finally macabre. But it is a Steinerian kindergarten in which children of this planet are taught, by bare experience and possibility, the conditions of hierarchical creation. They see what the animals are. This event goes on every minute, but we come to it at that eternal moment, which, except for delightful variations, time-space adjustment, is always the same.

* * *

The bamboo poles are split and set in each other in gradual declivity to make a trough, receiving a slice of the waterfall, carrying it into the garden, gently, a shimmering skin.

Ikebana. Delicacy of cause and effect. Secrecy of arrangement suggesting cosmic secret. If man disturbs the Garden, let him do so only as the world lines distribute the egg: hiding the personality of the maker in the anonymity of his effects.

When the water reaches the last trough it is diverted by the angle into a long narrow bamboo cup which, when the weight of the water overbalances, drops suddenly, spilling its contents in the pool, rises, hitting the trough with a sharp crack. It is called a Japanese deer-chaser, but whether it is to chase deer or pose before them a zen riddle is further hidden in the design.

* * *

When I first saw Denver, in the Sixties, it was the West. Isolated from the villages of Detroit and Chicago, its maternal grandparents, it lay instead in a sequence with Omaha and Salt Lake City, en route to New Mexico and Old Indian America. The rural suburbs outweighed the inner city; the black slums had a middle-class glow.

Boulder, to the Northwest, was a beer-drinking college town.

But Lindy and I travelled in the Southwest and saw the larger im-
pinging landscape: the Hopi mesas, the Mormon settlements, the irri-
gation ditches, the brightflower sandstone air. Plus another transition,
toward Texas and Mexico. Denver itself remained the newspaper office
in the approximate center, the bank.

When we came back in '72, we were picking up on a new energy.
Perhaps we got it inaccurately in the briefness of our visit and the
intercession of other things. We each read there, I in Boulder and
Lindy in Denver, which proved not so much that there was a larger
number interested in our work as that the street art scene had become
social enough to include the remoteness of our own geography in its
direct hospitality. The change was both incorporated and disguised
in the change of Lindy's father. By leaving home and wife, by moving
into the high energy downtown, and making his niche in the bars,
salvation churches, and used bookstores, he recovered the zany and
erratic powers of his youth, in the city that had chosen him and in
which he had chosen to make his ground. What we missed was the
awakening of Denver that seeded his revival. At first it seemed, on
Ogden Street and in Larimer Square, the transposition, onto Denver
life, of the American countercultural vision. It had a peculiar local
twist and style, but nothing substantially indigenous. This is perhaps
what Henry saw too. No longer did he have to seek New York, as in
the old days, for the scene; the scene was in Denver, and unless he
met it as a local artist and journalist, with whatever vision he had for
the years of gestation, he lost his precious credentials as a resident
of the city in time. This he no doubt intuited when he set out on
his own. If he did not know Denver intimately, the rest would be-
come equally obscure.

The American revival played in Denver too, and it eased the city
into its own native jive. Denver could no longer be the Sears-Roebuck
office building for endless pueblo suburbs. From all directions the
forces converged on her, desert and mountains, Roaring Fork,
Platte, and Pacific Watershed. San Francisco in the West, Los Angeles
in the other West, both seeking an inland focus for dances that had
become too cosmopolitan and sociological. Salt Lake, Mormon capi-
tal of the world, a minor chord in Denver's ear, of mission bells and
lay priests. To the South, Mexico, and the American chichimec, its
oil and mineral wealth, reaper of the Mesozoic: Texas, Oklahoma,
Arizona. Tulsa. Albuquerque. Galveston. Summed up best in Russ
Stevenson's odyssey from a theosophical family in Mission, Okla-
homa, to teaching abstract art at San Jose State, then to Denver, the
temple, as a spiritualist, where he painted the last extant portrait of

166

Henry W. Hough, showing his face at death three years before the final hollowing.

To the West, also, Las Vegas, the Shoshoneans, Honolulu.

To the South, also, mescalito, Don Juan, Shiprock, Portuguese Brazil (the new North American West).

To the North, Montana, Idaho, Wyoming, South and North Dakota, the direction from which Houghs came, a Lewis and Clark wilderness, resettled by New Englanders.

To the East, the buffer zone of Eastern Colorado, and the various planetary influences of the cities on the way: Kansas City, St. Louis, Des Moines, Chicago, Indianapolis. You wouldn't think that one would get help up in these halfway houses en route to Denver or San Francisco, but then you can't account for taste. People might think of themselves as going further, but then get hooked someplace, at first an evening, then having to spend a lifetime resolving it.

Along global lines of force Denver has aenoic sympathy with the mountains of India, Nepal, and Tibet, the Himalayas, reincarnative notch of the world's religions, Buddhist when Colorado was Ute and Cheyenne. The raw conditions of ascension in any space.

Just as Denver, in time, received her visitors and goods from Tulsa and Red Lodge, she now receives forces and intelligences from the East, the global East. The spiritually unsettled trails up and thru the Rockies become a silent hierarchy of paths and monasteries, recalling Asia. Until then, mediums and spiritualists hang out in the downtown and outlying mining districts, responding to accurate cosmic sympathies, to clear the stage, to set the stage, to sing the arena-opening dawn-creation hymns. And then the Asians come, to join the Mexicans, the Yaquis, the Hopis, the Americanos, the San Francisco Chinese, the African-South American blacks. Guru Maharaj Ji, on one extreme, in lush suburban Denver, his home decked out in Christmas lights to celegrate his marriage. Chögyam Trungpa in the Mountains, Naropa, with Guenther at his side, translator from Saskatchewan, to make of that old football town a center of Tibetan learning. And the rest of the folks engaged in Reichian Military reconnaissance, of interplanetary things, seen in the skies.

The old Denver can no longer contain the forces, either internally or externally. The mining and Wells-Fargo industries that settled it have been washed over, as the era-ending floods that just a few years ago filled the creeks and streets, into the gypsies that are gathered to any mature city, Damascus, Peking, or Marseilles. For the American Indians, many of them socially disoriented and dispossessed, this city is the nearest zone of the American manifestation, a procedure, like the striating of minerals in the wet core of the land,

167

that has bled them out. The Blacks from the Syrian temple congregate on downtown street corners. Mexican migrant workers around a diner. Westerners with their cowboy hats leaving the air-conditioned steakhouses, AEC types and bankers. Hippies, so-called, mixed of local Denverites, from old and new families, and those headed back into the geography from the West Coast. And the New Englanders, Lindy's family: Houghs, Downers, the Reverend Alex Lukens, Sr., and Jr., of Southwest Harbor, Maine, Philadelphia, and St. Barnabas Episcopal Church, Vine Street, Colorado Territory.

The Hare Krishna people, male and female, with their single braid, drums and tambourines, dance thru the streets of downtown Denver, playing loud holy music and chanting — as if blown, for they are spinning thru the crowds and are given to the forces of history, as they turn on their different axes, the people variously attending and ignoring them. They are not old enough to be anything more than choir boys of the church that has set them loose to leave in the mind of the city Denver, and America, this image, from another city, of being outside of time, of being in touch with the irrevocable seasons that measure the Earth and its cycles. They submit, as an exercise; and they put that submission on display, a lesson in morality and humility before gods. They are different than, are not the adopted children of the Tibetan Buddhists, who wear business suits and whose task, like that of the miners and oil prospectors, is to undergo America, to take initiation from the nameless masters, to pass it on, and not become pawns of the myth or image and be blown thru the streets, as Mexicans, Navahos, Chicanos, are, struggle to stand up, not to feel the pain, outside the bars, nameless hits on nameless streets, bent back, and thus also are not like leaves in the wind.

Now the planetary storm is kali yuga wild, and the spores of Earth ancestry, in the Caucasus, in Southern Africa, in Malaysia, are blown to all other lands. Quasha speaks of the pod that was Tibet, ripe mountain fruit, hybrid India and China — which the Red Chinese sword, its conscious side Maoist, Marxist, German, burst open — the unconscious side, yin, now seeds the world, as the Navaho and Arapaho scramble like hard pollen thru the streets, take root in the backland heaps and abandoned genetic fertilities, the old lesson from Sauer, of weeds and men. In the center of the city are the high-rises, protected by locks within locks, and the Denver Country Club is still kept, like an orchid, by those who pay to keep it. But the rest is a wildness, like rye, and buffalo, and Comanches, and the city chosen to rise in this spot, puts on her robes, and begins to speak to the legions of men.

The memory will not come, but it is everywhere, in the city, and in my thirty years, and down the long hallway, and thru the dream of the car trip over farmland hills; Lindy and I turn in our continuously-renewed sense of each other, a passion, regardless of what brought it — as far back as we explore its first and intermediate causes, it is now whole and as the sun; it no longer matters that it was thru an accident we met, that we barely made it: already our first child is a person, our second child a baby racing thru its first months like a fish, its eyes alive with the woman that will fill them, fills them. I simply come here, and I know you do, for we are beyond wondering why. Wandering thru farm country and over hills, we are led by our softest sepals and essences. The tension of me is water, but it is not water, and the feeling, which used to stop at the desire, now goes as deep as I will allow it to go, until it inverts, a summer pond, the full-grown frogs around it. Some of it is warm, some of it is cold, and at its bottom is a springfed grotto, and at *its* bottom is the solar center, the nickel-iron star we are. And beyond us is the globe: not ecology, not geography, but Indian people, Iroquoian, growing corn on the present site of Montreal.

Either the feelings become more, or the sun on them becomes intenser and more textured, or *I* go deeper into the water and see the isoetes plants, the young tadpoles in their nests, the fish.

I want it to be deep. I want it, despite me, to be everything. I have to fight you to be here. I have to absorb the preconceptions of our imposed harmony thank god, and this alone is a grinding, like eternal sound, in a residuum, beyond the dreams of depth psychology, our sesame into oil.

* * *

In the window, above the tenements, the indoor orange tree makes sweet chutney, drinking Denver's sun. The Rockies white and rough beyond. Jonathan lived in this city, wandered on Larimer Street; Lindy's father spent his life here. Without a clue. We ship his belongings to Vermont from the old Terminal Post Office at Wyncamp, the air punctured by the long squeals of coupled trains; the cartons fall down a chute into the depths of the station.

The trees are becoming green and white with their essence, the sun as overseer. The ashes of the human body sparkle with magnesium. Turnabouts in history happen so slowly, and for those who care, Mayor Speer included, the death of liberalism is in the air, and

America is changing, not as men wish, but from the restless depths of what men are. The clustered row houses are visible, the aerials, the chimneys, the wires. The sun rises from Kansas. The wind passes from Wyoming. The rush of commerce bears the quotidien street, threads that vanish, threads that return. There is a softness of old summers, whose blossoms are dust, the ambergris perfume Lindy wears, from the Botanical Gardens, fragments, fragrance of Mitchell and Joanna, stoked and swallowed by thousands of young couples, their cats on the lawns and on the porches, their children crawling in the morning light.

On the radio Frankie Laine sings "Moonlight Gambler," and the hot spring nights of New York static apartments come back..."*You can gamble for matchsticks; you can gamble for gold....*"

It's all strung out. Nothing is withheld, to happen yet, or to have happened then. We drive these streets in the rebirth of our lives together, think of home.

Old Goddard is a moral wreck, desperate operatives destroying each other in greed for the last remaining resources. Pimps and educational vulgarians, at the curtain call, hoping once more to be consulted by the experimentalists in Washington. It is all committees, yachts, mini-coursers, false radicalism; they are traumatized; they cannot go thru the wind tunnel again.

But I do have a choice. Here in Denver it does not seem like the end of the world, not does it in Africa, I am sure. The Spanish, western, square streets flash by in an early lush and watered summer, with a grace and charm that cools me out, via the counter-image of the stormy North Atlantic and its Viking ports. Such brilliant masks, on which are painted scenes of intense and objective beauty. We have nothing but our courage. If it will stay sunny enough.....

"*....the stakes may be heavy or small....*"

And the exchanges are open, Sunday in the heart.

* * *

A young guy in a blue shirt and shorts stands on the upper porch of the Victorian house, hunched over an hibachi with slow-breathing flame. The pigeons scoot along the roof they have spackled, over the peaks and along their tops; when it becomes too steep to walk, they fly up to the chimneys. The church bells are playing.

The hibachi-warmer puts his hand lightly over the effuse of the flame. His cat's tail tries the holes between the slats of the railings, goes in and out of them in sequence; now the cat sniffs the kitchen thru the screen and returns to be petted by the hand, which gives a little tug at the tip of the tail, sensuously changing the animal's direction. It sits in an opening between the slats, watching the birds in the Colorado maple.

The hibachi-warmer tosses the meat over with his hand and goes inside. The door slams behind him. He returns with a fork and flips it back. A young couple walks to their jeep, he holding a dozen hangers of colored dresses, mainly orange and yellow, the hibachi-warmer up above, in his turret over the front door, barefoot and barekneed in the sun and shadow. He has a plate. The pigeon flies up. He takes the meat off the fire. The jeep starts and rattles under the accelerator; he goes back inside; the door slams. The cat sniffs around the abandoned hibachi.

Down the street a cocker spaniel is chasing and retrieving a white frisbee, competing for it with a tiny black dog whose yips fill the air. The cocker spaniel brings it back to a girl in a long blue velvet dress; she is standing on her door stoop, tossing it out. The cat sits sunning on the high post.

* * *

Airplane

In the plane, suspense is the natural state. As we are moving down the runway for take-off, the stewardess gives her instructions. Like the opening of a play, the curtain rising. Whatever is happening to us, and however we choose to understand it, we are in it together.

Today we will see the whole nation, its clouds and farms and rivers. Those below are confined to the regions we pass over. The squares and lines of the West change to the denser interwoven patterns of the East. The meaning of the American settlement eludes us as surely as the worm in its cocoon, spinning outer dimensions only to achieve a tight space within.

* * *

In Stella's millesecond vision, UFOs come sequentially, they appear at different points of time, but on the film they cover only three frames and are synchronized in a smooth clockwork formation. There are qualities of lens, light, and film, which, if they are not sentient and manipulative as animals, are not as neutral as theory of optics would have them. This one, says Jule Eisenbud, is conceptually up for grabs. Does she film the UFOs on the edge of another dimension, their formation imposed by a disparity in time?, or does she project them from her mind onto the film? Is it something else yet?, the famous third party, mischievous as ever, Don Juan?

* * *

Clouds and land, banks and colors, angles hidden in angles: active and brilliant and overwhelming. The long thunderhead hangs in the atmosphere, and the pilot says we will make a detour south into Kansas to go around it. The engines play a different music and our direction changes. I see it hanging just beneath us, piling up and growing, the actual turmoil.

* * *

Spider and web, web blown away, spider remains. Wound together like an orange, Seth says, the nerves, etheric and physical, over-lapping at every site.

* * *

We fly over the rich inhabited circles of Massachusetts, and the mountains of Vermont stretch up to the North, darker and barer than we realized for living in them. They appear as the shadow of another age, cast into this one.

V

The seeds are blown thru consciousness, and they take conscious-
ness. The clouds release their waters, and lightning strikes beans in
the sky. Though the flowers come from the soil, their growth shatters
salt and iodide; forms retards them, as the body retards the dream.
Otherwise there would be no cotyledons, no ground clover and ivy,
no sheathing monocots or whorled dicots. They steal potassium from
stars, calcium from artesian dikes far below their roots. They fall
back, via the rhythm, thru the mysteries of shape, to the hand that
gave them movement.

And if this is the hand that gave our minds movement, did it do
so only initially, in the galactic explosion that foretells all Darwinian
science, does it reach us from star plasma to flayed atom to molecule
to mud to cell, repeated and recoded by the vitality, the uncanny
continuity of matter? Or does the hand, turning in a dream, give rise
to mind again each time, fusing it with matter at the historical mo-
ment? Are we the log, the negative exponent of the twelve lost tribes?,
or are we reborn refugees from the astral-vital plane? These two
possible interpretations, possible initiations, lie about us in mixed and
bastard decks. It is no wonder that our link with nature is unbroken
but indiscernible. The two merge, or we cannot distinguish them, and
if we are removed from creation by the inhuman scope of cosmological
history, and the billions of billions, we are equally removed by the
fusion of dream and body, in the moment of birth, whose number is
the mere binary from zero to one.

Fire and water meet in an androgyne and strike, ignite. The
principle of rain and sun and weeds and moss is reminiscent of Freud's
wondrous garden of dreams and prelinguistic seeds. To confuse
gardeners, though, in a search for common origin of mint and mind, is
to enter a labyrinth without thread. They pass thru aberrant geo-
metries, and their resemblance is the only fact of their intercession on
this plane. Some say we should strengthen our ego, and so come,
by creativity and sorcery, to the fount, where we meet the ancient
ocean. There is another path, not always the opposite, in which we
struggle to detach ourselves from ego, to dispatch the archetypal
messengers as we depart the narrow and sharpened band of conscious-
ness on which we receive a palliative for life. Perhaps it is a middle
voice problem. Perhaps it is a daily duality relieved by sudden entry
into the transhistorical zone, where spiritual events are eternal and
unwavering, and our sense of time is merely a means of descending from
the mountains to the cave, the eon in which its transmission is entrusted
to us. Ego is a koan to be solved, not a fortress to be built and decor-

ated or a barrier to be torn down and abolished. This far along, we could hardly renounce it cold.

I am dropped thru the center of a dream, and it is not like falling thru space. It is like sitting on a chair and having the chair topple over backwards, have it become that the chair was never a chair. As I reach out to steady myself or break the fall, I dwindle into a being too small to operate among objects this size. I am washed away. This identity, all a life, is a mask; take it off, and the black hole is waiting, thru which we vanish, calling out our last informationless word. Smash the altar and there is no altar; destroy the society and the conditions for building a new and better society are gone with the rest. Two stones of some size sit in juxtaposition; when one stone is moved, the space it fills disappears in me also. The speed of ejection is too fast for memory, too fast for belief in any of this, intercepted like an underwater column of light, without optimism, and without the sense that by passing beyond the physical I am entering a more beautiful and ethereal realm. It is the same everyplace, if not worse in the disappointment: the chronic recurrent shock.

They wanted so much. They had such fine utopian possibilities. Now they're gone too. And we are not the survivors.

If it was left up to us, we'd make a mess of it surely. That's why they don't allow us to handle such delicate affairs. Reality is our mud-pie, play and splash in it as we like. But don't for a moment act as though this is not important, because that's the only reason it's here.

VI

If there was once a sea of myth, all waters draw from it. Whispers of Atlantis at remote ports, the Atlantic itself a harsh and spiritual ocean, feral, barbarian, outside the Roman and Greek, hence defying the Christian. Irish priests sailed it in Mediaeval times, and saw it real, and saw in it the frontier waters of the Greek cosmos, the pre-atomic particles of unconscious creation, working like a mind, as they strove at the same time to reach what-is-now consciously North America, to contact pagan peoples, were thrown back into the mythical sea, the Isles ever of Brandan. They sailed upon translucent waters, over shells of stellar origin. They marked the sea of flatstone islands and dividing glaciers, of volcanoes which threw steaming lava, boulder size, into the waters. In the retelling of a Celtic legend, the glaciers became glass and mirror cities; the ocean blossomed with underwater mansions, herds of cattle driven thru it by submarine creatures; Jan Mayen Island of the geological North Atlantic became a harbor of angry smiths, sister to the isle of the Cyclops.

So the Irish Atlantic is lost by the *Voyage of Mael Duin*; the North American coast, visited later by Cabot and Verazzano, fades into an outreach of paradise and golden islands. The priests of the older logos wandered among the isles of the planet's history, until sea charts disappeared into lives of the saints. But the traceries and parchment astronomies remain like glacial outcroppings (the Phoenicians the last clue), a text wound back thru the telling of the *Odyssey*, gods turned into islands and storms, islands themselves into gods.

Until the sheer size and wateryness of it overwhelms them in a premonition of just how much pagan Jovian history lies between the creation and the temple of Galilee.

The immrama are not the only evidence of Irish voyages; for every spiritual log, lost in the Christian Celtic of Patrick, there is a raw physical arrival, whose transformation into the Algonquian leaves a landscape of a different order, alien to Saint Brandan or Homer. Sauer not only designates the forge at L'Anse aux Meadows as the work of Irish smiths, but cites the Algonquian rite of nailing a dog to a cross, (which later missionaries took to be the New World Incarnation or the apostasy of the Devil) — a mere Indian translation of a favorite Irish ritual.

Beyond the North Atlantic sit the cliffs of Newfoundland and the ice of Baffin Island, the shores around the Hudson, and the wild descendants of Asian peoples. This poor land, this linguistic sanctuary, took on the dreams and peoples of that Europe and pretended to resolve them, log-cabin-like in lotus-eater mythos, leaving technology in their place, even as the bluff of the single windmill in the fields of an older Spanish Holland — until once again now the portolan sailing charts are confused with the EROS photographs of the weathering Earth. We see *the planet* but our teacher is the cosmological map.

With Portuguese in the Azores and the Madeiras, the Cape of Good Hope rounded by Da Gama, the Eurasian culture vanished, and the islands of the Mediterranean were thrown into the jungle, beyond Europe, beyond the Mediaeval commerce Calvin smashed, and Galileo's telescope broke into mountains and valleys, of the Moon. The New World gained continental size as Jupiter sprouted moons, facts no one would deny, despite the destruction of rational numerology. To gain a new mode of seeing things is to lose an older one, and when properties could no longer be assumed from sympathies between objects, they became spaces and irregularities, Indo split from European, Sino from Indo, Uto from Sino; this the text of the present Earth.

The ship C.S. Lewis imagined in a fairy tale sails directly into the Sun, across the hingeline Earth. It is not the Earth we know, for the Sun grows larger as they approach it, and the sailors on the ship can look down hundreds of fathoms thru a freshwater sea. The shadow of their ship registers the topography of the bottom, and the underground cities rush past as the people of another creation seem dimly aware that something is transiting overhead. They move over the syntactic riddle, or the language barrier, because either common myth or shared speech origins allow it; as they drink the water they become physically lighter, their bodies almost transparent. The white sunbirds, arising in the East with the fire, pass them at more than supersonic speed, to meet the embodiment of morning. The ship sails in the strong Dantean current, until their passage into a sea totally of lilies holds them, Sargasso. They cease only when the active principle so outweighs the tension and weft of matter that movement itself becomes profane.

The archetypal has departed from science after three thousand years of mischief. We are bound now to a humanist anthropological quest. The Moon-landing has thrown us into the pure machinery, and if you think those men returned, at least as men, you are wrong; they took all of us with them and abandoned us there. Now it is simply the numbers, on the celestial harp, the seams in a seamless flow. Why, if form comes into existence with matter, do we have no notion of whence-form? And why do we assume its twinship with matter? Why, now, when the amorphous is more than just a prophecy?

As theogony became theology, the water of Thales poured from the nodes of an invisible objective world. When the elemental principles became distractions of physics, the gods returned, in Parmenides, not as characters, but the divine phenomenal life of the individual, who breathes Zeus and Saturn thru the pneuma of his soul, until that became a noose in Augustine, a monastic compulsion, a gambler's reform, released by Eckhart, Parmenidean, back to Thales with Luther and Calvin, who set the yoke the ships bore against the Western light, into the Indies and Americas, where Cotton Mather and Ben Franklin rebuilt the gross machinery and restored Olympus. Right into the House of the Lord.

Man can recall gods from the depths of his despair. It is they who stand, not the material world that conveys them; man brings gods into being as the gods bring man into being, and that moment, because it is timeless, can be repeated in its original form again and again. The nugget rests on the tongue of the bird who kindles the world from *armonia*, who places it glowing in the lips of time, who breathes it as fire down the long dark hallway. It is honey when in the hive or on the taste buds; it is perfume in bottles too small to see, that burst in forests after the rain. The world is made of corrupt texts which it grips like the stars a ship at sea, clothes them in form. The sails battered by the wind, the rags blown up from the deck, to hang upon the masts, all we see. Beyond the Ionian is the ionic, and beyond the ionic: the Ionian again.

Summer

Cape Elizabeth, June 12-13, 1974

I

The sky dark, the air moist, the sound of crickets behind Wells Road — the Dipper over the Terrien's house, where it was, season by season, even while we were away. The lights appear at the end of the field, by the ocean. And that they are mysterious is itself a mystery, and keeps coming in. I feel softness and passage, but the sense, that these are paths, itself must divide and fail totally before they are brought back together beyond the false profundity. Because the yarns are twisted, and the feelings are not even opaque as the bees gather honey, divest their bodies unconsciously of it in the perfect hive. For us it is uncertain, when the keeper returns, amidst molecules, whose honey it was, whose is the present flight of the shuttle. We are the wind-pollinated spores of high-energy cones, our minds ordered by a non-intelligence that yet knows more than all the rest of us, our intentions the endosperm for unfinished designs. And I think, as I watch all of us get older and change, that if death didn't exist for men they would invent it, or, if they were left to invent what they thought they needed, they would bring far worse into the world. This global culture is sufficient proof.

We live, almost unaware, in vibrations so robot and deadening, in a city so glib and devoid of gods, most of our possible psychic life is spent in not feeling what goes on. In fleeing the mind. And I will be done writing when I have gone back over my American childhood, in direct memory and incidental light, and recovered my vulnerability. When I have destroyed in me the global heresy. When I begin to find again a clear pool, despite the random taps, the dark lures. But if I stopped now, I would have only a wasting chaos, North America and its sciences in the center/its bashful corruptions, its superficial healing of our differences, its denial of an inner earth (for a cheap bounty of unusable treasures collected on a march thru territories whose seasons yielded also, and still do, 400 years later, berries, oysters, cacti, pigweed and maize stick-planted).

The dreams confound each other and cast purpose against purpose until each binds me twice, binds me thrice. I am not yet free to welcome the aeon, or even know what its therapy would relieve us of, tangled as we come, would open our feelings to — and where the new agrarian and decentralist societies would place our dying social body — what marriage will replace marriage, or how the herbal and visionary medicines of the millenium and the solar-tidal pulleys can cure us from: what still seems to be all we are.

So, from Cape Elizabeth, dictating back these notes, there remains some fucking majestic sense of my earlier books and of threads maybe spider filaments that pull throughout. If I show literary design, it is vestigial; there is not a conventional desire left in this body; I have put it all to the mill, and what comes out is a cloth, hammered as fine as the stars hammer information, as genes, between mutated and broken sequences of three, recover their triplets barely before unending manufacture of the living is lost. We need no other language; one strand of DNA rings the world. And even where their map splits, the artisans regroup and shuffle, from the eternal web, the single awakening lots across the limen of being. Despite the possibility of civilizations with different chemistries, our carbon is more than equal to creation; its vast ply, under the rigor of experience and number, is the proof of an alliance called biopoesis. It is too soon for us to marry our arts, but without this as possibility our circumstance is hopeless.

For we go on, sans text, as undrawn codons or the unlisted star observations of Copernicus, a lingering famine and dull we cannot even begin to gauge, megadeaths alone in the minds of the strong, who *are* afraid, and so, says a weary Henry Miller, what can we hope for the weak?

I loose the compulsion into the energy that breeds it, living always between the intimation that we are getting there (as the spirit and its sparks fly, and the design is sprung), and the terror that we are sinking more deeply into the slag than ever, as the joints harden, the rules become inflexible. I sacrifice this book to the technocrats and Madison Avenue aristoi, who stand before me, and demand production, Grossinger. And it is the wonder of my life that they will take it instead of bravado wealth and Calvinist fiction. And that He also wants it, raw as He gave it to us, that He will not separate, even now, because the athanor is too far, these living protean threads from the silver and the dung.

We have come far enough that our own texts are more frightening and seminal than those we inherit from hermetics of other times.

II

The trip from Vermont to Maine is almost entirely along 302. In Vermont it is postcard scenic, hills and farms and cows, small towns with churches. The New Hampshire mountains are different. Golf courses replace grazing ground; old hotels, bungalow colonies, and ski resorts overlook the highway, winding into the valleys, plenty of advertising. Near the Maine border, national forest takes over, and we enter the more elusive condition of the maritime zone: lake towns, beaches, small wooded islands. Miles of junk outside Portland, then we wait twenty minutes on the access road for two barely-moving trains to cross.

The city is as we left it: the University around the small field, the highway now completed over the park, the duck pond, children on bikes in among the trees. We drive by plumbing and supply stores, up past laundries and warehouses, around Congress Street, and down toward the wharf. A long new avenue with arc lights has cut thru the urban renewal district, purposely dividing the city in half.

Portland is a hard place to leave. When you're not there, no word reaches you. It's not like Ann Arbor or New York, which belong to everyone. Falmouth, Deering, Casco, Munjoy, Eastern Promenade: are anonymous and usable streets, for they are the streets of the fabled city we hope to build someday, the golden city on a hill, referred to more than once, and in more than one context.

We turn onto Center Street, en route, perhaps, to the Bridge, when, standing right outside his new store Sunshine, is Herb Gideon. He waves at us, then does a doubletake. We get out, quick embraces, and stand together on the street, taking in the cold salty breeze.

"Has it been two years?" he says, disbelieving. It has. So there follows a long rap, back and forth, about how we're getting older. "The thing I never realized," he muses, "is that business takes all your time. It's not like when I began. You got to know people. You fooled around. The store was just the thing that kept us going. Now, people like you come into town, are here and leave, and I never even know you."

All the times he couldn't get out to our house; yet he was there at the end to help us, on that scorching clear day, when we had to take everything, he and a few others, filling the truck and U-Haul, and what furniture we couldn't fit he took back to Erebus with him, and now upstairs, in the owner's quarters, sits the Morris chair, that came with the house anyway. I remember when we first met him, at Eddie Fitzpatrick's party, the surety then of a friendship we never had (the fish store that sold steamed clams overlooking the harbor, the tables ripped up the very summer we came, leaving, for the rest of our stay, only the posts). Some things were lost not just with our departure; they were being lost the whole time we were there.

The feds, in the form of income tax agents, have hit the store for as much as they could get, and overdue bills hang on the walls among the peace posters. The sense of luxury is wearing thin. "You just can't keep up stock the way you used to," Herb says. He urges us to settle down while he goes out to do some business. We put Miranda on the floor and make Robin a place to set up trucks and cars. I stare at postcards on the wall, vaguely irritable and impatient. A girl who is back in Vermont, which she calls *her* scene, likes the vibes here so much, and Danny, and the store, she hopes they'll come and see her. But I'm not sure they go anywhere anymore. Or maybe they do, as different people.

The afternoon passes, and Herb doesn't make it back. We get in the car and take the bridge into South Portland, on our way to Cape Elizabeth. The tankers below still pump their Venezualan cargo clear to Montreal, for Portland is an original North Atlantic city, and it has kept its secrets and geographical strength. Its people no longer want it, so with dignity it slips away, pretending to be their ravages when *they* are the ravages and *it* is the withdrawing body in time. The chop-squads work now on levelling the remains, to heroin, crime, and merchandise malls. The first uses I made here were so accurate: Levett entering Casco Bay, Olson reaching north to Quack and Pemaquid to stretch Maximus, the coastline west out of Mount Desert and the Cranberries (arriving in Portland from its own past as a fishing town), the wharf district and Commercial Street (back thru alchemy, James Fenimore, Cabot, and the Trojan promise of an isle in the Atlantic). I mapped and recovered archetypal Portland, but my connections to the present were thin. I operated between suburban Cape Elizabeth, the University, and Herb's street scene, a famous and doomed juggling routine.

We sneak a glance at our old house, pulling in at the Mullins' across the street. The roof is completely repaired; the front porch is repainted, circles of color on the centers of the posts. A large eagle sits at the top, hammered on. It's like coming back after life to see how what you used is used again, is simply artifacts, parts of other peoples' lives. We grew here like a beet, casting out wings. But what we left behind is left behind forever, worked back into the soil; what we took with us re-roots or dies. A metallic screen has replaced the barn door, and on the side of the barn are cages in which two large wolfhounds bound. The woman is gardening. It is heady. Even as we are spying on our own lives, we are spying on someone else. Unfair.

Kimmie is tall and slim now, shy of Robin, Robin shy of her. We are hung on continuity, and because there is a thread thru our minds to this spot, we think we can follow it and pick up talking where we left off. So Betty Mullins tells us about the neighborhood. There's a Portland-Gorham faculty member who used to live down the block; he's moved out and is sharing an apartment in town with a nineteen year old student; his wife's lost control of the daughters, and they're wearing lipstick and staying out late.

We drive down the road to the MacNeils. Minnie sees our car from the window and comes out of the house in tears. Lindy was the one person who dug, as a woman, what she was going thru, and the madness that could no more be hidden than the trees that grow up around her house, that everyone pretended no one saw. "You never should have left," she weeps. The fishermen's daughters have become teenagers, a little hesitant about Robin, who was their perfect boy-doll once. No doubt they missed him, and he missed the memory of them. But now that they have come back together, the connection has been lost; there is only what each has developed to replace the other in a world where nothing stays anyway, not in any big sense, just day by day and hour by hour. I go across the street and visit my old friend Mrs. Manual, the neighborhood artiste; she is designing sets for the Portland school theatre, and very proud to tell me; in fact so quickly does she get into it I know she has thought of me in this context many times since I left and regretted I was gone before I knew her triumph. The basic hellos are passed over, so she elaborates on the theatre. The teen-age son with whom I played ball, whose father coaches the Little League, sits there agreeing again and again, "It's sure good to see you, Mr. Grossinger." Which I could neither think of myself as, nor correct him on. And then the shift to my missing beard. "You've taken ten years off yourself," she says. And I wonder if that's also true of Plainfield, if the Cape was not as far as I got going that way, and since then has been working back.

III

Plainfield was wilderness when Portland was founded; train depot, farms and creameries at the heydey of THE PORT; then the farms dissipated, the bobbin mill burned, the railroad station was closed, the tracks pulled up (Robin and I came across the wreck of the factory, jagged and charnel in the brambles and high grass, raspberrying along the thickest stands into the fields until we were picking them from smashed windows and rotted autos). The college dealt the last blow.

Plainfield has since been recolonized by urban migrants who have come with the unrelieved burdens of SDS, the war, radical ecology, feminism, community health, free schools — fragments searching for a common and livable denominator, heaped up into a New World village, in the dream of making it over from the beginning. If only it were New Zealand, but it isn't, and they have no continuous acreage, only a map in their heads of what's already on the ground and what it might look like if they ever built the whole set.

The natives far outnumber the newcomers, but they are bitter and tired. Rural industry has faded, their own town map is riddled with holes; a few strong families hold onto stores and other businesses, supported mainly by Goddard. Whether they know it or not, they have a banquet of stones.

Main Street, all one block of it, is an unsettled mixture of local markets, student apartments, and countercultural establishments, Kellogg's is an old general store, whereas Bartlett's Market has attempted to modernize, and just last summer moved in a series of display freezers. They still keep the beer in the vault behind the meat and the Canadian bread, so marked, in an ice-box. Apartments are mixed with family houses, but they can be told usually by the assortment of motorcycles, sports cars, dismantled cars, etc., outside. The slaughterhouse is now a foreign car repair shop; behind it is the ruin of an apartment building, once owned by a missing ex-student; it burned two winters ago, trapping a girl for whom the Goddard health center has since been renamed. Packs of dogs travel the town regularly, and one knows, if only from a few specific cases, they are from Illinois, and California, and New Jersey; they raid the garbage cans, shit on the lawns, and leave general bad feeling, but nothing is planned. The students bring mainstream wealth, but in forms and tastes that twist the town apart, to meet their dollar, or shun it, and both happen, lot by lot. Those who are in business, say Freddie Fowler, with his earthmoving equipment, fire engines, city contracts, and blocks of rentals, are for modernizing, even the outmoded water system — new pipes, black sidewalk, revenue sharing, etc. The rest would like to play out the string and keep the taxes down. Up on Route 2, the Mobil station houses Mae's Store, while Boardman's Texaco is a hangout for auto mechanic freaks, and Earth Artisans, a little further out along the river, sells teas, flours, vitamins, and organic sundaes. That's where the big business between the college and the town happens. And those are not Plainfield forefathers out there; they're all from away.

Just beyond the dam, where apartments are rebuilt every few years to survive the flooding, the Methodist Church and Kellogg's Store face each other across Main Street. On the Church side are some native houses, Bartlett's Store, a laundromat, and, around the corner on Creamery Street, Fowler's offices across from his main apartment complex. On the Kellogg side are a hardware store, a barber shop, the Tigres-Euprates Women's Bookstore (named after an article in *Ms.* that oddly called Plainfield the Tigres and Eurphrates of the women's movement), original family dwellings, *The Country Journal*, the Grange Hall, and the fire station at Creamery Street junction. The *Journal* is run by politically-oriented migrants, with local kids on the staff, and 95% of the news no different than it would have been in a Plainfield newspaper of thirty years ago; it lies somewhere between complete receptivity and running for office in a conservative district; it also lies between the original it is modelled after and a pop nostalgic revival of same. A cooperative has bought the Grange Hall, and it is a food-redistribution center for the region, used for sorting and storing produce, but also crafts fairs, wood-heat clinics, self-realization classes, political meetings, contra-dancing, fiddle concerts, and so on. The theatre there is very much like the *Journal*: participatory, often a direct psychological or political exercise, always a touch of downhome in hope of getting the local people in with them. The natives feel just as strongly about luring New School kids to the summer Bible School.

The films are high entertainment, the crowd in overalls, as in the farm-belt on Saturday night. There is also a Two Penny Circus and a Mummers' Troop. The slapstick might pass for either good old God-given laughter or brilliant low-key satire. But a deeper alienation and schizophrenia underlie the performance; it is macabre in some totally unplanned way. Watch, as one battered ex-hippie gets up to do a Renaissance jig, announcing it by number and name in an appropriate accent, then does it, the expression on his face, while his feet move on the floor. I think of *Ethan Frome* and *Peyton Place*: if this is Jonathan Edwards and Anne Bradstreet, can they be far behind?

In the mountains around Plainfield, organic farms open, communes (New Hamburger, Pie in the Sky, their purposely ironic names), kilns, studios, glassblowing sheds, cabins; self-sufficiency is the cue, pre-capitalist model. If Marx is the prophet, it is in other guises; he is also the Nearings, Fritz Perls, and most obviously Mao. Because China, whether it is conscious or unconscious, as Third World model, is the only image there is.

The talk in Plainfield is of jeeps, four-wheel drive, wood-stoves, mulch piles, cross-country skiis, good hard work. It is a clarity which makes the rest of America seem vulgar and reckless. But it is also a mechanical chauvinism, a solemn righteousness, an indulgence in methodological jargon and hi-tech. Plainfield has no cultural illusions; it is hardcore, either way. The local people have basketball, church, town meetings, country music, auto racing, fireworks, cars, and t.v. The co-op people have crafts, direct theatre, and the tight aesthetic of their life-style. They have abandoned cosmology and art; their poetry must be addressed to women in the underground factories of North Vietnam. They believe the city lives off the fat of the country, and if they can't stop the buggering, they can break its habit in themselves. Most of them have been into drugs, rock, surrealism, Wittgenstein, academics, or labor politics, but at other times. And now these things are warning buoys: when they see them in others, they stay clear. They want to have just enough; they want to find out how necessary it is to live at all. And still live.

If the windmills and solar panels finally go up in abundance, they will be the pioneers. At very least, they are one half of our transformation, one half of the things we are now desperately concerned with, not only for survival, but as part of the dead reckoning of any spiritual path.

It is yet too sheer a drop for me. I keep a garden and seek a hard design. I try to untangle the webs of cultural desire and artifice. But when I hear talk only of wood, beans, manure, peas, nails, axles, I am reminded that they are also shells of fire blown into and out of being by a more powerful fire. They are essences, messengers, karmic clues. But they do not and cannot stand alone, without becoming material fixity, or just plain old-fashioned materialism. In 1930's Germany as well as China the peasant was glorified, his false innocence, that the strength and self-respect lost in a decadent culture be regained from the earth. But we have come past that point as a people, and we can no longer pretend, in primal scream therapy, to handle the complex by the simple; we can no longer pretend we know everything anymore. The farmers at the New Alchemy Institute

186

invite hermeticists also, translators of Chinese holy books; they don't want to go back to Iowa or the mechanical utopian century; they don't want to set the demon loose by hypnotizing themselves never again to remember the magic words.

We can have both, and we better have both, or it will be neither. For the guides lie on both our right and left hands; in our sloppy strength as surely as our damnable weakness, we shall fail.

IV

Where they meet the ocean, stars and sea are equal. Maine is an open astral system, ragged-edged and regenerative. Vermont is the cold mantle on which we vertebrates were whetted, hollow-cast in gypsum and secondary light. And I find myself asking, "Why did I leave the center?," without any sense of what the question means. The old excuses, so lucid and righteous then, fall away as if they were nothing, exposing me for the liar and rationalizer I still am.

Frank Hodges is delighted to hear from me; he's buzzing over our Anthropology-Geography Department and the major we're getting. After all, I'm the one who thought it up, rammed it thru, who saved his ass. Yet here I am, hardly the native son returned. I'm working for a college that may or may not fold before the summer's out, no assurance they care to keep me even if it doesn't, telling the chairman of a department I invented, almost whimsically, that he's on my reference list because I'm looking for another job. It's the American dream, and I'm glad to have fucked up in such a downhome re-orienting way. He's at peace, the kids, the garden, the cows, bigger every year. And he says, strangely touching in his manner, "gee whiz, Rich, I wish *we* could hire you. But we're after a geographer now, not an anthropologist."

Plus that I'm not looking to come back here, as I explain to Don, who bitches about what a farce the Anthropology-Geography Department is, hoping I will re-neg in private at least. But I'm pleased with their academic amateurism and clownish enthusiasm that makes my legacy to the rest of them, the mainline pros stuck in PoGoland, whom I also understand, a lesson in professional humility. My problem is not the blatancy of hanging a career together, job after job; it's understanding why I left and what was happening then. And knowing it so well I can be a stranger here again. What use could I get from blind assertions of progress, either way.

Don tells me, shit, if only you had played your cards right, you'd be sitting pretty now.

And I agree with him, in the sense that I didn't read the politics, or care to, when I was there. I wanted to be Zeus, world-creator, not some petty Roman judge. But since then Goddard has taught me I was wasting good etiological energy. Colleges are businesses, and, like stores, they have customers, and at faculty meetings you discuss marketing and educational products. It's just like hotels: the game is to fill rooms and keep their occupants returning. Goddard has even figured out how to make the degree as relevant as a bowling trophy at a singles' weekend. Now they are working on eliminating it altogether and going pure Hotel Vermont, with certificates of study, little tin Statues of Liberty to sell to the folks from Shaker Heights and Lynn.

But I don't want to have played my cards right *then*; I want to have not, and be here now, initiated by that error. Don says this because he has become record-time chairman of the Sociology Department, which itself is a more powerful alliance than I had the whole time there or have now at Goddard, especially since the President who hired me quit. And Goddard has ruined me for the system as thoroughly as any of its students; committee by committee and firing by firing I have worked out, painfully, exhaustively, the education I think my family tried to give me in place of the one they paid for, not realizing they are two different things. Looking back from these heights I know what they wanted me to be all these years, when they sent me to Amherst, when they started me out behind the desk at the hotel. And though I see why I can't and couldn't be it, I realize too it was and is for different reasons than I thought. Goddard is a hip second-rate Grossinger's, and both are on the skids. Plus that the world is just as banal and uptight as they said it was. Which I've got to face if I'm going to get any further.

Don is being like a big brother, after the fact. If I had stayed at Portland I'd have security, money, position. So it seems. But I know better than that. He's talking penny ante for a world like we've got now and the waves that are crossing it. After the fact, Goddard proves to be hardass millenial, aeonic. Vermont has ground all the hot shit out of me. Which is what it was when I bombed out of PoGo. I had a few books. I did some high readings out West. I though I wasn't being treated well enough for such a star, dragging my ass to the eight o'clock anthropology lectures, with *Rolling Stone* as a reference on fame. And I was right, prima donna that I was pretending to be. I wasn't appreciated. Somewhere out in the big wide world was my constituency to meet and love: it was a royal daydream. I was a fool.

I wanted to be employed by some transnational company that was going to move me up to a global position. (Zeus again). As though we had transcended nations, let along bureaucracies in all the small towns of the Bangor rail line. As though they wanted me to do anything more than process students. And when I failed the son of the secretary to the head of the Science Department, because he had missed all the classes but two, I got called into the dean and found it my word against his. Okay. But one part of it was brilliant and blind prophecy. If I hadn't left town, the madman might have shot me.

Because just two weeks ago he pulled out a gun, put a bullet into his wife, watched her die, then turned it on himself, and survived. That gun had been pointed at us. We had been told to get out of town in the best 1972 fashion. And as he's proven since, it doesn't matter if you're arrested and moved from the hospital to the court room. The other party is dead.

I had an intuition about that man, all the time unsure if it was paranoid, mythological, or the old third eye. Like at the Burlington Airport en route to Denver, when the speeding Goddard student freaked, turned on me, I didn't know who the hell she was, or that she was suspended from a place it's almost impossible to pull that trick at, and promised to take the plane down into the Green Mountains to pay us all back, singing, *"Hang down your head, Tom Dooley; hang down your head and cry . . ."* I was wrong. She didn't have the power. But this cat came all the way down the path. He worked on it for twenty years, and not as some ghetto kid for whom *bang! you're dead* was a local condition of planet. He needed pure schizophrenia; he needed to get so far out that shooting became as everything else among possible alternatives, to be tried at some moment that seems arbitrary, but is surely also in the stars. What we live out until there isn't any. When I mentioned it to the authorities back then, they laughed at me: the Black vice-chancellor with his eye on a better job in Maryland. "You have no sense of humor," he told me. And so from there on, we were on our own.

Not at all ashamed to admit that we were ridden out of town.

And Herbie says to me, first take on it, earlier in the day: "That was the fucking most ugly thing that's gone down here in a long time. Look who he finally shot." After all the years of public pistol-waving and boasting.

"Did you know him?" asks Mrs. Mullins.

I point across the street, to where the woman is watering flower beds we dug out of scrub. "Right there in that house, he pulled the same gun on us."

"The really disgusting thing," says Herbie, "is that the newspaper writes it up like he was a hero. They list all his awards and publications and prizes, as if he won the Nobel Prize."

And none of it is true. He made up that press. It was his own invention of a big career. Typical Brandeis jive. And the fact that local people believed it — which shows up again in the last edition — only fueled his psychosis. I mean, he thought it was a real coup to convince a town he had a *Times Book Review* national following. Easier than getting one. But he dug that hole, and then he had to go lie in it. And even this one won't make the nationals.

It's easier to sell Portland a shyster, a crook and a murderer, than a gentle herbal doctor (like my friend Mr. Enslin out there at the end of the road). Or a good native surrealist like Mr. Bemis. And I speak not of the Portland I love, but the mediocre Portland, of the newspaper, the school, and that long brown avenue they just laid in. Corrupt Boston creeping down the coast.

There is so much I don't understand, and what I do seems less and less, as the precisions grind out a world more deadly and more accurate everyday. I can't tell if conditions are getting worse or if I'm finally coming to see them as they are. The powerful of the world seem *so* powerful, and I know, at last, they care nothing for us and our dreams. I no longer fear losing the angels; one morning, or was it just *this* morning?, I awoke to find them already gone. I miss them, but they can't be my angels any more than the Martians can be my Martians. I can do better. And I have to. For my biology contains no dream-time rocket launches, no millenial Atlantic hibernations. I have only mistakes now to guide me.

V

When we came to Portland in 1970, Herbie's store was the local center of San Francisco culture. Despite the rednecks on the block, who got the police to slap a ticket on everything that didn't look as though it came right out of Portland Motors, his proposition thrived. Center Street was half a transplant of some other renaissance, half a realization of Portland's own calico and jade inheritance. Herb was no wandering freak looking for new territory; he was a native, son of a West Indian sea captain who settled there during the era of global sea commerce. He inherited the international disposition.

The respectable stores on Congress Street didn't just spring up like flowers after the rain, or from generations of money; they were owned by people who sold goods and who paid the rent by the goods they sold. If the goods didn't sell, the store closed. City Hall didn't come to the rescue. Herbie read the message and brought it home. In Berkeley, as in parts of Cambridge, it might have seemed the counterculture was itself a landed class, which impressed Portland passers-thru only with the futility of their own scene. But life and vision are the same in Cumberland as Marin County, and Portland's children were returning from America to a city they knew and could enclose. Erebus was Herbie's personal commitment to being back and digging in. The others were not so much his clientele as his spiritual justification. The real patrons could not be local freaks and heads. They had to be the wealthy Cape Elizabeth and Falmouth matrons, either out of some acquired appreciation of hip style, or because their sons and daughters led them there. Plus the up-and-coming young professionals. They could afford triple-layer prices; in turn, Herbie could let the important people hang in for free in exchange for hours in the store or decoration of the set. The rents were low enough for the church mouse, and Herbie was generous with his community. The Chamber of Commerce and businessmen's alliances mainly wanted to tear everything down, wipe out the old city, and get something modern and suburban, something they wouldn't be ashamed to invite their clients to. So nobody spent their capital on what was already built; they had far too much to waste. It wasn't long before Herb and associates figured out you could buy a good-sized city, complete with apartment buildings and storefronts, for what a suit might cost you in New York.

What Portland lacked in 1968, when Erebus began, damned the San Francisco transplant, almost immediately, to a career of mediocrity and dalliance. There was no culture underneath, in the deepest sense, to sustain a commercial aesthetic, so the grand event which, on Haight-Ashbury, followed an inner awakening of the people, on Center Street tried to bluff that inner awakening with a sparkly shell; it became paisley and waterbeds, pipes, teacups, and jive suits, within hours of the creative unfolding. Herb was a patron, and an honorable one, but the salon was one-track, and porn millionaires hung in the wings, barely titilated by their summer palace, by Bill Bemis' erotic cartoons and posters.

I don't understand how Maine gets bought out from the very beginning always; I don't understand it in the counterculture any better than in the Bar Harbor motels. But while it lasted and stayed high, the locals made the most of it, and there were times when Portland came alive from hill to hill under Herbie's vision and political cool. Erebus, *and* the City of Portland, invite themselves to the Sunday rock concert on the Promenade over the ocean, week after week, a civic event of no minor consequence. Then Herb hires out-of-work young carpenters to turn a building into studio space for artists, many of whom lacked even a place to sleep.

As popular a man as he became in some circles, he was also a mistrusted figure, and the implied, semi-feudal title of Hippie Capitalist was both wittily accurate and outrageously cruel. How much (and how soon after the initial innocent opening) drugs fucked things, and how much drugs were symptomatic, and then aura-spreading, of the original confusions, is hard to guess. There was an implicit decadence from the start. The scene cried out for art and vision and inner space; without them, the psychological and sociological implications were too bitter, too thorny. But when no substantial sprout of local consciousness responded to such blatant revivalist vibes, drug vision and jargon replaced it, perhaps to justify the heavy merchandising. Things became psychedelic, distorted. The grounds of their original unhappiness now strewn with an archetypal darkness (origins far beyond Portland), people blasted thru the outer territories (they now knew they could reach) to a deadlier frustration with the limits. As far as they got, an inexplicable barrier made the price in pain greater than the ecstasy for which it was paid. They needed patience and wisdom. How else to translate such omens of mortality and eternity. But there were no local guru-guides, and warning-points were crossed in a strange oblivion. The gold faded, which they had painted once to advertise the gold they proposed to make. Any business sprung from such a mulch was bound to embody its componential nightmare. For Center Street, that meant back to the banal realities of civic Portland, back into a debris those buildings housed before the bright new hangings and mandalas. The moral is not that we shall never get past the decay and greed of the fundamentalist American city, but that it takes currency of the most precise and impeccable specie even to begin our transit along the aeon. The same crap can do only the same tricks. And we know them well by now. That's our hypo-thetical life.

My participation in Herbie's Portland was fly-by-night and shal-low. I was amazed when I heard from Billie that Herbie thought I should quit my job at the college and run the Great Works Outlet. But suddenly I knew the artificiality by which I had come to town for a teaching job and how much was needed if I was to work my-self back there a second time. I found the store itself, with the rock music pounding away, hostile and hinged on unfulfilled violence. Among the artists I felt heavy-handed and patrician. The work I was doing cut me off not only from their radical chaos but from the excitement and comraderie they enjoyed in coming to terms with new forms. In one sense I was past it; in another sense I had never been thru it, and longed for its freedom and romance: to be at the beginning again, standing before the archetype and the ocean. If the longing became too great, I couldn't work at all. So I stayed out. Or I grazed the surface, part of me pretending to be too old and advanced, the other part boylike and innocent. And the Cape was one place no one visited; we were living in a tabooed district, and our unawareness of that made it impossible for anyone to lay on the antidote. As Billie put it when we left: "You are actually just as far, for my purposes, where you are as where you're going to be. So it's not as though anything's happening."

What the scene needed was native accuracy, intuitive local wis-dom. What I brought was outside intelligence, as exotic as Erebus, and in a form I could not yet live myself, and thus could not bring them on the level they were living. I was so accurate going one way the frustration coming back the other was devastating. But I never stopped once, except perhaps at the very end, to examine, just to examine, how detached from it all was my life. I had only mo-ments: a couple of gala experimental film evenings, like those I had run in Amherst and Ann Arbor before; a series of knockout poetry readings, one of them my own, and then Kelly, Snyder, Irby, Creeley, Dorn, Raworth, Duncan; a few brilliant classes, turning people on to Olson, Lévi-Strauss, Jung, Melville, Reich, Sauer; and the students who came from those transformed, on their own paths — many of whom lie now between India and Kansas. And none of it survived. They were ridiculous tropical flowers, lovely by their own intensity but incidental to the unfolding of the town. The bookstore has been replaced by the Good Day Market, with some of the stock pushed to the back where it forms a small browsing section for an ongoing organic food concern (a serious inroad in Herbie's empire), the bulk of it in storage, including a carton of all the *Io*'s and my books. The University of Maine Book-store returned their stock long ago, and even the library, at the very place I taught, tried to return a full set of *Io* thru their subscription agency. Before the movies and readings, the gun-wielding sadist controlled the arts at the school, and downtown was mainly rock and posters and drugs. For a moment, in the collegium cast by the visiting poets while they were there, the town and the college were joined, in the Mediaeval sense, and the rock music touched and was touched by a hieroglyphic ancestry (without which it was doomed to the zoo).

But I seem to have expected instant conversions, as much as I would have denied it at the time, as impossible as I knew that to be. The moment of Robert Kelly looking over Casco Bay and citing Olson with blazing accuracy was my moment, not Portland's. I had worked for it five hard years. And it was *my* walk along the beach with Tom Raworth, following the hitchhiker to his hut and col-lecting wood from among the stones. I stuck it thru with Creeley and Snyder, for I alone desperately required them. The town was not going to rally around events whose causes and ramifications they not only didn't understand but were still coming to in some absolutely different and appropriate way. And yet, as I carry the carton of *Io*'s back to the car, I feel I must have left something here. As I sit in the dungeon of the cafeteria with Don Anspach and David Fullam, the Sociology Department, eating the stale hamburgers, while the students queue up for their beloved behated grades, I imagine that the sheer twists and inspirations of my dilem-ma, my play for that one ounce of consciousness that would be the city also, must have left some sparks in the parapsychology of its air. And I also face that it may not be true, that the scales may be lighter than that, that such may be the slum principle of the world.

* * *

I sit with Billie in his loft. Things are worse than ever, he tells me. Boyfriend gone, no money, the dishes unwashed, the remodel-ing job around him half-finished in Beardsleyesque splendor, the rest crumbling brick: about to begin as a waiter in a lobster joint. He's losing the battle with Portland, yet where else is there? He can't just go to L.A. or New York anymore.

"What would feeling better mean?" I ask him. "The only reason we feel better is to delay our knowledge until we can handle it. Eventually we'll have to know every fucking thing."

He puts his arm around me as we walk up the stairs, the whole set of ambiguities between us. And a model, Tuta, who arrives while we are talking, treats our conversation from an aery perspective, like so many buttercups in the meadow in the sunlight, so many and too many and enough for enough to go on forever. It's damn painful, no matter how jivey we make it sound. She will pose for Billie on the roof when we are done. Until the real thing, it is just so much time wasted. Or because Billie feels that, I feel it, and her silent presence overwhelms us, as if we had a giant bird there and were pretending to talk about anything but surrealism. Pretending we could change any of this by our profound chatter.

VI

Around Exchange Street, Portland shares more with old Montreal than suburban Boston. When Billie and Erik began their great loft, it seemed like an eagle's palace in a slum. But my own vision was deceived by the Erebus masque, the mellow familiarity of the Center Street shops. Exchange Street had a small meeting-place park; stores of crafts, carpentry supplies, and sea materials; and local grocery markets; it was practical and self-sufficient in a time of excess. When people were really down and out, or beginning a precise new exercise, this was the place to nest down.

The Hollow Reed has opened Exchange Street to the public in the years we were away, serving as a reference point for the underlying cooled-out condition that spawned it. While a typical American organic food restaurant, with a social esprit Center Street never had about things like food, it is also a gourmet shop, right out of international Montreal. Erebus and scene remains moored in Haight-Ashbury commerce. And the whole issue of a boutique, which was the problem to begin with, is coming home with the swallows, bringing the wan appearance of the used furniture stores that made up this downtown wharf area at the end of another era, and from which these buildings were so optimistically reclaimed. Merchandise which was mildly irrelevant two years ago sits on the shelves, unbought, outrageous in the present context. Even Sunshine, Herb's trip back to used goods and reclaimed threads, is baroque, stylish, and high-priced. The jeans are washed and sewn, hung on rush hour racks. The cashier is the seamstress, and sits at the front desk sewing minute colorful amulets into the retreads, making them works of art.

Herb is sunning outside; he has the seamstress scratch an itch on his back. A longhaired kid from Ohio introduces himself, holds Herb's hand for a long time to check out the vibes, then asks where he can pitch a tent, his girl standing beside, silently spaced. Herbie suggests a farm in the country to the north. The kid stares at him hard, nodding. "They said you were the person to ask. Guess so."

A college professor from western New York State looking for a place by the ocean to camp with his children is the next to come looking for Herb; he is sent to Bath. Someone throws a rock thru a window in a condemned building; the glass falls behind the opening.

Who's that?

"He's the local Arica head."

The sense of violence is everywhere, but the rock seldom gets thrown. It's mainly sweet innocent smiles, hip jive. Herb runs his stores like fishing wharves, seeking out high school classmates and old friends, setting them up in positions the way the dealer lends his buddies boats. It's not that he digs being overseer, but the role is there and he takes it on assumption of his own benevolence. And he's been damn decent, given the way it usually goes. But we're all becoming thirty. The middle years of indecision are up; the conservative and genetic characteristics are winning out. Herb's vision was real, if only he could transfer it to new terrain. I sense that this is the height, and we'll work down from here, even as on the first meeting he flipped about our work, and then it came to mere regrets, expressed only years later. Our time is up.

The needle has not left the record on Center Street, but soon only the shell will remain, as velvet and ornate as the shells of the last commercial Portland. The Hollow Reed district touches on the possibility of a Third World city, its carpenters and young plumbers, its pottery studios and mimeo publishers, its medicinal psychotherapeutic bias, its co-op spirit and tie to the farms. The people work for less but retain the possibility that what a place makes and sells is commensurate with the world they live in. Center Street seems a blasphemous luxury: the confused relationships among people a direct result of the commerce. Those of the old crew do not travel back anymore. There are no hard feelings, but unless they keep to the integrity they have barely gained, they risk losing their sanity too.

* * *

The lobster fishermen of the first Cranberry Island text are the radical farmers of the final volume. The mediation lies in our use of either of them. And Portland sits in the middle ground, coastal city of an Abenaki-Hittite intelligence we can only imagine now, and that by the light of a candle long since snuffed.

VII

This is the summer, at Goddard, of the ecology revival meeting, and we are visited by Wilson Clark, sounding aeonics, end of fossil fuel, monocrop, disease, agriculture of famine. There is no way of knowing whether Wilson is as accurate as he is hot, but there is no disputing the ritual implication of his message or its connection with some real necessity that hangs in the summer air. If he offers no solutions, it is because he believes there are no solutions. He doesn't think solar conversion can pull it any better than nuclear fission; there is no free energy left. And that's also true, even without an accurate resource ledger: it is intolerable to go on taking their manna without the psychic acuity to measure its real planetary cost.

The New Alchemists follow Wilson: John Todd playing Robert Fludd. They propose a healing of nature, an exercise of humble sufficiency which, though futile against a general poisoning of the planet, seems the minimum clarity if we are to be human and responsible in our time. "You've all heard Wilson Clark," John says, "and he's probably taken ten years off your life." There is nervous laughter. "I think he's telling the truth. The bonds that hold life together are coming asunder." He speaks of deranged birds, psychotic fish, seas driven crazy. "If we can't save it any longer, we can at least depart with some nobility."

Their blueprints are of fish-pond cycles, aquaculture, small diverse farms with careful species and pest records, windmills, solar heat, methane engines. Their logos, though, lies in the precise consciousness of the human seeker, who is not a professional botanist but a lay scientist, in the tradition of those Mesolithic followers of Hermes who discovered the wandering gardens and orchards of the clone, ziggaruts in root hairs, proving, as we must prove, again, that the inside is larger always than the outside, and man stands only as a litness over the dark well of galactic and numerical unconsciousness, holds to it a stubborn flicker, his own being born a bare chicken's scratch from the abyss. No point any longer, says Crowley, in seeking the origins of tarot or the impossible conference of rabbis and mathematicians necessary to devise a ceaseless formula of significant connections. They must never have been. Those who bring gardens and card games and chess boards into this world know nothing of the source or novelty. The kings and wands, the knights and olive trees, if that's what they are: fill with unsuspected light just as their reigns would appear to be ended. We receive these things as we receive consciousness, and though we can certainly stand on ceremony, and refuse to budge, proof is not forthcoming. We may fulfill only a particular lineage; we may fulfill ancestral design, or the concurrence of our many lives. The atoms may die a total death upon leaving the body and entering the Sun. Our power is undiminished. We light the candle because we are able; nothing will tell us how or why. Nature lies in the same chaos and irresolution on either side of the imaginary veil, and the gods owe more to Horus than the impossible survival of Christ.

The old alchemists sought to perfect what nature had left imperfect in herself, but in so doing, they worked by indigenous principles, and kept to these, in the drama of the Stone, even at the expense of immediate success. Because they tapped the riddle gently, their resource was a dark and ever-dividing wisdom, in touch with the origins of ceaseless energy, the flow of numbers and pagan forms upon the surface figures of a slumbering creation. The new alchemists must be alchemists too. Yet they cannot recover the landscape of Hermes, nor can they ignore the cleverness of the materialist repairmen. They must find the rules as they fall to us now, the Emerald Tablet to be recovered from the beautiful but uninterpretable language in which it has come to us from holier times. Each time the domed fish-pond system fails a necessary attribute of heat or nutrition, moisture or predator, they adjust it only by recourse to initial properties of the system, its original resilience and health. They may not borrow a technological short-cut, however simple and proven its application. They may not intercede with heavy-duty machines at any stump along the way. They must be monks, beyond reproach, trying, like Greek middle voice verbs, the forces implicit, the trace minerals in stone, the bare heat of chemical conversion, open ever to the unknown properties of matter, the possible and famous consciousness of plants and even stones. This faces them prophetically, opaquely, and squarely; it is a true Sphynx.

They know all about poisons: lethal conditions breed stronger predators — a warning so clear it is written into every law of this planet from volcanoes to revolutions. They must write, or rewrite without reference, a lost Neolithic text, cataloguing in their own

Alexandria the genetic identities of billions of weeds and cultivates, the old gardners knew as wordlessly as the passage of goats and seeds thru mountain passes, in a memory system no Babylonian computer can replace. They must restore the ledgers of plant variety, microenvironmental adaptation, to a planet that wrote them, that continues to feed the sybil her lines. They are not in it per yield of vegetables and unit of protein; Paracelsus is their mentor, spurning Scott Nearing and Buckminster Fuller. Know it or not (and in time they will have to), they petition an ancient gnostic science whose messengers have been slaughtered or are asleep (or never were in the first place and so must be made again from the beginning of possibility), whose gods have forgotten us, if they were gods then; they petition it with no more hope of returned communication than the senders of 43,000 year intergalactic messages, without even knowing that they believe in such mysteries or want to. All those worries and doubts fall by the wayside as more and more their lives become valuable for inner reasons, as they can no longer waste them. They must be hermeticists first and farmers second, if they are to be farmers at all. For the puzzle they submit to the whirlwind is truly insoluble, either as an abstraction or in sheer numerical jackpot. Only by the direct access of their locale can they petition nature to heal herself; they have a voice as long as they are more into its articulation than the image of themselves as good physicians in a bad time. Hence, raise flowers along zigzag paths, indicators of playful submission equal to any whoring after agricultural and communal success. This is the only way the masters of pollen will hear them. Clearly they will be suspicious, for our whole lifetime at least, that anybody is trying to reach *them* and not the goods after the present run of treaty violations. *Just one more medicinal herb* must sound as heavy to them now as *just one more barrel of oil*.

Energy will not help the new alchemists, certainly not in the modern dwindling sun-star sense of the word; energy is too much and for the wrong reasons, an exercise in cornucopia and/or deprivation. The planet cannot sustain further extraction without some bitter inquiry.

They may arrive on the set with American laboratory skills, but soon after they are students of the Chinese science of feng-shui: there is an always-unknown balance of hills and waters, trees and open fields; there is an energy in the land for which the word energy is a ludicrous misnomer. Mental harmony and sexual rhythm wind with the streams thru the countryside, tipping their dragon breath to the graveyards, the garden mounds, the man who is, or by his deeds stands in place of, the heaven-annointed king — and how many nines (each made of two integers in jointed crossover) are ethically established by community lineages. Even as they climb, metaphorically, the golden staircase of Zosimos, they lay the peach-flower stream of Tae Ch'ion. They seek the graves of the boat people, but they do not know it. They seek the pyramids the pyramids of Egypt disguise, the granaries the rotten strawhouses of the Dogon stand as only reminders of; yet they cannot seek them until. Their goal is dragon trails, star-courses, a replica body made of shell and stone thru which nerves yet run; their goal is still, on paper, the garden of the rural counterculture, the Whole Earth Epilogue check-list. It is a wonder of our present age that the translators must join with the ecologists to reconstruct the Garden.

They are now in India, Mongolia, Central and North America, but it was at San Diego State that Todd took a class into the hills around that costly city and mapped the land, catalogued the species, depth of taproots, sources of water, the long-forgotten fact of there being a landscape at all. How poorly trained they were as biologists, though graduate students in a science of the name: so that their discovery alone became their training, their initiation, and, in the American sense, their radicalization. They found the shadow that sustained the desert, the aura of dug-in life around dessicated stone; they laid the plans for a village that might belong there, its windmills and terraced gardens. But the bulldozers followed them, tearing out feng-shui, laying the dead synthetic foundation for a development of luxury homes.

The fish piss into the garden, to grow the sunflowers, to feed the pigs, to feed the people, to feed the fish. It doesn't matter if it's good rock music or if the audience digs it all the way. It doesn't matter if the singer thinks he's Apollo. It has to hold up by itself, without recourse to some other system of innoculation that may not be around on the maiden voyage. It has to be *direct use of the Sun* in a sense that surely yet eludes us, and certainly not these secondary and lethal suns we have been using and petition now almost hysterically to bail us out again.

* * *

And in Boulder it is the summer when the Buddhists gather with their own translators at Naropa, in continuity with a Tenth Century university of Northern India. In this age of spiritual darkness, as the saying goes, they must recover the texts, despite the romantic fallacy of such a saying. Not a joyous astrodome celebration of

peace and love, but in preparation of the dharma for the passage
thru the darkness, thru kali yuga. Although the different lineages of
Buddhists mingle in the grace of the tantra, because America has
made this emergence possible and direct, there is no answer, no
historical or personal resolution; it goes back thru the psychocul-
tural web, conscious and unso, from which individuality must arise,
in the precision of Tibetan and Mongolian terms, to the rightness of
the vows. "Do you mean I have to devote my whole life to this?"
one student asks Trungpa after a lecture.

"You got it," he says, with a smile and mudra.

Experience itself is the pale genosis, the many-colored gnosis
cannot draw them out of, even for an instant, into a brighter light.
In this muddled time, terminology is more crucial than ecstasy.
Bare attention to the planet, the cause of sorrow and joy. The Al-
chemists prove this when they collect data on the resistances of
cabbages and bean species to pests and fungi climate by climate,
world zone by world zone. Which is exactly how they must go back
and forth from Sanskrit to Tibetan to American to the silence be-
yond the words. To the source of the wisdom, even if it has never
existed as such on this planet; no better time, no other time. It is
not just the deliverance of all sentient beings, that boddhisattva
function; they must contact the bare possibility in which deliver-
ance poses itself as a mission, without the agonizing sacrifices of the
savior. There is no such thing as a moment of spiritual darkness.
But it would not be upon us if we did not require it.

* * *

The centuries have flown past, in our false historical conscious-
ness; the debris of civilization occurs now in piles so huge we cannot
see them, and we have lost the patience and wisdom to sort and
reuse. We act as though our lives are somehow more hypothetical
and guaranteed than the lives of those who came before us. But
nothing can be left off the life-raft if survival is to be anything but
problematic. Psychoanalysis is peculiarly conservative, and if it is
the culture at stake, it becomes a sociology, damned to an accept-
ance of wearying urban symptoms. That very junk which turns in
the wind as the blade of a windmill comes to the aid of the dreamer
at the moment his dreams lose him, in the form of an Eighth Cen-
tury text, as syntactically subject to wind resistance and subject-
object steering. What was once a gluttonry, a painstaking clarity,
is now but a hollow reed, and the music we play thru it, in the full
reduction of its substance, in the knowing we were promised it once

instead of this, is so much more to us than our livelihood, even should Grandfather Clock be restored. I could write it as a science fiction story beginning on the Lower East Side; more people would read it, but the hopeless certainty of such a plot, running the full gamut from *Childhood's End* to *The Night of the Auk* would leave us back in the precise modernism of Godot. Better to abandon the thread while it still lies in murky waters. If it's even the thread.

VIII

I sit in the Terriens' backyard and play with Miranda in the grass, pulling her up and down, letting her grip and tear at the stalks and blades. I lie with my head beside hers and roll with her down a small hill.

There are passes of patience and tenderness, almost solar in their generosity; they are followed by perverse rutted breaks in attention. She cries long and hard and nothing I can do returns the calm.

The children tunnel their cars under the unplanted garden, a damp red earth, worked into roads and villages. The bees wander from flower to flower, their ranges crossing, coming back across the pastures to Suzi's hive. The gulls hang out beyond, and the sweet dew and mist from the last rains and moons is blown thru the air, either directly off petal surfaces, or from tubes inside flowers, which have begun to turn them to sugar and fruit.

Suzi is melancholy; her talk is of fatal diseases, how people she knows are dying. She says we are not living as long as we used to. Maybe the poisons are getting to us. Yet she speaks from a distance, as though considering an idea for the first time — but which idea?: that she is no longer a child?, that she is as fragile in her mortality as in her emotional tangency? Her husband lies in the next room, hung over from his midnight stomach attack, not coming out from there our whole visit (her voice still in my ears, waking us, whispering in the darkness how good it is we are here to watch the kids while she takes him to the hospital). I thought then, as I do now, how *we* were the cause of his malaise, perhaps the sole immediate cause, the acuteness of it the acuteness of his unrevealed discomfort with our lives — realizing also they would not accept that version because, for all the talk of them these days, no one believes in vibrations; no one wants the pain of living among them, or to feel their pueblo responsibility to keep a sun alive in their hearts (even the origin of life in the sea, which is still the sea).

The Terriens are troubled for reasons in the world I intuit but have no words for. They are the reasons I am troubled, but also not the reasons. I know that a life grows within us as the powers of our formation shrink into their final orbits, those rings of the million-fold zodiac, whose million is the sky, and whose millionth is our identical bodies. All extraneous furniture is removed, and the house becomes a sanctuary. I know marriage is a fragile bark, and every marriage is windswept. What else is possible if we remain on the Earth and share planet-wide influences? The rap against staying to-gether is heavy now, and accurate in our range; it would seem more practical, even more responsible, to love everyone. They need it so much more, and so do we. Yet we take on new science only at the cost of old science. And the most ancient text becomes the most despised. Its Palaeolithic clarity is scorned in the current scheme that cave-dwellers abandon forever the origins and necessities of Choukoutein, Lascaux — that new forms will keep us from the legacy of such tyrannical kings, that our choice of freedom makes us free. As if we had the option, let alone the right.

Just like everyone else we sit around watching each other, hoping to pick up clues, praying we are doing it right, or not so wrong we won't know what happened. At least let us know what happened, so we don't have to come back and do it again.

The troubles we have with each other, Lindy and I, are more painful than the troubles we have with anyone else in the world, because they are the residue of deep and acknowledged engagement over ten years. They are what persists when novelty and compro-mise wear off, as the courting wanes into a garden filled with fa-miliar weeds, and we do not have the energy to keep weeding at the height of summer when the apple tree calls us too. To assume that we could break apart and go with other people, and thus evade the problems, is to forget, conveniently and naively, that what we have come to, together, is what each of us, more or less, will come to with anyone after this length of time. Now is the real beginning, now that we have gotten beyond the formal chamber. There are thousands of cults and temples, but we have chosen this one. And sexual energy, which calls us everywhere, is a truly unknown power in our time. It can be used for whatever we will use it for. It has neither to be the sun nor the whole of passion in life. Yet it can swallow these if we want. Or it can work in tiny spaces and against the vast and numb inner weight. We are literal only in our despair.

* * *

We spend time picking out trinkets at Erebus in exchange for our books, big goblet beer glasses. We eat at the Hollow Reed, and get into the spirit of squash and bean soup and carob-date milk shakes. With only Miranda, the years seem to have gone backwards. We don't feel young, but the feeling of ourselves as a young couple with our newborn child is restorative. We can't keep the innocence, and we can't, if we are to survive as a family, scorn the sources of its gentle virtue.

We visit the old places; poor Rocky's Sunoco has been sold twice over, and Rocky is gone. Wilbur isn't at the post office, but the postmen gather around me and shake my hand. They are marvellous. They make me feel it may all yet be possible. In the old days they sang songs suggested by the names of bookstores to which I shipped *Io* and formed rowdy chorus lines, arm-in-arm, leg-kicking, from window to window, while the public, in their vertical lines, applauded, nobody begrudging the time. The South Portland post office is a joy, and I choose to honor it here so I won't forget elsewhere, and honor Wilbur Tucker, of Kansas City, and believe it or not, Plainfield, Vermont ("Keep coming," he said, as I broke down where we were going into more and more specific locales). They had another option: to be as sour as the people in the Montpelier bus depot. And by choosing this one, they opened the world to the same sunlight that is inside a deck of tarot cards, if we would but use them. Because that light is everywhere, and comes, on the side of the angels, from taking life as holy, and everywhere responsive to the light that brings it into being. The old sun lit the South Portland Post Office on the day that Wilbur Tucker and his gang read Black Sparrow off a package and ran around tweeting like blackbirds in a field of grain, then joined arm in arm for a chorus of "When the Swallows Fly Back to Capistrano." My applause, Wilber; four years later, after seeing many an establishment stand there and hassle its already-haggard clientele with the indulgence of their own irritation. I consider the South Portland Post Office a school of higher learning and a shrine.

IX

Beda and I sit there looking at each other. I'm not sure what I feel or what it is about her that moves me so deeply. I am moved simply because she is there, and time allows it.

In the beginning I took her calm and spiritual devotion as the link between us. We were pilgrims on adjoining paths, paired in some previous hypothetical existence. Now it seems odd I even thought of spiritual things in that way, or sought to legitimize our friendship by calling it spiritual, and reaching, as I do, for science fiction stars when there is earth beneath me, solid strength-giving earth, subterranean powers beneath again. The path is the path all beings are on, no matter their expressed concerns. It was not Beda's spirituality or my cosmic vision. We abandon those hoaxes willingly tonight; we have our meeting in oblong secular space, disorderly rattly time, and yet the link remains. We seem now, in the best sense, twins. Enough has passed for me to know her entry into my life does not break my link with Lindy, nor does it remove her; she was always gentle, un-dire. ......has passed for me to know there is no other such person. She is not the invention of my discontent and romantic questing. She fulfills none of that.

Either I don't know who she is, or she is one of the only people I know. I seem to have said each thing a moment too late for it still to be necessary. She jars me out of Portland solipsism. She makes each moment critical again. I have wasted two years fearing a choice, which was just another of my exaggerations, hanging life on a wall like a picture and forgetting it. She is not someone who would write or call, and in the end I have to go see her, despite finding out too late where she lives, despite the eleventh hour drive to Scarborough, despite her present constellation with a man. The gift is to see her, to have her see me. That's where we left off. If I miss on it for reasons of emotional confusion, I might as well sell out to the emotions altogether. Instead, I find that things are far more possible, far more hopeful and like me than I feared.

The childhood is over: in the sense I have said — *I had a childhood*. I no longer want its history or to be the brazen recovery from sad loveless years, relived in recurrent symptomatic form. Perhaps I saw when I was nineteen I couldn't make it, certainly not all of it. So I set some things aside, the most scarred and irresolvable, and took the energies I had, the calm objective knowledge, the intimations of stars and history, the tarot cards, the books I loved, the emotional open-ness from having fought the whole time against having them take my vulnerability too. And the rest: the terrors, the men, the hauntings, the disembodied broken-ness, could be left behind, to serve, at best, as negative energy for a life. I felt, maybe even, I would never have to meet them again, if I was lucky. I had no desire or necessity to be whole; if I could live at all, I would gladly sacrifice it.

And all these years that other material has taken on shapes and tried to reach me, and I have met with the shapes and eased them back. I have allowed them to exist, in the best of detentes, because the alternative was worse. I have built their altar and can build it no longer. They are now stronger than me, and I have a kingdom worth invading. There are no more deals. What if I do want to live the life? What if I want to defy the doctors and rise from the premature coffin? What if it is not the false sorrow but the false assurance of happiness that binds me?

Just because they tried to kill me doesn't mean I have to survive in some bastard way to assuage their guilt in a gradual or mediocre process of the years.

And now, as then, she stands at the top of the stairs, looking down at me thru the hole in the spiral, smiling. And when I reach the bottom I look back up at her once more. We have come as wise goatmen to each others' desert births, bringing gifts the stars hold in keeping for us only because the Earth cannot; we would not want the Earth to and so confuse our lives again for mere omens and signs. I will never understand it and I will never change it. It will be that way forever, and I can always go back to it. The grace and restraint are astounding in such a pagan dance.

X

The Take on Mount Desert, June 15, 1974
(Bernard overlooking Bass Harbor)

Chipmunk runs into twisted tree bottom. Grass and wind turn in stray influences of sun, devil's paint brushes in full bloom, red-orange to the shore. The fields above the wharves are abandoned. Their dirt is punctured by rocks so large and frequent it seems a single stone; the topsoil is that thin. Classic glacial till. Coarse sandy loam busted by the bedrock, firmed in the Holocene present. The sea is the real garden; the sea alone stands above an older archaeology (re: Sauer's claim that the Atlantic around England is more fertile per acre than her planted fields).

Luxuriance aside, what is in the undergrowth comes up. Old matter of older science. What is in the atom burns thru the molecule, and the molecule lights the aura of the cell. The soil is the palpable medium, the carryover. The Greek in us holds to chemical and physical properties, exclusive. Fire and water work upon it, from within as from without; ash and rust are carried thru the equation, until the elemental is crowned again. And worms breathe; there must be nitrogen; there must be air.

The trees are bent and usurped. It is not clear if it is the composition of the soil reflected in the arches, or the total atmospheric condition — gravity, light, moisture — driven thru the dancers in their dance. Stunted apples. Evergreens trapped among the deciduous. Pine and birch, cedar and quaking aspen. Fallen against rooted trees. Old man's beard hangs everywhere in the branches, among the candles and blossoms, as the wind shifts and turns thru them, its last notes caught in the nerves of the aspen, which alone continue to play them when the wind is gone.

The undercropping is granite and pegmatite. Diorite is the basic island; dark diabase lies in its veins. Spike moss and staghorn moss grow upon the stone, markings of the fragile loom. Where the stone yields to the ground, forests of groundpine and groundcedar form, themselves swallowed in rib grass and migratory orders. The stone reappears always, with new veins, flashes of mica, silicon, calcium, and upon that barely animate surface, lichens of various colors, purple and white and light green. If they are like craters on the face of the Moon, it is a relationship of acquired motions, thirsty fungus splotches in harmony with cold geologic puncture and crack.

A grape red ant walks across the stone.

The tide flows into the harbor in regular waves, their reflections

on the boatsides like flocks of silver undulating birds, rising and
falling about a fixed point in another dimension. The gulls call out
as they cross the harbor, move from perch to perch. Their voices
begin with an animal earthiness, rise thru a human tone, and pass
out into something jaggedly alien. I seem to hear the dialogues of a
tribe of incomplete people, crying to each other, hungry and aroused,
yet mastering geographies whose speed would leave us breathless.
And — with the flowing of the water, ceaseless, the same of the
Moon's mastery too, the continuous bird language and wind music,
the irregular passages of breezes, falling leaves, and petals, the dash
of the chipmunk, the eternity of light, color, gravity, and locale —
it seems almost that *we* are the objects that are in the way. We are
the impediments. Without us, consciousness flows.

* * *

Kevin Roth brings his boat into the wharf. I learn his name from
Norwood Peabody, an old lumberman still hanging around making
himself useful. "He's not your usual fisherman. He's from the Bronx,
New York." At sight he's a healthy ageless forty, sprouts of red hair
and stray beard. It's a new mystery to me why the others tolerate
someone from so blatant a carpetbagging origin. Two years have
passed in a supposed research study, and I realize I know little again
about what's really happening, or was then. The very search for mean-
ing obliterates it. Should I count traps or wait out my unproven ob-
servations? What will the old guard say?

Kevin finishes his business with Jasper down below, and then
works his way up to the dock where Norwood helps him unload.
The study is over. I'm not going to return with note-pad and pen,
from the old days. I feel silent, even silenced, in some very final
way. I work on the unloading; the traps are waterlogged and still
bear their weighting flatstones; I can barely lift them, so half-lift,
half-drag them along the wharf. There is an additional problem; for
as Jasper joins us, bad back and all, he begins muttering about the
wasteful amount of twine used. Kevin is cheerfully embarrassed.
Jasper is saying something like: "So much netting you can buy us
out and we'll sell you the front door."

After the job is done, Kevin says he'll answer some questions. He's
not overjoyed about it, maybe a bit bemused. I find out he had a
supervisory job in engineering in New York, does some of the same
in eastern Maine; he lobsters when he can. He says he moved up
here with his wife a few years ago, but had been coming before that
for fifteen years. It's only later and from another source I learn that

his wife has owned a house in town for a great many more than fif-
teen years, and there was another husband. Which is how he's seen:
the man now living in that woman's house, a point of reference
they always keep on islands.

My final question reflects my own weariness as much as his. Do
you like lobsterfishing?

He hunches over and nods many times, pure macho. "Look, man,
I don't do anything I don't like."

* * *

There's a new hired man, Silas; Oswald has left to drive the
school bus. The fishermen are paid now once a week, with credit
taken out of each payment, instead of the old way, every load, in
cash, with the books upstairs: out of sight, out of mind. Cashflow
is tighter. And many of the fathers are no longer fishing; their sons
have replaced them. Aubrey Fowler works for the park, but Jim
Fowler goes, and though Fred Beal has heart trouble, he still lob-
sters, still eats hot dogs and candy bars. "Just because I'm on a
special diet doesn't mean I've gotta go without good food." Later
he tells me, "There ain't no lobsters out there to catch, but I'll bet
you every man at this wharf is fishing twice as much traps as he
was when you was here before; it's human nature." More traps, less
catch: both absolute figures, nothing relative, nothing to ameliorate
them.

Wendell has taken *his* traps up and is about to go handlining with
Marlon Bridges, who has a boatload of fancy new radar. A lot of
good that does Jasper. His business is lobster, a few scallops on the
side, and in season. But the real story of Wendell is his work out on
the islands and beyond. He takes a group from College of the At-
lantic whale-observing past Mount Desert Rock; another group goes
with him to Little Duck Island, bird-watching and tagging. "There's
quite a population in the area." What were markers at sea have be-
come colonies, respites, even enlightenments — for those fishermen
who will realize there is more than fish out there, always was.
There's a gestalt therapy group on Great Duck; the man who bought
the island years ago has returned and brought with him a method-
ology, filling with intense hard-working people a land that has been
empty since the farms were abandoned. They face our collective
mental illness, with the shags and gulls. They realize our lost thera-
pies lack insight, but our original principle recovers what it can. They
will form groups and work toward clarity, personal freedom. They
will entertain people from mental hospitals, hoping, with the sea,

to erode coarse barriers institutions have imposed to obscure those of society. There is a family from Albuquerque Wendell is ferrying over, or did yesterday, and now has been invited there for tea and lunch in the midst of hauling his traps. It is not that times change; it is that the essential location of places among places is realized. Wendell is a new age ferryman, for an ecological college, for scientists mapping bird-migration and whale-population, for collectors of solar data and gestalt therapists. His affinity is Hermes, Mercury is the metal; he is the go-between for remote but approaching connections. He has a steady income for the first time in his life (except for the 36 hours he lasted at the sardine factory after his marriage, handing out fish to the cursing women, battered like the doughboy, until he took his ship out into the water and fished the offshore shoals). It is not only money; he is learning things he finds he cannot any longer do without. With the I Ching, Dane Rudhyar, a garden, and a mulch heap, he is keeping late late hours for an easterner, but the discipline remains, subtly removed, and some of his older fishing partners, after abandoning him as loony, are looking again. Wendell is getting very smart very fast in a dangerous and holy text. It may not be fish, but it does recall the fishermen's lineage, when Marduk was king and Tiamat was the abyss. He'll be a true Phoenician hardliner, if he survives, not just the aroused sea and fragmented rocky garden, but the later rebellion of the family and the mind.

One day, when he came into the wharf for gas, boat empty, but a good day's ferrying on the islands, an exasperated Jasper, hungry for lobsters, exclaimed: "You, you, you bird!"

* * *

Kevin is trying to steer his boat over to the lower wharf to the pumps, but the tide is bothering him. He keeps missing the angle and going back out to try again. Then he smashes into the corner of the lobstercars. Jasper watches with majestic scorn. Norwood turns on the gas above.

How did he learn lobsterfishing?, I ask Jasper.

He gives me a good long look, then says: "He didn't."

* * *

The objects are waterlogged; the surfaces are scarred and pitted; the buoys hang muted from the sheds. The wooden els are collapsing, twisting apart; whole sections of them have caved in and lie upon the wharf; the beams and planks are chipped and cracked; the tops

of posts are mashed and splintered. Salt has come out of the sea
and covered the facing with the intricate corrosive delicacy of a
lathe. It is too late now; it is doubtful that any of this can be re-
placed or done over again. We make it from here with what is left.
Or we don't make it from here. The same. The roofs are littered
with crab shells and gull shit. The ocean bears a ripe and rough de-
bris; pink blastulas swollen from germ cells, fine lithe underwater
plants, wood and glass and stone and shells, smoothed and lightened
eaten thru with tiny holes. The spirals retain their basic spiral shape,
and the urchins that shoot out spiny harden about the yoke, their
arrows forever slung. There is a darkness on the beach, of tar and
oil and heavy rags, boats pulled up to dry and be reskinned. There
is a continuity of work enmeshed with the continuity of time. And
between the large and the small, there is the ceaseless rushing of
shape into shape, holes into solidity, branching into mass. The sea-
weed covers the stones and has dried into a topsoil; the bubbles
oscillate with potency at a speed slower than we can see; other
speeds are more rapid, if discernible at all. The engines clatter, the
hammers pound, never solidly striking the nail, however flush they
hit. There are sudden drops of metal and bursts of radio noise.
The engine catch and fly against their abrasive parts for spells. It is
all incomplete combustion, and human beings stand in the center
of that, almost oblivious of what it is, what it could be if it were
complete, or would rest in the silence of its imperfection. But no,
man makes it by activity, by absurd machinery, by his work. The
gulls continue to unleash their substance, and the tide brings the
water in as the background of every motion, broken by the boats
as it pours by them. I could have come back here at any time and
seen the same thing, from the sequence of different things: each
present serial compacted moment stands, against each other mo-
ment, and against the probable, and because it happens we see it,
and because it dashes itself out against the substantiality of form,
it dies gasping into the next moment, and the figures in the conti-
nuity sit motionless, as though waiting to be carried from zone to
zone of equal undisturbed light.

* * *

Sewall Alley's lobster place is under new ownership, its name
changed to Gull Stone; Warren Pinkham is the proprietor. "We buy
all kinds of fish now," he says, "not just lobster. Clams, shrimp,
flatfish, cod, haddock, hake, halibut. And we do the speculatin'
for the fisherman. Used to be he'd get the going price per pound.

211

If it was haddock he'd get forty cents. If it was grey sole, he'd get his quarter. The fish all went to Boston, and the speculatin' was done there. Then the fisherman, he'd get the blue sheet out of Boston and he'd figure we was cheating him. That sheet's a crock of shit. If it says haddock at fifty-seven cents, that means fifty-seven cents is the *highest* haddock got on that day, and it might have been there for just a few minutes. But you know as well as I do that all the fish doesn't belong in Boston. Now take your hake and cod; that goes to Baltimore where they make fish flakes out of it; you'd get piddling prices in New York or Boston, but it's black food, you know, the black people eat it. Now, grey sole. You can't *give* it away here; people say it's not a fish. Fillet it and take it to New York and it's a luxury. Send your herring to Chicago; the Polish people love it. I get my three cents a pound for packing, no matter what the price; I mean it takes the same to pack it. So I'm not competing against the fisherman. But I send it straight to the real market, and if that's Baltimore I know better than to get there thru Boston."

Who owns this wharf now?

"A summer boy. He's been coming to the Island a number of years and there's lots of family property around. He manufactures Rolls Royce jet engines, so you can't say he knows much about the fishing business; but he's interested in fishing, boats, the resources of the sea."

What did you do before this?

"I drove truck. All over the goddamn place. Nova Scotia, New Brunswick, Newfoundland, Cape Breton, Magdelan Islands, Prince Edward. I know the area pretty well. But I got tired of driving. I grew up in Manset right over here, so you might say I'm back close to home."

Is the owner trying to make money at it, or is it more for sport?

"Well, he doesn't have to make money, so he can afford to keep a business when the fishing's bad. I'm glad it's not my money. We take some risks. Over in Pretty Marsh we're growing our own oysters. We put in 100,000 seed last year and another 100,000 this year. It comes from California, all of it in a little jar, $330. We don't expect to make much money, but we're experimentin' with mariculture, and we're going to have oysters to sell."

How does it work?

"Well, you put them on trays with a screen, and you brush the algae off every now and then to keep the water circulatin'. After a month you go to heavy mesh; then in the winter you anchor it down in the deeper water. You pull it back out in the spring."

You must have to keep moving them to bigger containers.

"It's like a pregnant woman; she gotta keep wearin' bigger clothes."

What do you think's happening with the fishing business now?

"We're on bad times. The market's good, but the fish aren't out there. And the market isn't as good as it should be. Haddock should be up higher; so should cod; but it's not even up to last summer, and the fish are scarcer."

Why do you suppose that is?

"It's an unsettled situation. The real answer isn't here and it isn't in Boston or Baltimore; it's in Washington. The government's cut down on all the foreign aid to South America, but they were *really* subsidizing the American fishermen. Because Latins'd turn right around and buy fish with it. It was just one bank account to another. Now, with the food shortage and some of them regimes down there, it's all over. No more subsidy. Cod's ten cents a pound; last summer it was eighteen all the way up to thirty cents. They know it's gonna have to be sold here. When I was in Canada, I worked for United Maritime Fisheries. And that was a big company, the biggest, like a government corporation. Now when they knew Haiti and the Dominican Republic weren't going to get their dollars from Uncle Sam, they wouldn't send them any fish. They might as well drop them back in the sea because they weren't going to get paid."

Why do you think the supply's down?

"Well, as far as lobsters go, they're putting themselves out of business. There's no unity. At the Maine Lobsterman's Association, everyone goes and everyone talks; you have one idea and they're all shouting. They can't agree to representatives; they don't trust one another. Now in Canada, the government runs it; they say when you can fish and when you can't; and they work it so the fishermen catch more in two months of the year in Nova Scotia than they catch fishing the whole year here. And it makes sense. There aren't that many lobsters out there that you need more than two months. But they're greedy; they don't want anyone else getting them; they all want to do something about conservation, but they don't listen to one another; there are as many solutions as there are fishermen. Now the catch is off twenty five per cent this year. It may be a late fall like last year and things'll pick up. They're talking about regulatin' the lobster licenses, and I think now there's a limit; but people are buying them when the kid is age two, just in case they want to go fishing later on; they're payin' their ten dollars a year and deprivin' someone else. I guess you can't blame them. But if you ask me about the offshore fishing, it's clear it's the Russians that are catching all the fish."

Wendell Seavey says he won't believe it till he sees a hammer and sickle on the ship.

"Well, that's not hard. If you go from here to Nova Scotia you'll see the hammer and sickle more than you want to remember. You take the ferry, and that's all it is, a tour of Russian ships. It's a whole Soviet fleet. And you won't see a sea gull around those Russians because they leave nothing. They suck it right up, bottom and all, and they process it at sea. There's no waste. All kinds of fish go in there, and the racks and scales are ground up too. They make fish meal out of it. You see they've got these mother ships that have the factories right on them, and they're maybe six hundred, seven hundred feet long; then they've got the fishing vessels; they're two hundred, three hundred feet long. The fishing vessels go out and bring their catch to the mother vessel, and the mother vessel processes it and then another ship comes to take it back to Russia. They don't even have to fuel; the tanker just comes with its snorkle tube and fills them up. The crew stays out there fishing six years. And the only reason they come home then is six years is the life of the engine. When they've gone thru a spot, nothing lives. It's like running an army. Your private fisherman can't compete with that kind of operation. He's got maybe $10,000, complete investment. These ships have got the whole Soviet government behind them."

It's moon rocket technology.

"Right, and I'm competin' with my tin can and stick of dynamite."

* * *

In the back room of his place in Bass Harbor, Emery Levesque is cutting haddock fillets, one after another with his perfect hand. His thumb is heavily bandaged from a single miss. The knife's not the only thing that's sharp. Thurston Davis is hanging around looking for work after the weekend. He was on a fishing boat last winter when some high-hanging gear fell on his head. He carries a skull plate and keeps off the water. He's tending a garden, drinking a good deal of beer, the summer passes. He wants to grow cucumbers and give them away to the whole island. He's going to have really fat tomatoes. Emery cuts away, listening.

"Hey, how did you get those big tomatoes that year? Did you buy fertilizer?"

"No, just put manure in the watering can, poured that on them. They were so many I was giving them away."

"Grew like mothafuckas, didn't they?"

Can you use those?, I ask, pointing to the haddock racks.

"Not unless you want every woodchuck and cat on the Island visiting your garden," Emery says.

There's a long silence as the work goes on. I talk a bit about how different things seem.

"It's all the same," says Emery. "You might think it changes, but it never does. That's the mistake everyone makes. They think they see change. But they don't, not really." One fish after another, cutting them off and tossing away the racks.

Has the new wharf taken away any business?

"I've got all the fishermen I can handle. I don't want any new business."

You're not looking for more?

"There's no room on the wharf. It's so littered with traps where are we to put the cod flakes? One man pulled up four hundred yesterday to go trawling. You can't even walk thru."

"That Robert Torrey ain't too fierce, is he Emery," says one of the kids, hosing down the tables.

"Why should he be?" says Thurston. "He went out after haddock and came back with eighty pounds of catfish, at six cents a pound."

"The gill nets are doing something," tries the kid.

"They did last year," Emery says.

"You just set'em down out there like a trap," says Thurston. "It's a great way to catch fish."

"The trouble with fishing," says the kid, "is everyone's always fighting. There's no peace."

"Now Charlie Cleaves he jumped a boat out there on Long Island, didn't he?" Emery adds.

"Gun and all," says Thurston.

"They cut him for thirty pair," insists the kid. "That's a thousand dollars worth of gear."

The wharf is like a public park. They play out the life while they work, enjoying the details and turnabouts. It doesn't matter that everyone's heard Homer sing it. It doesn't matter who's boss and who's hoser and who's got a bum leg and plate in his head.

Outside the dirty window, sea gull wings flash streaks of light across the walls.

* * *

Jasper stands up by the gas pumps watching for his lobsterboats to come back in. There are only a couple out, the rest are trawling and handlining. "Well," he says, " the price of lobsters is going up to a dollar seventy on Monday, and that's gonna make these fellas pretty ugly, taking all their traps up."

How do you know?

"That's something that's hard to explain."

The wardens' boat arrives, new and official, looking like a police car. Jasper guffaws. "This ain't where they're supposed to be at the time of day. But I suppose you can't expect them to know that." The wardens stride onto the floating dock, packing guns, and stand by their boat joking with Jasper while the gas is pumped.

Some fishermen are talking about the time Oswald fell in the water. The son, just as big as the father, lost his footing on the edge of the lobster cars and handed Oswald the crate at just the wrong moment. "When he bobbed up in the water, first thing he said was: 'You stopped me in a vital place.' "

Young Ken Parsley, without a fishing father, is wondering aloud who he can beg traps from so he can get twenty to set out in the harbor and fish by rowboat.

"Jasper's always complaining about my lobsters," he tells me. "He says, 'What's wrong with that one? Why're you bringing me cripples?' "

On the other side of the wharf, someone is asking Fred Beal if he's going to see a doctor. "Doctor? I might, one of these days."

Now Jasper comes up the plank and stands by the gas pumps again. There is a man in a navy blue shirt driving his boat in toward the wharf. Who's that?, I ask him.

"That's a professor. Can't you tell?"

The professor ties his boat and walks up the plank. "Good afternoon," he says to Jasper.

"Afternoon? Around here this is known as evening."

The man smiles graciously and continues on. After a few minutes Jasper yawns and walks toward the bait shed. There is a car parked in front of it, inconveniently, and he gets in.

It was good talking to you, I say.

"Oh, I'm not going far." And, in fact, he's not. He sits in the front seat for a couple of minutes, thoughtful, then laughs it off, backs into another parking space, and returns to the pumps.

* * *

The sounds of the harbor echo in each other, and the works of man, as smith, as fisher, as dealer, go on. I feel alien to this Earth, and yet I am of the Earth for good. The Martian and utopian attraction is just the Earth in other ways. My mood is central, because for all I've thought and done, there is little I really know. And I am ready to admit it. I will sacrifice the angel to the restless hollow that precedes it. But I will not give up hope of its return.

It is not that I know nothing. If I knew nothing it would be easy. What holds together for me, what accuracy I have, drives me to the threshold of clarity. It seems just in front of me, the solution, the easing, an entry. If I am in a museum, the guards stand watch. The priceless treasure is in some hidden vault. Only its replica sits behind sealed glass. But they don't know that. They guard the whole damn thing. And I have no idea which vault or even by what number system the position is concealed. I might as well turn around and go back. The detour is a thousand years. Longer than I will live.

I cannot enter new territory, and I cannot retreat into old. The daydream I play over and over in my mind has no interest. I understand it too well. I understand the motivations. I would like to have it hold water. But then I would *never* get there.

In a conversation with Heisenberg, Neils Bohr suggested, very reasonably, that Darwinian theory was based on two *independent* assumptions. Only one of these requires nature's testing of living forms and seeming choice of the most viable; the other makes a brave assumption that new forms arise only in chance dislocations of genetic continuity, including, of course, the accidental occurence itself of a mode of biological replication. No doubt all this in the harbor has been submitted to nature, and if it has been found wanting, it remains in compromise, and if it is yet to be found wanting, it will not be able to survive. The undergrowth contains in it only the traces it does, and though our imagination is boundless, we are not the kings of creation, and we cannot set our own terms. Nor can nature steal wrongfully from us what we can maintain, even in excess. But has all this in the harbor, and I too, in this recording *of* it, come about by chance also, chance submitted to the prior victor of chance, and is that what my flight from gnostic vision has taken me to, a pessimism beyond despair? Or is that only how I must see it to understand how desperately precise the whole thing is, and how rooted in an actual science of forms these trees and flowers and emotions are? If it is to become as lovely again as it was, and if it is to lead me to the outwashes of a hermetic and golden kingdom upon the alfalfa-barley fields, I must know how to plant it by bare indigenous seed. There will be no more drab suffient labor or relic desire. Or there will be no second chance.

Until then, if ever, I will have to take it this way, as it is given.

I loved this island, but I have no sympathy for it, in the Mediaeval sense; medicinally, it drives me away, its unmitigated macho and human spoilage, even the therpaists flying gaily over the mountains in their $30,000 golden airplane. It is a poison I must swallow, oblique to my condition always, obscurely as the different paths to different wharves scattered in the undergrowth of Bass Harbor, the unoccupied house in their center. The confusion is exactly the impossibility of being encyclopedic about their origin, either botanic or human. It is the same confusion as not knowing which one to take, and by taking, to abandon the others. I stand above the harbor, master of a text the ground knows only as weeds, the fishermen throw back, by their voyages, onto an ancient windy Atlantic.

Obscurity of purpose, but exactness of purpose.

Across both sides, and the water between, in the tide and the motion of clouds and sky, yet invisibly, the letters come floating back into the world, to spell the world, and they are not atoms, they are not phonemes, but it is still: *the letters come back into the world*, washed as soft as glass is when the ocean delivers it upon the shore.

The shadows blow with entries of light. White petals litter the grass and stone, as in a kept garden. Up by the road are buttercups and clovers, herbal flowers wild and absolved of responsibility. Ants crawl in among the dandelion heads, sucking the orange out of them. Like bees they return to the hives, bearing all they find that is antlike, crumbs and seeds and string, and the bodies of other ants.

If it is hermetic, it is so by a different version than it is atomic and physical. Uncertainty principle does not mean *my* uncertainty; it proves only that in a certain procedure, in a defined sequence of activities, it is possible to come to a point, an absolutely external and verifiable point, that does not enter into the world's activities. The paradox is purely situational. The basic facts of matter are contradictory, if we are to be men. Not unknown, not unsolved, not that we are in need of more comprehensive procedure or better apparatus. They are observed, and observation establishes uncertainty as a fact, a condition of their substantiation, not an admission of ignorance. There is a veil between here and there at least as formidable as the veil between mental beings and atomic pebbles, never to be ripped from thence: *never*, with all that that implies. The uncertainty in Taoism and Buddhism, as well as the complementarity, is of another order, arrived at in a different physical space. There is hardly loneliness for teachers who have emerged from an actual inner universe to announce its obvious florescence and deceit. Their minds are where they left them. The scientists, though, have come down a hard and gritty road of molecularity; for them there is no tangential procedure, no personal device for constructing the heraldry of a painfully turbulent beast. Their paradox is historical, not eternal, and for that reason they have arrived, with me, at a point of terminal process. The Moon rocks and the neutrinos, the buttercups and the fishing boats, are not the shadows of shadows, by prior consent. They are the objects that cast the shadows, or the shadows cast by the objects that most resemble them. If they are on fire, it is in the most blatant perceptual and electrical sense. Their metaphysics comes only after the disappointment, even as it so unexpectedly produces it.

In my uncertainty, I am an Augustine: I cannot leave the laboratory, for I have submitted my problem to the fact of my being, and now I am stuck with it. The one solution is not even a solution. And there are no minor discoveries and tours de force along the way.

Against the tide, against the lichen, against the dark behind the blue sky the meteors travelling in their guise as stone, against the stone that burns and the fire within stone, and within water too, against my own traced currency, the blinding attention even inattention is, against the uncertainty and its moments of incredible joy, it seems that there is beauty, as there is vision, but all beauty is of a different order, and all lives come to it only as they can. Vast boulders of science, rolled thru the centuries, catch again the glint of Heraclitan flame. The particles fly on past, for they are not even particles, no more than the riddles we pose seemingly of other riddles which pose their bodies, our bodies. We cannot expect these paths to lead to our condition, for the microscope is not the zazen, and the sound of the water is not, though it imitates and guides, the crash of the engine. The planets tug upon their orbits only as dark barges, heavier always than the gigantic blankness we imagine them in, more sparkly and flamelike than the cameras we submit their remoteness and wilderness to, by the same properties of the same lenses that roughen maria of viral molecules upon helical lattices, submerged in the same blessed obscurity of fact.

Axiomatically, grapevines hide their support.

Men teach me these things. I go back to the fisherman-scientist-priest who holds the torch, and I ask him which way I am to continue. Beyond my texts is a garden I have planted, I now must tend. Its gardeners lure me to the splinter of a vagile stream.

What I know: I know, even if it won't help me, and this is true of all of them, the therapists as well. If I can recover from the cure, with its failures of optimism, its authoritarian bias, I can begin again, joyfully, even healed, in a space so small I never would have known. I feel the creature come to life again, wounded as he is. He is a worm and he is beautiful. There is something promised even this blast over the sea cannot destroy.

July 4, Plainfield

The parade goes by our house, first in straggles, then the main body — kids on bikes with flags, cars and trucks from the outlying farms and local businesses, families piled on them; teenagers in hot rods anxiously honking while the traffic jams up at the corners. The day can hardly hold them, they want so much to bust out somewhere. The streets rattle with hobo band noises and fire-crackers. The Atlantic migration that placed these people here is over, but they swirl in pockets and sputter, Scythians, Saxons, Huns. It is an incomplete Green Revolution, an erratic countercul-ture twisted upon an uprooted Eurasian church. The Massachusetts Bay Company has laid the trail clear to Madison Avenue and big time sports. And the water table cannot throw it off. Like Colum-bus' discovery of something else, the Revolution was also: lost be-fore we got out of the Seventeenth Century.

This year, for the first time, the town allows Bread and Puppet Theatre to participate. They come with a huge tyrannical Uncle Sam leading another figure on a chain, accompanying puppets, magnificent birds, eggs, ornate weirded Middle Americans, a death's head, et al. What are these wonders doing among marching children and rancher station wagons and flags? Though no one seems to know who they are or how they got here, there is vague delight in the crowd. An old resident turns to his crony: "They sure put in a lot of work this year."

The other agrees. "I think this is the best one we've ever had."

Around the corner by the ballfield, the State policeman is directing traffic. Uncle Sam and his comrade tower over him. "Hey little fellow down there? Where do we go?"

The trooper grins, looks up. It's three times his size and pure American, whatever freak is inside. The crowd is pushing and Uncle S. is impatient. "Little fellow, can you direct me please."

The trooper strides back to get a better look. "Man, I don't know *what's* going on around here."

Crazy crazy dreams.

I am in this dark windowless room. It is the attic and it is very old and no one has lived here for a long time. The vine growing thru the crack bursts the planks and throws them open, a silent explosion like rags, Milky Way everywhere. The stars are at the other end of things, but in their intensity upon me, their phosphorus brightness, they are suns. This is not the observatory from which men look thru glass into space.

Each night, towards sleep, the last dream settles back in, wanting to be dreamed again. The mind, or what serves as the mind, destroys it; this is no tea party. Not when we stand against a changeless source.

* * *

I am swimming to the far side of the lake carrying a picnic lunch in my hand. It is the camp lake, but it is also the lake at my father's hotel. The cold forest surrounds it, and mixed with the trees and clearings are apartments I have lived in, street-corners on which I have stood in wind, classrooms and bunks. I see them as clearly as events on old cosmological maps. The water in the lake is rough, like the ocean, but I have no trouble swimming. In fact, I am supple and quite at ease. Large chunks of ice are afloat, despite the warm summer sun. I push them away as I pass them. I sense they are colder than ice, they cannot be dissolved. My friends are all around me, bobbing and paddling, bearing their own lunches. There is a spiral or current somewhere, and, as I look just over the flat plane of the water's surface, our positions in relation to each other are changing independently. When the shore comes near, I swim to it and pull myself out of the water. We camp among prehistoric ferns, large as trees, and eat our lunches.

* * *

My grandmother is dead. This dream happens in the living room of her house at the hotel, now a guest building. They are preparing to bury her, but she is also present in the room, looking very pale. Her body is in the coffin. Or is it my grandfather in the coffin? Is it he walking behind the table of tiny sandwiches, pretending not to have died?

My father is standing among the guests, acting concerned. The position of authority has fallen to him without warning, and he must make quick decisions. He says that everything, absolutely everything, is different than we had thought.

He is going to sell the hotel, move to Alabama, and open a different kind of resort. In fact, it is not my father in my grandmother's living room. *I* am there; he is calling from Alabama, telling me about the beautiful country, so tropical, so fertile, acres and acres of it undeveloped. I wish I could be with him to see it, but I realize I am stuck up north.

The dream clears again, and I realize he has sold the hotel to the new president of Goddard, who stands in the living room looking stern and authoritarian. He is a businessman, not an educator, and when the previous, more freaky president resigned and he took over in the pinch, sales jargon replaced social philosophy at all the meetings. Goddard and the hotel have merged. I am suddenly working for a mere shadow of my father while my father is in Alabama, enlarging his own vision. The condition is softness, revelation, perhaps reconciliation: mild southern air. The condition in my grandmother's living room is hard and cold, northern cash, worry about fuel oil, high prices. My father has bought a religious retreat; he will learn. Staying here I see the vicious mask behind liberalism; I see the smile torn away; I see the new president smiling.

I am in Alabama, and the planned hotel is still wilderness. My father wants me to write a section of it into being. I marvel that my skills, after all these years, have a use. I can save this land yet, turn it into cottages around a temple instead of rooms and facilities around a main dining room. The president of Goddard knows as little about this world as my father does, perhaps less. I'm one of his goons. But in the dream my father finally knows what I am doing, early enough in his life that he can use it. The new hotel looks like the summer camp I went to as a teenager, the one he didn't approve of, like my writing. We start again. The hotel has become a school, a secret atheneum. There are no more colleges and universities. I am free.

* * *

I am playing with Miranda and she seems very fragile. Her head extends like a filament thrown by a spider. The more I handle it the longer and thinner it becomes until it breaks off and lies there in the grass. She is dead. I think rather guiltily: it couldn't have been helped. As if I could so easily do away with, mechanically and by choice, the things I have made and the things I love.

In the dream the dead master comes to me as a voice behind the world. The first stories about Florida will never be written, he says. I awake with a start from an unremembered dream and realize I am almost thirty; not everything I began or left in doubt will be gone back to, not anymore. Some things are gone forever, despite their importance once, despite the promise I made never to forget.

We are on a late boat to Menemsha, a ferry. We catch it by leaping at twilight from the wharf across dark waters. Now I explore the interior. Dona is aboard. She is huddled in a shawl. Everything is dark, and witchcraft seems to be present. But I know better. This is not a boat to Menemsha. We are in the East River. The islands of the East River are filled with grapevines; we are the first ever, back over time, to reach them, despite the mammoth city in this place. The whole voyage is Tyrian-Hittite. Dona is one of the fates; she is knitting another threadbare shawl. No, it is the one she is wearing, still connected to her needles. She is looking thru a scrapbook, the pictures and snapshots of our lives. I try to see over her shoulder, but, as I do, it changes to pictures of mid-American families. The boat continues; the water rocks us. It becomes subways, trolleys, taxis, a thousand stations and intersecting tracks. I don't see her anymore. The image is broken like an old black plate.

Things do change. It's not as though they go on forever as they were. Everything must first be repeated a hundred times and more. We must suffer it not working until we can longer bear it. We must be like the hero of a movie, in such desperate straits a happy ending seems impossible; perhaps it is the wind which changes, ever so slightly, perhaps the orchestra picks up a hidden theme.

When the seedlings are high enough, the weeds are covered with newspapers, day by day thru the early summer. Now the pages are washing away under dirt and rain and sun. Fires, cities, Richard Nixon, Henry Aaron, Henry Kissinger, soak thru each other, and sunflowers and corn pop thru the pulp. The squash serpent twines on an old advertisement for my father's place; the dot photos fade. It seems so long ago, like news of world that wish to overcome us, liar's news, newsmen's ego-driven folly. Its real life is shorter than a pea.

The only way is to destroy them, reduce them to a condition they serve, a sterner condition than they are. Then we see what the news has been all along, good news and bad. We see the numbers taking the numbers back to bed. The flowers bright and merciless, the stock market and classified disappear thru mud and ink. There is yellow squash spreading in buttons, a single pumpkin dumped upon a *Sunday Times* model in a nightgown.

Bright new fruits and pods burn, dreams catch nights of stars: these are the reality, the moment without nostalgia or terror, beyond a day of tasks I neither absorb gracefully nor understand. The room is filled with a story; fruits hang on soft limbs from the splinters; the cucumber blossoms along its axillary stem, the stem axillary to that. Purple-pod beans are tangled with violet-white flowers. Previous dreams crumble and feed the fire.

* * *

My brother and I are at a ball game. It is late in the season, and there are dozens of players we don't recognize, even their names. Something tells us we are truant, and between innings we try to escape thru a hole in the back of the stands. Perhaps we do not have the proper tickets. The crowd is enormous; there are a million people, more, and we are in the upper deck, twelve stories above the ground. On every level is another game, another whole season. We find our way out thru a tunnel into a subway station, but the numbers of the streets seem too strong, too final; they are magical numbers, not stops. There are bulbs leading in all directions and people moving in long lines. Some sections of track come to an end as wood; in place of rotted stumps we find them sprouting again, leaves and buds, a few flowers. Dead end for trains. We are forced to return in the other direction even to come back the way we were going. It was bad enough with trains going up and down on four avenues; now there are hundreds of whorls, many of them unexplored, and vehicles left over from other cities, run by pirates who have destroyed whole cultures in the past and are just as dangerous if we stumble aboard. The trains are off schedule in some collective fashion; they seem to be rushing to catch up, doors barely open before they close again.

* * *

I am running down the pebbly path to the camp lake, carrying
my towel. I think of the lost summer, when I went to my friend's
camp instead, the strangeness of the following year. This is like re-
turning from even longer ago. I look down at the man directing
activity at the waterfront. It is Abbey West returned! Like the first
day of camp when I was young. He'd make his opening speech and
we'd stand before the endless summer. He was a man few people
loved, almost no one sought out. From my own brambly path I
adored him. I went to see him in his house when others hoped only
that he wouldn't see them. He was the disciplinarian, but also the
only ethical authority in a camp run by two clowns from New York
who, for all their mockery and flamboyance, could not reduce his
dignity. Most people were charmed by the antics of the owners and
feared Abbey West. I saw in him the one wise man in town, and I
went to him to learn and honor that, whatever form Camp Chipinaw
made him have to take. He read me accurately and told me true
things, though now I remember not a word, only the lucid passage
of his voice.

And then they finally got rid of him. When I came back after
being away, he was gone and a good-natured lackey ran the place.
Everyone loved him. No one missed Abbey West. It was like pro-
gress, as if an eagle weight could be removed from the countryside
without removing as well the specific and holy motion of that eagle.
In the years since I have dreamed often of his return. And for all
whom he might symbolically be, in my life of fathers, magi, and
doctors, he is also Abbey West. I run down to the waterfront and
cry out, "Abbey, you're back!" And he turns; I see the lumpish
face; it is not him; it is only another tall man, younger, inane-look-
ing, annoyed at any mistake. I stand there weeping, for the dream
is a big one and the disappointment is final and real.

* * *

Samuel Cinamon has opened a new furniture store in Portland.
He and his chemist son are moving all the things out of the old store.
This time it won't be used furniture and antiques. It will be new
stuff, upholstered chairs. Lindy and I walk around in the setting
and realize how shoddy and false it is compared to the real place.
He is proud because, once a poor immigrant, he is now selling Ameri-
can products. When we lived in Portland, he lit up whenever I came
into the store because he identified with my grandparents and their

hotel. But hustling was all he knew, the only way he could communicate. What could he sell me that was right? From floors of piled heirlooms. How could I respect him as he was? Whoring after the buck. As I awake, he stands confused among crates, his son the only confident one.

* * *

Everybody is visiting, all at the same time, coming in thru the door. They are piling up in a crowd in the living room. David has slipped back in hoping I will not notice him. When I see him, I realize we are in a very social scene, and there will be talk only of practical things.

* * *

A doubledecker bus with a glass ceiling-floor. Up above the figures of my life look down upon me, women, as I look up at them. They are shifting their feet and laughing.

* * *

At the end of life is twilight and an icy blue pool. I bathe in it as the mist. I must relax now whether I want to or not. There is nothing more that can happen to me. At the beginning was a fierce yellow sun. I flee it. I try to get into the pool.

The pool is full of old men and women; they have worked their way here by long tenuous paths. I look back at the yellow light, and it is beautiful and warm and I wonder why I never saw it, I want to go into it, big and whole. I want to, but can't, swim in the pool.

There is something else in the sky that has nothing to do with the people bathing, something that must be more than a dream. The words of Jerry Quarry, the defeated boxer, ring in my ears, the sportswriters mocking him for having predicted he would win. "I had a dream. But I guess it was only a dream. Because I didn't have the strength." The plot thickens. It's going to be double jeopardy at least, all the way.

XIII

The world stretches out blue and light each day, opening thru summer, our senses seeming to tell us that the path is open, the radiance shorn of deceit.

Most sun is now stone. The rest falls upon the future into living systems it has nourished in the past. The winds follow the light. None of us are special, nor is the condition special. Behind the sky dark planets roam; and if they are not filled with creatures, intelligences, they remain, craters and stone. We cannot bargain with their condition. Humbly they meet us, as what they are, we are. The rest belongs in some other sky.

If global circumstance is ominous, we are still not any different than we have ever been. We live in the condition mankind is, behind a cheap screen civilization throws. There is nothing even the strongest of us can hold onto as the tide pours into the basin the Moon holds for it, the victim's blood. And it wouldn't even be courage. Saturn's rings grind out optically at best in glass.

I have taken my own safety as a priority without even knowing to what end it was granted, at what cost elsewhere in this mundus. Surely they are not my friends. This is not for free.

If they are not filled with creatures, they are filled yet with not-creatures.

I am an animal in the wide-open prairie; the Sun is a brute. A computer-wheel imbedded in stone, dredged up from Mediterranean waters, is itself — no astronauts or Atlanteans necessary. It can't be irrelevant, even when ignored by the pride of science. It is equally not an omen. It comes from the waters in which it has rested thru the accident by which it was found. It has its use. Which is not the same as an explanation. It is now in the world's ken.

Nobody wants me to be here any more than I do, and if I do not want to be here enough, I will no longer be here. It is not a matter of my wanting and knowing their wanting and knowing. If there are six-dimensional beings and allies, the information still reaches me cold and hot, visionary and numb, massive and light. It is my body. They must get thru that. And they *become* that. I cannot be reached.

Slaughter in the streets of small African countries, South American and Adriatic revolutions broken but respawning, Russia cracking Eastern Europe, brief skirmishes in a century of (Dorn) uninstructive total war. There are dismal signs in America which may mean, at this point, absolutely anything. Icarus and Kohoutek have passed, and those who say *whew!, no effect* must have been expecting total snuff-out or at least the loss of California. They might try counting resource tables or fallen heads of state. The bread we eat is bought in direct confrontation with the peasants of India and Iraq; the actual expense of running our garaged cars is transnational, takeover of native industries. The fine art we do is as dirty and grit-laden as the rest; it is folk art, glyphs, animal paths for sure. We are a mistake. These are the slums too, for all their IBM expressionist piazzas. As much as I seek to build the edifice made possible by Western science and the rich mythologies that meet in our global-finance streets, a gloss stands against it, a harsh babble of raw tongues. As long as I demand to live in my system, the parts paid for in blood, I am a piece in an invisible chain, given reason by dead weight. The big game is decisive. This local weather is a lion of blue sky and fast winds, clouds in fluid prospect, dashed to bits perceptually, leaving iotas in vastness, and still it stands, as the stars do, winds beyond sky. Geology is the only natural science: lava, crystal, and lime. Amethyst clumps about a dark egg. The bare planetary existence we were given can be no more, albeit the goldwork of Rome and glassblowers of Corning, the aerospace technicians, the living above our means, the fragile and transient beauty of the street fairs and puppet shows, slick optimistic dolls animated by theatrical consciousness, gyroscope backup. For all our seeing our minds as possibilities, I ask: as possibilities for what? Did I think the life I was living was not the real life?

If there is background noise, it is bones. My work up to here has been pure foreground. In one revision I am wild and dionysiac, laughing as I have never laughed, running wild in an initiation I have posited but never indulged; and if I did these things, I would be another person; I would have his joys, her joys, his life, her life. So I defend this self as if its existence were more than an accident. The fertility of everything winds along another parameter. It is easy to want, but its price is staggering. Wherever I look, across sections of being and creation, I see the long body, the planal shadow. It seems to be atoms and electrons, or molecules and cells, rows of photosynthetic suns, cultures strung in perfect hexagrams across their totemic adaptation to the ground. Change the scale and the meaning holds its peg. Tear out the peg and the scale is permanent. It is because we have put an image on it, dot by dot, that it can even be seen.

"We're not picking those berries to spill them on the ground again? It's not that type of game?" Robin half-asks, half-tells me.

For all the tinsel and pomp, the seriousness of the abacus stands out. We have lived our lives with the curse of pre-Oedipal trauma, in the birth, the circumcision, the subincision, the miserable families that spawned us, raised us, or died on us. We have accepted it, accepted how, in the subtlety of its pattern in our pattern, we cannot be more perfect beings, and have yielded to that imperfection in intricate and insoluble ways. And still we have not taken it seriously. We hoped to protect ourselves from the full consequences by pretending we didn't care, by pretending to soften in the face of life-destroying forces, as though we could take away anything they were able to take away, as though we could match their moves by killing ourselves quicker.

We cannot stand outside them even if our solar inventions conquer their present bite. We have no chance of escaping by submitting meekly to their fury. They drill their soldiers as hard and as cruel as any historical Prussian or Mongol. They want us alive. Those who fear them as the secret police and ecocidal warriors are both right and wrong, and they are wrong if they fear only the ritual robot motions, the Chicago killings, the arrests, the poisoning of Erie, the assassinations, the aerosols, the sulphur. We are self-sufficient from the beginning; we contain the full power that makes us what we are.

We have lived under successive threats, and the luxuriant decadence of our parents' hopes and beliefs, who sent us to zones of supposed education and life-exercise, while Hiroshima and Nagasaki left them more relieved than horrified. They stand us in poor stead before the garden that now must be planted and tended, and the self that must tend it. They staged it as a football game, a competition among our contemporaries, for honors without empirical base in self. We played as if it were interplanetary war. We played our guts out in Latin class and Watermelon League while others waited. We must start all over again, and this time without the advantage of being children, without their paranoia-less ability to learn, without the freedom to lie out vast under clouds, receiving energy. We have had taken away from us the one thing we were given for free, by those who pretended to be our guardians, our friends, our teachers. By drilling us they weakened us; by pretending to love us they fucked up the communes of the seventies.

We are sacrificial victims of a dying order whose lineage we were raised to carry on. This will stay with us, however eloquent our voices and cosmic our scope. The real tangle in the garden defies us, for the language with which we know it is as tangled again. We shall do no unknotting. We are the last heroes. There will be no heroes after us. And though nothing will allow us the possibility again, we must cultivate it, in place of any other means or way, at night and before sleep, to quiet even in the best of times, often in the worst of times, the buzzing in our brains.

The water that supports the garden is only water, and what it carries in it now, of unconscious data and detritus, cannot be removed. The free energy of carbon is over as a way of life. It leaves an undreamable and toxic residue in the microcosm, where no mogul can buy it out. We can no longer do by force what we cannot do by care and craft. And perhaps we are becoming gentler, for healing is a necessity at last.

The Oriental military may stand against us, and they are not a football team, or even an American army. At one time they were the Martians of Flash Gordon, alien and evil; then we gained political consciousness, and they were the Third World guerrilla fighters, noble, pragmatic, and strong. But what if they are neither?, if they refuse to relieve us of either our terror or our guilt? Then we stand equally shorn before the herbal gardener of the origins of agriculture and the Taoist doctor of the jewelled path. Our national leaders can worry about the amount of oil under Asia and the effect of that on our economic survival. I will always believe they are first in love with the apocalypse they protect us from. It is a subtlety, like chi, which concerns me, for nothing can free us, even as armies, from the responsibility of being human. Playing possum now is just the continuation of our oldest game. Because, while they were learning to grow rice and fight the people's enemy, we were made petty capitalists and varsity pawns. But we have already lived half a life under nuclear bombs, and they have reined our possibilities as surely as iron bridles, though this savagery be hidden in the seeming burst of freedom that atomic fears and hopes have spawned in our midst, the happy-go-lucky antics of those who no longer care. And Barry McGuire sang "Eve of Destruction." Even when we snapped their bind on our every ease and found Reich at the temple door, urging tenderness and flow in the face of techno-murder, they replaced it with ecological doom, the same dreary apocalpyse-monger landscape, the same wiped-out Earth. The fallout shelters of the fifties are gone because they were hopeless, and we laugh, and rightly so, at that kind of foolishness. The swords are still drawn, but the hiding is over. We can see what they are trying to do to us. The message is clear. If we are going to live these lives against the forces that hold them back — and they are as terrible as they seem — then we are going to have to go right thru that storm, not at sea, amidst poisoned currents and laser submarines, but as we are the sea. We are going to have to live *because of* what we are, not despite what we are. The trauma will become like the Sun and other stars; it will no longer be our psychological history except as the big horoscope of our having been at all; it will twist with the tree and blow with the branches in the wind. This is all, even if there is more.

In ourselves the sword hangs to split the rabbit's throat; we alone can remove it by daring to strike. We alone can outlive and unlive the heroes against the anti-wind, when our last hope is gone. In us: the utter and primal force, not to waste in a scream, a holocaust of past and present, in hope of victory-like clarity or oblivion; by our consciousness — cupped as lightning bug its light — we suffer the riddle imposed in thought; we are the gods whom those in darkness have set against the darkness, and the agony they pose for us is not to stumble blankly back. When we signal them from this bare turf under the complete cosmological sky, their answer is the obvious one: terror is a luxury too; behind the panic is a witch who will not seduce us no matter how we submit to her. But then we are all afraid of the same thing — that we will not be afraid in time.

There is no other life, not only for us to live but to refuse to live. Better to plunge, to risk being pulled up like a rat on the end of a cyanide pole.

In 1938 Raymond Chandler wrote: *"A single drop light burned far back, beyond an open, once gilt elevator. There was a tarnished and well-missed spittoon on a gnawed rubber mat. A case of false teeth hung on the mustard-colored wall like a fuse-box in a screen porch."*

And yet people lived and died there. It wasn't even bad theatre.

"Plenty of vacancies or plenty of tenants who wished to remain anonymous. Painless dentists, shyster detective agencies, small sick businesses that had crawled there to die, mail order schools that would teach you how to become a railroad clerk or a radio techni-cian or a screen writer — if the postal inspectors didn't catch up with them first. A nasty building. A building in which the smell of stale cigar butts would be the cleanest odor."

Which is a lesson to the purists among us. By 1938 the enemy had us surrounded, the atom bomb a *fait accompli*. Then they died and something replaced them. They reside now *in us*, in the sheer ac-cumulation. We have never had it to begin again with windmills. We have never had it to do over, psychically or without DDT. And what if the so-called life behind the life we live is simply this one?

"An old man dozed in the elevator, on a ramshackle stool, with a burstout cushion under him. His mouth was open, his veined temples glistened in the weak light. He wore a blue uniform coat that fitted him the way a stall fits a horse. Under that gray trousers with frayed

cuffs, white cotton socks and black kid shoes, one of which was slit across a bunion. On the stool he slept miserably, waiting for a customer. I went past him softly, the clandestine air of the building prompting me, found the fire door and pulled it open. The fire stairs hadn't been swept in a month. Bums had slept on them, eaten on them, left crusts and fragments of greasy newspaper, matches, a gutted imitation-leather pocketbook. In a shadowy angle against the scribbled wall a pouched ring of pale rubber had fallen and had not been disturbed. A very nice building."

Raymond Chandler made Phillip Marlowe that way, after he lost his oil wells in the last depression, he turned to writing, like a monk to the bloody Latin scrawled across his time.

* * *

The lightning bugs float in the night air. Their lives are short, a few weeks; but all lives, the great books tell us, are of the same length. In the quick successions of images that flash in their sensoria, they see everything, they know all there is to know. They are not alienated from their creation, though we stand outside their zone and watch them as if a tragedy, disappearing and reappearing in broken arcs.

It is all held together on a thread, great suns as well, each one, where they are, across our system as galaxies across a band of telescopic haze. The fierce edge of creation cuts the hierarchical arrangement of existences. Yes, there are messages, sent between incommensurate realities, but they are no different than the rest. The things happening are the messages — lightning bugs, memory, stars, their staccato and rhythmic order, is all that meaning can be. Things reach us and are disclosed only in the most explicit and sensible fashion; they are the same things we did not see when they passed us before, dumb and random. This is all the initiation we will have. We are no different than bioluminescent bugs; at times of being brought into being we lie in an eternity untouched. This is the due opposite of Chandler's conclusion to *The Big Sleep*; it is also, by the translator's fangs, his very words.

"What did it matter where you lay once you were dead? In a dirty sump or in a marble tower on top of a high hill? You were dead, you were sleeping the big sleep, you were not bothered by things like that. Oil and water were the same as wind and air to you. You just slept the big sleep, not caring about the nastiness of how you died or where you fell."

The lights go on and off, and where the lives we experienced cut across the darkness, we see everything, and whether we remember it or not, we endure. We cannot be everyplace. The big sleep stalks us, but our death is not the lightning bug either.

Robin and I climb the back hills and woods of Plainfield, just beyond the Biggam's house. We pass thru the pine forest along the old stone fence; I carry him over the rusted barbed wire boundary to the edge of the sugarbush. We rest on the dismantled wall. Wild growth reaches our knees; its constant drag leaves us exhausted. But he discovers wild strawberries, each so tiny it is only a taste. When I pick him up, he smells like one.

The world, even in its natural condition, is sweet, and after this experience there will be no convincing him otherwise. I tell him that sometimes people mess up real badly, but he cannot accept it as anything but secondary to the fact of his life and all there is to learn, the sun, the flowers, because the speed of his being outweighs the considerations that swing in the balance beyond it. He is absolutely accurate to his time.

I look out at the vastness of forest and valleys, the mountains ringing those, the clouds active across the sky. When I open all the way and let it in, it is more terrible than beautiful. I smell rusty grasses and bitter herbs, decay amidst fertility, fertility played only thru suffusion and decay. Chamomile grows sweet and tame in the scoured dust of the driveway, a traditional tea, but here are hundreds of budding and unbudded plants, large sour leaves, wild nightshades, vines crawling away from domestication, poisons that no doubt contain powerful powerful medicines, if our wisdom were greater, if our fear of being reborn, of living this time, were not so great. As we crumple the vegetation under our feet, the aroma rises, not perfume. It has the true stench of mutation, chemical mystery strung thru wire and bone.

Sex is about the sweetest it gets, because we are drawn overpoweringly, to want to be there and because we come from there. In our plowed garden spinaches and peas grow, and melons among musty leaves; we eat mindlessly a raw salad, and are nourished. But there is no essential sympathy, no chemical link. Sap and sugar are acrid. Our hunger blurs the cannibalism, the barbarian lineage of crops. It is just the world and the world is pagan; we not only have a defective uncle; we lack, St. John's wort, a true Christian ancestor on either side. Seduction is enough of an ambiguity, but compared to the alien sweep of most of this planet's carbon and non-carbon chemistry atop the metals and uncoded stone, it is one magnificent luxury. As it is to eat the garden, to grow calm foods. There is a Devonian curse on this, like Frankenstein in clone. So warriors battle their hunger, fasting, refusing to be seduced; they know finally, in the wearing down of life, our seductions are bitter weeds also, bitter in the way we are bitter, and the lives of other people are broken across our life, in numb sensual affinity, jointed where we fall together. Even if it is raw fate, blind chance, it has cast this broken branch, this nub and twaining. And I can reach the bare edge of it, I can just about see that it is there. Were it a whole tree: it could be no more.

My writing has run the course of its preferred vision and of the golden light in which I have chosen to steer. The songs have been beautiful. I have loved them, but I have not listened to them. I have been the instrument, not the player. Now that I know the music, I am tightening the strings — raw edge of bare harmony. It is a wild risk. But I am not bluffing. As I come to seem vulnerable in the work, I feel less vulnerable in my life. There is no mistiness to the vision anymore. And yet the vision is, even at the beginning, woven from a song of the dumb celestial harp, equal and beautiful. Just as the bountifulness and goodness of the world amazes me, its ceaseless imagery from whirlwinds out of whirlwinds — so does the severity. And unless I submit this exercise to the law and ride it hard to its false conclusions, I will go nowhere.   I am turning the ship into the storm.

* * *

Before Robbie will swim in the pool, he wants me to clean out of it the insects that have fallen there. I take a big kitchen collander, yellow in its optimism, and strain them out of the water, both living and dead, shaking them out into the grass. Those that are still able scramble away. Now he points to the animals on the bottom; he wants me to get rid of just the really big ones. So I strain up the dead grasshoppers, frozen in their last mask; they are light and drift without turbulence thru the water. They end up in the grass. He watches very carefully, taking in what is happening and what has clearly happened.

Minutes later, from up on the hill, I hear him crying; I leave my work there and come running down. He is standing up in the pool rubbing his eyes, his hair dripping, howling away.

"Did you hurt yourself?"

"No."

"Then what's wrong?"

"I fell under the water. All the way. I closed my eyes. I got water

235

in my mouth." Each statement separated from the next by crying.

Seeing the grasshoppers on the bottom drew him to that mask in pure phobos and imitation. We begin doing that, and we think it will be easy to stop. We spend our lives thinking that, while they chuckle and blunder, holding the sword over our heads.

XIV

Deep Numerical Music

Those who lived in beehives are gone, and the wind of centuries blows dirt against their stone relics. We are dolls, doll-like fragments of their incomplete design, winding roads that evade the object, yet return again and again. History is not enough. "After this life there's another life," Robin says decidedly, but he has too much confidence to see the dismantling that goes on all around us, that destroys nothing, that parts no thread. The nut we pretend to crack plants only further trees in the distances, and as the forest becomes deeper and orientation more vast, we wonder how it ever seemed simple, how we ever imagined we could tame it as a garden. When I call Morgan on the phone, the sound, he tells me, is like the Buddhist gong, in the center of meditation, calling him back mercifully into the world of things. The bats at twilight, irregular in the windows, wear bats. Rigel, Capella, Aldebaran. Faint Pleiades. There is no fresco dripping, there are no masks; the form seals even before the blue glaze reflects it, the circle pouring from the hidden wheel.

We live now between a supercivilization that sprays the cosmos with messages and prophecies, blueprints of a golden age, and a Buddhist revision in which we renounce not only the outer space gambit but our own Rosicrucian city. Their intergalactic beam wheels thru creation, spreading seeds and notes that translate as possibilities into any particular world; this is the connectedness, the refuge from loneliness. Atlantis merging with Andromeda. But if we stir to the panpipes of Saturnian magi or trust Clarke's overlord-guides and the possibility of "childhood's end," these are desperate acts, our priests tell us. For even if they have the machinery to build cities as large as the Sun, to accommodate our restlessness till eternity, they cannot pull us, when body and soul mean to divide, from the

236

abyss. And surely they do not lie beyond it. They do not: or that would be the same thing.

Their music is everywhere, promising us life, tempting us to be what we think we are, to use our materials courageously, despite their obvious incapacity before the task. They do not deny death, but their spacecrafts, operating at the speed of light and archetype, turn time into cream, and drink that cream, as the body's fuel, the machine's big non-entropy thrust. They litter our laboratories and telescopes joyfully, trying to initiate us by the sphynx of cosmic cities. Yet how's that different, asks Gary Snyder, than the whole trip of America to the original Indians?

We stand between Buckminster Fuller guardians and the new farmers and hunter-gatherers. The technology is not the real prize of the west. It couldn't be, not with its reliance on cheap underground energy and its ramshackle agricultures and medicines. It just doesn't work. Its clear sight, its vision of a furnace sun, is a darkness most of creation will never know. The real prize is a methodology we do not even begin to understand — a methodology that creates while it destroys, which, at the same time it makes the planet toxic and unfit, draws more and more fantastic occurences from a Biblically-sealed shell. The enigma of our age is that we cannot separate the parts that work from the parts that do not. We have made a machinery that cannot hold even itself together. And we have built a beautiful and sacred factory and given it nothing to process; its fleet lies abandoned and ignored. So they fill the trucks not even with dung and waste, but with each other, and drive them into gullies where they come apart and are washed away. And what they preserve, in their tinhorn pride, is a dime a dozen in this galaxy. A cheap two-bit robot breeding cancer and insanity. We could do so much better with what we have. We don't really know what we have. And even then, whispers the other voice, does it matter?, do we really care?, knowing how all this is going to end. Yet if we really don't care, it is going to be more than the Buddha's stunning reversal. This is all going to disappear with a rapidity to make us wonder who ever went thru the trouble in the first place.

Sam warns me not to forget the music we heard in college. He came to Vermont for a rest in the woods, but he's got those Ecology Conference Apocalypse blues. "Who wants to play the piano if the whole thing's coming down." Because that's all they talk about now. Their radical anger is vented in their hopes that the war-makers are going to put under their own machine.

What is the music?, I ask him. It's a refinement, he says. A refinement of what, I don't know. It is subtle. It comes from faraway.

There is no archetypal melody. It's all built up, tune and association, from what's here. But still, he says, I feel as though I am transferring notes of a great code; I *am* helping even if I'm not building windmills. I am bringing things into existence at the lowest denominator. So low no one could possibly recognize them. For years, maybe centuries, to come. But how else are they to get here? Surely not by the literal discussion of community and societal rebuilding or by hi-tech elaborations upon the gargantuan and everpresent machinery. There are things we don't even know to know about. We can't begin to want them. We can't imagine where they come from. Their perspective sits beyond a point beyond Pluto, *at* a point. They spray the androgyne as fertilely as tassels dust the wombs of corn. We must selflessly and subtly serve as their agents. Wherever it comes from, do not look to the visible cosmos. Do not look for friendly astronauts. The sky is but a metaphor, accurate in its astronomical and astrological boundaries, for the source. If we don't allow them to find us, if we don't lay ourselves bare at every stage of the way, even our mistakes, our evasions, connecting the themes as they come to us in one long symphony, then speculation is for naught. That's what the music is all about. You don't have to play it on radio-telescope vibes and beam it at Cassiopeia to get that. The discovery of *our* muffled drum is so much more important, Mahler, Schoenberg, Cage, than *their* discovery of us.

We are writing alchemical instructions, in our confusion of amulets, techniques, and texts. This is the famous historical confusion; the alchemists were not the only ones who mixed molecules, gods, psychic processes, and technology. Our contribution to solving the riddles *is* the riddles, even as the Mediaeval attempts upon Neoplatonic riddles upon Egyptian riddles upon the Palaeolithic heritage upon the origin of language in call systems upon the mute wild planet upon the zone of moons and suns. What is lost we will never know. What we maintain is the basic bare continuity of the present, even whose attack upon hermeticism is a hermetic text.

XV

Dark blue summer/end coming. Twisted red leaves, and memory, and wild grapes. Golden pumpkins in the grass.

Here in the North we have these Newfoundland summers. There
are no long untended emotions; the break comes before we are aware
of it, so that we find ourselves always one step behind. The stone
wall is never repaired; the railroad tie steps are not replaced; the
house continues to peel: all day the sun low in the sky, embracing
both dawn and dusk. By now, like the golden cloudberries of the
palaeo-peoples to the taiga, we must be hundreds of years older; we
must be that much closer to wisdom.

Chuck and Anne pull up carrots and take the few red tomatoes
from the vine. We have swum in the lake in the hot afternoon, and
seen thru the eye the inhibitory nerves as well, where the image
breaks down into less and less as it passes thru the retina into the
brain, into what we see, all of us alternately bathing and sitting in
the mud — the children playing on rafts made out of broken skids. I
go under in bundles of water, seeking the other face, out past me,
the mirror a muddy frogpond, silver once. The torch underwent
the flask of vinegar long before creatures ever crept from rusty rain-
water and torpid hay. I know I am getting near the bottom. The
water is colder, my fingers touch mud. I open my eyes for a bright
morninglike flash, the grains streaming by the curtains. The tadpole
carcass is not the archetype, even my own vestigial strokes and buried
gills. The genetic language has been written. Now there is only water,
and a white bird. My head wants to shake clear with forest around
it, sky, my lithe taut body resting on the grass. I keep going under.
Without that, daylight would be a cheap display.

I look among the glossaries, but it doesn't help when the words
are lost. Naomi comes again, dark and reminiscent of everything I
am not since childhood, because she went a different way. Bearing
Miranda's chart, as she bore Robin's once. The conditions that allow
this lie back in a priest's hands. Byron Dix alone cools out the sleek
highway with his motorcycle, down from Newport, bearing photo-
graphs of the overgrown hives and huts and stonecutting marks of
peoples, ancestral to us, who lived in New England in obscurity be-
fore Babylon or Greece. These two bugs flit across each others'
paths in the late afternoon. A mammalian vision guides the parallel
lines of modernistic sight, leading us thru caves we do not see. The
fatness of the fly's body as senses wing between ganglia, and nerves
join where the gap is bridged, only because there is a gap. The magic
is real, and though my friend declares: "There ain't no other incar-
nations," all these exotic forms hang from the same banana tree, as
far from here as Easter Island. There is one universe, occult and na-
tural, for reasons of state. The other universes we sought, in mega-
lithic peoples, in disembodied astral voices, are like the moment

239

before knowing, more valuable than what it leads us to. Exchange it for proof and we are dead. We are just as free to leave this trap as lobsters who do not thru 90% broken laths. But the dark water-stream rushes out of the tunnel, past the moment when revelation would happen if it were going to, into the world.

The pool is visited by swallows. We sit until twilight with our meal, and then go back in for wine and talk.

Norman shows his "Morning Prayer" film: the girl, gently in the rocking chair, becomes the bearded man, Norman himself, continuing to rock, to his own voice singing a Hebrew creation prayer: *Anakhnu modim . . .* And this is the temple: the feeling itself of not being able to enter. I walk back to the house, where I have lived the last two years, and the stars are full in the Vermont sky; we can see almost every one of them we need to see, the zodiac written only on the broken belt, Anselm hiking up the hill beside me, big steps, cool air. The days keep on coming, bright as flowers.

Back past the Pillars, but not of Hercules, not of Ceres, our origin abounds. The stone North American glacier is born without a name, comes from the stars with caribou and goat, and ranges well past this clime. The pools we bathe in are bare scrapes in the surface, are sensoria filled with rocks. No matter how small they fall before the Sun, we can wear them again and again, whole.

We sit on the grass with Kenward and Joe, Anselm up on the steps, Harvey crouched, sweet borage tea. The stone wall Joe drew, piece by piece, stands at the end of the garden. Sunflowers nodding over the fence. Miranda's bright eyes shine in the grass beside Lindy. High up above, making a line that cuts open the sky, leaving a sound behind itself, a jet, minute, almost transparent, its trail etched in a wet sky. And Harvey says: "About nine hundred miles an hour. Do you think he's having fun!"

Glacial calcium glows in the fields, beside tractors, rusted giants. Past the darkness, past the divider, this could be so sweet. But it *is* sweet.

Do you think we're high? All the time!

I find no one who remembers me, but the river, grinding in its bed, is a consciousness as thoughtless and eternal as the one behind mind.

XVI

Grapes, just ripening, are twined around dark red withering choke-
cherries. Grasshoppers rub their rough bodies against the husk. The
breeze is too wild for song. The river is tarnished, and the sound of
bells hangs in the continuity of the nymph's pitcher — corroded pots
of a lost bronze age — in the eternal and precise autumn light.

Leech Pond has touched the sewers; the lily pads fizz and bubble
brown. And in the basement cruel fungus dismantles the tomatoes.
The berries of summer have dropped, but huge blackberries form
in the cold sun. Along the edge of the forest, squirrels eat the hazel
nuts, single and from the branches, a thieving wind. The white quartz
lies broken on the forest floor.

Time will never be the same, Robin Grossinger. Our child who did
not come on this walk over the log bridge into the fields beyond
Norman's cabin. Because we did not wear boots and did not go in
the morning when dew was in the grass. Carting Miranda along the
tire trail, exchanging her between us — and I wanted to know then,
as now, as I want you to know, of what radical and unstable light
this love is, is also made, Lindy's and mine, how uncertain and
flickering, even the singleness of the sun in a billion angles, from
which you push out, pip and mystery. Of a thread softer and more
durable than any we utter for all our talking, all our fluency. It is a
mute god.

The time was not time at all, and has not passed, in the rushing of
a chill wind which embraces all warmer and colder winds, in whose
octave the season moves not as a squirrel or geese or the hen's blown
feathers, but a bear, swaying above the pelvic cavity. If there is a
moment on two legs, the descent is still on four, always. So close
we are, so delicate, along the margin, this line of second-growth
trees is both jagged and smooth. And the rest is abandoned villages,
shires and flumes that have sunk to the bottom of a pit of light.

If damage has been done, if we have done damage, it is so great
and so long ago we are no longer responsible. Dire prophecy about
our time and coming times, which reaches out like a hooked claw
and seems to get us, itself melts back into the glaciers, and the
present is left, the rabbit standing at red dusk upon the entry to the
house.

The forest is filled with robots; they are invisible, forerunners of
a new aeon. Five hundred years early, right? These are good times
because they are uncertain times. If we knew more we might live
less. What does "proven" mean to Jack who wants to *grow* the
beanstalk, whose fear-desire is that his dream may, like a vine, engulf

the world it is attached to by his mind?

The stream contains our making love, and the desire to go beyond, is neither your nor my desire, even when it divides us.

Two dark pines stand on yonder hill, black trunks at the core of their visibility, branches flowing darkly upward. Beyond them, bent back in the September air, a cloud is coming apart like a galaxy, its material released, thin pieces, threads, then beyond. The bells ring in the water as at the beginning of this piece, and nothing will stop them as nothing will locate them. However large the Sun is, however far it has come into this autumn, towering above us, its arch and tangled yarn are what we have, nothing more plentiful or absolute.

There are fragments of raw science and busted equations, rising and descending, mixing upon the strings like monkeys. I do not remember whether I am young or old, a child or a man, whether the water is beneath the ice or summer, whether the light is revelatory or dim. And in not remembering, I am at the sentry of another system; the hollow rumor of its transactions echoes upon our finished walls.

XVII

Robin comes home from his first days at school with lists of words on yellow lined paper: zebra, spaceship, kangaroo. At night, before bed, we read the Narnia kings, making it impossible that he should ever, in year to come, forget. Dr. Cornelius leads Prince Caspian to the top of the castle to show him a planetary conjunction, to reveal his dwarf ancestry, to show the Prince the forest where his destiny lies.

The station wagon stops at the edge of the driveway and lets Robin out; he plays with trucks and cars and dirt till nightfall.

Aslan the Lion glows like a second sun; his footprints turn into pools of delicious water; each thing part of the lost design.

I sit in the living room by the fire reading Raymond Chandler's description of the gambling ships in the ocean beyond Bay City, California, the smell of sage rising from the pages, as mystery sheathes mystery, leaving, beyond those the detective solves, those in the book itself. The murder victims are themselves clues of another agency.

Jovian fire in the night air.

XVIII

The Ashley is brought out of the barn where it has sat, boxed, for
months. The conical free-standing fireplace leaves, trailing loose ash,
and creosote drips from the open stovepipe onto the floor. It is a two
day job, involving new pipes, sand from Brook Road, steel brushes.
Tire chains are swung from a rope against the inside of the chimney,
and then the mirror catches Chris' face perfectly squared against
the blue. He sits on the upper roof, his voice muffled, asking if it is,
in fact, a square.

The dead leaves are turned into parchment. No two are alike, and
before the words on them are read the words are erased, text
crumbles into ashes, seed for seed, that will return, years hence, as
a full tree in some other brightening summer. Perhaps then there
will be priests. Perhaps the dharma will have disappeared, will be
the same as everything else.

The church fades in the sun, less and less paint each year until a
thick new coat holds the image, or winter by winter the furnaces
reducing these single dwellings to diamond coal.

At twilight the warmth hangs to the Earth for a moment, low
ground fogs, their chemistry active over the fields. The stars receive
our rhythm and give back an eternal tone. Because it does not
change, you can always look at it. Because you can always look at
it, you change.

* * *

Summer seems to have returned. The second false flies come,
and hornets swarm at rooftop against the boarded attic windows,
the green shutters. This is so much more what we are than summer.
It is no wonder we don't remember, and what we do reminds us
only of what it must have been like.

* * *

The t'ai chi classes begin one night in the karate studio in Barre,
fall shopping festivities outside, the streets crowded. This room sits

alone in the upper world. The teachers move in fine willowy paths, but our own bodies are at stake, not theirs. I want to be able to do this so much I shouldn't be having so much trouble. But then it wouldn't be worth shit. I'd lose the tough and difficult room, the crumbling office building. I'd lose the opportunity of being totally unable, from the beginning. Now I must change myself in a way that is not apparent or suggested by watching Carolyn and Andy. As unfamiliar as their movements are, where I begin is familiar to me, rough and painful. Find the axis. Adhere. Yield by taking yourself away. If you want to learn, you have to do it. The long-indulged fear I have no center is dismissed, forcing arduous realignment. Which is deadlier, by far, than any simple cosmic deprivation.

What is lost is re-acquired always; that was the promise, wasn't it, in those best of times that were really the worst of times unto those worst of times that are no doubt the best we shall ever know.

A late spring? Perhaps.

Or perhaps we do not need spring anymore and are ready or not to face the darkness.

Memory of hollow Y rooms, against my will, *by* my will. On these cold floor boards I sustain a break with many useless tired-nesses, pre-Third World gestures of industrial fatigue, visions wasted by being visions too long. I learned nothing at the Y, except weary-ness of living, after the game is won and lost, after the quaff of chocolate and hot radiator pipes and woolen sweaters and buses taking us home. And that's why it haunts me now: it has had all the years of my life in which to become the stand-in for myself.

Waking from dreams with a jar because the two worlds are always dissonant, their brightnesses lit from a divergent source, at which the seeming body lurches. One moment secure in an event of central importance, even final meaning, then cracked into another morning of this continuing world, the sky blue and leaves blown down upon us as we run, chasing. The fallen sunflower is visible thru the window mist against the tree trunk. In the forge, in the Western World in the forge; so vast and broken, the wind and dead trees and decaying lands are themselves bare stop-gaps. Even granite Barre, its bakeries and State buildings and quarries, big holes that history will not continue emptying and cannot begin to fill.

* * *

On the cold wet lawn at Sunday church-time, above Plainfield village, beside the apple trees from which they drop, battered thru the branches, into the pile of them, mulched on the ground, while the wagons of manure pass, families downhill from farms and trailers to church — Carolyn and Andy, beside each other, measuring the years of their lives, go thru 105 moves. In the stillness of whatever sun there is. As an energy source? Or is the energy something else altogether? Rising from the ground in which we were born, against a gravity that makes our planet home.

* * *

Wendell writes: "Time flies — or maybe time stands still and we fly!"

I am found in myself wandering outdoors in the moonlight, angrier than I have ever been and not knowing why. This is no trick but some essential blueprinting.

I find myself wondering what the last months have been, in their heat and productivity, their spreading thru the fields, that I, in no actual sense, am required at their harvest.

XIX

Swift sky. Bare maples blown. Village of Corinth below in the valley.

The rain is cold and penetrating; at first the lamps of my body are dim. But as I move and work a warmth arises. I see the transparent spots in the cloud-cover, twisting at the Sun.

Smoke rises from the cabin and the day is passed by others inside. I alone have gone from there, the chatting unbearable. Even being out here, and seeing what I see, it is no more available. The wind is, the light is, and my vision of it is, half again as much. But who would have thought it was easy, that it would happen only for being here. I know just one of the imaginary paths by which I come to this impassable sea.

Thru the protection of the trees, the rain soaks me. I tear out rotten stumps and throw them down the hill, in honor of the abandon of childhood, precisely because it will not work, it will not free anything. The muscles that hurt when they hurt are exactly those that hurt also when they do not hurt. The procedure is learned for times we think are neutral. So there is something to do, instead of standing here, untaught, not so much braving the elements as using, misusing the elements to quiet, by counter-tension, the storm in self. Would that the thing I did on the hillside in the rain were t'ai chi. But that would have been a different hill. It could not be t'ai chi, not after two classes. It was formal and controlled movements, to make an offering to t'ai chi, to take my mind off throwing rotted wood, the falsely cathartic, to replace it by resisting it.

Porcupine albino in the undergrowth. Caught by boys in a box trap. Exhibited at the roadside market. So is everything wed by dream to dream, language to language, the translators and interpreters standing so close we do not see they are links, in another chain. The convoy passes between old lands we believe have vanished — in a ceremony at which the ring itself is priest — and we are wed, stuffed into it not because our death is imminent but because meaning is only continuous — billions of wet leaves beneath my feet, blanketing a bacchic decay whose voice sizzles; and on the side of the dead tree a woodpecker, who knows what he is, who doesn't know what he is, and so goes on with his tree-nicking, sucking the creamy mite in the fire of that eternal moment.

XX

After a summer of no baseball at all, the poets from South Londonderry come, rouse me, and I am standing in the outfield with Mørk while Shepherd Ogden, in his West Virginia sweatshirt, name and number on it, hits them out, high and tiny into the sky. I start to do usual baseball warm-ups, but I find myself in a combination of them and t'ai chi, then only t'ai chi. The game comes alive, and I feel speed and breath. I am an animal running. I throw the forever daylight of my biology back. Is this what baseball was? all the time? simply the body? and dancing free and wild? across intermontane flatlands mixed of rocks and mantle beneath the garden and centerfield weeds?

There is no chi involved. But the chi, with its Asian and medicinal lineage, its surety of a life current in a body of veins and arteries, is a clue to the sequence of motions, *baseball isn't neutral either*, not while I'm alive, while I'm scooping, flung beyond myself, glove to the webbing, tumbling as I snag it, the missile of disintegrating time.

This is Vermont and October, and I have never played before. I have never known how big the Indian games were, for the real plains,

246

their bumpiness and scars, and not just the calm village green, how farflung the spaces, the chase of sewn and bound objects, the flow and slink of deer and beaver and weasel, stopped from the pellet center of animal selves. I collide with the ball for the moment it is solid/I am whole, running it out of impossibly blue sky, the few clouds, the sun intense but fallen, the leaves red and ochre, the cold breath of those who have lived into the eleventh month of their thirtieth year. I love the field of play and its realness, its grassness and that it is prairie; I love the ball as a pinpoint, a connection, a sting. There is rhythm and orb and breath and deep awe of sky, whether daylight here of its inner phenomenal splay or night-blazed with our whole history, strung out in eternity, true faces of those who would be our gods. And though the ball is not a planet, and a meteorite only in a lark, it is a sky object for the way it loses itself in the blue and then comes down on the parabola I can measure without a second's thought, that precise occuluded moment at which we come together, because I learned to do it, the t'ai chi class a recent memory, the sparrow's tail of what we can yet become.

I want the scar-tissue to open, the fear and desire to mesh, where autumn is more brilliant than left-field, *and* the only spectator, fire in my blood, the imaginary applause of iron, running in my ears, as at twilight Mars sings and a hundred stars appear sultry, subtly, the billion that do not, like the suffusion in liquid/life once was, coacervate warm on the dilute robes of the missing dakini. All these things have to do with baseball, stars and cells and deer and Indians and rough sewn objects to stand for the whole of creation, their worldness, their cosmological completion; don't ask me why; I don't think of it while I'm playing. They make their way into my baseball piece always, by stealth and association; it's a wonder they don't take it over, and leave me frozen and silent, a player on some remote field where the game has either ceased or not yet been invented, because everywhere else I am a historian, a gimp astronomer — there alone am I the magician and the prince.

Mørk says: "When you catch the ball it's like you're catching the whole world," and so opens for me a kind of wonder I have suspected all along, that is greater than my knowledge, and I have fled because it made me a forever child. I lie bare and arms open, before the powers of sky. Did I think I was playing some kind of jock adult game, when I was dancing openly, writing baseball liturgy and myth?

Now it's gone. And I am proud to stand with Shep and his brother Lash, talking shop on the big stone by our house, kicking the autumn leaves. Let the trees like giant men enter into their discourse with the stars. We will stay small, and shy, and imperfect, for we are approximations anyway, and if we are babes, these are our rightful toys.

XXI

Cold drizzle in the leaves, all emptied of color and light. The black metals clank. What's over, I don't know. It seems to have happened a hundred years ago, a summer of apples and hay.

By mid-afternoon the sun comes thru a window in the air, and water glistens on the corn tassels and blackened cauliflowers, drips from the eaves. The light flows unimpeded thru the skeletons of apple and maple, down over the hill; it shows the rain on the bark and leaves, hung, dropping, replaced, as if some more fantastic and precious element: our mistake. It is water that is the fantastic element, whose vertical brilliance is time itself, whose proof we are, while clouds stretch across the flat horizon.

I slept and dreamed and bobbed at ocean's edge between 1:30 and 2:00 today, only half an hour, but swift and intense. My complications and I spun together as fragments in an eddy, broken tissues. At first we were events and people; then we were long complicated geometric forms, diamonds and snowflakes, x-rays of gem structure and coral reefs; in the end we were archaic spiders and crabs.

The wind blows the maple leaves to the ground in drafts so sudden against so buoyant a shape that Robin and I cannot catch them. But the samaras, with their long rudders and seed-anchors, are easily plucked. Everytime the wind blows we dash, arms out, across the driveway, five points for a leaf, one point for a seed.

Now I remember in my dream last night I was the person they sent to the Moon. I passed all the exams; I was chosen by the fearful intelligence computer and then welcomed as if I had won an honor. There I am, being put aboard; that whole part of the dream either mechanical, or never happened, now forms to explain the rest.

A giant body fell beyond me on the video screen, then in the actual window. There you are!, they shouted thru all my wires and telepathies. They had worked to put me there. They had sent me against my will. They hung on my every word.

I got out the chart and made plots of position. It was quite un-
necessary. I knew at once that it wasn't the Moon. It was something
else, perhaps part of our ancestry, an incomplete astral connection.
It was hollow, or concave; it was built up by parameters of time,
not by forging and bombardment in space. Which meant I couldn't
reach it or see it because I came only at the moment they sent me.
It was neither frightening nor mystical; it was simply the bend in
space which got me, that it could be so torqued and twisted within
twists. Suddenly the Moon appeared right before me; I was in the
Moon. There! I shouted at the top of my head. There's your Moon.
And they lay in bed, I could see them, all of them, waiting, waiting
to stop waiting, until it stopped in them. And the texture-suck was
amazing; for every point in me there was a point in it — discon-
tinuous and regenerating.

The whole thing was accidental, even my courage. The Moon was
where no Moon should be. From staring at it so many years and
imagining its surely palpable geography, I had lost the reason why
Earth and Moon were originally separate, and how stringent that
was when it was done. Big and raw in its vacuum, afloat as a relic
on which I make the barest scratches, not even scratches, with my
fat hulky fingers.

Then I was the person back from that Moon, the only one back,
to teach them how to make the shot again. I knew they couldn't.
Its position was receding beyond ours faster than knowledge of how
to reach it was growing. Each attempt would be more dangerous,
though not to life, more necessary, than the one before.

An unknown man from North Montpelier comes in his truck
with his three kids and asks if they can collect the leaves from our
yard; they want to take them home and stuff a Halloween "person."
it seems a most touching poverty, in Vermont, not to have leaves.
Yet he and the kids work with a hilarity and delight, aslant the
tension I feel these days. I find myself with unexpected tears, for
both their joy and their dispossession. As they leave, the back of
the truck plump with blanketsful from raking, I give them pump-
kins and squashes they receive with delight and hold as treasures
from the world beneath the sky. I am thrown back on the ambiguous
sorrow with which it began, for there is no real poverty. We are on
opposite sides of an experience their visit allows me to feel. As if
they were sent for that, and are not real, the blue truck turning out
of the driveway. Awake!, someone tells me. Awake before it is too
late.

There is some still poorer person who comes to me formed as
myself. There is some poorer self who waits on me, it seems so

long ago.

Now the sun comes out and a thin mist hangs over everything, 4:00, Lindy returns, the air cool enough to breathe, cool and not cold. The birds call in the many dimensions and expectations of daylight they inhabit. The more I listen the more they are.

There is another feeling, and its only certainty is how intense it is and how far its roots go in my veins and sinews. The summer went by so fast, but it was not fast, it was at an angle so sharp I can now see only the arc of its turning, the railroad bed beyond the washout, the colored leaves on the ground. And though it is gone, perhaps unfairly, it has moved me to another place. I stand here, and wish to have it back again only because I don't wish to have it back again. No way. I am relieved it is over forever.

The few days in the mountain pool naked, the Platonic and Keplerian classes, Harvey's DNA lectures, Chuck's reading of *Maximus*. I am here without the hay, without even gathering the last pumpkins from the hunt in Central Park. There is no richness of reaping or intense and remembered sun on which vague and unknown figures form. There is something more valuable, something wild, beneath, and far.

And a week ago, in the cold and because I couldn't reach you, and went past you into the still-bleeding spaces, for the first time in ten years, I cried and it all came out, out of my chest and back, torn from anxiety to compassion, and then that other thing, neither.

Going down into a fiery red glyph, the old hermetic sun at the horizon, hanging, signature as a lion, fission body in deep space.

Bringing in armloads of wood from the back porch, dripping with it, bark and splinters on my sweater, into the fire.

First wet snow. Snow images return. Clinging to the limp maple leaves. Covering the aluminum cat bowl a passing dog has chewed and left in the grass.

Winter waits as always, in brilliant and obscure rags.

Mid-morning down highway 89. 11 at Springfield, to London-derry. 100 south along the West River. The meeting place over the bridge on high ground. All of us are there, company in the forest, bushy familiar bodies. Chuck. Harvey. Ken Irby back from Den-mark, sitting by the window, an older gentler man. Michele writing in her book. Shepherd, Lash, Mørk, Tinker, Norman, Veronica, Max, filling the tables of this collegium.

South Londonderry, Vermont. The wedge in time, the feet shuffling, the beer from the tap. The ice river. Thin blasts of rain. Large lunch platters of pancakes and nutty breads. Thank you, Mørk. Thank you, West Bank Tavern, and friends.

An almost ritual moment this is, we have come together, with-out preliminary phone calls, without reassurances. We are part of someone else's obsession, as we used our obsessions once to shape the lives of our elders.

One poet after another reads. At night the river rolls by, a blan-ket of light; it is only lanterns, wine, and Lindy lays it out in her own rich voice, by the candle, what she has gone thru, the mellow-ing and inwarding revealed.

We gather ourselves, and with Norman, drive back to Plainfield, where our life is. 89 again, at night, nervous talk, then silence, until I am pushing 90 into the starless hood.

Cold rainy Vermont morning. Going house to house in the station wagon picking up the kids for New School. Buried behind these mountains: in her pendant orbit. A village. Creamery Street to Brook Road to Barre Hill Road to the Dailey Apartments to Main Street to Maple Hill. Faint steam on the river, single leaves blown thru the visible, cover the pond surface. The wipers run, the motor: runs. On the car radio, Eric Burden singing "San Francisco Nights," so few years ago we rose like glow-worms, if not to the song, the idea — "... *feel all right. on a warm San Francisco night* ... " The kids, shiny in their slickers, one by one into the back of the car.

May, 1973 — October, 1974
Plainfield, Vermont

Work by Richard Grossinger

The *Solar Journal* series

Solar Journal: Oecological Sections
Book of the Earth and Sky
Spaces Wild and Tame

Essays

Mars: A Science Fiction Vision
Early Field Notes from the All-American Revival Church
Martian Homecoming at the All-American Revival Church

The Continents

The *Cranberry Island* sequence

Book of the Cranberry Islands
The Provinces
The Long Body of the Dream
The Book of Being Born Again into the World
The Windy Passage from Nostalgia
The Slag of Creation

Current Work

The Planet with Blue Skies